A GRAIN OF TRUTH

Also by Christian Unge in English translation

Hell and High Water (2021)

CHRISTIAN UNGE

A GRAIN OF TRUTH

Translated from the Swedish by
George Goulding and Sarah de Senarclens

MACLEHOSE PRESS
QUERCUS · LONDON

First published in the Swedish language as *Ett litet korn av sanning*
by Norstedts Förlag, Stockholm, in 2021
First published in Great Britain in 2022 by MacLehose Press

An imprint of Quercus Editions Limited
Carmelite House
50 Victoria Embankment
London EC4Y 0DZ

An Hachette UK company

A CIP catalogue record for this book is available from the British Library.

ISBN (HB) 978 1 52941 660 2
ISBN (TPB) 978 1 52941 658 9
ISBN (Ebook) 978 1 52941 657 2

This book is a work of fiction. Names, characters, businesses,
organisations, places and events are either the product of the author's
imagination or are used fictitiously. Any resemblance to actual persons,
living or dead, events or locales is entirely coincidental.

Typeset by Jouve (UK), Milton Keynes
Printed and bound in Great Britain by Clays Ltd, Elcograf S.p.A.

I

NOBEL HOSPITAL
Thursday late morning, 7 November

The young mother with the pram finally managed to extract her cheese sandwich and the woman swiftly took her place. She knew what she wanted and how much it cost. Two ten-kronor coins in the slot. Then a glance at the chairs over by the reception.

For one second, when time seemed to stretch out, tearing apart her very being, she went into free fall, struggling to get air into her lungs. Her chest tightened.

"I'm hungry."

Spinning around just as the jingle of the second ten-kronor coin died away deep in the bowels of the vending machine, she felt the boy's warm, dry hand in hers.

"Where . . .?"

The boy looked worried.

"What? What's the matter, Mamma?"

"Nothing."

She breathed out, closed her eyes, pretended to rub one to remove something, inhaled deeply and opened them wide again. Felt an urge to crouch down and hug the boy, as if to make sure that he was real, that he had not just appeared in a dream. She resisted the impulse. Her neck was sore and, when she filled her lungs, a weight settled across her chest. Something was broken, she knew that, but it was too late to try and fix it, nothing could ever be mended again.

"Wait, darling." She keyed in the right number and the machine responded with a thud. She reached in and removed the cold bottle, which felt slippery against her sweaty palm. "Here." Her mouth was parched all the way down to her vocal chords. She coughed up some phlegm and swallowed it.

The boy took the bottle. Did not seem to notice her shaking hands. He walked slowly back to the red plastic chair. The woman followed him.

"Why do we have to be here? There's a horrible smell."

"We . . ." She faltered, looked at the boy's lined boots, at the laces that had been dragged through the slush. There were grey mud stains on his navy blue trousers, and the light red down jacket had been mended in a few places. "You'd better take off the mask so you don't scare anyone."

"But . . . Iron Man's one of the good guys, Mamma."

"I know. But please just listen and do as I say."

Reluctantly, the boy pulled off the gold mask and held it firmly against his body.

"Come here," she said and leaned forward. She drew him towards her. He stood still, peering into a cubicle where a patient was lying on a bed and breathing into a mask. A monitor above the patient's head was beeping.

The woman felt cold. A piercing cold. She had to get her pulse down, try to seem normal. Surely a hospital ought to feel more secure than this, isn't that the basic premise? What can have gone so badly wrong, even here? She removed her jacket and wrapped it around the boy.

"No," he insisted.

"Aren't you cold?"

"No."

He shook off the jacket almost in a panic, as if it were on fire.

"Sure?"

"Yes." The boy sounded annoyed. "Don't do that."

"O.K. Sorry darling. I just don't want you to be cold."

"I'm not cold."

"O.K., O.K." The woman took back her jacket and began to walk. The boy followed her, his boots squeaking against the plastic floor.

The sound jarred her. She was shaking so badly that the pain shot all the way down to the base of her spine.

They made their way along the corridor, weaving in and out among nurses who were darting back and forth between cubicles and opening and shutting doors. She liked the way there seemed to be order in this chaos, like a big factory where everyone has a set job to do.

The woman searched her way systematically through the ward. She wanted to avoid asking questions, attracting attention. That much she had learned. It is what *he* always said: "Whatever you do, keep a low profile." If only she could rewind the tape, start all over again.

In one room, a nurse was putting a plaster cast on a young man. In another, a family was sitting next to a woman whose eyes were red from crying. Her make-up had run down her cheeks.

Eventually, the woman realised it was pointless. She was drifting about in a world she did not understand. She walked up to the desk, had to make an effort to separate her tongue from the roof of her mouth. Coughed. A blond woman looked up from her computer and straight into her eyes.

"May I ask if you've admitted any people who were injured in a car accident?"

The nurse nodded. "Are you family?"

"Yes."

"They're very busy at the moment. I don't think you should go in right now." The nurse pointed to a door marked Emergency Room 1. Then she added: "The older man is having a C.T. scan, then he'll be taken to K 81."

"Is he going to make it?" The woman cast a worried glance towards the emergency room.

"Who?"

The woman pointed to the door. When she saw how badly her hand was shaking, she quickly brought it down again. The nurse looked puzzled, turned her head and seemed uncertain as to how much she could say. Relatives must never be left without hope, yet at the same time, one should not promise too much. "Don't know . . . But the older man is in a less serious condition, he's not intubated."

The woman said thank you and stepped back before the nurse got a chance to ask her if she herself was alright. She wiped the sweat off her forehead and felt an unpleasant searing pain down her spine.

Oddly enough, she was quite intrigued by all the symptoms affecting her body. They were new to her. Apart from the terrible period pains she had always suffered from, she considered herself healthy. But now that something different was manifesting itself every minute, like the numbness in the fingertips of her left hand, she could not help stopping, noting and being fascinated.

"What's a ward?" the boy asked.

The woman reflected. "A corridor with lots of rooms. A bit like a hotel. Or like . . . Princess Leia's starship."

The boy's eyes widened. "Are there toothbrushes in plastic packages?"

"Maybe."

"And chocolate?"

The woman felt a rush of warmth when she heard the boy pronounce the "ch" in chocolate, as if he were clearing his throat. As if he had a mouth full of soft, warm chocolate.

"Don't think so. Are you still hungry?"

He nodded.

"Come."

They left A. & E. and set off up the stairs. She tried to remember what the nurse had said: K 81. All in good time. She had to get it right. Mustn't leave any unfinished business when they then disappeared for good.

They stopped when they reached the entrance level. The ceiling was low. She felt trapped, almost a sense of panic. The floor was wet and covered in grit. The boy looked over at the Pressbyrån newsagent a few metres away.

"Can we buy something?" he asked.

"Absolutely. Sure we can."

They made their way past stationary prams, drab processions of bulky winter coats and two women in white who were slowly pushing a transparent box on a steel frame with wheels. Their shuffling steps bore witness to many sleepless days and nights on the front line. She thought she detected a whiff of acrid sweat.

The sweet, warm scent of cinnamon buns inside the newsagent's made her feel sick. She felt a pressing discomfort in the left side of her groin. "What would you like?" the woman said.

The boy looked around. "I want food."

"Food?" the woman asked before remembering that he had not touched the lunch they had been given at the house. He had only picked at the potatoes. The woman went to the back of the shop where they had a variety of ready meals. "Lasagne?"

The boy shook his head and made a face.

"Beef and rice?"

The boy considered her question. Then nodded slowly. They took the box of food, paid and left the shop. On the way out, the woman noticed that the smell of sweat was actually coming from her. It was sour and rank. She hadn't had time to wash with soap that morning, only splashed some water onto her armpits. If she thought hard enough, she probably knew why she stank. And yet she couldn't quite remember. Only feel the nausea. Over what she had done. Her stomach hurt. She needed a toilet. Her body was drained. Her head pounded, thoughts bouncing about between the hard cranial bones.

She needed to stop for a few moments and make an effort to work out where she was. Her clothes felt heavy, as if they were drenched in something. She imagined it to be petrol. She looked at the boy, who was walking along holding the box with his meal. The woman became confused, thought she was seeing two faces in one. Foreboding dulled the sense of security that had come from having the boy with her, a feeling that she was all by herself. Then another stab of pain hit her in the stomach. She had to hold her breath for a few seconds, try and think away the pain.

"I wonder what he's doing now," the boy said. He was dragging his feet, the grit scratching the floor. Why was the boy thinking of *him* now? Why couldn't he just be content to be with her? After all the time they had spent together. It wasn't fair. She felt a violent rage that she struggled to contain.

"Don't know. What do you think?"

The boy shuffled on.

"What?" he said.

"Nothing."

"You're weird, Mamma."

"Am I? How do you mean?"

"You say funny things."

"What sort of things?"

"Don't know. You're just weird."

"Wait here," she said, she couldn't hold it back any longer. She dashed into a toilet. Maybe she should have taken the boy in with her, but it was too late now. Even as she sat down, the contents of her bowels emptied into the toilet bowl with force. She flushed, washed her hands and pushed the door open. Coming out she found herself staring straight into the Iron Man mask.

"Well done for staying."

They walked on, reached some stairs, paused and stood aside for two people dressed in blue. The boy kept staring at the floor.

"What's the matter, darling?"

"Nothing."

"Go on, tell me." And then in a lower, gentler voice: "Tell me."

The boy turned towards her and flipped up the face of the mask. He responded to the quieter tone.

"Well, you're saying kind of strange things."

"Am I saying things you don't understand?"

"Yes. And you're talking to yourself."

"Don't be silly."

8

"Yes you are."

The boy looked uncomfortable. She doubled over as another piercing pain shot through her stomach, but she breathed through the spasm, which left her with a lingering feeling of nausea. Her field of vision suddenly shook, like when a pitching boat hits a wave and then settles back onto a steady course. She thought she understood what was going on, but there was no alternative. She had to hurry up, do what had to be done.

The boy folded down his mask again. And said, his voice echoing inside it:

"Come on Mamma."

"Right, boss," she said. "Let's eat now before we die."

"International Men's Day."

"International Wednesday?" Tekla asked.

Viola smiled and held open the door to the emergency room. "International *Men's* Day."

Tekla went in, put on a plastic apron, a face shield and double plastic gloves, then slipped her ID card into the computer. "Didn't even know there was such a thing as Men's Day."

"It doesn't work," Lisa, the head trauma nurse, proclaimed drily. She was by her standing desk, where she had a laptop, a blank patient file and a can of Diet Coke. Tekla punched in her code for the third time.

"They're replacing it with some sort of device that's meant to recognise fingerprints," Lisa added, taking a sip of Coke.

Tekla looked at the gruff nurse: dyed blue hair in a rough plait, rolled-up sleeves and broad shoulders.

"Fingerprints?" Tekla said. "Why not voice activation while they're at it?"

"They're making the same idiotic mistakes here as on the other side of town," Lisa said and went over to pull the string that opened the double doors separating the emergency room from the ambulance bay. One of the doors got stuck halfway but Lisa simply gave it a thump, as if it were a punching bag at the gym. "They think fancy technology can do our job. They've forgotten that human beings aren't cars. The last time those idiots engaged their brains, it was all about lean business models, wasn't it? And what became of those millions? They could make a start by fixing that door."

The nurses Viola and Johan went out to meet the ambulance staff. Tekla thought about the text she had received the previous day, which she had still not answered, but relegated it indefinitely to the back of her mind.

"How am I supposed to access the patient file then?" she asked.

"Not possible right now," Lisa said, throwing up her hands in despair.

"Maybe a good thing." Tekla fished a can out of her pocket.

"You should perhaps complain to your immediate superior."

Tekla considered it briefly, but that only reminded her how exasperating her new boss was. "Thanks, I don't think so. Let's focus on the patient for once."

She finished her drink in five gulps while walking towards the ambulance crew.

"Hit and run in Stuvsta," the male paramedic said.

Tekla raised a hand. "Just a second. Is his airway clear?" She turned to the woman on the team who was holding an Ambu bag over the battered face, but she couldn't see much because of the neck brace and all the straps stabilising the patient. Two feet covered in blood stuck out at the bottom of the stretcher.

"Yes," the woman said. "But he needs oxygen."

"O.K.," Tekla said, turning her attention back to the ambulance crew, while Johan and Viola together transferred the patient to the hospital's own stretcher. "Carry on."

"He's probably around forty, identity unknown. We found no wallet or any other clue as to who he might be. We just got a category one call for a car accident at the bus shelter in Stuvsta, near the commuter train station. This one and an older man."

Looking over the shoulder of the paramedic, Tekla could see another ambulance pulling into the bay.

"Ragna is standing by in Emergency Room 2," Lisa said.

"Is that really a good idea?" Tekla was worried, but at the same time she felt oddly confident. Ragna Sigurdsdottir could look after herself. It was Ragna's pregnancy that she was concerned about. The anaesthetists appeared behind Tekla, a woman and a man. They put away their kick scooters and donned plastic clothing and face shields in silence.

"When we got to the scene, the patient was lying on his side. Lowered consciousness but revivable. G.C.S. five. A passing jogger who had reported the accident was waiting at the scene. Free airway but traumatic injury to the face. Bleeding from the head and mouth. Saturation 90 during transport with 10 litres oxygen through a mask. Blood pressure around 80. Increased heart rate between 100 and 120. Nasty lower left leg fracture which we've immobilised." The ambulance man looked up from his tablet. "That's all, I think. Except that he's had a total of twenty milligrammes of morphine."

"Why weren't they taken to the N.S.K. trauma centre?"

"They already had a case. You can't expect a hospital that cost fifty billion to deal with two trauma patients at the same time. Are you out of your mind?" the paramedic said with a smile.

A quick look at the stretcher told Tekla that everything was being done properly. The head stabilised. The anaesthetic team had the airway under control. "What about the other man?" Tekla asked.

"His condition is far less severe. A fractured forearm and a blow to the head, but he's responding."

"Thanks," Tekla said, pulling down her face shield. She approached the patient. It was clear he was badly injured. Hit by some driver who fled the scene. Maybe drunk or stoned. A senseless act if ever there was one.

"And we don't have a name?" she called out to the ambulance crew who were moving towards the exit.

"Sadly not. And there was no-one around who knew who he was."

"What about the driver?" Tekla called out.

"A white car, a station wagon, which drove off. The police arrived at the same time as us."

"Let's hope they catch the bastard and lock him up for good."

Tekla began at the top. The man's blond scalp had been torn

away on the left side so that the bone beneath shone like dirty marble under the strip lights. The left half of his face seemed to have been pushed in and looked rubbery. When Tekla carefully palpated the cheekbone, it gave way and the globe of the eye sank in. Nasty fractures which would require the skills of many specialist surgeons.

"This is going to be tough." A film about reconstructive plastic surgery at the Mayo Clinic played in Tekla's mind.

The man was in deep sedation from the morphine, and unresponsive. Probably about forty, normal height with unusually long muscles across his right upper arm. Tekla grasped his right hand, which felt somehow rough, as if he earned his living doing physical work. All of which matched the outdoor clothing he wore and his suntan, which was unusual for the time of year. Tekla cast her mind back to her childhood in Edsåsdalen. She used to love picking up logs and balancing them on the chopping-block. With a cigarette in the corner of his mouth, her father would swing the axe up into the bright blue sky and, at the last moment, say: "Now keep your paws out of the way or there'll be bangers for supper". Tekla would quickly pull her hands back and watch the log split in two. She remembered the sound of the axe sinking into the block. How they then laughed, working away until the basket was full of firewood and the ground strewn with cigarette butts. She missed that comforting silence when darkness slowly crept in from the woods.

"Saturation 88," Viola said and upped the oxygen.

The anaesthetist and her nurse were talking nearby: ". . . need to intubate . . ." and ". . . is going to crash . . ."

"Do you need any help?" Tekla asked.

The name of the anaesthetist was Helena Gray, a 31-year-old registrar who carried herself straight as a ramrod and still had half her specialist training ahead of her.

"Uncalled for," Gray said. "What about you? Might be a good idea to call in the cavalry before the patient snuffs it."

Tekla ignored her and carried on with her examination. A

gurgling sound came from the patient's airway. "Do we have a blood pressure reading?"

Nurse Anki was just releasing the cuff, which let out a hiss followed by a scratching sound when she tore off the tourniquet. "60 over unmeasurable."

Tekla felt the patient's wrist: no pulse. She applied two fingers to his groin. A very faint, quick pulsation. "Have we got a cannula?"

"It's not working," Johan said. He was kneeling beside Tekla, looking for veins in the man's brown forearms. It was pointless, there was no blood in the vessels, they had collapsed. Tekla noted that the suntan only went as far as the man's upper arm.

"Hand me the intraosseous drill, please," Tekla said, turning to Lisa. "I think we need the on-call surgeons," she added, and she thought she detected a smirk on Gray's face just as the anaesthetist was holding up the laryngoscope to intubate the patient.

"Which category is that?" Lisa asked, picking up a telephone. She went over and ran her finger down a laminated list hanging on the wall. "And, most importantly, what colour and number do I call?"

"Oh Jesus!" Tekla exclaimed. "Just get the switchboard."

"They probably also have a colour and a number," Lisa said drily.

"Tell them you need the on-call surgeon over here."

Anki began to cut open the man's trousers with some large scissors. "Tell that to the management team, my dear. Their orders are that we stick to the new guidelines right until the end of the trial period."

"Do you think it's category one, red?" Lisa said. "Regenerative Medicine? Isn't it supposed to be called Surgery? Or am I meant to search within a unit? There's a red unit too."

"Just call the switchboard," Tekla hissed. She noted that there was less noise coming from the left lung. The right one sounded normal.

Anki went through the pockets of the bloodstained rags. She held up a small piece of paper for Tekla to see. "Can I chuck it away?"

"Go ahead," Tekla said, glancing at the receipt from Tempo – a

14

food shop – and went on palpating the liver and the spleen. When she applied pressure to the left abdomen, the patient moved one leg.

"Ketamine ready," Rikard, the anaesthetic nurse said.

"We still don't have a working line," Johan said in a surprisingly calm tone. He tapped the patient's hand, changed the position of the tourniquet and then moved down to the feet in his continued search for a useable vein.

"Let's see who gets there first," Tekla said.

"I bet you it's me," Johan replied, looking up.

"Intraosseous drill," Lisa said. "And Klas Nyström is on his way."

"Oh dear," Gray exclaimed behind Tekla's back.

Tekla was startled. "Is *he* the person on call?"

"That's what the switchboard told me," Lisa said, holding the receiver at arm's length, as if it suddenly smelled bad. "And it *was* red unit."

"This could get really exciting," Rikard muttered, writing something with a felt-tip pen on the syringe he was holding.

Tekla saw that the stethoscope in her hand had started to shake. "O.K. Didn't know he'd already started." She wanted a bomb from her Lypsyl tube, but now was not the right time. She felt the patient's bare belly. Anki had managed to remove both the trousers and the checked shirt, thus revealing the extent of the man's injuries along his left side. It looked as if the car had driven over him lengthwise. Dark patches of blood, gravel and gaping wounds ran down his abdomen to the lower part of his leg, which was broken in two, with the bone protruding through the skin. It almost looked as if someone had stuck a ski pole into it – actually pushed it in. The skin was a map of dark purple islands, the subcutaneous haematomas. "We may have to call in an orthopaedist as well."

"What colour would that be?" Lisa asked without a trace of irony.

"Don't think Klas Nyström needs an orthopaedist," Gray said.

Tekla ignored the comment and picked up the intraosseous drill. She drove a needle into the patient's right lower leg. He hardly budged. "We have a line."

"I'll do the Ketamine, then," Rikard said and got a nod from Gray.

The door opened and Tekla relaxed for a second when her quick glance revealed the grumpy but familiar face of Piotr Nowak, also an anaesthetist.

"Has he been intubated?" Nowak asked, walking over to the head of the bed. He kept his hands behind his back.

"We've only just got a cannula in," Gray said. "Do you want me to have a go?"

Piotr nodded.

"50 over unmeasurable," Viola said after measuring the blood pressure once more.

"Giving Ketamine," Rikard said.

At the very moment Gray was unfolding her gleaming laryngoscope to find her way through the pool of blood and phlegm into the patient's windpipe, the doors to the emergency room were flung open and Nyström stepped in.

NOBEL HOSPITAL

They moved along a glass walkway. Every now and then a gap between the buildings gave a view onto the courtyards below. Most of those they passed in the corridor were dressed in either white or blue. Doctors, nurses, assistant nurses on their way to the changing rooms after yet another day's work. The others wore ordinary clothes, just like them. Occasionally they would pass a child and each time she noticed how that caught the boy's attention. Often it was some older child and there was longing in his eyes, a craving. He had been isolated for so long. He yearned for a real life, to play, to laugh. The woman tried to distract him by pointing out boring busts in the corridor. She was unable to bring them to life. They remained statues. Surrounded by walls that were cracked after years of general indifference. How was it possible to work in such an uninspiring environment without going mad? The urge was back. She needed a toilet again. There was a burning in the roof of her mouth and her tongue was throbbing. She needed something to drink, could just about swallow an ocean.

They stopped in the next lift lobby. She read the signs: the names of the different departments, some of which she partly understood. Haematology was to do with blood. And Endocrinology with hormones. But did that include kidneys? Then right at the top: K 81 – Orthopaedics.

The lift pinged. A monotonous and metallic female voice announced which floor they were on.

"Where are we going?" the boy said.

"We're going to visit someone."

She reached for the boy's hand but it was busy playing with the lift buttons. "Fo-ur, f-ive, s-ix . . ."

"There." The woman was seeing double but her finger managed to locate the real thing and she pointed to the button for the eighth floor.

The boy pressed it.

For a few seconds in the silence of the lift it dawned on her: she knew where she was. Was she predestined to end up here? Had she gone wrong somewhere? She felt that the decisions she had made at every stage of her life had been carefully considered. But did her perception correspond to reality? Wasn't the fact of them being there, after all that had happened, the very essence of a failure?

"Eighth floor," the robotic female voice said. The lift stopped; after a few seconds the doors slid open. Together they read the sign: K 81. This was it. So much was at stake. Maybe failure could be transformed into something else, something with a slightly more forgiving tone.

There was a sour smell when they entered the ward – of something like excrement. It offended the nose. The woman nearly retched. She hoped the boy hadn't noticed the stench. By the door to the first room there was some hand sanitiser on the wall. The woman hesitated. Would she be told off if she helped herself? She pressed the bottle quickly twice and rubbed her hands hard. Then waved them vigorously in front of her. She felt a stab of pain in the stomach. She would soon need the toilet again. And the nausea refused to go away.

"Why are you doing that?" the boy said.

"I'm disinfecting my hands. It kills the bacteria."

"Do I have to do it too?"

"You haven't touched anything."

"I held your hand."

She smiled, trying to tell if the boy was doing alright. He hadn't complained. "That's true. But you . . ."

"Can I help you?" a woman asked, emerging from a larger room with a number of patients sitting around different circular and rectangular tables. Two men in wheelchairs were watching a huge flat screen T.V. with the volume turned right up, so that the applause of the studio audience and the jovial banter of the programme host could be heard.

"We're waiting for a patient. A relative." The woman wondered what had made her say that. It was not like her to improvise. But then nothing resembled anything any longer, nothing would ever be the way it used to be. And now, just as they were entering the ward, there was no turning back, no way out, it was too late.

ACCIDENT & EMERGENCY, NOBEL HOSPITAL
Thursday, 7 November

"Good afternoon, everyone." The voice was as soft as silk. "How's it all going here?"

Tekla loosened the tourniquet on the patient's left thigh and stole a look at the hospital's new star surgeon. She noted that the fabled Klas Nyström was nothing like what she had imagined. The tales she had heard had blown him up into a larger than life figure. Even her colleague Tarik Moussawi had spoken in hushed tones in the break room when he told them how Nyström had sacked a registrar on the spot in the operating theatre because they had been too slow handing him the forceps. Professor Nyström was also responsible for the annual conference on organ transplantation in Brussels, and the only person with his own parking spot, right by the entrance. The most hotly debated topic, though, was how Monica Carlsson had managed to lure him to the Nobel Hospital. No doubt with large sums of money and plenty of perks.

Nyström was a man of normal build, around fifty with thick, fair hair parted at the side, an enquiring look and a smile more suited to a parents' evening than an acute trauma response.

Tekla felt warm liquid on her glove, looked down and saw the blood pulsating.

"Oops," Nyström said, placing himself by the patient's feet and making a pleading gesture with his hands. "Suggest we try not to waste those little red blood corpuscles."

Ashamed, Tekla tightened the tourniquet. "Sorry."

"Is he alive?" Nyström asked.

"So far, he is," Tekla said.

"But not much longer if you carry on like that."

"I beg your pardon?"

Nyström leaned forward and looked at Tekla's badge. She caught a whiff of soap. "Tekla Berg."

Tekla went to get the ultrasound machine but could feel the surgeon's light blue eyes on her neck.

"Emergency doctor, right?"

"Yes, why?"

"Excellent. Excellent. You know, in the new organisation that Monica and I have put together, expertise will descend from the top, in the shape of yours truly in other words, in precisely the same way as here and now, and take over from the generalists once they've done their bit. Imagine a spaceship with advanced technology suddenly landing among stone age people."

Tekla switched on the machine, picked up the probe and performed an overall ultrasound to see if there was any free fluid in the lungs or abdomen.

"Haemothorax in the left lung and free fluid in the abdomen," she announced after thirty seconds.

"Intubated," Gray said, pulling out the guide wire from the laryngoscope. She listened to the lungs. "Breathing sounds, but less audible on the right-hand side. You did say it was fainter there, didn't you Tekla?"

"Would you bet your medical licence that it's a haemothorax?" Nyström asked, taking a step towards Tekla.

"Yes, what else could it be?" she said, backing away from him.

"What if he already had pleural effusion from cancer or an infection *before* the accident," Nyström replied.

"Unlikely," Tekla said, but she could hear the uncertainty in her voice.

"Sloppy work," Nyström said with a smile that actually looked genuine. "May I?" he said in English, holding out his hand. Tekla gave him the ultrasound probe. Nyström pulled on a glove and carefully placed the device against the patient's skin, which was covered in blood. He quickly changed a few settings on the screen. "Impedance 0.3. The latest study by Levy shows that you can distinguish blood from ordinary fluid with a ninety-eight per cent degree of certainty. Clever or what?" He tossed the probe back to Tekla.

He turned. "Lisa who keeps horses in Nykvarn."

"That's right," Lisa said, nodding. She was impressed.

Nyström looked at Tekla again. "Building a hospital from the ground up. Just like the Egyptians. Anything else is unthinkable. Imagine if the first stones they laid down hadn't been straight, what would the pyramids have looked like?"

"50 over unmeasurable," Viola said.

"Set up another line and shove in two litres of Ringer," Nyström said with a gentle smile.

"Shouldn't we be giving him four, four, one?" Tekla objected.

Nyström thrust his hands into the large pockets of his white coat. "What did you say your name was?"

"Tekla."

"Well I never . . . Tekla. Exciting name. Do your thing, stabilise and all that, but don't venture out onto thin ice."

"I see," Tekla said. She wiped the perspiration off her forehead with the crook of her arm. "The Crash-2 study says to give blood, plasma and thrombocytes in a four, four, one ratio."

"Don't know if you saw the latest circular from management, but there's a blood shortage in Stockholm."

"I did, but . . ."

"Not that I expect to solve the problem within the hour, but my lab's making great strides. Synthetic blood, how about that, my friend?"

"Well, of course, it would be great if something could be done about the shortage of blood in the world, but—"

"We already have the patent," Nyström cut in.

"O.K., congratulations, but right now we have a *patient* who's about to pack it in."

"And run a trauma C.T. scan on your way to Surgery," Nyström added. "You saw the free fluid, didn't you?"

"Absolutely," Tekla said. "And that's why it would certainly be a mistake not to go straight into theatre."

"Who's going to operate on this patient?" Nyström looked around as he posed his rhetorical question.

"You, I suppose," Tekla said.

"Spot on," Nyström said with a broad smile. "I want to know exactly where to place my incision, rather than carving him up like some old cow." He spread his hands. "Look, you've done a fantastic job, all of you. Let's see if I can save this poor fellow's life. He doesn't look all that old. Might he be a parent? That's something one must never lose sight of when talking about massive budgets, restructuring and the like. It's what I always tell the powers that be; at the end of the day, don't forget who we're doing all this for."

Nyström held up one hand like a charismatic preacher. "The patient first. Never forget that." Then he turned to Tekla. "Two litres of Ringer and then to Surgery via C.T. I'll go on ahead and prepare the team for action." He went over to the patient and, before Tekla could stop him, the world-famous surgeon from provincial Linköping placed both hands on the man's pelvis and pressed down, as if wanting to close a large, stubborn toilet seat.

"Wait," Tekla shouted.

"Dear girl, we need to see if his pelvis is unstable."

Tekla resisted the urge to haul Nyström away from the patient.

When he was done, Nyström pulled off his glove and dropped it on the floor. "Right. Nothing to worry about." He walked out of the room in his neon yellow, sporty sandals. Like a Greek god flying off with something burning under the soles of his feet, Tekla thought. The door banged shut.

"50 over—" Viola said.

"Give him two bags of O negative blood," Tekla cut in.

"But you heard what he said?" Lisa objected.

"And order up another two, plus two bags of plasma and a unit of thrombocytes." Tekla picked up the intraosseous drill, driving it into the patient's right shoulder. "There we are, two cannulas."

"You're insane," Gray said. "Do you realise who he is?"

"I've heard the stories about Busuttil and his collection of Ferraris, yes."

"Pretty mediocre surgeon," Nowak muttered. "Saw him fumble with a drain yesterday."

Tekla smiled. The Polish anaesthetist had nailed his colours to the mast.

"He did his fellowship with the world's best liver surgeon at U.C.L.A.!" Gray exclaimed. "They went skiing in Aspen with their families."

Tekla raised her face shield, which had fogged up completely. "Nice for his wife. Now we're off to Surgery."

"But—"

"You look after the airway and make sure he stays alive until we get there," Tekla said, staring into the eyes of the anaesthetist. Sigurdsdottir's voice could be heard from the other side of the sliding partition.

"You do realise what this is going to lead to?" Gray said.

"She doesn't seem to care," Lisa added with a grin. "Perhaps Tekla isn't so interested in sports cars."

"Off we go!" Tekla announced as she strode towards the door. "I just wonder which route we should be taking."

"You can't leave until you've coded the patient," Lisa called out.

"What are you talking about?" Tekla snorted.

"Coding the patient," Lisa repeated. "Under the new guidelines, no patient may leave A. & E. before the receiving category or unit has provided a code that can follow the patient on their hospital journey from admission to discharge. They're meant to have a bar code which the organisation—"

"I'm not having anything to do with that bullshit!" Tekla yanked the string that opened the doors to A. & E. "Come along now before he pegs out. I don't give a damn about their bloody guidelines. He's young. He doesn't deserve to die because of something so meaningless."

"Are you suggesting that there's a meaningful way of dying?" Lisa said.

Tekla met the eyes of the quick-witted nurse with a smile. "Good point."

ORTHOPAEDICS DEPARTMENT K 81,
NOBEL HOSPITAL
Thursday, 7 November

The nurse set down a tray laden with dirty dishes on a trolley in the corridor. The woman saw people go in and out of a door a few metres away, probably leading to a ward office.

"Has he or she been admitted to this ward?" the nurse asked. Her mouth barely moved. The words were pressed out of a narrow slit in the taut, suntanned face.

"I don't know. Or, rather, I suppose so," the woman corrected herself. "We've come from A. & E. They said he was going for a C.T. scan and then he'd be brought here."

"But has he been admitted here, to K 81?"

"That's what they told us in A. & E.," the woman stuttered, managing a smile.

"Do you have a personal identification number?"

"Only part of it." The woman lowered her voice and gave the old man's name, or at least the name by which he had introduced himself to her.

"Wait here," the nurse said and went over to the place which the woman assumed was a ward office.

"What's going on?" the boy asked. He hadn't been following the conversation, his attention was focused on the patients' dining room and the large T.V.

"We have to wait."

"I'm tired. How much longer do we have to stay here?"

"Sit down," the woman said, pointing to a chair by a small, round table. The boy slumped onto the chair. Pulled off his mask in a bad-tempered movement.

"Aren't you happy to have me all to yourself?" She knew he didn't understand irony. All they had been doing, for far too long, was spending time together, just the two of them.

The boy did not answer.

A few moments later, the nurse came back. "He's not registered for K 81."

"Perhaps they haven't got here yet."

"He's still on the books in A. & E."

"O.K. Is it alright for us to wait here?"

"He could end up anywhere in the hospital. It's the coordinator who decides."

Fascinating, she thought. Amazing how unsympathetic people can be. The nurse spoke without any feeling, a look of disgust on her face.

"But is it likely he'll be brought here? The nurse in A. & E. did specifically mention K 81."

"I have no idea," the nurse said, already heading away both physically and mentally. Only routine held her back: yet another difficult relative who did not appear to understand what she was saying. "It depends what he's in for and if there's space."

"Are there any free beds on the ward?" the woman insisted.

"I don't know."

She considered asking if she might go and see for herself, but realised that this would annoy the nurse even further.

"He's been in a car accident." There was a smell of smoke mixed with the stench of faeces from the corridor.

The nurse was no longer able to hide her irritation. Her body was as tense as a drawn bowstring. "I still don't know where they'll take him. You'll just have to wait and see. If I were you, I'd go down to the entrance hall and get a coffee. Then return to A. & E. and ask them where he's being admitted."

But you're not us, the woman thought. If you were, you'd be running for dear life and screaming for help.

"Mamma, I'm hungry."

The woman took the food container out of the boy's hands. His fingers were ice cold from holding the frozen meal. "Can I just heat this up in the microwave? The boy hasn't had anything to eat for ages."

The nurse's first impulse seemed to be to say no. Her whole body exuded resistance, some sort of disgust for the woman who was so incredibly stubborn. As if she wanted to tell her what a disorganised, chaotic mother, person and relative she was.

But the woman didn't care. She wasn't bothered by what the nurse thought of her as a mother. She felt totally comfortable in that role. Ever since her twenties she had known what kind of a mother she would be. The man she was living with then simply didn't possess the basic qualities needed for parenthood. At the time she wasn't aware of this, but in hindsight it was lucky she did not get pregnant back then. He was not worthy of a child's love. But she was, and she still was now. Inside, at least. After that, circumstances beyond her control had influenced events, but she did not see that as her own fault. She actually felt sorry for the nurse standing there, sorry to be the cause of her annoyance.

"I can heat it up for you," a new voice said.

A woman dressed in white with a blue hairnet and a warm smile put out her hand. In the other she was holding a ladle filled with something dark, it could have been chocolate. She spoke with a strong accent.

"Thank you." While the woman held out the box, the first nurse turned and walked off to the reception area without a word.

There was a sofa over to the right. A two-seater standing by a low, round table made of light wood. A corner in which they could hide from the suntanned nurse. The woman knew that she would soon need to find a toilet. She searched the room for something to drink, struggling with her double vision.

The boy put his feet up on the sofa.

"Not like that," the woman said, placing his feet firmly back on the floor.

The boy was struggling to sit up, kept sliding down into a slumped position. As if his muscles were no longer functioning. The woman saw how close he was to a breakdown. His blood sugar was far too low.

The image of the nurse with the tanned face was etched on her retina. She felt a sudden burst of rage at her attitude, but it quickly subsided, no longer bothering her half as much as the intermittent blurred vision. She was trying to suppress what was happening inside her brain.

She looked around. There were three thermoses with pump tops standing in the middle of the room next to a basket of white cups. She had to narrow her eyes to be able to focus. A steel jug, two bottles of mineral water and a carton of semi-skimmed milk had been set out on a cooler plate. A window gave onto darkness. She felt sorry for the venetian blind that had got trapped, askew, between two panes of glass. All she could see outside was sleet and dirty concrete.

The woman stood up, feeling dizzy as her blood pressure fell, faltered, regained her balance and walked over to the cups. She poured a glass of milk for the boy, not caring if anyone in the room was watching. She pressed the burning palm of her hand onto the cool aluminium plate and, as she was about to turn, spotted a knife lying by a plaited loaf of cardamom bread on a carving board. An ordinary bread knife, maybe a bit on the short side. Black plastic handle. She reached for it and held it in her hand for a moment before taking a napkin from a pile and wrapping the blade with it. Then she put the knife into her jacket pocket and poured herself a glass of water which she drank in large gulps. It tasted of iron and left a thick layer of mucus on her tongue. She wanted to scrape it off, but had some more water instead. She went back to the boy, who hardly lifted his hand but still managed to take hold of the glass of milk, which he slowly began to sip. He was oblivious to the urgency – his body needed energy.

The nurse with the hairnet arrived with the food on a plate. She had added a peeled carrot and made a butter and cheese rye sandwich.

The woman had no idea if it was for her or the boy, but either way she appreciated the gesture.

"Thank you so much," she said, meeting the eyes of the nurse. She wanted to ask what her name was, where she came from, how long she had been working on the ward, who she was and from which secret source she drew her kindness. And under normal circumstances she would have done just that. But life was not normal right now. Hadn't been for a few hours. Before then, there had still been some logic in the chaos.

The boy gobbled up the whole meal in less than two minutes.

"Be careful you don't get a tummy ache again. We had to go to casualty not so long ago. Do you remember?"

The boy did not answer, just finished his milk and asked for more. He seemed calmer now. There was an interior design programme for children on the T.V. She took the boy's hand in hers. This time he let it lie there. She saw two programme hosts, yet only wanted to see one, unable to control her vision. Closed her eyes instead. Thought about everything that had happened. She hadn't understood a thing. It had been there all the time. An uncomfortable truth hiding in a corner of the bedroom, one that had not been visible from her side. She had to get to the toilet before she exploded. Shifting on her chair, she felt the hard handle of the knife in her pocket.

NOBEL HOSPITAL

Thursday, 7 November

Tekla was waiting for the anaesthetists to fit monitoring equipment to the patient when, suddenly, the door to the second emergency room opened behind her.

"Have you coded the patient?"

Tekla swung around. Sigurdsdottir's attempt to impersonate Carlsson, the hospital C.E.O., fell flat as soon as her lemon yellow trainers came into view. There was a broad smile on her face.

"You need to practise that more," Tekla said.

"Complete bloody waste of time," Sigurdsdottir said, tearing off her plastic apron.

"That doesn't sound convincing either."

Sigurdsdottir, who was Tekla's only true friend at the hospital, got out her second double Japp bar of the day and stuffed some of it into her mouth. "God, I thought I was going to faint there, for real," she said, holding out the chocolate.

"No thanks," Tekla said. "I'll pinch a banana in the ward later on."

"You do know that they've put up surveillance cameras in the patient pantry?"

Tekla stared at Sigurdsdottir's deadly serious face.

"Only joking!"

"I didn't think you should have taken on the emergency in Room 2."

"I know," Sigurdsdottir said. She pressed her hand into the small of her back, leaned backwards and wiggled her hips a bit. "But I do so enjoy it. And soon I'll be missing your blood-smeared cheek."

Instinctively, Tekla put her hand to her face. "Have I . . .?"

Sigurdsdottir laughed and stroked Tekla's cheek. "Not at all. Just a bit too much blusher."

"Great." Tekla sighed.

"You're so beautiful without it," Sigurdsdottir said. "Why can't you see that?"

"Rubbish."

"When I'm back, you and I are going to go dancing."

Tekla failed to bring up any pictures in her mind. Sigurdsdottir was holding the door open for her trauma team, who were leaving with their patient.

"How did it go?" Tekla asked.

"Nothing serious," Sigurdsdottir said, with ill-concealed disappointment. "Fractured left arm and concussion. With a bit of luck he's got a subdural haematoma which I'll get to drill, but I don't think it's going to happen."

"You're sick," Tekla said, shaking her head. A dull headache was making its presence felt again and she took out another can.

"And you ought to cut down on the energy drinks," Sigurdsdottir said. "What about your guy, how did you get on in there?"

"Much more exciting," Tekla said. "Nyström showed up. Did you know he'd already started?"

"How could you have missed it?" Sigurdsdottir exclaimed. "I saw him this morning wearing full body Spandex. He comes in from Nacka on his bike – he's done marathons in twenty capitals. Also said to have Europe's largest collection of toy cars . . . well, maybe the biggest in Nacka anyway."

"How do you know all this?" Tekla asked, fascinated.

"You just need to keep your ears open. And ask a few questions now and then. Why not give it a try, there's more to life than reading articles and dedicating yourself to your patients. When was the last time you went to the theatre or the opera, for example?"

Tekla thought about it. "Twelve years."

"You do realise that we're meant to use *both* hemispheres of the brain. If nothing else, you can justify it by saying that you'll be a better doctor if you also do other things, get a bit of perspective."

"There may be something in that," Tekla said with a smile. "I'm just terrified that Nyström is going to have a say in the reorganisation and do what he did in Linköping."

Sigurdsdottir's grin revealed her irregular row of teeth. "You have no idea, my friend. It's way worse than that. It's the very reason he was recruited in the first place."

"What?"

"He and Monica are going to be in charge of the whole process. On top of that, he's been appointed to the R. & D. council because he's a professor. Several of our senior staff now feel threatened, but Monica would never let even one of them go to the N.S.K., she hates their C.E.O. Hanna Parida so much."

Tekla felt as if the sky had fallen on their heads.

"All we need now is for him to open a clinic for assisted dying."

Sigurdsdottir narrowed her light blue eyes.

"What?" Tekla said.

"Something else that's doing the rounds."

"You're kidding?" Tekla exclaimed. She could see in her mind an article Nyström had published in the medical journal *Läkartidningen* two years ago, in which he advocated setting up centres for assisted dying across the country.

"No."

Tekla did not want to entertain these doomsday scenarios. She pulled the door open and called. "Come on, we're off." She met Sigurdsdottir's look. "I've got to . . ."

"But of course, dear. See you," Sigurdsdottir said, waddling off behind her team to the C.T. scanner. "Look on the bright side. It could be worse. Some consultancy firm could have got their hands on the hospital."

"How's it going?" Tekla said, taking over the bed as it appeared from Emergency Room 1. Rikard, the anaesthetic nurse, was pumping air into the patient's lungs every now and then. Gray got onto the team's kick scooter with the pharmacy trolley and Lisa followed as the back-up from A. & E.

"So-so," Rikard said and upped the speed at which they were moving. "Blood pressure about as stable as the stock market right now."

"No idea you were saving for retirement," Gray called out, keeping up on her scooter.

"Well, it's not as though they pay us nurses a fortune," Rikard said, sounding dejected.

Tekla's mobile pinged. A text from Sigurdsdottir:

And don't forget your date tomorrow ☺

How the hell could she forget something so awful? She replied: Don't worry, and put away her phone.

"Shall I run through all the instructions you've chosen to ignore?" Gray said from her kick scooter.

"Don't bother," Tekla said.

"First you went against Nyström's prescription by giving blood, plasma and thrombocytes."

"I'm not deaf," Tekla said.

"Then you disregarded his request for a C.T. scan," Gray continued. "He's going to be livid – he'll have to operate blind. You might as well start looking for a new job."

"For any real surgeon, that would be standard procedure for a trauma with free fluid in the abdomen," Tekla countered.

"And Monica's bound to find out that one of her senior A. & E. doctors openly took a stand against the new procedures."

"Just imagine," Tekla said. "They may have to write out a regular patient wristband. By hand. Perhaps the bar code thingamabob will blow up right in their panic-stricken faces."

Gray smiled. "You're going to get so much shit for this."

"I'm happy to have been able to put a shine on your day."

"It's as bright as—"

"Bloody hell," Rikard exclaimed. He stopped. Tekla looked at the monitor, which showed a pulse of 130.

34

"Pressure's decreasing. He's bleeding like a pig."

"That's not what I meant," Rikard said. "Well, that too, but look." He pointed down the corridor. Tekla thought her migraine had got worse, but then realised that the passage was sealed off with a plastic sheet behind which scaffolding had been erected.

"Damn," Gray said. "We'll have to go around it."

"That'll take too long," Tekla said. "It'll have to be the service tunnel."

"Are you sure?" Rikard objected. "Isn't that even longer?"

Tekla had already begun to push the stretcher back towards the lift lobby.

"Aren't you going to give him some ephedrine or something?"

Gray looked at Rikard. "Yes. He's about to crash."

Tekla turned the bed. As they waited for the goods lift to arrive, all eyes were on the patient, fighting for his life. Tekla felt a pulse in his wrist, as slight as the sheerest thread. The left hand was not injured and she saw a smooth golden wedding band on his ring finger. It occurred to her that no-one had mentioned any family, but at least there was a partner somewhere. She thought about the text from Lundgren, suggesting they meet. Her instinct told her to decline. Of course. But then, on the other hand, when would she ever dare? Never seemed like a pretty appealing answer.

Her stomach rumbled. Tekla put her hand into her pocket – only two cans of energy drink left. Luckily, D.H.L. had sent a message that morning that her order was on its way.

The doors opened to admit the patient and the entire team. Rikard injected some drugs through the intraosseous access.

"We have to fix a C.V.C. the minute we get to Surgery," he muttered, sounding irritated. A black shape was now visible on the relatively undamaged skin of the patient's upper arm. Tekla wiped away some coagulated blood and saw that it was a transfer tattoo of Darth Vader with parts of the helmet peeling off. So there was a child in the picture too. A whole family? A wave of nausea hit Tekla and she emptied the can in a few gulps.

The lift door opened and they set off along the empty service corridor.

"Pulse is increasing," Rikard said.

"Pressure's falling," Tekla countered.

"It was up at 70 for a while, but now it's back to 50."

"And oxygen saturation's falling," Gray called. "Would be too bad if he crashed down here."

"At the same time as a power cut," Rikard said.

Tekla could not help admiring the anaesthetic nurse's dry sense of humour in such a dire situation.

"Wait," Tekla said, pulling out her stethoscope. She listened to the patient's heart.

"Shit!" she yelled. Her voice echoed through the service tunnel. "He's got a tamponade."

"How do you know that?" Gray asked.

Tekla pointed to the man's throat. "Distended jugular vein, muffled heart sounds and falling blood pressure. Beck's triad. Cardiac tamponade."

NOBEL HOSPITAL

Thursday, 7 November

"Those toilets stink," Carlsson said with an imperious look at Ulrika Westin, a medical secretary. "Typical public sector!"

Westin took a deep breath and waited for the six division heads to walk past with their cups of coffee. "You think so?"

"Are you suggesting I'm wrong?" Carlsson was indignant.

"No, of course not. I'll get Locum, the property managers, to see what the problem is."

"It reminds me of that disgusting Swedish tradition of eating tinned rotten fish. I was hoping we might have made more progress with the new plumbing."

Carlsson motioned to the secretary to go in and then she herself shut the door before opening the weekly meeting of the management team.

Everyone was sitting in their designated place. Carlsson was not especially bothered either way, so long as the man she shunned above all others was seated on the uncomfortable chair squeezed in behind the high computer desk she was using. Sadly, she couldn't get away with gagging him.

"We have a very full agenda so we might as well kick off," Carlsson said. She chose to remain standing by her laptop so that she had full control over what was being projected on the screen behind her. The slides had been prepared by Westin. Not quite museum quality, but Carlsson only needed them as a prompt. Oral presentations had always been her strongest suit, whether as president of the students council or deputy chair of the Young Conservatives in her local town, during a short spell as president of the student union at Karolinska and then during her meteoric rise through the medical world. There was zero competition on the various speaking platforms in the hospital universe – doctors as a rule not being known for their eloquence – but Carlsson was aiming much higher than that anyway. She was not giving up on her ambition to become C.E.O of the N.S.K., a job she had missed out on by a whisker. And she could think of no better place from which to attack the hospital to the north of them than the top floor of the Nobel Hospital. Soon enough the N.S.K. management would come crawling back and ask her to take over.

When she reached for the mouse to right-click, her finger seemed to stick in the air and suddenly felt numb. She stared in surprise and clenched her fist to release the locked digit, but it stood straight out. Then, just as suddenly as it had stiffened, it loosened up again and she was able to click through to the first slide for the meeting agenda. Carlsson tried to see if anyone had noticed, but they were all focused on the screen behind her, like obedient pupils on the first day of term. She wiped some perspiration off her upper lip and drew her hand across her white silk blouse, pretending to straighten her scarf, before carrying on.

"You can see for yourselves how many items we have to get through so . . . I'm going to get stuck in right away." Carlsson glanced around the room. There were rarely any problems with the six division heads. They had agreed to the funds allocated to them and, luckily for Carlsson, seemed unaware that it was possible to argue for more. Or else, they were resigned to the fact that it was Carlsson who decided how the cake was to be shared out.

She clenched and unclenched her right hand a couple of times.

"Let's deal with a few straightforward matters first. As you know, Göran has been appointed the new senior consultant and Hampus Nordensköld will take over from him as head of A. & E. I'll be announcing all this at the general meeting tomorrow morning."

She met Göran Collinder's eyes and saw that the poor fellow had aged ten years in a matter of months. It must have been the loss of status and the realisation that retirement was creeping closer. Nordensköld, on the other hand, appeared to have made straight for the men's section at the N.K. department store and bought himself an expensive but fuddy-duddy tweed jacket with a discreet, matching dark green tie.

"Göran will be perfect for the new post. Thanks to his extensive contacts, both inside and outside the hospital, he can help to oil the wheels when the machinery seizes up."

Or keep troublemakers and idiotic trade union representatives at bay. Carlsson couldn't stand them. She got out a salt liquorice car tyre and quickly popped it into her mouth .

"Am I right, Göran? A fitting conclusion to a fantastic career. What could be better than three tranquil years before taking up golf full-time?"

Nordensköld and Emma Nyrén, head of communications, chuckled for a few seconds, as if they were sitting with the French horns and had just had their own little cue from the conductor. Collinder managed an unconvincing smile as his eyes narrowed to two slits in his tanned face.

There was a brief silence, broken only by the sound of Nyrén's long fingernails dancing across the computer keys, producing a sort of morse code. She sat bolt upright on the edge of her chair with one foot tucked back at an elegant angle. Every now and then she would toss her blond hair so that the long fringe landed perfectly above one eye. Carlsson saw herself in Nyrén, with that thick straight hair, the flawless complexion and a smile that never seemed fake, albeit a version that was twenty-five kilos heavier.

She avoided looking at the man opposite Nyrén.

"Next item: the renovations. We delivered on the I.C.U. this spring and it really was a tremendous success. I had a delegation from Bologna here this week and they were extremely impressed."

Nyrén graced the whole of the long meeting-room table with her smile. Even the women looked enchanted.

"And you can't have missed the fact that we're now working on the entrance level," Carlsson went on. "We regret that this means you'll have to take a bit of a detour for a while, but it'll do some of us good to go the extra mile, so to speak. And now for the annex," she added, with genuine pride in her voice. She turned to Nyrén, who took over seamlessly.

"I gather from the construction manager that the residential part is completed. I went there on Monday to have a look and they had just finished painting the walls and sanding the wooden floors. It's going to be absolutely top notch." Nyrén sounded as if she were describing some fantastic destination hotel. "The reception and entrance areas will be finished in the course of this week. I'm going over this afternoon to check that all the furniture and bed linen has arrived."

"Good," Carlsson said, clicking to the next slide. "That means we're now ready to receive the first cases. We have the staff standing by and one patient in the pipeline. Right, Klas?"

Nyström straightened up and nodded slowly. "But I'm not allowed to say anything, am I?"

Carlsson returned Nyström's smile, which had not escaped anyone's notice. "That's correct. We'll obviously let you all know as soon as the first patient is admitted, but right now we have to keep it to ourselves. This sort of thing does tend to leak out."

"And when they actually get here, you can be sure you'll hear about it," Nyrén added. It was obvious from her attitude and the fawning smiles that she was enjoying making a big secret out of all this.

"What do you mean?" Göran said.

"We'll be holding a press conference to announce our transplant programme. A key component of our new business plan. I'm going to organise a monthly session with the media on a trial basis. To talk about our renovation projects as well as progress on research and the cases of the month."

"Cases of the month?" Ellen Cederholm, the head of the sensory organs division, asked.

"One interesting case from each of your divisions," Nyrén said. "Every four weeks, you'll have to find a patient who's willing to share an account of their condition and treatment with the media."

"Are you ..." Cederholm was trying hard to find words that would not displease the C.E.O. "That sounds very American."

"Precisely," an enthusiastic Nordensköld exclaimed. "You know, like Trump standing there on the podium with all his serious-faced staff lined up along the wall and that cool, round logo in the background."

"I'm glad you see the potential, Hampus. Perhaps not exactly like Trump, but it's important to be on the front line when it comes to developing healthcare in this city." She looked at poor Ellen.

"Do you have anything against progress?" Carlsson said, moving a step closer to the woman, who was looking in vain for support from her fellow division heads. Not one of them seemed prepared to extend a helping hand.

"No."

"Good." Carlsson returned to her desk. "Not even the N.S.K. does regular press briefings."

"Except when they have some announcement to make about famous Italian researchers," Nordensköld added with a smile.

"For example," Monica conceded, but she refrained from giving Nordensköld any further encouragement. He was about to burst with smugness.

"Item three. The very core of the hospital's new programme." Carlsson paused for effect and looked around. Nyrén touched up her lipstick and went on tapping at her laptop as if nothing had happened.

"Our new liver transplant unit under the leadership of none other than Klas Nyström," Carlsson solemnly proclaimed.

The division heads nodded obligingly.

"I had a call from the C.E.O. of the N.S.K., asking for a meeting to discuss transplant activities in the whole of the Stockholm area. As if. Basically, it was to tell us not to go ahead with our liver transplant programme. And there has been complete silence from Göteborg so far."

Monica saw her index finger stiffen and stand to attention again, only to fall back onto the table three seconds later.

"Maybe they realise they can't stop it anyway," Nyrén suggested.

"Probably," Carlsson said quickly. As if that really were the case. As if she really called the shots when the National Board of Health and Welfare's working party decided how to allocate highly special-ised care facilities in Sweden. She pushed her short, black fringe to the side and helped herself to two liquorice wheels.

"That brings us to the last item on today's agenda. The I.T. pro-curement process, which I believe is running ahead as—"

"Maybe I should come in at this point," a voice said. It was the man behind the high computer table. Carlsson had so far managed to avoid looking at him. Her finger locked into an angle.

"O.K., well as—"

"My name is Ludwig af Petersén, for those of you who don't know that you've got a new C.F.O. And I took up my position, when was it Monica, I'd say about—"

"I'm not sure, Ludwig, but it's probably not all that important," Carlsson said drily.

"A month. Call it a month," af Petersén said. He had to squeeze past Carlsson and the podium she was standing on. "I've just left PwC, where I was senior advisor to the board with a focus on health-care issues. The hospital management recruited me to build up the new Nobel and help establish it as the leading hospital in the county."

"How about being a bit more ambitious than that?" Carlsson snorted.

"Are you suggesting I take over your role?" af Petersén said with a chuckle.

"Well, no, obviously not," Carlsson said. "Why would I . . ." She stopped herself, realising that she sounded bitter and angry. She was not known for her sense of humour.

"Only joking," af Petersén said. "No, of course we need to aim higher than that. The Nobel Hospital should be a world leader. A hospital which continues with its core business – emergency services – but also offers something else that really stands out, namely a brand new liver transplant unit. A programme which is seen as a benchmark not only in this country, but internationally."

"That's not something you can make happen just by pushing a button," Cederholm objected, having apparently got a second wind.

Af Petersén went over and put his hands on her shoulders.

"Too right. You're absolutely right, dear girl. Under normal circumstances, that is. Under *normal* circumstances. But we have a secret weapon. When you have a star surgeon of Klas Nyström's calibre, you can build the entire business around him and feel confident about announcing great things at press conferences, because you know that you're going to be able to deliver on your promise to be a world leader in the field. We may have to cut back on some of the other research groups, but we'll come to that."

"But are you planning to try . . . to go for privatisation, is that what you're telling us?" the division head asked. Judging by the tense silence in the room, there were others who had had the same thought but not dared to put it into words.

Af Petersén took his hands off the woman's shoulders and folded them in front of him.

"Absolutely not. Let's not get carried away . . ."

"All in the fulness of time," Carlsson added, suddenly feeling the whole of her right arm go rigid. Not only did her index finger stand straight out, her arm had gone stiff all the way up to the shoulder. And also numb in an unpleasant way. At first she thought it had gone to sleep because she'd been leaning on it and some nerve was compressed. She let it hang down by her side and swung it to and fro casually, but nothing happened. Instead, she realised that she was losing the feeling in her left arm as well. She tried to stay calm, wondered if it might be a panic attack, but her breathing was regular. Her pulse was perhaps slightly faster than usual after af Petersén's annoying intervention, but nothing out of the ordinary. The worst thing

43

was that he was so good. She saw that the fear in the eyes of the division heads had given way to eager looks and relaxed smiles. They were taken in by his baloney. He was more of a politician than a C.F.O.

She let her arms dangle, shook them to try and loosen them up, but the unpleasant numbness and stiffness lasted for several uncomfortable seconds. Then the symptoms vanished just as suddenly as they had appeared. She raised her hand and reached for the mouse again.

"Right, I think we're beginning to run out of time," she said, as another wave of anger engulfed her. It was important that she not appear cross and resentful.

"Many thanks, Ludwig. We are delighted to have you here as our new *finance* officer. At long last we'll be getting some control over the numbers. Am I right, Emma?"

Nyrén nodded, smiling at the division heads.

"But I suggest we leave the details for later when we'll have made more progress in our work." With an open hand she gestured in the direction of af Petersén's chair. He appeared to hesitate for a second. Was he going to object, make some closing remarks?

"Certainly, Monica," af Petersén said, and this time he walked all the way around the table in order not to have to bend double to get past Carlsson's podium.

"We were actually supposed to be discussing the I.T. procurement process," Nyrén said, in an attempt to get things back on track.

"That's right," Carlsson said. "But maybe there's nothing new on that front. We have a bid from a well-known international firm who are going to be awarded the contract."

"Well here I think we have to back-track for a moment," af Petersén said as he sat down and opened up his laptop.

"Is that so?" Carlsson said. "How come?"

"A competing Swedish firm has lodged an appeal with the Administrative Court."

Carlsson struggled to keep calm.

"And you learned this . . .?"

"This week," af Petersén said, looking worried. That, at least, was what he wanted to convey. Carlsson did not find it convincing. He really ought to be apologising for not having informed her straight away.

"O.K. And how do we move forward on this?"

"It could take some time."

"I disagree," Carlsson said stiffly. "We'll stick with the company we've decided to use."

Af Petersén still looked worried. He nodded and drew his hand across the edge of the computer screen. "I don't think so. I've been told by the Board that this has got to be done by the book. No funny business that could get us bad headlines. I'm sure you'd agree with that, Emma, wouldn't you?"

For the first time, Nyrén looked uncertain. She glanced quickly at Carlsson. "No, obviously, we must ensure that we have the Board's backing on all important decisions."

"Wise words," af Petersén said. His long pause was eloquent.

Carlsson's brain went into overdrive. She knew that she was unlikely to win this battle, that it would be smarter to just let it go. She needed to regroup and come back with renewed strength, not rush into something that might backfire.

"Well, that's all we have for you today," she said. "As usual, Ulrika will send out an e-mail with the minutes within the next twenty-four hours."

Carlsson was the first to leave the room. She waited outside for Nyrén to appear, clutching her silver-coloured computer to her figure-hugging blazer. They walked in silence until they reached a secluded area in one corner of the building.

"You look . . ." Carlsson could tell that Nyrén was casting about for something kind to say. ". . . different. Just . . . good."

"You mean I've lost weight."

"No, I—"

"That's exactly what you mean. And I suggest you refrain from commenting on your boss' appearance."

They walked on to the end of the corridor and stopped by the windows.

"Well, what can one say?" Nyrén asked, pushing back her hair with the nail of her index finger.

Carlsson thrust her hands into the pockets of her black slacks. Straightened up and looked outside. She saw the Tax Scraper towering halfway between the hospital and Slussen.

"Wise words."

"What?" Nyrén sounded puzzled.

"You were commended by Ludwig. Did you hear that?"

"Oh I see, I—"

"Emma," Carlsson interrupted the head of communications and turned to face her. "I hired you because you're loyal and have the same vision for the Nobel Hospital as I do. Right?"

"Absolutely, but I—"

"No buts, my dear." Carlsson pushed aside Nyrén's fringe. "I think your hair is fantastic. You must spend an awful lot of time on it."

Nyrén stood silent, waiting to see what would come next.

"Never call my authority into question in front of anyone else. Ever."

"Of course. But I wasn't questioning anything in there."

"Dear girl. So naïve. And you're supposed to be in charge of communications." Carlsson patted Nyrén's cheek a few times. The last one was almost like a slap. "Get a grip. No more idiotic remarks that undermine my authority. Do you hear me?"

"I hear."

"And?"

"I promise. It will never happen again."

"Good," Carlsson said with a smile. "Let's get some coffee."

NOBEL HOSPITAL
Thursday, 7 November

"Look," the boy called out, pointing to the corridor.

The woman caught a glimpse of the old man gliding past on a hospital trolley. The boy jumped to his feet and rushed off after him. The woman carried the tray over to a rack for dirty dishes. She could barely stand and the stabbing pain in the pit of her stomach was back. She staggered out of the dining room and saw that the old man had his hand on the boy's head. Like a silent blessing. She wanted to scream but managed to restrain herself. Everything had to be controlled. There was too much at stake.

Two nurses, or maybe assistant nurses, steered the stretcher into a room that was marked with the number 4.

She followed them. The boy was hardly aware of her, he was completely absorbed by the old man on the trolley and his escorts. They entered a room for two divided by a simple, sliding partition. An elderly patient lay there, sleeping. The old man was wheeled over to the unoccupied side.

"You'll have to wait while we get organised," a short, blond girl told them. She was probably only about twenty but had a dominant attitude that suggested she was the boss of the universe. She must have been the person who brought the old man along to the ward from A. & E.

They transferred him to the second bed in the room. One person by his head, one by his feet and two who were pulling at a sort of bottom sheet lying on a blue plastic film. Presumably to make it glide more easily. They laid the old man down gently.

Suddenly, the woman doubled up with terrible stomach pains.

47

She felt sick and looked around for a waste paper basket. After a few deep breaths the nausea disappeared. She was desperate to fend off thoughts that crowded her mind. Knew what she had to do. At the same time, she was beset by a terrible doubt. She tore herself away, overcome by a vision of a small coffin, about a metre long. Mounds of flowers. A flute playing a sorrowful tune. An overwhelming grief gnawed at her insides. Another life. Another world.

She met the old man's gaze for the first time. Struggled to hold it. She walked over, but stopped half a metre from the bed, afraid that a hand would be held out and she wouldn't know what to do. The old man's eyes were dull. They seemed confused. Probably the drugs. A veil of morphine, a thin film that wiped away the threatening look she had seen there that morning. There had been a different resolve. Now those eyes were on the woman, now looking down at the boy and then back to the woman again. He made an effort to say something, but all he managed to produce was a cough. He fell silent. The mask over his face stopped him from speaking – he was, after all, a casualty. He turned away and looked out of the window. His lips were purple, his breathing rapid. His snow-white hair was ruffled, it needed to be combed.

"I'm afraid we must ask you to step outside for a moment," the assistant nurse said.

Clearly the woman looked surprised, because an explanation was forthcoming. "We're going to insert a catheter."

The assistant nurse was interrupted by the arrival of a doctor, a young woman, blond straight hair perfectly tied up in a ponytail, fringe and a prominent belly announcing the imminent arrival of a baby. She was pale and looked tired, but her face broke into a broad and friendly smile.

"Are you family?"

"Yes."

She introduced herself and held out her hand. It had just been sanitised and was damp, but the woman's spontaneous reaction was to hold on to it, enjoying the feel of its pleasant warmth.

48

"I only wanted to say hello and welcome to our unit. And, while I'm here, check out his lungs."

"Is it serious?" the woman asked, wiping the sweat off her forehead. The light from the fluorescent tubes had a paralysing effect on her. It felt like it was searing her face. The doctor was bound to notice how unwell she was.

The doctor lowered her voice, speaking to the woman so that only she could hear amid the surrounding clamour. The boy did not move from the old man's side.

"He had a guardian angel. Probably the car only brushed him and wasn't going all that fast. His forearm is fractured and in a cast. He's broken a few ribs and he has a lung contusion, which is when fluid accumulates in the lung after a blow to the chest, that's why he needs oxygen and diuretics. But it's his head we have to watch carefully. He has pretty bad concussion. As I said, his guardian angel was right there with him. At his age, he could just as easily have died. The other one is worse off."

The woman stiffened. She waited to hear more, but nothing came. In the end she forced herself to ask if he was dead.

The doctor rested her slim hand on the woman's arm. "Miraculously enough, not. He's in surgery right now. If he survives, he'll be taken to the I.C.U. We'll keep you informed."

Once again, she felt the pain in her stomach. A shiver ran through her. I.C.U . . . He was still alive.

"O.K. But what do you think—"

"The prognosis, you mean?" the doctor filled in, looking in the direction of the old man. She was used to this. The woman nodded, even though she hadn't meant that. She could not care less about a prognosis. Didn't want any figures. Wasn't interested in anything to do with the old man. There would be no prognosis. She would see to that.

"Yes."

"I don't usually do forecasts, that only happens in American T.V. series. We take one day at a time. Just now he's not doing too well.

We've got to begin by trying to remove the fluid from his lungs, giving him diuretics and using a mask that blows in air so that he breathes against a resistance."

"I see," the woman said, sounding both unconcerned and understanding. She went over to the boy, who was lost in his own world. A world consisting of the old man, a thin sheet and the smell of disinfectant. The doctor left the room.

The tall, blond, rather chinless nurse – it reminded the woman of some syndrome – gave her a significant look. A glance at the nurse's nails told the woman that she did not spend a lot of time on them.

"We just need to tidy things up a bit here."

"We can wait," the woman said.

The blond nurse looked up and caught the eye of her colleague on the other side of the bed. She was shorter and her dark hair was pulled back in a ponytail. They seemed to be silently debating whether to ask the woman and the boy to leave the room again. But something told her that they had agreed not to. As if there were some unspoken rule in the unit whereby relatives of such a seriously ill patient, who might die within hours, could decide for themselves. And stay if they wanted to. Perhaps some psychologist had even done a study showing that families of people who are dying actually *ought* to be present as much as possible, because it helps with the grieving process. Maybe these findings were recently presented by a dedicated department head at a staff meeting and the two nurses were now implementing the new guidelines.

She said again, mostly to herself, but loudly enough that no-one in the room could possibly miss it.

"We can wait. No problem."

For whom? she thought. Not for her. For the staff? Presumably. They had to watch their language when family were present. They need not worry about the patient in this case. He was drifting in and out of consciousness.

The boy was lying across the armrests of the only comfortable chair in the room, playing on a phone. He had his back to the old man's bed. He had managed to find one of the hospital's open networks and was busy with his favourite game, competing against others online. The boy was utterly absorbed and did not appear to be registering anything that was happening in the room.

The woman sat down. The boy's long fringe flopped over one eye. The good thing about never having been to day-care was that he never picked up nits. Not once had she had to dig for lice with a comb under the kitchen light.

The nurses were working in silence to prepare for the insertion of a catheter. The natural thing would have been to tell the woman what was about to be done, but a compact silence had settled and was not about to be broken. The blond nurse left the room and immediately returned with a shallow aluminium basin. She went into the bathroom to fill it with soap and water. When she came back, a tall head of foam was swaying over the bowl. She had put on a plastic apron and gloves. So had the assistant nurse.

The woman wondered when they would be left alone, if there were only a few more minutes to wait before it could happen. She felt the tingle of sweat in the palms of her hands.

"30 over unmeasurable," Rikard said after once more taking a manual blood pressure reading.

At that very moment, Tekla's mobile rang. She was on the point of declining the ill-timed call when she saw that it was Carlsson.

"Monica, we have a bit of a situation here, do you mind . . ."

"I just wanted to say that I've been told that you and Klas have met." Tekla could hear that Carlsson was chewing on something. "I had intended to introduce him at the Monday meeting, but he turned up a little earlier this week to gently ease himself into the system. It's truly—"

"Sorry to cut you off, Monica, but I have a very unstable patient here."

"Alright," Carlsson said quickly. "Fine. Patients first. I won't keep you from your duties, let's talk later." She hung up.

"We've got to hurry," Gray said.

Rikard blew air into the tube. The patient's ribcage rose. Tekla's brain was whirling, but her body had already decided. Blunt thoracic trauma with potential cardiac arrest as a result of tamponade.

"We won't get there in time."

She knew the way by heart. Four hundred metres to the nearest lift lobby, waiting time by the lift, the risks involved in doing what she had in mind in a lift, then another three hundred metres to Surgery, some hassle with the new passes, waiting for someone to open the doors, and then into theatre. At least six minutes. After four, the patient's brain would be starved of oxygen and he would, by definition, be brain dead.

"Give me a scalpel."

"What are you doing, Tekla, we've got to—"

Tekla had already bent down and was pulling on fresh gloves. She took the bottle of hand sanitiser that was on the bed. "Could you please just hand me a scalpel?" she said with some restraint. "Surely you've got one for acute C-sections."

Gray shook her head. "Well yes, but . . ."

"His pulse is racing," Rikard announced. "He'll be gone any second now."

"What are you doing?" Lisa panted, setting down the emergency bag.

"Going in," Tekla said as she ran through what she had to do in her mind.

"Going in where, Tekla?"

After some searching, Gray produced a disposable scalpel from a side compartment of the kick scooter and held it out with a trembling hand.

"The ribcage. Once I'm in, we'll need to move carefully but as quickly as we can to the lift lobby over there. Will you call Surgery, Helena, and tell them to have a room ready for us."

"But . . ."

"Stop saying 'but' all the time, anyone would think you work for the County Council."

"He's crashing," Rikard said, letting go of the Ambu bag.

"Start compressions," Tekla said. "Not that it will make a huge difference. And it certainly won't save his life."

Rikard left the head end of the trolley and began carrying out compressions while Tekla tore open the wrapping of the kit for acute C-sections. She sprayed hand sanitiser over the man's left thorax and, using disposable pads, tried to wipe off most of the coagulated blood that had trickled down from his battered face. She was searching for some area between the ribs that was not mottled blue, but the injuries to the ribcage were both internal and external. She had to accept that there would be bleeding regardless of where she placed her incision. Though he couldn't have much blood left in his circulatory system.

Just as she had decided where to cut, Tekla stopped and pushed a bloodstained hand into her pocket. She got out a can, opened it and swallowed the contents. The other three stood in silence, mesmerised by the mad doctor down in the service tunnels of the Nobel Hospital.

Tekla looked at the transfer tattoos on the patient's upper arm and let her eyes wander down to his ring finger.

"You're going to be drowning in shit," Gray said.

Tekla opened her eyes wide and aimed the incision at a spot above the sixth rib, extending all the way laterally down towards the flank. At first, there was hardly any blood. She made the cut longer so that it looked like a big mouth across the man's chest. "Now it's going to bleed. Can you give some adrenalin?"

"Certainly," Gray replied. She began to fiddle with her syringes.

"What do you want me to do?" Lisa said. Tekla smiled to herself as it became obvious that the team had accepted the new situation.

"Hook up a Ringer, maybe," Tekla said. "There's no more blood and we need to work up as much pressure as we can. Lucky he's young." She imagined a child sitting at a kitchen table – or maybe he had more than one, who all needed him. The first incision was made and she pressed the scalpel down deeper, just above the rib. Suddenly, fresh blood was spilling out over the bed.

Next came the difficult part: separating the ribs by hand, without any equipment. Tekla put down the scalpel and pressed three fingers in between the ribs. It was tight and difficult to move them apart but they yielded, millimetre by millimetre, and her fingers went in further and further.

While Tekla was pulling and tugging, Rikard was trying to do compressions. Her task was made all the more difficult as her fingers were squeezed between the ribs whenever he put pressure on the thorax. Tekla shifted and applied all her strength. There was a sound like that of a slim branch snapping. Some ribs must have broken off the sternum. Finally, she managed to insert her right hand and feel the heart. The pericardium, the thin sac surrounding it, was like a blowfish, full of blood which was not meant to be there. It was constricting the heart so that it was unable to fill up and relax with every heartbeat, resulting in circulatory failure.

Tekla started pumping the heart with her hand and told Rikard to stop his compressions. "I'd rather you checked if you can get a femoral pulse."

Rikard applied two fingers to the patient's groin.

"Good pulse."

"And the pupils?" Tekla asked Gray.

Gray shook her head but pulled out a torch and looked into the patient's eyes. "They contract."

"He's alive. Let's get moving."

Gray stumbled over to the scooter while Lisa carefully began pushing the bed in the direction of the lift lobby.

Tekla felt her mobile vibrate. A new text. She thought about the message from Simon saying that he wanted to talk, had something to tell her. Tekla had grown accustomed to that reassuring, uneventful weekly conversation with him from Spain when he would rattle on about Miguel, Javier and all the others he had got to know during five months of rehab on the Costa del Sol. Tekla's savings would only last until Christmas, but she had not yet sprung that on her dear little brother. Right now, she was just enjoying the fact that he couldn't cause any trouble back home. She was planning to go and see him between Christmas and New Year. Then she would tell him that there was no more money. That he had to come home.

They reached the lift lobby and Tekla tried to shift to a new position to relieve the pain in her back. Lisa checked oxygen saturation and Gray once again got out her torch.

"His pupils are still contracting. Surgery are expecting us."

"But pressure is unmeasurable and there's virtually no pulse," Rikard added after briefly stopping the ventilation.

With her eye firmly on a green door some way down the corridor,

Tekla had no trouble pulling up *Difficult Decisions in Thoracic Surgery* from 2007 in her mind. A mammoth work by Mark K. Ferguson, which she had glanced through during a stint in specialty training in Uppsala several years ago. Tekla remembered how envious her fellow students always were, saying that she never seemed to revise yet always passed exams with flying colours. Haemodynamic instability. Operative manoeuvres, page 984. A stylised illustration.

"Can you put on some gloves?" she asked Gray.

"Sure," Gray said. The lift arrived with a ping.

"Hold the doors," Tekla told Rikard. And to Gray, who was holding up her hands: "Pull the ribs a bit further apart. I need to get my other hand in." Tekla could feel warm fluid inside her right glove. Blood had seeped in since her arm was so deep into the man's chest.

Gray tried to get a hold, groping carefully with her fingers next to Tekla's bloody arm.

"You can forget the kid gloves," Tekla said in a calm voice. "In principle, he's dead, so anything we can do is a bonus."

Gray looked terrified but pressed her hand in between the ribs and pulled. There was a crack when they broke away from their attachment to the spine.

"Thanks," Tekla said, thrusting her second hand into the man's thorax. She felt her way across the smooth surface of the respiratory muscle until she found two flabby structures, one slightly larger with more elastic consistency than the other. She took a stranglehold on something that felt like a punctured bicycle inner tube and squeezed it.

"There we are," she said. "Could someone check the pulse now." She was pumping the heart with her right hand.

"Better!" Rikard burst out and, for the first time, the deep furrow between his eyes disappeared. "What did you do?"

"Compressed the aorta," Tekla said.

They pushed the bed into the lift and pressed the button for the fourth floor: Surgery.

ORTHOPAEDICS DEPARTMENT K 81, NOBEL HOSPITAL

Thursday, 7 November

The old man's eyes were closed. His face looked strangely empty. Were it not for the unabashed treatment he was getting from the two women, he might have been asleep. They rolled him onto his side and turned up his backside and thighs so that the blond nurse could get to work, rubbing, scraping and stripping off the dried faeces. There was no hint of disgust on her face. Her expression was gentle and neutral. They worked away for ten minutes until the woman could see the redness right across the old man's buttocks. They replaced the plastic and put a clean bottom sheet on the bed before buttoning the white patient shirt down the man's spine.

He was lying on his back again. The monitoring device emitted a beep and the dark-haired assistant nurse pressed a yellow button, which she could only reach with difficulty. She saw that the woman was worried, and said quickly:

"Saturation tends to drop when we're busy with the patient. It'll soon go back up again." She went on straightening the bed. The old man was bare from his stomach down to his feet. Knees slightly bent. Kneecaps as large as grapefruits, skinny shins. His calf muscles dangled like oblong pouches from his lower legs, purple blotches marked his greyish white skin. This was not the same person who had met her at the Central Station. How could it be? How could such a commanding presence crumble in just a few hours?

A musical loop kept playing over and over again on the boy's phone. Small explosions and shouts could be heard when the hero died and the game began anew. The boy was completely focused.

Now and then he quickly raised his left hand and rubbed his eyes. There were some faint dark shadows under them, maybe they were affected by the dry hospital air.

The assistant nurse pulled up a steel table that had been standing in a corner.

There was a packet on it, the size of two shoeboxes. She tore off the paper wrapping, revealing the contents to be a complete catheterisation set.

The old man's private parts hung between his thighs. The nurse placed them on his stomach and began washing. She took some clean compresses and wiped the shrivelled skin on the testicles. Her movements were mechanical, routine, effective. Her face wore a bored expression, mouth closed, eyes empty. In her thoughts, she was miles away. Picking up a syringe which the woman imagined to contain some anaesthetic, she quickly inserted the tip into the urethra. The woman felt an ice-cold shiver run down her spine as, for the first time, the old man showed some sign of discomfort, tilting his head backwards. The nurse injected the contents until a transparent, viscous fluid began to seep out of the urethra by the nozzle of the syringe. Then she rubbed her nose with the crook of her arm. The woman spotted three tattooed stars curling down her throat from behind her ear.

"Mamma?"

"Yes?"

"Can I play some more?"

"Why wouldn't you be allowed to?"

"You don't usually let me play for more than half an hour."

"You can go on," the woman said, cupping her hand over the back of the boy's head. "But we've got to leave now. There's something I have to do."

She held his hand when he helped himself to some sterilising gel from the bottle by the door.

"I don't want to catch anything," he said with a smile.

It struck her how easy it was – the relationship that had developed between her and the boy. It made her feel proud. She paused for a second, remembering that it had been anything but a foregone conclusion. Could she now call herself Mamma?

Once they had left the room, the woman began to feel dizzy. Nauseous. She had to sit down on a chair in the corridor and take some deep breaths. Once more there was a pungent smell of excrement. Her bowels were straining again. Suddenly it was as if they had only just arrived in A. & E. As if she had gone back in time and was reliving her conversation with the staff at the reception.

"I need to go to the toilet," the boy said.

"Oh dear." The woman looked up. "Let's go and find one."

"I'm going to wet myself."

"No, you're not. We'll make it in time."

They walked towards the ward office. The woman kept having to steady herself against the wall, the floor seemed to fall away. Through a window, she spotted a young man with a shaved head and thick black spectacles who was speaking on the telephone. She knocked on the glass, reluctant to open the door and simply march in. The man looked up from his computer, telephone in one hand. He held up a finger and nodded. Did that mean just one minute? That he would soon be available? She decided to be a model of patience.

"Mamma, I have to pee *now*." The boy stood with his knees pressed together tightly. He was pulling at the woman's down jacket.

Once again, she tapped on the window pane and pointed at the boy. As if the nurse in there would understand what she meant. The woman looked around for someone else who might be able to help. Her eyes scanned the corridor for a sign indicating a toilet, but there was nothing. At the far end of the passage, a member of staff was standing by some sort of locker, maybe a place for storing valuables.

"Come."

"I can't."

"Come along, you'll be O.K." Her tone was much sharper than she had intended. She was annoyed with herself for making the boy feel that it was his fault for not telling her in good time. But he could handle it. She had prepared him for something like this – they had practised, run through scenarios. What to do in a panic situation, if someone arrived, if they had to flee.

"You wait here, I'll go and look." She rushed over to the female staff member by the cupboard.

"Excuse me, is there a toilet here?"

The nurse pointed to a door further down the corridor. The woman turned to the boy and waved to him to join her. He took a few stumbling steps, but it looked as if his legs were tied together at the knees. After covering half the distance he stopped. His shoulders sagged, and his knees slowly separated until they were about ten centimetres apart. Then she saw a dark patch spread slowly down his jeans from the flies to the thighs. The woman ran up to the boy. Knelt down and took him in her arms.

"It doesn't matter," she whispered.

She hugged him tight, smelled the urine.

"It's alright."

She could feel her tears welling up. Could not remember when that had last happened. She embraced the boy for a long time, thought she felt his rapid heartbeats before realising, after a few seconds, that they were her own. The thuds resonated right up into her head. Images popped up. From the lake where they used to pick mushrooms. She thought back to the rare times *he* had accompanied them, in the very beginning, when they had moved house once and ended up in what she felt was the perfect place. But after only a year they had to move on. She never found another mushroom place that was as good as that one.

The boy kept his eyes tightly shut and raised his head slightly. His arms once again hung limply by his sides. Mouth shut. Nostrils flared from the heavy, slightly forced breathing. The tears trapped inside. The Iron Man mask was in one hand. He put it back on.

Slowly, the woman released him, leaving one hand on him so that he would not feel alone. "Don't worry. We'll fix it." Inside, she was angry and irritated that he had not warned her in time. But she had learned that accusations and making someone feel guilty hardly ever make things any better.

She took the boy's hand and, reluctantly, he allowed himself be led over to a patient bed standing by the wall. She lifted him up onto it, hugged him again and whispered, "It's going to be alright," before walking off to the office. On the way there, she drove her hands into her jacket pockets, feeling the blade of the knife through the paper napkin. She quickly pulled them out again, as if she had burned herself. The time was not yet right.

The door opened and the male nurse with the black spectacles emerged. "Can I help you?"

The woman opened her mouth to say something unpleasant but changed her mind. She even made an effort to smile.

"There's been a little accident. My boy has wet himself. Do you have any trousers we could borrow?"

"Only adult size for patients."

"Could you please get the smallest ones you can find?"

"Sure." The male nurse turned and left, disappearing through a door.

The woman swung around. The boy was sitting immobile with his eyes fixed on the floor in front of him. She didn't go straight over to him. Something held her back. They should have been far, far away by now, and by rights she ought to be in a paralysing state of panic because they weren't, but for some strange reason she was not. Maybe because it was all preordained?

They were by an antechamber leading to two patient rooms. Yellow coats were hanging on hooks. She saw two face shields. Maybe these were some kind of isolation rooms. One of the doors opened and she waited for someone to come out. It was dark in there. Pitch black. The door was opened wide but then closed slowly. She shuddered. No-one stepped out. And there was no-one inside either. She had a clear line of sight into the room and saw only an empty bed and a bedside lamp which was not lit. But not a living soul.

Her hands were shaking. Had they been doing so even before the door opened? These past few hours, her body had been sending out signals she'd never experienced before. It frightened her.

"Here," she heard a voice say, and turned.

The nurse seemed impatient. He waved a pair of white trousers in front of her face and thrust them at her.

"Thank you," the woman said, taking them from him. Her hands were still shaking. She felt a sudden urge to punch the man in the nose, knew exactly how to do it, it would be so simple.

SURGICAL DEPARTMENT, NOBEL HOSPITAL
Thursday, 7 November

The lift doors slid open without any fanfare or flash bulbs, just a robotic female voice saying: "Fourth floor."

"We need help," Rikard called out. The cavalcade emerged slowly and stopped outside the large hall with the airlocks leading into the theatre suite. Every so often, Tekla had to let go of the heart for a moment to flex her wrist and rest the muscles in her hand. "I need someone to relieve me as soon as possible."

"Which room?" Rikard called.

One of the nurses ran into Surgery while the other one went up to Gray. She looked in horror at Tekla, who had both hands inside the patient's thorax, all the way up to her elbows.

"Yes, she's insane," Gray said. "But in a good way, today, as it happens. He'd be dead if she hadn't opened up his chest."

The other nurse was back. "Room 3." She ushered them into the antechamber.

They were joined by several people in green. All staring at Tekla, as if she were cradling a sleeping leopard in her arms.

"May I suggest you get a move on?" she said.

A short woman with heavily made-up eyes, her hair tucked inside a blue scrub cap, stepped up and seized the end of the bed with whitening knuckles. "We've located Klas Nyström. He's on his way."

"O.K.," Tekla said. "But can we get going now?"

With a combined effort they lifted the patient onto the operating table. The theatre anaesthetics team placed a central line on the throat, connected tubes and started up the monitoring devices. An assistant nurse with a black nose ring went around collecting everybody's phones. She put her hand into Tekla's pocket to fish out hers. Tekla crouched down and shook her arms, hoping to summon up a last tiny shred of strength.

"I think you'll be needing an orthopaedist as well."

A few minutes later, a tall man with a large nose and piercing eyes arrived. He was holding up his hands and waving them to dry the sanitiser. One of the nurses held open a pair of gloves into which he drove his hands. With his head on one side, he stared straight into Tekla's eyes.

"Are you a thoracic surgeon?"

"No," she replied.

"So you're just a plain bloody moron."

Tekla turned towards the head end of the bed, where an anaesthetist was standing, completely impassive.

"And you certainly don't look like a surgeon," she said to the room, in her mildest voice. "Perhaps you were on your way to the delivery room?"

"Klas will be here any minute now," the tall man with the large nose said, while appearing to check the equipment that was being laid out on a cloth next to him. "I'd hate to miss his reaction when he sees what you've been up to."

Tekla kept on pumping. She was trying to think of some quip about that enormous, monumental nose of his, but decided to focus on the patient. "Shall we swap sides so I can begin laparotomising?"

Someone put a mask over the tall man's face and Tekla could only see his small eyes. They had ended up far too close to the top of his nose. Tekla suspected that might make it difficult for him to judge distances. In fact everything about him struck her as a bit awkward. She couldn't help wondering if he was a good surgeon. Presumably, since he was Klas Nyström's advance guard. Maybe he was just that and nothing else: a sort of administrative battering ram who rolled out the red carpet for the great surgeon.

"What's your name?" Tekla asked.

"We're done now," the anaesthetist said from behind the cloth that marked the separation between white and green by the patient's throat.

"Olof Törnqvist," the surgeon said, peering down at the abdomen, where he seemed to be planning to begin. "But you can call me Senior Lecturer. Don't think there are any other ones in here."

"Right, Olle," Tekla said. "Blunt trauma to the thorax. He was packing it in when we were down in the service corridors, so I had to open him up and do manual cardiac compression."

"I'm not blind," Törnqvist said.

"He has free fluid in the abdomen and an open fracture to the left lower leg," she continued.

After watching the theatre nurse disinfect the abdomen, Olof the surgeon picked up a scalpel with his long fingers. "Making the first incision," he announced in such a loud voice that none of the seventeen persons present could possibly have missed the greatness of his deed.

"I'm writing sixteen thirty," said a female voice on the anaesthetic side of the bed.

"And, in case you were wondering, I haven't felt any hole or anything like that up close to the heart," Tekla said as she saw Gray sneaking in to stand by the head of the bed with the anaesthetists. It was obvious that no-one wanted to miss this, the hottest performance of the year.

"I wasn't wondering," Törnqvist said, working his way through the different layers on his way into the abdomen. "But let me give you one last piece of advice."

"Don't need it," Tekla said. "But thanks anyway."

"Whatever you say when he comes in, don't even mention the liver. Klas Nyström is planning to give the Nobel Hospital a world-class liver transplant centre. Objectively speaking, he's probably Sweden's best surgeon and the most distinguished liver specialist in the Nordic countries. So you'd better be bloody well equipped if you're going to discuss the liver with him."

"Do you think he knows how many lobes it's got?" Tekla asked in a serious tone.

Törnqvist's nose shot up – and then down again when he understood that she must be pulling his leg.

How does one measure a surgeon's competence objectively, Tekla asked herself. By the number of operations? The number of successful operations? The number of reoperations within ten days? Or is it enough for a sufficient number of people to say that you're the best, and then by default you are?

The door opened and Tekla's pulse shot up. She looked around, but it was not Klas Nyström, it was an older woman. Judging by her sun-wrinkled face and careful, halting steps, she looked to be about eighty. With the picnic basket she was carrying, she could have come straight out of an enchanted forest. The old lady methodically lined up some test tubes which she filled with blood from the C.V.C. in the patient's throat. One almost expected her to start humming the theme from *Madicken*. Then she left the room. Tekla thought of moss growing in the shade under the pine trees around the house in Edsåsdalen.

"Agneta-gneta," Törnqvist muttered with a grin.

"Klas Nyström's research nurse from Linköping," the theatre nurse explained.

"Scrubbing!" someone called out from a corner of the room.

Tekla had no idea what was meant by that, but it must have been code for something, since several people sprang into action. The theatre nurse standing next to Törnqvist even took her eyes off the open wound for a moment.

"Where's the remote?" Tekla heard from behind her back.

"Should be over by the monitor," the chief nurse snapped.

"Here it is," somebody else said.

Tekla still didn't know what was going on. She concentrated on one thing alone – not letting the patient die because she no longer had the strength to go on pumping his heart. The pain in her hand was excruciating.

In the middle of it all, a ringtone could be heard from one of the phones collected by the anaesthetic nurse. Someone picked it up and announced: "Magnus."

"That's mine," Tekla said. "You can decline it and switch it off."

She avoided meeting anybody's eyes.

In a teasing tone, the nurse added: "Magnus has texted you twice, as well."

"Thanks for letting me know," Tekla said through gritted teeth. "I'd appreciate it if you'd stop checking my messages."

"Oops," the anaesthetic nurse said with a smirk. "Touchy. Shout if you want me to read out what he said about getting together soon."

Tekla restrained herself.

"You can let go of the aorta now. But carefully," Törnqvist said. He seemed to have managed to staunch some of the haemorrhaging in the abdomen. He held up a dark purple mass which looked a bit like chocolate pudding. "One burst spleen removed. Was bleeding profusely."

Tekla first gently loosened and then completely released her grip on the carotid artery.

"Pressure hovering at about 70," the anaesthetist said.

"Which one is it?" someone standing by a large screen on the wall called out.

"Number three," said the chief nurse without taking her eyes off the hook from which all the intestines were hanging.

"Stand by," the voice in the corner called out.

Törnqvist turned around. "Well switch it on then, for God's sake."

Suddenly music sounded from the loudspeakers in the ceiling. Muted string instruments followed by a male choir. The doors were flung open. And had Tekla not been so exhausted, she would have joked that someone forgot to dim the lights and switch on the spotlights.

NOBEL HOSPITAL
Thursday, 7 November

The boy was wearing the white staff trousers, which the woman had rolled up at the ankles. The fabric was stiff, as if it had been soaked in syrup and left to dry. The woman could tell that he was uncomfortable, but that he was being brave. She would have done anything to swap with him, to put on the scratchy trousers and give him her own. She sometimes caught herself almost wishing for an absurd, completely unrealistic situation, where war had broken out, the city was besieged and someone was holding a pistol to the boy's crying face. And she then heard herself saying that she would take his place. The pistol was turned around and she saw the expression in the boy's face shift from fear to horror. She smiled to herself, held the boy's hand and shut her eyes.

"Mamma . . ."

"Are you O.K.?"

The boy nodded, almost imperceptibly.

Over his shoulder she spotted a woman dressed in a long, brown coat coming into the unit. Her shoulders were wet and so was her white fur hat.

A sharp smell of perfume trailed behind the fur-clad woman as she walked down the passage to the secretariat. She enquired about something before turning, walking a few steps back and opening the door leading to the old man's room.

The woman's ears were filled with a rushing sound. The noise of the T.V. in the coffee room and the boy's small voice had vanished. All she could hear was her own heartbeat. Something was happening to her hand, it was the boy tugging, pulling.

"Mamma!"

"Yes." She gave a start. It was difficult to see beyond all the lies. Thoughts about the boy were so intricately linked with the man, but now disentangled and wound into a separate skein.

"You're not listening to me. You're so weird."

"What did you say?"

"Aren't we going to go into his room again?"

"Sure."

They went back. Stopped. The handle looked sharp and hostile. The boy reached for it and walked through. The antechamber was dark and the door to the patient's room closed. A woman's voice could be heard from within. The boy was already by the second door.

She wanted to scream. Close her eyes. She followed the boy into the room. The fur-clad woman stood with the old man's hand in hers, speaking soothing words which were drowned out by the hissing of the ventilator. The walls began to crack, great big slabs came loose and fell like ice floes into a dark sea. The floor swayed beneath her feet. She grabbed hold of the washbasin.

The boy went and stood beside the fur-clad woman, who stopped talking and looked down at him. She had not yet noticed the woman.

"Hello," she said.

"Hello," the boy said.

"And who are you, dear?"

The boy turned to the woman, who was now exchanging looks with the fur-clad visitor. She was heavily made up with dark red lipstick and sharply drawn eyebrows, framed by an attractive mass of toned hair spread evenly across her shoulders.

"And who are you?" The fur-clad woman's eyes were red from crying, they had interrupted her performance. It looked fake. Was she the one they had been waiting for, was it her bathing costume?

The woman opened her mouth but stopped herself. They had quite simply got there first. She knew what had happened, knew that they only had a limited amount of time, like ice melting in her cupped hands.

The nurse came into the room and broke the tension.

"How nice that you could all be here."

They looked at each other.

"At times like this, it's always comforting to be together," she went on.

The fur-clad visitor wiped away some mascara that had run from her eyes. The woman stared at the old man. Realised that it was too late. Realised that the fur-clad woman had come to his rescue. That the opportunity had gone. She turned and left. The boy ran after her.

"Mamma?"

She didn't reply. Kept walking towards the exit. Mustn't look back.

"Mamma, answer me."

She was floating along. Her legs felt numb. The floor was swaying.

The door closed behind them but then opened again. The young nurse came out.

"Wait."

The woman stopped. The nurse approached. "Who are you?"

The woman looked at the boy.

"Hello. I'm talking to you. Who are you? Apparently she's never set eyes on you. Do I need to call security?"

The woman was paralysed. Her mouth was so dry she couldn't even open it. She stared at the nurse.

"You're not a relative, are you? What's your name?"

Instinctively, the woman turned. She took the boy's hand and walked towards the lift lobby. She heard the nurse calling something after her, but didn't catch it. They were already in the stairwell, heading down one level. It was too late. She had had her chance but she'd failed to take it. She slowed down, her hearing was coming back again.

"Stop it now. Please, Mamma. You're hurting my arm."

She came to a halt, and let go of the boy's hand. They were in a side corridor running parallel to the main one, on a floor that was colour-coded green. There was nobody else to be seen. The signs on the door behind her indicated where they were, but she couldn't understand what they said.

"I'm sorry," she stammered. Swallowed over and over again. Managed to get rid of the thick layer on her tongue. "I didn't mean to hurt you . . ."

The boy sank to the floor and leaned his frail body against the wall. The woman crouched down, tore off her down jacket. Sweat was trickling down her spine. She ran the flat of her hand across her forehead. Wiping tears off the boy's chin, she happened to scratch him with her nails and he jumped. "Sorry."

"Why did she say that?" the boy asked, did not seem bothered that her nails had grazed him.

"Why was she angry? Tell me, Mamma."

"I don't know."

"But why did we hurry away?"

"Sometimes you've got to . . ." She stopped herself. The words sank in. All she wanted was to go back to the old man and finish it off. They were wasting time. She had to get past the obstacle. That other woman. The one with the eyebrows. A nameless, prehistoric animal.

"Mamma, what's the matter with him? Everybody seems to be cross with him."

"No. Not him."

"Then who?"

The boy was asking questions she could not answer because they no longer had a common language.

"No-one. No-one at all. Nobody's angry."

"I don't understand."

"You don't need to. The important thing is that we're together."

"I want to be with Pappa."

The woman felt another excruciating spasm in her stomach.

"Later on. Not now."

"But what are we going to do? I want to go home."

"Soon. We just have to . . . see him. But let's have something to

71

drink first. Don't you want that? Aren't you thirsty? I am. Incredibly thirsty."

She tried to stand up, but all the blood was stuck in her legs. She had to straighten them out, centimetre by centimetre, so as not to faint. In the end she got to her feet and leaned against the wall. "Must have something to drink." She looked around for a toilet. So unbelievably thirsty. "Come on." She helped the boy up. Thought she heard somebody behind her and turned but saw no-one. "Let's go." She put her jacket back on again.

"Mamma."

"Yes."

"Why can't I go home to Pappa. Have you had a fight?"

"No. Or rather . . . we had a bit of a discussion. But that's not the reason. I want to have you to myself today." She could feel the knife through the down jacket, still wrapped in the paper.

"Why?"

She stopped and turned the boy to face her. Carefully, she raised his chin and looked at him as he reluctantly returned her gaze.

"Because I love you. I love you with all my heart. I always will. And because . . . I would do anything for you. Absolutely anything."

The boy twisted away, did not want to listen. He made a face. Swung the golden mask to and fro.

"I won't keep on about it, you know all that already. But it's important that you believe me. Do you understand? Look at me. Please. Whatever happens."

Grudgingly, the boy looked up.

"Do you know that I love you?"

"Yes."

"For sure?"

"I said yes. Can we go now?"

They stopped for the boy to go to the toilet. The woman stood guard outside. She also needed to go but restrained herself. He came out without flushing. They went back up the stairs to a blue storey.

The door to the ward was closed. She knocked on the fireproof

72

glass. A cleaner let them in, and they made their way towards the old man's room. Out of the corner of her eye, the woman saw a nurse approaching. She tried to make it to the door unseen, but she wasn't quick enough.

"You can't go in there."

There must have been a change in staff because this was once more the chinless nurse with the frayed cuticles, rather than the shorter one. Her body language was determined, the tone of her voice harsh and metallic. Strained.

"I just need to—"

"No." She stood in front of the door. "I'll call security."

She looked around.

"Who are you, anyway?"

"Can I just go in and see him, one last time?"

"Absolutely not." The nurse looked this way and that, as if searching for someone. The woman raised her arm and put her hand on the nurse's shoulder. The nurse screamed and knocked it away with all her strength.

Pain shot from her armpit down to her hand. She raised the other one and took hold of the nurse's tunic. Why had her hand shot up? Why didn't she simply back off, withdraw from the impending disaster? The floor was swaying, the corridor and the whole world too. The nurse ran away. The woman grabbed the handle, pulled open the door. Fell headlong into the darkness.

She stood in front of the bed. The old man was asleep. Only the tubes, wires and drips kept him tethered to this world.

The woman approached him. Placed her hand on his stomach and felt it rise and fall with his breathing. She was sweating, felt that she was running out of air. Tearing off her down jacket, she took a firm grip on the knife, closed her eyes and thought back to his kitchen. Saw the meal they had eaten there. A stew. Potatoes. The boy . . . did he really not eat any of it? No, he'd had a sausage, hadn't he? She couldn't remember. Then the men had left the house. She'd searched, found the containers in the garage.

The door behind her opened. She saw the boy, his eyes fixed on the old man, and then several nurses including two men, who were evidently there to remove her. She slipped the knife inside her shirt.

"We've alerted security. You need to leave the ward," one of the men said.

The woman turned to face the old man. All sorts of images flickered before her eyes. The knife being drawn. The boy alone in a room. Then two hands seized her by the shoulders and pulled her back. She nearly fell but managed to regain her balance. Picked up the jacket. The nurses ushered her out of the room so roughly that she was unable to resist.

A crowd had gathered out in the passage. She saw the pregnant doctor with the fringe in the background and several new faces. All staring with harsh looks. Many seemed afraid.

"Stay here," said the male nurse who had pushed her out.

She began to move towards the exit.

"Let go of the boy!" the doctor barked, catching up with her. And then, in a milder tone: "We only want to help you."

Ignoring her, she kept walking towards the doors. She had a tight grip on the boy's hand. That was the only thing that mattered now.

The doctor who had shouted at her overtook them, ran around her – not without difficulty – and blocked the way just as they were leaving the ward.

"Please. We really do want to help you. I think you need to see a psychiatrist. Don't you agree?" The doctor's voice was soft. Almost like song.

"What medicines are you taking?"

The woman stopped in surprise. She was fascinated by the doctor's pleasant voice. They looked at each other. Was she trying to trick her into staying? But this woman doctor's face shone with sympathy. She must already be a parent herself. Wanted the best for the child. And in this case, the way to the child was through the mother.

"Come on. Let go of him now." She stroked the boy's hair.

All at once, it was as if a bolt of lightning shot through her body.

The doctor's features contorted into a grimace, a spitting feline face. A claw-like hand reached for the boy. She recoiled. Heard a hissing sound behind her as she set off at a run. The noise became harsher, like a bark. It slipped around every corner, every pillar. Now a new threat appeared from her left: a guard came running. His bulky frame swayed from side to side, keys and chains jangling as he went. His body filled up the corridor, growing larger with every step, transforming into a terrifying animal.

The woman charged off in the opposite direction. She pulled the boy along, deaf to his screams. She pushed her way past a hospital trolley, and raced for the lifts. Away from danger.

Thursday, 7 November

Professor Klas Nyström's hands were up by his ears, as if he were holding an invisible astronaut's helmet. "Time to save some lives."

Tekla could imagine that this had been his opening line ever since he decided to become the most famous surgeon in Northern Europe, when he was about four years old and sitting at the family kitchen table.

She had to change her position so as not to faint. Her vision was beginning to blur, but she saw Törnqvist, with his hands clasped in front of him, move back to allow the conductor to take centre stage. The male chorus swelled from the speakers.

Nyström approached the patient and looked down into the surgical wound. Then he slowly turned to the anaesthetists to check that everything was in order, gazed around the room where his attentive audience stood ready, and finally rested his eyes on Tekla.

"Well, I do declare! Look what the cat dragged in. A little house mouse. Tekla Berg, if I remember right."

Tekla would have liked to straighten up, but she had to continue squatting in order to keep pumping blood into the patient's arteries.

Nyström held out his right hand into which the heavily made-up theatre nurse deposited some forceps. His other hand was drawing shapes in the air while his body swayed in time to the surging male voices.

"Gesang der Geister über den Wassern, for male choir and piano, Opus 167. Do you know who the composer is, house mouse?" Nyström said.

Before Tekla had a chance to answer, Nyström himself expounded.

"Franz Schubert. Performed by the Lund University Male Voice Choir. Sends shivers all the way down to the cauda equina, doesn't it?"

Nyström poked around in the patient's intestines and abdominal organs with the forceps.

"Looks pretty dry."

He handed someone the forceps and carefully shifted the liver aside.

"All the damage is on the left side."

He leaned forward and lifted one of the lobes of the liver.

"If the job isn't done properly . . ."

Nyström looked up and caught Törnqvist's eye.

"Did you see that the liver is bleeding?"

Törnqvist's cheeks turned beetroot red.

"It can happen to the second best of us," Nyström said. "That's why Donald *always* goes down and does the clamping himself. Even if everything else is prepped, that final touch of his is vital. A sort of insurance for what is basically the main source of income for U.C.L.A."

Tekla assumed he was referring to Donald Bigoti, the renowned surgeon, and his medical skills and not to what he might be doing to the carburettors on one of his famous collection of Ferraris.

All at once, Nyström's fingers began to dance across the liver. As if he were playing a jaunty piece on the piano. Now and then he would point at an instrument, occasionally making a little movement with his fingers in the air, to which the nurse would respond by picking up an implement from the table in front of her.

"100 over 40," the anaesthetist said.

"Can I stop pumping?" Tekla asked.

"Did I hear someone squeaking?" Nyström said.

"Can I stop?" Tekla repeated.

"*Jawohl*," Nyström replied. "But don't vanish down that hole of yours just yet."

"She did actually save the patient's life," Gray piped up from where she was standing, two metres away.

"Is that so?" Nyström said. "I was told that some maniac tried to murder a patient by opening his thorax down in the service corridor. But I guess that must have been some bizarre cock and bull story."

"The patient was crashing and if it hadn't been for Tekla, there would be no-one here for you to operate on," Gray insisted before leaving the room.

Slowly Tekla unfolded her body. The pain radiated from her right hand all the way up to the neck. Eventually she managed to stand upright, gripping the operating table to stop herself from falling. She watched Nyström try, in vain, to get hold of a bleeding liver vessel.

"You need to pack that liver and get the patient to the I.C.U.," she said.

Nyström's hands stopped playing. He looked up at Tekla and she saw the famous surgeon attempt a smile behind his face mask.

"What are you doing afterwards?" he asked.

Tekla could feel all eyes on her. Even the male voice choir in the loudspeakers quietened.

"I was planning to go back to A. & E. and—"

"After you quit working here at the Nobel Hospital tomorrow, is what I meant," Nyström shot in.

"What are you talking about?" Tekla asked. It was over an hour since she had her last can of drink and her brain was not keeping up.

"House mouse finished. Tekla Berg finished. Over and out," Nyström said.

"Oh, I'm with you," Tekla said, with painstaking clarity. "No, I'm not leaving the hospital."

"Who's your boss?"

"Hampus Nordensköld," Tekla said. She refrained from adding "unfortunately".

"Call Hampus Nordensköld," Nyström said, "and inform him that Tekla Berg has just left her job."

Tekla wanted nothing more than to get out of the room, but she was not going to do so at the expense of the patient. "Don't try to mend a traumatic hepatic haemorrhage. You're supposed to pack it with sterile pads and then hand over to the I.C.U."

"I don't think you . . ." Törnqvist ventured.

Nyström shook his head and lowered his hands to the instrument tray. The chorus was back, rising to some sort of crescendo.

Suddenly, Nyström grabbed a fistful of gleaming surgical instruments and hurled them across the room. An assistant nurse only just managed to step aside to avoid being skewered by a scalpel.

The male voices came blaring out of the loudspeakers above a carpet of strings – violin, cello and double bass.

The door opened and another person entered the room.

"I'm the orthopaedist," Urban Wikström said. "The hit and run, is that here? Some lower leg fracture that needs fixing."

The whole room breathed a sigh of relief as the doctor with the heaviest wooden clogs in the hospital stomped over to the operating table and pulled on some gloves unaided, as if he were about to slit open a wild boar he had just downed in the forest.

"We have an unstable abdominal haemorrhage," Tekla said, avoiding Nyström's murderous look. "It only needs packing. The patient has to go to the I.C.U. now."

"Makes sense," Wikström drawled. Then he looked down at the leg. "What about that?"

"An open fracture. You're welcome to nail it back together again," Tekla said cheerfully.

Nyström stripped off his gloves, threw them on the floor and marched out.

"Who was that?" Wikström asked.

"Some new surgeon from Linköping." Tekla couldn't help smiling behind her mask.

"Oh, O.K.," Wikström said and coughed. "Has he had a bad day, then? Ah well, in that case I think we're going to need a hammer and some nails now."

Tekla met the eyes of the theatre nurse. She didn't seem to know what to do next.

79

"Afterwards we'll have to send the patient for a C.T. angiogram," Tekla continued. "Are you going to write the referral or shall I do it?" Tekla said, looking at Törnqvist. When the big-name surgeon's flunkey also threw in the towel, or rather his gloves, and left the room, she realised that it would be down to her.

Tekla put on fresh gloves, then packed the patient's abdomen with sterile pads while Wikström stabilised the lower leg fracture and glanced at the patient's face.

"A bit too challenging for my simple brain. We'll have to get E.N.T. to come and have a look later on."

On her way out of the operating theatre, Tekla spotted an all too familiar face. She still associated the cocksure smile, the shiny, wavy, chestnut-coloured hair and the side parting with the workshy, incompetent registrar who had been her colleague during the first year at the Nobel Hospital. For some completely incomprehensible and in many ways tragic reason he was now her line manager.

"Tekla, Tekla," Nordensköld said, crossing his arms. He was dressed in a light blue shirt tucked into black jeans and a pair of shiny black shoes.

"That's me," she said.

"So I'm supposed to kick you out?"

"I think that's a dumb idea."

"But I gather you managed to make Klas Nyström so angry he went straight to Monica."

Tekla was taken aback. "Did Monica ask you to fire me?"

Nordensköld looked at her in fascination: "You do know who your boss is, don't you?"

"You." Tekla suppressed a sob.

"That's right," Nordensköld said, triumphant.

"And?"

"So it's me who decides if you get to stay or not."

NOBEL HOSPITAL
Thursday, 7 November

The world around her had changed. All the lights had been turned right down. Ahead of her lay a tunnel of darkness – she could barely see one metre. The only thing her body told her was that she had to get away from the ward.

The doors to one of the lifts were open. Two people stood there, waiting. They had pressed a button which had lit up in a shining, digital number five.

The woman slipped in. Pressed up against the mirror, she held the boy between her and the wall. Closed her eyes. The doors shut. She counted. Got lost at six. Tried again. Muttered the numbers. Could feel the boy's body with her hands, but didn't hear what he was saying. A wave of anguish rippled through her, and then sorrow. She was already mourning her own death. She looked down at the boy, tried to persuade herself that from now on they would manage on their own, but she was not convinced.

The lift stopped. The seconds before the doors opened seemed endless. She threw herself out, ran to the right. Didn't want to look back. It was still dark, but people teemed around her, immobile pillars, like ancient trees in the night.

Her lungs hurt, forcing her to slow her pace. She carried on at a trot, remembering the board on the wall in the entrance lobby: ninth floor, B-building. She read the signs but had to make a real effort to compensate for the double vision. A long passage. Dodging people like traffic cones. The boy stumbled along behind her, sobbing and snivelling. She tried not to run, not to draw attention to herself, but how can you walk slowly when the world is ablaze?

Lift lobby B. A ping. The doors opened, she dragged the boy in. Pressed the button for the ninth floor. Inside the lift she slumped forward, took deep breaths and tried to ignore the pain. Did her best to stop the contents of her stomach from bursting out of her body.

The lift stopped. The secretariat was straight ahead, a sign on the wall read "Intensive Care Unit". Some glass doors to the left kept opening as people dressed in blue came and went. She avoided catching their eyes. Walked in. And on. Reached a large, open room. The white light screamed at her. She flinched. Took deep breaths.

"Mamma . . ."

"Not now." She looked down at her Iron Man. Then, in a whisper: "Not now. Later."

The boy fell silent.

A short, plump woman approached her with a smile on her lips.

"Can I help you?"

The woman tried to open her parched mouth. She couldn't.

"Are you looking for someone?" the nurse enquired.

Her jaw made a cracking sound. "Has the patient from the car accident been brought here?" It sounded halting.

"I see. Are you family?" the woman asked cheerfully. She pointed to a group of people around a bed about twenty metres away. "Pretty much a miracle. Shall I get a doctor?"

The woman tried to pull herself together. Make a decision. But the boy's hand kept getting in the way. She began to back away. "We'll come again later." She turned and left the room through the glass doors. They nearly bumped into a doctor who rounded a corner, a woman with gentle, almond-shaped eyes and short hair. She said something, seemed taken aback. They hurried on. Took the lift by the next staircase down to the ground floor and walked to one end of the building.

They reached a T in the corridors. A door on the right. A stairwell. She went through, nearly tripped up, caught hold of the boy and managed to make her way down. Opened another door. They entered a dark passage. She could see better now. Heard the boy sobbing.

That made her stop and let go of his hand. Again, she saw people all around her.

"Sorry. I'm so sorry."

"Please stop it, Mamma."

"Look at me."

The boy covered his eyes. Crouched down. The mask in his lap looked heavy, as if it were made of solid gold.

"Come along. We have to keep going. Just a tiny bit more." She had no idea where they were heading, but she felt threatened. They needed to find shelter. She helped the boy to his feet and took his hand. It was cold and sweaty. They carried on to the end of the passage. She opened a door that said "Staff Only". Yet another stairwell. They walked down some narrow steps and opened a heavy steel door. Now they were below ground. And she felt that she could begin breathing again.

NOBEL HOSPITAL

Thursday, 7 November ·

Tekla was tense with anticipation as she sat staring at the door to the changing room, but no furious boss or aggrieved senior surgeon came storming in. She got to her feet and let the bloodstained clothes drop onto the grey linoleum floor. Then walked over to the only mirror, which was fixed above the washbasin, got some fragrance-free soap out of the pump dispenser and rubbed her upper arm to rinse off the blood. The patient had been given fourteen bags, which was a lot, but not a record.

She washed her face, pulled some paper towels out of the holder on the wall and dried herself slowly. Pressed the rough, institutional grade paper hard against her eyes and then looked at herself in the mirror. Lowering her gaze, she noted that her ribs were more prominent than ever. Who was she to accuse the staff at Grangården of not giving her mother enough to eat? She averted her eyes and went over to the shelves where someone had left obsessively neat little piles of blue uniform tops and bottoms.

Tekla felt cold, put on two tunics as usual, one over the other, and tucked the trousers into her white tube socks. She briefly considered removing the one that had bloodstains on it, but decided not to. Sank onto the varnished pinewood bench by the lockers and stared at her phone, resting her head against the blue metal cupboard door. A padlock rubbed against her neck. She shifted and eventually managed to relax.

Her phone pinged. The delivery had arrived. She needed somebody to help with the carrying, but that would have to wait. She went on Google instead, to pull up an article she had not had time to finish that morning. A headache was pounding away at her temples. The reason for that, she realised, was that she had had no solid nourishment for more than ten hours. Her shift had ended an hour ago, but she did not feel like meeting the silence in her flat, not just yet. With her phone tucked into a pocket, she left Surgery and took the stairs to the ninth floor. Entering the I.C.U., she nearly bumped into a woman with a boy who was holding a gold-coloured toy mask in his hand. She jumped out of their way and watched them hurry on. They seemed quite distressed, almost as if someone were chasing them.

Tekla looked over at the cubicle with the hit and run patient, who had just come back from Surgery.

"How is he?"

"Thanks to you he actually is, rather than chilling out in the cold room," Eva Elmqvist said.

"How about his blood pressure?"

Elmqvist walked slowly towards the cubicle, where two syringe pumps in their holders were blinking in time with the monitors.

"Like the weather. No hope, no-vember . . ."

Tekla saw that his blood pressure was at 70, notwithstanding the large amounts of noradrenaline flowing into the poor leaking blood vessels.

"Blood count holding up?"

"We've just redone a blood gas, but the answer is probably no." Elmqvist pointed to the bandage on the patient's right side, already soaked in blood.

A nurse handed Elmqvist a tablet. "It's sinking like a stone."

"He's losing blood," Tekla concurred. She stared at the lab list. "The only question is, where's it coming from?"

"Let's just finish off here and then we'll do a C.T. scan. At least one thing to be proud of after the renovations," Elmqvist said, referring to the I.C.U.'s newly acquired scanner.

Tekla ran through the numbers in her head. "He's already in A.T.C."

"A.T.C.?" Elmqvist asked.

"Acute traumatic coagulopathy."

"You mean D.I.C.?"

"Not according to Kushimoto's 2017 article in *Intensive Care*." Tekla shot a look at Elmqvist who was running her fingers through her curly hair. "But what do I know. You're the expert."

Elmqvist screwed up her eyes and looked at Tekla. "Now you're doing it again. What were the liver results? And don't lie to me."

Tekla hesitated, thinking back to her school days when she deliberately gave the wrong answer so as not to reveal her photographic memory. But that did not fool the bullies. They had seen through her and their envy had already taken root, too deep to eradicate.

"Asat 4.2 and alat 7.1."

"How do you do it? So quickly?"

Tekla looked over at the patient. "Why are his liver values so high?"

"Circulatory failure," Elmqvist said.

"But what about the liver function, the high I.N.R.? It's not logical."

Elmqvist picked up the tablet again and looked at the lab results. "You're right. Don't know." She went to the syringe pumps. "We'll have to increase the noradrenaline and order more plasma."

Tekla inspected the patient's hand. The fingers were swollen. "The albumin level was 18. You'd better remove that ring now or you'll need to get out the bolt cutters."

Elmqvist pulled off the golden ring and held it up to the sharp light of a lamp on the wall. "My eyesight has got so bad. Could you . . .?"

Tekla took the ring and had a look. "All smooth. No inscription."

"Strange," Elmqvist said, handing the ring to an assistant nurse who was collecting the clothes that had been cut off the patient in a plastic bag.

"Have the police been here?" Tekla asked.

"Not yet," Elmqvist said.

"What kind of monster runs over an innocent person and then drives off?"

"A man?" The laconic suggestion came from Elmqvist.

"Well, but—"

"A drunk one," Elmqvist added.

Tekla remembered her father's yellow eyes. The taut swollen belly and the purple blood vessels around the navel. The shaking hand reaching for a glass of water on the bedside table. She saw every mole on his chest, each yellow stain on the crumpled sheet covering his spindly legs, but she could not conjure up the smell, which must have been a mixture of acetone, urine and laxatives.

"I suppose so," she whispered in response. "I'll be back later to see what the C.T. turned up."

"Aren't you meant to be off? And isn't he Klas Nyström's patient?"

Tekla ignored Elmqvist's searching look and made for the I.C.U.'s luxurious coffee room. White walls and ceiling and no handles on the kitchen cupboards and drawers. Even the floor was white, sur-faced in some impractical rubber material that squeaked under her trainers. She selected a double espresso and got out her phone just as it started to ring. Grangården, the dementia care home. She declined the call and instead pulled up Moussawi's number.

"At the back, opposite the staff car park," she said to him, ringing off when Anita Klein-Borgstedt, her oldest colleague and the person she admired more than anyone else at the clinic, appeared.

"Is the coffee better here?"

"Faster machine, that's for sure," Tekla said. She went over and pushed in a cupboard door which popped open. "How cool is that?"

Klein-Borgstedt shook her head. "You know how I feel about progress."

"What brings you here?" Tekla asked as she placed her coffee cup in the dishwasher. In a hospital, failure to comply with kitchen regu-lations was the second most dangerous thing to do next to talking shit about the nurses. And rumours spread fast. About female doctors, that is. Because a man who put a cup in the dishwasher was more likely to be seen as either feeble-minded or ripe for retirement.

"I'm the consultant for a rheumatology patient." Klein-Borgstedt managed to get a regular coffee out of the machine. It rattled as it ground the beans. "But I'm so glad I bumped into you. I want to invite you to a small do at my place on Friday in two weeks' time."

Tekla visualised a big house with a gravel driveway and cars pulling up by a flight of stone stairs, where servants greeted the guests in the warm glow of outdoor lighting. She could feel the sweat stinging the palms of her hands as she went through the contents of her wardrobe in two seconds; a white blouse from Lindex was the most elegant piece of clothing she posessed.

"How lovely," she managed to utter.

"I'll give all of you the details nearer the time."

"Is the whole clinic coming?"

Klein-Borgstedt got a mischievous look in her eye. "I can't tell you if they'll all show up. But they're invited."

They left the coffee room together. Klein-Borgstedt stopped by the entrance to the large, open I.C.U. room and lowered her voice. "How old are you, Tekla?"

"Thirty-six . . ."

"Good. That's good," Klein-Borgstedt said.

"What do you mean?"

"You have thirty healthy years ahead of you."

"To do what?"

"When I was thirty-six, I had no idea how medical care would develop. None of this existed then." Klein-Borgstedt looked around the room with nostalgia in her eyes. "I had hardly even heard of ultrasound and magnetic resonance."

"There's a lot going on," Tekla said.

"A little too much," Klein-Borgstedt said, laying her bony hand on Tekla's arm. "Don't forget the most important thing of all."

Tekla was not sure if she was meant to answer. She took a chance and said nothing.

"They're perfectly capable of saying that the patient comes first, without meaning it. Because they don't, believe you me. All that matters is the bottom line. Forget the empty rhetoric, at the end of the day it's all about money and careers. Climbing up the ladder until you reach some sort of meaningless summit. But for you and me it really is a matter of putting the patient first. Don't forget that, Tekla. Never forget it."

Klein-Borgstedt let her cool hand slip slowly off Tekla's before ambling over to Elmqvist.

Tekla allowed her words to sink in. Moussawi had texted, asking where she was. Tekla rushed out of the I.C.U. and hurried towards the lift lobby.

BASEMENT CULVERTS, NOBEL HOSPITAL

Thursday, 7 November

They were standing in a long corridor. Thick pipes in different colours ran along the high ceiling: brown, white, black. A few yellow ones. A dull buzzing sound could be heard, like electricity locked up in a metal cupboard. For some reason, down here it felt safe. Two cleaners came by, pushing a large cage trolley full of black rubbish bags. Curious, they took a good look at the woman and the boy.

"Let's go this way," the woman said, moving slowly towards another opening in the passage. She was troubled by the humming noise from the tubes up in the ceiling and wanted to get away. They continued along the service corridor until it was crossed by another pathway, where the floor was painted yellow. Before long it occurred to her where they must be: it was the main artery of the hospital, which extended several hundred metres in both directions. A narrow steel groove was set into the floor.

A driverless vehicle with a blinking yellow light came trundling jerkily along, stopping from time to time. It seemed to wait for some sort of all-clear signal before lurching on again. The boy stopped, fascinated, and watched the cart as it crept closer.

"That's so cool," he burst out suddenly. "Can I ride on it?"

"No, only look."

The boy stamped his foot demonstratively. When the woman looked at the robot, the flashing light bothered her, it stung her eyes.

"Come on, let's go."

"Wait."

"O.K. But only for a little while." She spotted two men in building workers' clothes approaching them. Although they weren't looking in their direction, their presence felt threatening. The hacking noise made by the robot carriage stopping, starting and stopping again was going round and round in her head.

She gave the boy's back a gentle shove to indicate that they had to go.

"Stop pushing me!"

"Sorry. But we've got to leave."

"Why?"

"Because . . . well, we just have to."

"No."

"Come along, now."

"I don't want to."

"I understand that those carts are fun, but I don't want us to stay here. It's not safe." That wasn't quite true. There were several kilometres of yellow robot corridor ahead of them and they could easily have stepped aside when the carriages rolled past. Standing where they were was not dangerous at all. Besides, the vehicles were bound to have some sort of warning system that stopped them if they were about to crash into someone. But the woman wanted to get away, the whole of her being needed them to go to a more secluded place, so she could do what she had to do.

"We can look at them from over there too. Come on, now." She set off, knowing the boy would follow her. However exciting those carriages might be, he did not have the confidence to stay. He crept into her bed at night. The distance between them when they walked together, side by side, was less than it had been six months ago. At the same time, it felt as if each inhabited a different universe. When she shut her eyes, images from the cottage appeared before her.

More carts rattled past, going both ways. Sometimes, without any warning, a jerk would send them off in a different direction. One suddenly stopped in a sort of depot. Another turned and vanished through an opening in the wall. The vehicles must be running along other routes as well, which they could not see. But there were no other people around.

At last the woman began to feel a little calmer and was able to think about something other than her headache. Then a new feeling overcame her: fatigue. Her eyes were bone dry. She wanted to lay down her heavy body.

They left the main passage and went back into the green service corridor, passing yet another lift lobby. A nurse all in white stood there fiddling with her phone. Her shoulder bag glittered with gold buckles and she seemed oblivious to their presence.

"Mamma, I'm too tired to go any further."

"We're stopping soon, but not just yet."

"I can't. I'm going to faint."

"Then I'll carry you. To the end of the world."

"I don't want to go to the end. I want to go home."

"So do I," the woman said. "I really do." But at the same time she was thinking: I'll never make it back there.

The woman spotted an open door leading off the next passage-way. All the ones they had passed so far had been closed, and she had assumed that they were also locked. Now she saw one that hadn't been fully shut. On it was a yellow sign with some black numbers. No indication as to what might be found inside.

Carefully, she pushed the door open and entered the room. It was lit up and surprisingly large, a bit like a classroom. And empty, apart from two piles of what looked like white laundry bags. In one corner, some thick pipes rose from the floor like tree trunks and carried on through the ceiling.

"What are we going to do?" The boy seemed worried, twisting his body from side to side.

"I need to rest for a bit." She looked around and saw a few chairs standing in a corner. She went to get one. It was made of steel, quite heavy, and she pushed the backrest in under the door handle. It fitted perfectly, like a big wedge.

"I don't like this place," the boy said. He did not seem to consider why she was barricading the door.

The woman went over and hugged him. Her back hurt when she bent down.

"There's nothing to worry about. I'm here." And then she added, as if she could tell that was not enough: "We have each other, after all."

"Can't we go home?"

"Soon. Soon we'll go home." She rubbed her dry eyes and walked over to the pile of bags. "Look, it's just like our old play area with all the cushions."

Reluctantly, the boy followed her. It seemed he would rather be near her than stay standing in the middle of the room.

They sat down on the soft sacks, which smelled of detergent. Under normal circumstances, the woman would have thought twice about sitting there. Her brain would have seen them as a threat, a potential source of bacteria. But her brain had lost the battle against her tired body.

Slumped on the laundry bags, they lay looking up at the ceiling. Rows of cables that had been painted over ran alongside the strip lights. Two narrow pipes curled out into the centre of the room and then took a sharp turn towards the wall before disappearing through the ceiling. The humming noise was less noticeable in here. That left her with more space for her thoughts.

"Can I play?" the boy asked.

"I don't know if it'll work down here." She got out her phone and was amazed to see that she had two bars.

"Here you are. But turn down the volume."

The boy took the mobile and pressed on the side to lower the sound before losing himself in the action on the screen. She looked at him. He raised a hand to rub the corner of his eye. She thought she could see tiny ants crawl out of his eye and scurry into the thicket of his hair. It sickened her more than it frightened her. What about the man, she wondered. Was he still alive?

NOBEL HOSPITAL
Thursday evening, 7 November

Tekla took the stairs up to the ground floor and cut across the main entrance hall.

Sigurdsdottir came waddling along by the Pressbyrån newsagent and her face lit up the moment she spotted Tekla.

"Would you like some?" the Icelandic woman said, holding out a large chocolate bar.

"No thanks," Tekla replied. "How did you get on with that trauma patient of yours?"

"Do you ever stop thinking about work?" Sigurdsdottir asked. "There is such a thing as small talk, you know, about the weather or chocolate or Instagram."

Tekla was silent.

"I heard what you did down in the service corridor, you lunatic," Sigurdsdottir said. "You do realise that'll have consequences."

"Did he have a subdural haemorrhage?"

"No. Concussion and an ugly radius fracture requiring surgery. But he certainly had a guardian angel."

"No doubt about that," Tekla agreed. "Seems unfair, though, doesn't it?"

"What do you mean?"

"Well, my patient is younger, has more years left. Yours was quite old, has had a longer life, and should perhaps have been the one to die, if one had to choose."

"If one had to choose, that is," Sigurdsdottir said. "You're pretty disturbed, Tekla."

"Surely it's only logical. I'm certain that Nyström and his rational

94

mind would agree. Maybe your patient ought to be transferred to him for euthanasia instead. Perhaps he's got some healthy organs that could be harvested."

Sigurdsdottir ate some chocolate and considered the matter. "Interesting thought."

"I saw Anita in the I.C.U."

"Did she invite you to her farewell party?"

Tekla stopped. "Farewell party?"

"Didn't she say?"

"You're joking."

"I wouldn't joke about something so serious. I know how much you like her. She's resigned, didn't she tell you?"

Tekla could see the house of cards collapse before her eyes. Klein-Borgstedt stood for so many good things – in Tekla's eyes she was something of a legend. A role model when it came to taking a perfect medical history, doing a thorough and well-reasoned clinical examination and drawing together all the facts to arrive at a sensible differential diagnosis which did not call for a whole raft of expensive tests and x-rays.

"That's not possible."

"What's not possible?"

"Anita's our rock, for goodness' sake," Tekla said.

They walked in silence past the patients' library and then turned left down the corridor.

"But why?" Tekla said.

"You'll have to ask her that yourself," Sigurdsdottir replied.

"But you know, don't you? Has it got something to do with the reorganisation?"

"You ask her."

Tekla sighed and left Sigurdsdottir standing outside the Urology secretariat. It had stopped raining, but the humidity lingered in the late afternoon gloom. Tekla was shaking so badly that it hurt all the way up into her spine.

*

"I guess this must be it." Moussawi took a last drag at his cigarette before flicking it away into the darkness.

"Looks about the right size," Tekla said. She had a quick look at the shipping label and nodded.

Moussawi bent down to pick up the large box. Tekla took hold of the opposite side. They carried it into the lift lobby and put it down.

"To your office?" Moussawi asked.

"You haven't asked what it is."

"I've renovated a fair few houses in my time," Moussawi said. They'd become friends after he'd done her the favour of driving a massive drain into Victor Umarov's thorax without any anaesthetic the previous summer. As a result, the gangster boss had stopped terrorising her brother.

The lift doors opened and they carried the box in.

"You seem to be in a bad mood," Moussawi said.

"I've just heard that Anita has handed in her notice."

"No wonder."

"But surely we need to fight back. We're all upset about the reorganisation, but none of it has been decided yet."

Moussawi smiled.

"What?" Tekla exclaimed.

"You're so naïve."

"What are you talking about?"

"Did you really believe it was only for a trial period?"

"What else would it be? They've announced that it's for two weeks, and there'll be an evaluation after that."

"So naïve."

"Cut it out, will you?" Tekla spat. "What do you mean?"

"It's all window dressing," Moussawi said. "The hospital administration already decided on this restructure ages ago. It's our new way of life. And, as union representative, Anita knows all about it."

"You're joking?"

"Unfortunately not," Moussawi said and bent down.

They picked up the box and manoeuvred it into Tekla's office.

They managed to squeeze it in beside the desk. Tekla was wiping the sweat off her forehead when her phone rang. It was Lundgren. She declined the call and put away the phone.

"You do know that there's a life out there?"

Tekla looked at Moussawi in surprise.

"Ragna has a habit of telling me just that."

"And with a good work–life balance, you become a better doctor."

It felt odd to hear the tall doctor from Iraq analyse her private life.

"I think you ought to pick up next time your phone rings."

Tekla said nothing, but ripped off the plastic and the cardboard. Crawled round to put the plug in the socket. Then she opened the door. A cool light spilled out onto the black fitted carpet.

"Great," Moussawi said. "Only question is, what are you going to fill it with?"

Tekla closed the refrigerator. "You'll see."

After Moussawi had gone, Tekla thought back to the week after Lundgren had come out of hospital last summer. She had gone to his place every day. In the end she stayed over. For several nights. One morning at around four they had sex. She remembered how skinny and rigid he was after the operation. How gently he caressed her, how impatient she grew, how she wanted the foreplay to end. She took the initiative, straddled him. But it felt as if he was holding back. They changed positions, she wanted to ask him why he was not in more of a hurry, why he would not let himself go like she wanted him to. Then she noticed that he kept touching her between the legs. Eventually she asked him what he was doing. Lundgren froze, explained that he thought she had her period, that there was a smell of blood. They stopped. He went to sleep and Tekla left the apartment. They never discussed the incident again. Tekla went back to working hard. She kept Lundgren at a distance – something had broken that morning.

Tekla called the I.C.U. "You've been trying to get hold of me."

"Just wanted to tell you that the patient's haemoglobin level is falling. Thought you'd want to know," Elmqvist said.

"What did the C.T. scan show?"

"Diffuse pelvic haemorrhage."

"Incompetent bloody idiot!" Tekla said.

"I beg your pardon?"

"Not you. Klas Nyström and his cack-handed compression of the pelvis in A. & E."

BASEMENT CULVERTS, NOBEL HOSPITAL

Thursday evening, 7 November

The woman shut her eyes. It was almost an effort to close the dry eyelids. Her hips were hurting and she shifted slightly to one side, finding a softer spot on the sack she was lying on.

She let go of the boy's upper arm, which she had held in a firm grip ever since they'd entered the room. Pictures of a submarine popped up in her brain. She could hear a low-frequency rumble from the engines, a crackling noise from the tannoy. Waiting for something. To make a getaway, to confront an imminent threat. She was in standby mode. Active rest. Sleeping, but only to a depth from which she could be easily roused. At the same time, she felt an indescribable fatigue. She was one of the submarine crew. But a member who could be replaced and did not play an especially important role. She was far from being the captain of the vessel. She remained lying where she was. Tried to delay the inevitable. Slipped her hand into her jacket pocket. Found the knife, still wrapped in the napkin. She felt the sharp steel through the paper. The tip of the blade.

Another image: her father as a young man. Or was it a photograph? She couldn't remember. Her brain might be playing tricks on her. But never mind. What did matter was the warmth and the feeling of loss conjured up by the images. His restrained but glowing smile. Although it wasn't directed at her, it nonetheless filled her with joy. He was reading. Or at least holding a book in his hands, a thick, important book. He had removed his spectacles and was putting one of the temples into his mouth. He was looking away, gazing out of a window next to the high-backed armchair in which he was sitting. Was she spying on him from somewhere further off? He was

99

unaware of her presence. A lump in her stomach. She wondered what was on his mind. Would have loved to ask, but did not dare disturb him. Then he quickly put his thick black glasses back on again, lowered his eyes to his book and the smile disappeared.

Freezing, she rolled onto her side and grabbed a half-empty sack to try and cover her legs. The boy's body gave a little warmth. His thumbs skittered across the screen, now and then he had to use one index finger, drawing it slowly over the glass. Then back to the dancing thumbs.

She was shivering now, and tried to warm up by rubbing her palms against her thighs. It had probably been about an hour. She didn't know. Suddenly she panicked – she had no idea what time of day it was. Tried to recall images from the past twenty-four hours. Only saw fragments: people turning around and watching her with a menacing grin as she walked along with the boy next to her.

The humming continued, and now she could also hear a very quiet thumping noise. As if someone were kicking a wall somewhere far away.

The boy was still playing on her phone. He looked tired, about to fall asleep any minute. Eyelids heavy.

Suddenly he got to his feet. Wiped some snot on the sleeve of his jacket.

"Come," she said, reaching out towards him. He went over to the door. "You're staying here." She heard her own voice as if it were coming through waxed paper. Hoarse and dry. An unpleasant, dull, cawing sound.

The boy remained standing by the door for a few minutes before slowly returning to sit with his back to her.

"Can I have the phone?" He gave it to her. "Lie down and have a rest."

The boy lay down and pulled his knees up to his chest, breathing heavily.

She stayed sitting like that for about half an hour, stroking the boy's hair until he fell asleep.

100

With her other hand she slipped the knife out of her jacket pocket and placed it beside her on one of the laundry bags. Taking hold of the napkin, she pulled so that slowly the knife rolled out, ending up exposed, next to a heap of paper. The strip lights reflected off the shiny steel. She felt her heart beat faster. Her breathing grew heavier and heavier. She picked up the knife and squeezed the handle. Her other hand was still caressing the boy's hair. He was not aware of what was happening, deep in the world of dreams. She heard the thumping more clearly now. Wondered if the high levels of stress had sharpened her senses. There was a distinct frequency to the humming, almost as if she could see it in one colour and the thumping noise in a different one. The boy was sleeping silently. But she could feel his relaxed body beside her. He had rolled down towards her when one of the sacks they were sitting on had slipped aside. She was still gripping the knife, the palm of her hand was throbbing.

Tekla passed the deserted I.C.U. reception area, her heart skipping all the way up to her larynx. She stopped briefly and checked the pulse on her wrist with two fingers. Alarmingly high, she thought, putting it down to the crazy levels of nicotine in her body. Her phone rang.

"Hi, Tekla," came Lundgren's soft voice. A wave of calm enveloped her. Like a warm sleeping bag settling over her shoulders and slowing her pulse down.

"Hi."

"Have you given any more thought to my suggestion?"

"Not really."

"There's no rush, but—"

"If there weren't, I don't suppose you'd text and call me on the same evening," she interrupted him. It came across as harsh and unkind, but there was no way of taking back the hateful little words that so often popped out of her mouth.

"No worries, Tekla," Lundgren said, in an effort to smooth things over. "It's only because I was thinking of booking accommodation—"

"O.K," she cut in.

"O.K. what?"

"Book. It's fine."

"Are you sure? I'd be very happy if you came along."

"Don't keep asking. Or I might change my mind."

"I'll stop, then. But what are you doing tonight?"

"That was a question," Tekla said.

"Sorry," Lundgren said.

"I've got to go. I have a patient who's not doing well in Intensive Care."

"Understood. Just don't work yourself to death."

"Rather that than getting run over by some drunk driver."

"Well if that's the alternative, then I agree," Lundgren said and added: "Look after yourself, Tekla."

She put away the phone and walked into the largest room in the I.C.U.

"What's the blood count?"

"Good job you came," Elmqvist said and turned her attention away from Törnqvist for a second. "Latest blood gas came in at 55. And acidosis going up, 7.18."

"That's bad," Tekla said. "Like a lemon."

"What are you doing here?" Törnqvist asked, placing his long fingers on the patient's abdomen.

"Eva called," came the curt reply. Tekla wished she could tell this lackey of Nyström's to wipe himself off the surface of the earth once and for all. She turned to Elmqvist, who was standing with a telephone in her hand. "But what about the liver, no haemorrhage then?"

"Not as far as the radiologist could see. But it was an oral report."

"Lucky for Klas," Tekla said to Törnqvist. She stood on the opposite side of the bed from the young surgeon. The patient's thorax rose and fell in time with the airflow from the ventilator. Once again her thoughts strayed to her father's deathbed. She remembered the drawings Simon had done for him. They were taped to the yellow wall above the headboard. Boats and fishing scenes. There was one showing Tekla and Simon standing either side of their father, with their arms around him. And, revealingly, Simon had drawn their mother sitting on a chair next to them with a cigarette in her mouth.

"Don't you bad-mouth Klas," Törnqvist said. "He's—"

". . . the best surgeon in the world," Tekla interrupted him. "I know what you're going to say. I bet he can play the flute, recite Faulkner and go backwards on a unicycle. Am I right? Anything else on his fantastic C.V. that you'd like to tell me about?"

Törnqvist ignored Tekla, as if she were an irritating five-year-old on the Tunnelbana.

Tekla went over to Elmqvist. "Have you called the vascular surgeon?"

"Not yet."

"Can I have it?" Tekla took the telephone from Elmqvist's hand. "The on-call vascular surgeon please."

"Which division is that?" the operator asked.

"Division?" Tekla said. "What difference does that make? Can you just get me the vascular surgeon. Surely there's a common on-call hotline for all of Stockholm?"

"I need to know which division and which colour code I'm supposed to be looking for," the operator said in a matter-of-fact tone. "Everything's been changed according to the new—"

"You can't be serious?"

"Wait," the operator said. "What if I just ignore the guidelines?"

"Yes please, do just that," Tekla said, shaking her head, resigned.

After a long minute the call was put through. "Adam Frölander, on-call for vascular surgery."

Tekla realised that the switchboard never told her which hospital was on call that day. "This is Tekla Berg at the Nobel Hospital. Can I submit a case?"

"Is it urgent?" the vascular surgeon asked. She could hardly make out what he was saying, there was such a wind blowing.

"Yes it is. We've got a young man in the I.C.U. here at the Nobel Hospital with an unstable pelvic haemorrhage."

Frölander raised his voice. "What do the orthopaedists say?"

"We're going to get them here, but it'll take a while. Right now we need you to stop the bleeding. The patient is unstable."

"Have you tried to stabilise him?"

"I don't know what you mean, but we've done all we can. Blood, plasma, thrombocytes, packing, but the pelvis is still bleeding."

"Has the patient been seen by a surgeon?"

Tekla had to restrain herself; she felt like throwing the receiver at the wall. "The surgical backup operated and fixed a haemorrhage in the liver, among other things. I wouldn't be calling if we didn't need you to come."

"How old is the patient?"

"About forty. But we don't have his identity."

"Could it be a homeless person?" Frölander asked.

"What's that got to do with it?" Tekla said, sounding irritated.

"I didn't mean it like that."

"So how did you mean . . . Oh, forget it. Can you just get yourself over here?"

"Well . . . it'd be better if you sent the patient to us. We have more advanced equipment."

"Us?"

"N.S.K."

"What kind of advanced equipment?" Tekla said, just as Nyström entered the I.C.U. He went over to Törnqvist, who briefed him on the situation.

"A hybrid operating room. You don't have one at the Nobel Hospital. Using a C-arm is a problem, the images are less good."

"O.K., I know nothing about that," Tekla said. "But it's going to be difficult to transport the patient in his current condition. Actually, impossible."

Frölander had run out of arguments. He would simply have to cut short his walk or whatever he was doing and get on with his job, however reluctantly.

"Try to top up the patient and boost him while I go in and begin prepping the room. Get him over to us with blue lights and we'll do the rest."

Once her conversation with the vascular surgeon was over, Tekla knew that she would have to take on the next Neanderthal in line.

"So, the liver's doing well," Nyström said with a smile.

"Yes, isn't that a relief," Tekla said.

"And I gather the vascular surgeon is on his way," Nyström added without looking at her.

"No, they want us to send the patient to the N.S.K."

Nyström walked slowly over to Tekla. Standing up close to him, she could see that he had juvenile acne along his hairline. "Why on earth?"

"We don't have a hybrid operating room here."

Nyström's eyes fixed on Tekla's chest. She felt completely naked, as if she had just stepped out of the shower. "Tekla, Tekla. How much damage are you capable of doing in twenty-four hours? Call that vascular surgeon again, will you."

Tekla did as he said but this time her call was declined.

"He's not picking up."

At that point the next disaster came walking in, dressed in a light blue shirt and white trainers.

"What's up?" Nordensköld asked, stopping at a safe distance from the patient's bed.

"Good," Nyström said. "I could do with some male leadership right now. We need you to get that vascular surgeon over here, he's insisting that we move the patient to the N.S.K."

Nordensköld smoothed down his neatly parted hair.

"That's not my job."

"Aren't you Tekla's boss?" Nyström said. "I called through the switchboard."

"I'm first line manager for the blue division but not operational boss between four and nine p.m."

Nyström was about to let rip with a few well-chosen words when it dawned on him that he was a member of the hospital management team which had just devised this new system.

"Well who is, in that case?"

"No idea," Nordensköld replied. "Call the switchboard again," he suggested as he left the I.C.U.

Nyström struggled hard to keep up his sanctimonious smile but his cheek muscles were beginning to feel the strain. "Would you please try and phone the vascular surgeon again, Tekla?"

She was more successful this time and handed Nyström the receiver.

"Klas Nyström calling. Where are you? In Waxholm? What are you doing there? You have twenty-nine minutes to get yourself to the Nobel Hospital. Otherwise I'll make sure you're sacked before the week is out." Nyström gave Tekla the receiver. "He's coming. It's pretty naïve of you not to have realised that Frölander was just trying to buy time. I'll bet you he was sitting on his veranda in Waxholm with a glass of red and it was more convenient for him to get a taxi to the northern side of town. Call X-ray and ask them to prepare a C-arm. Everything needs to be ready when Frölander arrives. And give him some more blood in the meantime."

"His blood pressure keeps decreasing," Elmqvist said. "I really think you need to come up with some surgical procedure that will stop the bleeding."

"R.E.B.O.A.," Tekla exclaimed. She lowered her voice and said it again, sheepishly. "R.E.B.O.A."

They all stared at her as if she was standing there stark naked.

"R.E.B.O.A.?" Elmqvist said.

"An aortic pump, just to stop the pelvic haemorrhage. There's no point in giving him all this blood if it only leaks out into the abdominal cavity."

"And who do you suggest should be doing a R.E.B.O.A.?" Nyström asked in a friendly voice that was in stark contrast to the expression in his eyes.

Once, during her specialty training in Uppsala three years before, Tekla had assisted at such an intervention.

"Me."

"You? Interesting," Nyström said with something like genuine fascination in his senior consultant's face.

"Are we going to continue this discussion or do you think you two could get on with saving the patient?" Elmqvist butted in as she went across to the computers. She picked up a bright green apple and took great big frenetic bites out of it.

"We're taking him to Surgery in any case," Tekla said. "I know where everything is."

"And how do you know that?" Törnqvist asked.

Tekla ignored him and began to help Elmqvist disconnect the patient from all the tubes. All of a sudden she noticed that Nyström had crept up behind her and was standing about ten centimetres from her back.

"You do realise that this will be your last act at the Nobel Hospital?"

She could smell the star surgeon's breath. Sweet and nauseating – she could have done without it.

"I was planning to save the patient. But you're more than welcome to do the procedure yourself," she said.

Nyström took a step back and, with a deadpan face, said: "Be my guest."

Tekla turned her attention to the patient. It was obvious that Nyström didn't have a clue what a R.E.B.O.A. was.

BASEMENT CULVERTS, NOBEL HOSPITAL
Thursday night, 7 November

She had stopped shivering, no longer quite so cold. The air in the laundry room was cool, seemed to be circulating, there was probably a powerful extractor. She was calmer. The people out there were less threatening than before. And it felt good that this would be the place where they spent their last hours together. They were alone, with no-one and nothing to disturb them. If only she could find some words. But she did not know what to say. As far as she was concerned, everything was falling into place, but maybe not for the boy. He was being given no chance to express his last thoughts. But she was fairly sure he understood. He had to. There was really no alternative. She was doing the one thing that was right for both of them.

The thumping noise was more audible now, and it was becoming more frequent. She raised the knife, her hand only shook a little. But it was alright. Stable. She held what was left of the future in her fist. She stroked the boy's back, pulled down his jacket so that the skin of his neck was clearly visible. The heavy breathing. A motionless body. The room felt cooler. She reached out, searching for the man's hot back in the darkness. As she had so many times during all those nights when the pitch-black cold outside had defeated failing boilers.

Slowly she sat up, her knees stiff. The boy did not move. She lifted the hand holding the knife, ran a finger over the serrated edge of the blade.

The boy woke up. Lazily he rolled over towards her. He didn't appear to see the knife she had in the hand that was turned away from him.

"Mamma?"

She had no answer. So far as she was concerned, they had exchanged their last words. Still drowsy with sleep, the boy looked around and spotted the knife.

"Why have you got a knife?"

She looked at it in surprise. Her body felt numb. Something warm trickled down from her nose to her lip.

"Close your eyes," she said to the boy.

"I don't want to. Mamma, what are you doing with a knife?"

"Please shut your eyes."

The boy raised his hand to ward off the knife.

"What are you doing, Mamma, why do you have a—"

"Shush," she said gently, lowering his arm with her free hand. She could see the other one, the one holding the knife, in her peripheral vision. As if she had another person standing beside her, assisting at an operation.

"Close your eyes," she repeated as the tears welled up and blurred her vision. She let them run, then wiped her face. There was blood on the back of her hand.

"I don't want to shut my eyes," the boy said, and he started to cry as well.

"You have to."

"Why?"

"You've got to trust me," the woman said.

"But why do you have a knife, Mamma? Please say. I won't tell Pappa."

"Why would you do that?" At the mention of the man, her anger flared up and she gripped the knife even harder.

The boy looked over at the door.

"But I heard Pappa—"

"Pappa isn't here. It's only you and me. Now do as I tell you. Close your eyes."

Suddenly the walls started crowding in on her. The room felt cramped and stuffy. With her free hand she reached out towards the boy, who tried to defend himself, but his head came up against a laundry bag. Tears and snot ran down his face.

"Darling, shut your eyes now. Relax."

"What are you going to do?"

"Help us."

"What do you mean, help?"

It seemed as if the boy did try to relax. Maybe he recognised the panic in her face. Maybe he realised what was about to happen and felt that there was nothing he could do. Maybe he was simply too tired to resist.

The boy closed his eyes.

By the time they got to Surgery, the patient had virtually no blood pressure. The anaesthetists administered every drug they could find to boost the collapsed blood vessels. The fifteenth and sixteenth blood bags were each hanging on an I.V. stand and there were more on the way. Assisted by the duty theatre nurse, Tekla was making a mental note of everything she would be needing. She surveyed the instrument table that was covered in a sterile sheet and began to clean the man's groin. Pulled the ultrasound machine into place and requested a sterile cover for the probe. "Gel, please," she said as she began searching for the femoral artery. It was difficult to distinguish it from the vein since all the blood vessels had collapsed. Tekla altered the setting on the machine until she finally got a good image.

"Where were you planning to place it?" Törnqvist asked. He was standing opposite her, all scrubbed up.

"There was no bleeding from the liver, was there?" she said.

"No."

"So I thought I'd insert it into the iliac artery, making it as distal as possible to avoid bowel infarction. Putting it higher up towards the thorax would be a risk in terms of both the intestines and kidney failure." She measured the distance from groin to navel.

"How long can it stay in place?" Törnqvist said.

"Ideally as little as possible, but fifteen minutes at a time, then we relieve the pressure which sets the blood flowing."

Tekla pushed in the needle and got blood return. "Think it's the artery."

"You think?" Törnqvist asked.

"Think pretty much for sure," she said with a smile. The man with the large nose seemed incapable of smiling. No doubt he was still sore that an emergency doctor was leading an intervention in his operating theatre.

Without another word, Tekla inserted the guidewire before pulling out the needle.

She followed this up with a dilator and a large 12 French introducer and then slipped in a balloon catheter and injected fifty millilitres of sodium chloride to achieve the right degree of resistance.

"Pressure's going up," said one of the anaesthetic team.

Tekla rested her hands on the patient's thigh. She had managed to move the balloon catheter from the femoral artery up to the aorta. Since this now blocked the flow of blood to the patient's legs, pressure increased and ensured some supply to his brain and heart, buying them a little time. She looked at the monitors, which were displaying better curves. "Now you can give some more blood and check gases again," she said, turning around. "It's been forty minutes. Any sign of the vascular surgeon?"

No reply.

"Could someone call the switchboard and have him paged?"

An anaesthetic nurse helped Tekla dial the number and switched to speaker mode.

"Adam Frölander. Vascular surgeon."

"Tekla Berg calling from the Nobel Hospital. Where are you?"

"What do you mean?"

"You're supposed to be here for our patient with the pelvic haemorrhage."

"I'm waiting for you."

"Waiting?" Tekla exclaimed.

"Yes, at the N.S.K."

"Are you joking?"

"No, I discussed it with my boss who said he'd talk to someone in charge at your end and get the patient transferred to our hybrid room."

Tekla saw Törnqvist standing on the other side of the table, panic written all over his face. "We thought that you were on your way. You've got to come, I've done a R.E.B.O.A."

"R.E.B.O.A.?"

"Yes."

"Who did you say did this R.E.B.O.A.?"

"Me."

"And who are you? A surgeon, I suppose."

"Tekla Berg. Emergency doctor."

Silence at the other end.

"Hello?" Tekla called.

"You'll have to talk to my boss."

The telephone clicked and Tekla saw Törnqvist's large nose nodding in the direction of the window to the operating theatre. She turned to see Carlsson and Nyström standing out there side by side, looking as if they were admiring a painting in an art gallery. The only thing missing was glasses of champagne in their hands.

Tekla stepped back from the patient and asked one of the assistant nurses to open the door for her. With her hands held in front of her, she backed out of the room.

"How's it going?" Carlsson enquired. Tekla noticed that the hospital's C.E.O. had dyed her hair pitch black since the last time she'd seen her.

"The vascular surgeon is standing by at the N.S.K."

"But—"

Tekla cut Nyström off: "Well, he said he'd be coming over but . . ." Tekla looked at Carlsson. "Apparently they spoke to some big shot here."

"Not me." Carlsson considered the matter for half a second. Tekla spotted a fleeting smile on her lips before she got out her phone.

"Monica Carlsson calling. I believe there's been a small mix-up, but your vascular surgeon is refusing to comply with the on-call agreement. He's gone to the N.S.K. but we have an unstable patient in Surgery over here at the Nobel."

Carlsson listened for a few seconds, then said: "If you don't get that surgeon into a taxi within the next five minutes, I'm calling the evening papers to give them a little story I've saved up from last year. The one about your trip to Helsinki. You bet I will. So what's it to be? Good. We're waiting here – let's just hope the patient pulls through."

Carlsson put away her phone and smiled at Tekla. "He should be here within fifteen minutes. Otherwise you call me. O.K.?"

Tekla nodded.

"And please keep the patient alive." Carlsson put her hand into a bag she pulled out of her pocket. Tekla noticed that she was shaking. Carlsson threw a handful of liquorice into her mouth and chewed feverishly. "I'll be in my office." She left Tekla with Nyström in the anteroom to the operating theatre.

"Who was she talking to?" Tekla said.

"Hanna Parida."

"Wow," Tekla said.

"Yes, when it gets choppy, you're better off sitting in Monica's boat."

Tekla wondered whether the C.E.O. of the N.S.K. herself would be calling a taxi for the vascular surgeon.

An hour and a half later, a subdued vascular surgeon with a sweaty brow arrived and, with great concentration, set about staunching the haemorrhage in the small pelvis. Once the patient's blood pressure and blood count had been brought under control, the orthopaedic backup was called in to stabilise the pelvis. Tekla saw no reason to stay and watch the repair job, so she left Surgery and went down to the on-call room in the service corridors.

She didn't feel like going home. She was starving but had managed to still her hunger by eating two bananas taken from the staff canteen at the I.C.U. Although there were bloodstains on her trouser legs, she did not change out of her hospital clothes. She crawled into bed under three yellow blankets that smelled of damp. Turned off the light and looked at her phone. It was half past midnight and she felt as if she had been awake for forty-eight hours. Her knees hurt and her head was thumping.

The room was in pitch darkness. The only sound was a dull banging noise from a pipe somewhere in the background. The room was cool. For some mysterious reason it was colder than out in the service corridor. Tekla had a vision of her mother the last time she went to see her, two months earlier. She'd been the same as always, slim as the long cigarillos she still smoked out on the balcony with the other "ladies", as she called them. She didn't say much, hardly seemed to recognise Tekla, but smiled anyway and looked her straight in the eyes. Tekla had hardly ever seen her mother so happy, even during her healthy days. It was as if all her troubles were forgotten, no husband or children around to remind her what an unsatisfactory mother she was. No guilt about the smoking. Perhaps her face could finally relax, allowing the muscles around her mouth, which she had kept in check, to contract into a genuine smile.

Tekla tried to hold on to the image of her mother's softened face but, before she lapsed into sleep, it was replaced by Carlsson's sharp look and tight mouth.

NOBEL HOSPITAL

Friday morning, 8 November

Her first thought was that she had gone blind. Then she realised that her face was pressed into the laundry bag. Gradually began heaving herself up. There were bloodstains on the white fabric. She could feel the boy's back against her own. Turned slowly. Saw the motionless body.

Once again, the woman wrapped the knife up in the napkin. Tucked it away inside her shirt. She picked up some unwashed hospital trousers that were lying on the floor and wiped the blood off her nose. It went on bleeding. She looked at his back. Shoved his legs, but he showed no sign of life. Her stomach cramps had started again. During the night, she'd emptied her intestines three times into a washbasin which she had managed to climb onto with great difficulty.

Suddenly the boy moved, turned and looked up in surprise.

"You've been snoring," she said.

He didn't answer. Rubbed his eyes.

"You were such a good boy yesterday when I asked you to close your eyes. And if anything bad happens today, I want you to do the same again. Shut them tight and put your hands over your ears. Can you do that?"

The boy nodded.

"Good." She tried to get to her feet, but felt the blood drain from her head. Saw black spots in front of her eyes. She needed to drink something. Her nose was running. She knew she was bleeding, but let it drip. She made another attempt at standing up, inch by inch, until she stood there, swaying, next to two long pipes labelled "hot" and "cold".

"We have to get out of here."

"I want to go home."

The woman took the boy's hand. "I know."

"Why can't we go home?"

"Soon." She pulled him to his feet. He held the golden mask in his hand, still wearing his jacket. She staggered over to the door, making a huge effort not to faint. The handle was ice cold, the door heavy. They went into the corridor.

"Are we going home now?"

"Soon," the woman said, finding her way to the lift lobby. There was no-one to be seen. It was probably very early. Maybe still night. The numbers on the display counted down until the bell rang and the doors opened. The light was bright, she had to narrow her eyes. Trying not to catch sight of herself in the mirror, she pressed the lift button and drew the back of her hand under her nose. Light blood mixed with darker clots.

The lift stopped on the ninth floor. The woman stepped out. The door to the intensive care unit was closed, but she could hear voices from within. Looked around. Nowhere to hide. Once again, it felt as if the walls were caving in on her. She took a few steps towards the door, heard light female voices on the other side. Suddenly it opened, and two nurses in blue uniforms and green caps came walking out at a brisk pace. The voices grew harsher all of a sudden. The nurses looked at her and the boy but hurried on. The woman did not hang around waiting for questions, she walked in with a firm hold on the boy's hand.

First they got to an airlock with a rubbish bin containing blue shoe covers. She was unable to focus. Her field of vision grew narrower and narrower. A familiar voice sounded in the distance. Suddenly it forced its way into her consciousness.

"Mamma?"

She pushed open the next glass door.

"Mamma?" she heard the boy calling while pulling at her arm.

"Yes?"

"What's the matter with you?"

She looked along the corridor before them. A glass cubicle on the left. No people. Voices far ahead. A hydraulic hissing sound could be heard as the doors closed behind them. She set off.

"Mamma!" the boy called, but his voice did not get through to her. It disappeared back down into the water, replaced by a loud whine. All she could see was a narrow strip of light ahead of her, which she walked towards. A hand kept pulling her back but she strode on. In a flash she knew that it would all be over within seconds. She must not look down. Not meet his eyes. Anybody's eyes. Just follow her inner voice.

She reached an open door. Inside the room, night still lingered, a dense darkness surrounded the beds, but the patients were picked out by the warm yellow glow of a lamp at each bedhead. Like spotlights on a stage. She moved past a rectangular nurses' station with no walls or ceiling. She knew where she was going. A shape dressed in white stood by the bed.

She was walking through snow. Trudging through tall, wet grass. The whining sound in her head had grown more intense. Her temples were pulsating. A twitching, prickling feeling crept up towards her face. She could feel herself go numb. It was as if half her body were paralysed.

"Mamma!" a voice called out far behind her.

Friday morning, 8 November

Tekla was woken by the sound of hysterical laughter outside the door. She sat up. Her arms were frozen and stiff. The display on her phone said 5.30 a.m. She had actually managed to get some badly needed hours of undisturbed sleep. She was amused by the fact that someone could be laughing down in the service tunnel so early on a Friday morning, and so hard as to almost choke. She fell back onto the squishy, damp local-government-issue pillow, picked up her phone again and texted Lundgren: Looking forward to the weekend trip. Let's discuss details. Then she got up, left the on-call room and made for the main entrance.

The kiosk in the lobby opened at six and the scent of fresh danish pastries was already wafting across the newly scrubbed stone floor. It was still clean; no patients with November slush on their shoes, no prams with gritty wheels had yet had a chance to dirty it.

Tekla was so hungry that she had a hard time deciding what to buy. She helped herself to two chocolate wafers, one yoghurt, four breakfast rolls and a litre of orange juice. And then put back one of the wafers before paying at the till. Sitting on a sofa, she wolfed down the whole lot, leaving only half the juice. At last, some energy splashed around inside her. After throwing the wrappers into a bin, she headed for the lifts to the I.C.U.

"You're early," Elmqvist said.

Tekla took a seat on a chair next to the intensive care physician. "So are you."

"I was on night duty. What's your excuse?"

"I didn't go home," Tekla said.

"Even though you weren't on call?" Elmqvist sighed. "Haven't you got a life?"

"You mean apart from the thing I'm most passionate about?"

Elmqvist ran her scarlet fingernails through her hair. "One part of me would like to see everyone as dedicated as you are, Tekla. But the other half feels really sorry for you."

"How's it going?" Tekla asked, looking at the cubicle with the patient.

"Fingers crossed." Elmqvist pulled down her reading glasses while clicking on the patient's lab results. "Blood count is steady at 80, which is fantastic. Let's hope for the best. The liver values have shot up, but that's perfectly understandable after yesterday's circulatory failure."

"Lactate is still high," Tekla said.

"Yes, that's worrying. And as you can see, blood gas hasn't gone back to normal."

Tekla ran her eyes over the test results. "Are you doing another C.T. scan today?"

"Not sure it would be all that helpful. Right now we need to get his kidneys going and control coagulation, which is getting out of hand."

"I can see that," Tekla said. There was something odd about the liver tests. She couldn't put a finger on it, but it was definitely not just a consequence of circulatory failure. She stood up and went over to the patient. Elmqvist followed her.

A nurse checked all the syringe pumps, topped them up with meds and wrote something down on a piece of paper.

"Has he started urinating?" Tekla said.

"No," the nurse answered.

Carefully, Tekla lifted the sheet. She looked at the fake tattoos on the right arm. Half of Darth Vader's body was now gone, but you could still see the distinctive helmet and upper body. "Has anyone tried to get in touch?" Tekla said.

"No," Elmqvist replied. "The police were here last night asking the same question. We've seen no relatives. And no-one has been reported missing."

"Strange," Tekla said.

"Perhaps he really is homeless or a junkie, after all," Elmqvist said.

"Well, there was nothing like that in his blood," Tekla said. "Or anything about his clothes or the condition of his skin to suggest that he was some kind of vagrant."

Something didn't add up, Tekla said to herself. There was the transfer on his upper arm. The ring on his finger. This was no ordinary down-and-out, if indeed there was anything normal about being homeless.

She was so deep into her analysis that, at first, she failed to notice the person who turned up in her left field of vision. In hindsight she wished that she had raised her eyes by just a few centimetres, then she could have taken that step, that decisive step to prevent the disaster. But because she was concentrating so hard on trying to explain the rising liver values on the basis of the scant clues she had managed to get from the patient, Tekla didn't see the woman who was now only a few metres from the cubicle. Or that there was a small boy behind her.

Maybe it was the simple fact that Tekla was unusually calm and relaxed after her good sleep in the on-call room and did not therefore have her radar warning system switched on.

In the end it was the boy shouting "Mamma" that startled Tekla out of her reflections about the patient. At that, she turned and spotted not the woman but the boy beside her, who had his hands in the air. In one of them he was holding something that Tekla couldn't identify – it was a shiny golden colour.

The woman raised her hand. At first, Tekla thought that it was for a handshake, a greeting, a gesture of gratitude for everything they had done for her husband. Or brother, or best friend.

The woman looked to be somewhat over thirty years of age with straight, dark hair in a simple updo. A narrow, somewhat sunken face, but with a kind of melancholy beauty. Wearing jeans and sturdy shoes. It all seemed perfectly harmless as she approached the doctor and the patient in the cubicle. No reason to see anything other than a hand extended in cordial greeting by a grateful relative.

Then Tekla saw the knife.

She recoiled and took a step back to protect herself.

"Pappa!" the boy could be heard screaming in the background.

Taking one last step, the woman brought the knife down in an arc from the perfect angle to achieve maximum speed as it hit the man in the bed. Tekla watched as it was driven in right up to the handle. It was almost comical to see what looked like the black plastic grip of an ordinary kitchen knife poised on top of the left side of the patient's ribcage.

The woman turned, seemed to want to get closer to the boy, who was standing a few metres away, but began to shake uncontrollably. She fell against the steel frame of the bed, bounced back onto the wall and slid to the floor.

Once again, Tekla stared at the knife. It was stuck squarely into the heart of the man whose life she had been fighting to save.

II

ST PETERSBURG
Some years earlier

Yulia Mikhailova's journey from shy suburban teenager leaving "School no. 4" with mediocre grades to well-paid 25-year-old on a special mission to Sweden began at the vegetable counter of a grocer's shop in Gatchina outside St Petersburg. The owner valued her for the way she applied her "sense of aesthetics" to the vegetable display, and promised her a raise when she turned twenty-two in April. Not that Mikhailova was any more artistic than the next person, she just arranged the fruit and vegetables in an orderly manner and in stylish pyramids. Her real strength lay in her social skills; the customers loved to chat with her about this, that and the other. Families with children and elderly people had a particular tendency to linger in her part of the shop, giving their views about everything from allergies and nappies to low pensions, local politicians or even just the weather. Her best friend, Larissa Neverova, was usually at the checkout and showed no particular interest in children or pensioners. She did, however, enjoy nipping out of the back entrance of the shop for "a breath of fresh air" with her chum and, in between frenetic puffs, she would fantasise about a better life in Europe. Neverova showed Mikhailova pictures of capital cities which she said they "absolutely had to visit before they got married", and she was especially obsessed with Paris. "There we can shop until we drop, they'll all be green with envy," she said. But Mikhailova did not yearn for any life other than the one she had in Gatchina. She loved her town, its leafy surroundings, the harmonious population. She had been together with Pavel for three years and had tried to get pregnant, but so far hadn't succeeded. They had no idea whose "fault" it was, talked about doing some tests, maybe getting married first, but routine got the better of them and the uncertainty became the norm. A fertility investigation would cost money, which they did not have. Pavel always said that they should stop worrying and simply enjoy themselves.

Mikhailova did not need to enjoy herself, at least not in the way Pavel had in mind. He liked to party and spent a lot of time watching action films. She really only had one dream, and that was to become pregnant. Ever since her teenage years she had known that she wanted a big family, at least two children. How she would actually go about providing a secure home for herself and her children mattered less to her. But time passed, and Pavel was anything but enterprising. Mikhailova was twenty-two and feeling more and more pressure. Many of her former classmates already had one or even two children.

She knew that Neverova had a second job as a dancer in some clubs in St Petersburg and that she earned good money. Working as a checkout clerk at the grocery was just a cover for her parents' benefit. Mikhailova added up her roubles and saw how much more was needed for a fertility investigation, not to mention in vitro fertilisation if it came to it. She had no wish to get drawn into the nightlife she had heard so much about but Neverova constantly nagged her about it and, in the end, she found it hard to resist. One evening Mikhailova agreed to accompany Neverova. They had a good time in St Petersburg, in the company of self-assured men with loud laughs and black cars, of a type she had never previously encountered. They were given champagne and they danced. Mikhailova was not dressed as provocatively as her friend. Neverova told her that it was unnecessary because she was "drop dead gorgeous" anyway, unfairly so. "It doesn't matter what you wear, you look fabulous in anything." As Mikhailova started going out more and more, she noticed that men couldn't take their eyes off her, as Neverova pointed out with envy in her voice. "You could go far," she said. Neverova started going out with a man who had a large apartment in St Petersburg, where they often spent the night. It took an hour, sometimes more, to get back to Gatchina. The town felt increasingly small and cramped, that much Mikhailova was prepared to concede. But her dream, first and foremost, was still to become pregnant, not to go shopping in Paris over the weekend.

Then Maxim entered Mikhailova's life, a man with a more restrained smile, of whom the others appeared to be afraid. It was Neverova who introduced him to her. The way he looked at her was different, more thoughtful. He began with her shoes, then studied her height and the colour of her hair before concluding: "Neutral." She thought she understood what he meant; something good, something that could be modified if necessary. He offered her a job. "You'd only need to work at weekends," he said. What he meant was obvious, and she refused in no uncertain terms. Maxim did not insist, he was polite and gracious. "Get in touch if you change your mind. It's up to you to set the limits for what the clients are allowed to do. We're professional, there's a code of conduct. You never have to be afraid. By the way, could you look after my daughter?"

Mikhailova was taken aback. Maxim's three-year-old daughter was ill and he had brought her along to the office, a copy and print business. She was with the girl all afternoon until Maxim came back from a meeting. She was paid more for those few hours than she could ever have imagined. "Let me know if you change your mind," he said.

But Mikhailova gradually dropped out of city life and, for a while, she and Neverova were no longer quite so close. She worked away at the grocery counter, and her wages did indeed increase by a few roubles on her birthday, but she couldn't stop thinking about the big money Maxim had offered her. Eventually, she and Pavel managed to scrape together the sum needed for an investigation. They were told that she had endometriosis. "For you to have even the slightest chance, you will need in vitro fertilisation," the doctor announced in a matter-of-fact voice. She realised that she had to raise the funds somehow and got in touch with Maxim again. Neverova now had her own apartment outside St Petersburg. She lived there with an older man who had made a fortune buying up failed health resorts in the southern part of the country and converting them into extremely luxurious spa facilities for the growing upper-middle classes. Neverova waxed lyrical after visiting one of the resorts. "We bathed in champagne," she exclaimed. Mikhailova wasn't sure if she meant that literally, but she also went along once and was equally impressed by the opulence.

Maxim had her come to his office, which clearly dealt with more than just copy and print. "The city administration is my biggest client, in more ways than one," he admitted, offering her *pechenye* and chocolates as he explained the rules. "Remember, we're not some kind of brothel. The people we deal with are from the top drawer. In Europe it's known as an escort service. Nothing else. And you are my main asset. If you're not happy, the client won't be happy. And if the client isn't happy, I won't be happy either." He gave her a persuasive smile, which reassured her. "Remember that." Mikhailova felt nervous, but not afraid. "And you're welcome to look after my daughter again."

The first client was a young businessman from Germany. He took her out to a restaurant, made stilted conversation about his investments in Russia and spoke at length about his wonderful wife and his two fantastic young children. Mikhailova hardly registered what he was saying, she was so busy smiling, nodding and trying not to think about what would happen after the meal. After they had walked back to his hotel room, soon ending up in bed with their clothes on, he said that he wanted "more than just a little petting". She refused, but was prepared to go along with some flirting and kissing, if indeed, as Maxim had told her, that was as much as was needed. The German businessman seemed disappointed, but knew what the deal was. One of Maxim's men had followed them and was down in the hotel lobby in case there were "any question marks". She had her phone close at hand.

She spent two years working for Maxim and his men. Occasionally she would take care of Izabella – that was his daughter's name. At first she was impressed by Maxim's lifestyle, he seemed incredibly rich and well established. Then, after a while, she realised that there were people who were considerably more powerful than Maxim and his lackeys. It also became clear to her that he worked for someone who in turn worked for someone else and that, right at the top of the hierarchy, there was a person they all spoke of in measured, respectful tones. Mikhailova could only guess at the size of the *organizatsiya* – or the network, as they called it – but judging by the cars, the money that flowed and, above all, the professionalism, she knew it couldn't be a small, local, gangster outfit. She wasn't told the name of the man at the top. Someone called him the boss, and another time he was said to have *blat*, which meant that he had connections. What might that imply, she wondered. Did the mysterious man at the top of the hierarchy know a person high up in the Party, maybe even the President?

There followed a few years in the fast lane, which she enjoyed, although she never lost control. She only used cocaine on the more special occasions, otherwise she kept well away from drugs. She managed to avoid sexually transmitted diseases and abuse. Maxim's men were always nearby, leaving the clients in no doubt, they knew where he drew the line. And she could set aside some money in a bank account. Her new friends called her *khomyak*, the hamster.

One day, Maxim came to see Mikhailova with a man who was somehow in charge of the boss' accounts and finances – she had already come across him a few times. They wanted to discuss an assignment in Sweden. Her mother was from there, as she had told Maxim, and Mikhailova had grown up speaking Swedish. "It will open up doors to the West," her mother had said. But to go and *live* in Sweden ... She had never been there, did not know any other Swedes and was unfamiliar with the culture.

Then Maxim told her more about the job and who was behind it: Anatoly Mischenko. She already knew him, indeed had been his escort for almost a year and was therefore the most respected girl in the group. He was the big boss. At night she was taken by car to various apartments around town, rarely the same one twice, where she would spend a few hours with the head of the organisation. She hardly ever thought anything of it, except when the other girls showed their jealousy in some way. When they were in bed together, beneath the covers, Mischenko was just an ordinary man of normal build, about fifty years of age, who yearned for love and rubbed expensive creams into his silky soft hands before they had sex. He whispered to her that she gave him something he'd not had for many years. She rarely saw him in any of the restaurants, and never once met him in daytime. She knew that he was married and had a child, Kolya, but that was all. She had met the boy, a year old now, in one of Mischenko's restaurants. A young girl had brought him along in a pram and Mikhailova recalled that she had wondered where the mother was. She also remembered the two massive bodyguards, who never left the nanny's side. Maxim explained:

"The mother was killed in a car bomb a few weeks ago. It was the second attack this year. Somebody also fired a missile into their garden this spring. It exploded in the pool house."

"Was the child in the car with her?" Mikhailova ventured to ask.

"Fortunately not," Maxim said. "But he was the one they wanted to get." Mikhailova had heard about the attack on the car, but this was news to her.

After thinking it over for a few days, Mikhailova asked to see the boss, but in more formal circumstances this time.

She was taken to his heavily guarded *dacha* outside town. She had never seen so many weapons all at once, and understood that some sort of conflict was brewing, though she had no idea who else might be involved.

She was especially nervous, wearing a smart blouse which Mischenko's chauffeur had dropped off a few weeks earlier. She could tell that it was expensive, silk as soft as a baby's cheek. They sat down together on a large sofa. A man with a machine gun stood guard outside the window.

"Do you understand what I'm asking of you?" Mischenko said,

folding his hands. He was dressed in a brown knitted jumper and black trousers. She thought he had aged, but then she had never before seen him in daylight. He still had the same intense look in his eyes.

"I think so."

"He's my only child," Mischenko said.

"How long will we stay there?"

"I don't know. Let's take it one year at a time."

"A year?" Mikhailova had imagined that she would be looking after the boy for a few weeks. Maybe three months, at the most. "I don't know if I can be away that long."

"Because of your boyfriend?" Mischenko said.

"Yes." It was strange, really. Obviously he was aware of her private life, and those of all the escort girls. But she could not help feeling that there was more between them, that she received special treatment, because of something Mischenko saw in her.

"He won't be able to come along. But did Maxim tell you how much you'd be paid?"

"No."

Mischenko named the sum. In her mind, Mikhailova saw what that money would allow her to do, how it would change her life.

"Sleep on it," Mischenko said, getting up.

"Why are you asking me of all people?"

Mischenko paused and looked at her. Then he smiled, a pained smile. "You remind me of someone. And Maxim has told me how good you are with Izabella."

She stood up and walked over to him, taking his hand. She didn't care if a bodyguard saw it, let them step in if they had to.

"I heard what happened to your wife—"

Before she could finish her sentence, Mischenko slapped her face so hard that it took her breath away.

"Never mention my wife again. Ever. Do you hear?!"

Mikhailova gasped. "I'm sorry."

Mischenko left the room. Mikhailova was driven home. Sleep

did not come easily that night, but she'd already made up her mind back on Mischenko's sofa. She would accept the assignment, the money was too tempting, she'd never have to work again. And there was no dissent from Pavel. So she broke up with him, it was obvious that he wasn't planning to wait for her. He suggested that she take the job and send money back to him, which he would "manage while she was away". Not likely. He was a rat, had always put himself first. She had no intention of supporting him. He was so feeble that he could not even be bothered to protest when she told him it was over. She was almost disappointed at how easy it was.

Suddenly, Sweden no longer felt quite so alien. Moving there seemed like a good way to get some distance, work things through, recharge the batteries and think about the future. Save all the money and return to an affluent life in St Petersburg, study languages or maybe law ... She had time to consider it. Life offered so many opportunities, but you had to play your cards right.

She was to live with a man by the name of Alexander Kozak, or Sasha as he was known, who seemed nice. He was a few years older than her, had been one of Mischenko's closest bodyguards for many years and seemed less narrow-minded than many of the men she had met. They moved to Sweden with the boy.

SVENSTAVIK

Three years earlier

"Are you tired?" Mikhailova asked after taking off her shoes in the entrance and hanging up their jackets.

"Hungry. Toast," Kolya said.

"Coming up. And maybe some hot chocolate before Olga arrives?"

Happy, he nodded.

She went into the little kitchen. It was smaller than the one in the last cottage but, on the other hand, the sitting room was bigger. Before they moved, Kozak had said that there weren't all that many houses to choose from, "but this one has a fireplace and I know you like that". By now she had grown accustomed to her new life, accepting that he made the decisions, that he had a plan for them, all controlled by Mischenko of course, but it still rankled. "Only one more year," he had said, and she had chosen to believe him. At first she'd missed her friends and the pulse of the city, but now she was happy to live in the countryside and enjoyed the calm. Nor was she bothered by the fact that they had to be seen to be living a simple life, which was absurd given the money they had at their disposal. "But that is something we have to keep quiet, otherwise we blow our cover," Kozak insisted. She knew that he nevertheless tried hard to make life as pleasant as possible for her. He got her a new laptop and the right service provider to give her a good connection for her series, and she had plenty to eat. But there could be no question of fancy cars or clothes that would stand out. She understood that. What made her unhappy was that he was incapable of seeing who she really was and what she really liked. She wasn't particularly keen on fireplaces, never had been, and if he'd ever asked her any meaningful questions, he would have known as much.

The kitchen was usually tidy, but now there were dirty plates in the sink. A carton of milk had been left standing on the table. Large lumps of butter oozed onto the spider pattern of the dark grey counter top. The air was stuffy, there were cooking smells from the day before. This was not like her, she usually kept the house clean, but neither she nor Kozak had had the energy to put things away before going to bed, it had been too late. She'd wanted sex, yearned for closeness or at least tenderness, and at first he seemed willing; he told her that her hair looked great and that he'd always loved the fact that she was so "slim". Unlike . . . She tried not to go there, to stop analysing his words, and lap up the compliments instead. For a long time she thought it would lead somewhere, but once he had downed his fourth glass of vodka he turned surly and went back to harping on about her "constant unreasonable demands", and went to bed fully dressed.

"Demands," she thought in the bathroom. She had got ready, washed her face, rubbed soft cream into her skin, put on her flannel pyjamas and snuggled down beside a snoring Kozak. She had con-templated joining him under the covers, but then decided to curl up on the other side and try to sleep. All she wanted to know was what the future held in store for them. Three years of her life had flashed by and the dream of having a child of her own had become even stronger thanks to Kolya.

The flight left Umeå early. He was only going to stay away for a few days. Usually it ended up being a week, at least. She found his absence less difficult to live with now than she had in the begin-ning. She looked forward to the highlight of the week: coffee with Olga.

Mikhailova got some butter out of the refrigerator. She took two slices of bread from the freezer and pressed them down into the toaster on the window sill. She filled the kettle with water and switched it on. A turquoise light shone in the dark. She didn't bother to turn on any others, it was too much of an effort to banish the autumn gloom settling around the Jämtland lake outside.

Kolya came into the kitchen and sat down on a folding chair by the oval table in front of the window.

"How come it's so dark?"

"Don't you think it's cosy?"

"No, I find it scary."

Mikhailova lit a brass lamp standing in the window. It gave off a faint, yellow light.

Snow had started to fall outside.

"Why is Olga coming?"

"Olga is so much smarter than me. And she's also studied more. And she's older."

Then she added for her own benefit: and because she's extremely well paid for home-schooling you, maybe right through your entire school career, but I can't tell you that, my lovely Kolya.

"She's strict."

"Sometimes it's good to be strict. She knows so much and she's so keen to teach you a whole lot of things."

Kolya didn't look happy.

"Would you like to take a bath? Or are you too tired?"

Kolya thought about it. A hint of a smile emerged. She was always working on it, trying to draw out his carefree side, the joy within him that was all too often obscured by his brooding. No four-year-old should be that worried, she told herself. He was, admittedly, precocious and serious by nature, but she really wished that she were able to get him to laugh a little more often.

"Yes."

"Good. Let's eat first."

"O.K." Once again, disappointment that everything in life comes with conditions.

Mikhailova buttered the toast and made herself some tea.

"Do you miss your friends in Bräcke?"

Kolya chewed.

"No."

"But maybe you miss . . ." She searched her memory. "Anton?"

Kolya shook his head. He looked over at the window, just as he always did when he felt shy. It pained Mikhailova to see him so uncomfortable in her presence. Had he been like that from the beginning, she wondered? Probably, yes. For as long as she had known him, since his first birthday, when they moved to Sweden, he had been a careful child. Of course he missed his best friend Anton. She cursed the arrangement that had them moving house so often. According to Kozak, they were simply following the plan. She disagreed and argued that they had the situation under control. "How dangerous can it be?" she said. Kozak sneered: "You're so naïve."

Maybe she was. But he didn't spend even a tenth of the time she did with the boy.

Mikhailova reached out and stroked the boy's head, then gently scratched his neck until he squirmed away. She leaned forward and kissed his hair, took a deep breath.

Kolya was taking time over his piece of toast.

"Thirsty."

"I'll get it. Water?"

He nodded.

She poured some into a glass, took two sips herself and filled it up again before handing it to Kolya.

"Even if you haven't yet made any new ones here, you know that I'm your friend."

"You're Mamma."

She bit her tongue. "But also your friend."

"No." Kolya raised his head and gave her a sly look.

"Come on," she said. "Time for your bath."

Mikhailova turned the taps on full and poured in shampoo instead of bubble bath.

Kolya sat cross-legged waiting for the water to rise. He was playing with two empty bottles and seemed fascinated to see how far he could squirt a jet of water onto the tiles beyond the end of the bathtub.

Mikhailova perched on the toilet lid, watching him. She felt tired. The trip to the airport and back had taken it out of her. She disliked driving on the slippery main roads.

"Be careful. Don't put your head under water."

"I won't."

"Promise."

"Yes Mamma," he sighed.

"I'm not saying it to be mean, it's just that—"

"I know," Kolya said, exasperated.

Yes, you know, she said silently to herself. Of course you know.

She heard her phone out in the hallway. At first she couldn't be bothered to go, figuring it must be Kozak, just calling to say that he'd arrived. She got up, then changed her mind and let it ring. Went back into the bathroom and leaned her head against the tiles. Shut her eyes. Images began to flicker before her.

Who was she really? She often asked herself that. Her mother had once told her that she was hopeless when it came to showing her true feelings. It was a sort of self-fulfilling prophecy. She hardly ever let anyone in, keeping strong emotions at bay. Although she was drawn to boys and had grown up with two immodest older brothers, which taught her all about male anatomy and psychology, she was fourteen before she managed to get close to a boy of her own age. It was on a school trip, and she was almost as awkward as he was. Even though she had all the theoretical knowledge, down to the last detail. She only needed to follow the mental map. At last they found themselves alone in a room at a youth hostel. She managed to control her tongue and kiss him on the mouth. The fact that they got no further just then did not matter. She saw it as a victory, she had managed her first step out into the real world. There followed the occasional sexual encounter with older men who were completely absorbed with satisfying their own needs, and then she met Pavel at a party at Neverova's house. He took his time – they both did, prepared to wait out the unease in the room until, eventually, it got up and lumbered off. Sex with Pavel was wonderful, she thought. He guided her with a light hand and her body followed, smoothly, like on T.V. Until he began to show his darker side, the jealousy and the fits of rage. She never considered the men she saw while in Maxim's service as real encounters. They were soulless bodies that were shifted from one place to another. Like sacks of potatoes moved around in a storage room. And she never let them enter her shell. But she had allowed Kozak in. Because she had believed him to be different, capable of giving and not only taking.

Mikhailova opened her eyes. A sound had caught her attention. Or rather, the absence of sound. Kolya was lying in the bath with his head under water. She launched herself at the bathtub and pulled the boy up, who stared at her in surprise.

"What?"

Mikhailova felt her heart pounding. She was shaking.

"I told you not to go under water."

"But you're here."

"Yes, but it's dangerous." She held him in a firm grip, which he tried to resist. He was still standing in the bath. She tried to control her shaking.

"You're not allowed to, do you hear me?"

"Ouch, you're hurting me."

He struggled to escape her rigid hold.

"I can't keep an eye on you all the time."

"But you were sitting right here." Kolya looked terrified. He began to cry and turned away, crossing his arms.

Mikhailova lifted the boy up, felt the warm, wet body against her blouse.

"You mustn't—"

"O.K.!" he shouted, wriggling in her arms.

"Calm down. I just don't want you to drown."

"I said O.K!"

Carefully, Mikhailova set the boy down on the bathmat and kneeled beside him.

"Do you want to get back in the bath?"

He shook his head.

"You're allowed to."

"Don't want to."

"I'm sorry I shouted. I got so frightened. Do you want to get back in?"

"No."

"O.K. Let me dry you then."

Mikhailova took the largest towel off a hook and wrapped it around Kolya. She sat down and dried every inch of his slim body. Avoiding his willie, which she was afraid to hurt, letting it dry by itself. Then she picked him up and carried him from the bathroom to the bedroom, setting him down on the bed.

"Do you want to watch something?"

Kolya nodded.

"Avengers?" she asked with a smile.

Kolya nodded again, looking pleased.

There was a knock at the front door. She left the boy alone for a moment and, with light steps, went out into the hallway to open the door. Olga was standing there in the rain, holding an umbrella.

"Awful weather," Mikhailova said in Russian. "Come on in. Tea?"

"That'd be great," said the 63-year-old lady from Östersund as she stepped inside. "Here." She held out a plastic box. "One needs a little bit of cake to go with the coffee."

Mikhailova experienced the same joy as she'd felt as a small girl when *babushka* visited them. "I'll put the kettle on."

SVENSTAVIK

Three years earlier

"Yesss! Santa Claus is coming!"

Kolya leaped to his feet and sent the cup of hot chocolate flying. He didn't even notice it, but ran into the sitting room and danced for joy.

"Is he really?" Mikhailova whispered, trying to catch Kozak's eye across the kitchen table. "Couldn't you have told me earlier?"

Kozak got to his feet. "I only heard last night."

"There you are. Perhaps you should have said something then." She wondered why Mischenko never contacted her directly, after all that had happened before she moved to Sweden.

"I didn't want any fuss and you were so tired."

Mikhailova picked up the broken cup and mopped up the chocolate that was already trickling through the cracks in the floorboards underneath the rag rug. *Didn't want any fuss,* a fascinating euphemism for the masculine head-in-the-sand approach.

"Any idea how many will be coming?"

"He didn't say."

"Was he the one who called?"

"Yes."

She was surprised, it told her something about Kozak's relationship with him. Rather than analysing this information, she simply accepted the fact and went off to Åsarna to do the shopping. She tried to think large quantities, knowing that a lot of alcohol would inevitably be consumed. When she got back to the cottage, Kozak and Kolya were out on the brand new snowmobile. She went straight to the kitchen and stayed there until eleven o'clock that night. She emerged exhausted but satisfied with the buffet, which stood ready to be served up the next day. She crawled into bed beside him. Tired but happy.

"Can we buy another radiator?"

"Certainly." Kozak turned out the light. "As soon as they've gone."

"Are they staying for several days?" Mikhailova exclaimed, sitting up in bed.

"No idea."

"Oh my God."

She didn't get to sleep until the early hours of Christmas Eve, after getting up again to creep into Kolya's room and fill his stocking with Star Wars trading cards. He was still as keen on them as ever.

Christmas Eve began quietly. The temperature had dropped below minus ten but there was no wind when Mikhailova went out to clear the snow that had fallen during the night. She had asked Kozak if their guests were planning to stay the night, but all he said was that it would be O.K. Maybe for him, but what about her as hostess? And it was the first time she would be seeing the boss here in Sweden, whose name they only mentioned when they were alone, outdoors, in the woods. She wasn't sure how much of her story Kozak had been told.

The first car arrived around lunchtime. Mikhailova spotted it through the kitchen window and immediately called out: "Here they are."

Kolya was the first to reach the door. He jumped into his boots but didn't bother with a hat or jacket. "Wow!" she heard him say and she soon realised why. Another three equally large cars pulled up, S.U.V.s with tinted windows. She hoped that the farmer who lived two kilometres away had not seen them, but the chances were he had. How would they explain it, when they were trying to keep such a low profile? She knew what this meant: moving to another cottage, far too soon.

Several men in leather jackets got out and looked around. Kolya stood motionless on the front porch, observing the party. She heard him whisper. "Where's Santa Claus?"

She wished she could say "soon", but she remained silent as she had no idea what he would look like, or whether he had got dressed up in some way. But she knew at once when she saw the elegant suit on the man in the third S.U.V.

The boss, that is Mischenko, walked calmly towards the house and did not take his eyes off Kolya until he had reached the front steps. Mikhailova sensed the boy pulling back, almost sheltering behind her, but she pushed him forward.

Mischenko had aged, more than the three years it had been since they had last met in his *dacha* with the armed guards outside the window. He bent down with his arms outstretched. "Kolya?" he said.

The boy nodded cautiously.

"Do I get a hug?"

"Remember what I told you," Mikhailova encouraged him.

The boy put out his hand.

"Not like that. A hug," she whispered loudly.

Kolya leaned forward and gave him a hug.

"What a tall four-year-old."

"Yes, I suppose he's got good genes," she said rather boldly.

Mischenko gave her a steady look and reached for her hand.

"Yulia."

"Welcome," she said. Her hand felt damp in his. He drew her to him, still holding her hand. There was the familiar smell of tobacco and aftershave. It all came back to her now, strong feelings welled up as she heard him whisper: "Thank you."

Then he greeted Kozak. Mikhailova tried to hold on to the feeling of his embrace for a second or two and wondered what he had been thanking her for. Leaving home and moving to Sweden? Sticking it out for three years? Taking care of Kolya? Or was Mischenko thanking her for their . . . *relationship*?

Several men followed Mischenko into the small red cottage. He walked around, humming to himself, and stopped in the kitchen where she had laid out the buffet, which looked to be more than sufficient now that she knew how many of them there were. Mischenko smiled at her. He had a weather-beaten, clean-shaven face and a neat haircut with the occasional grey strand. Was neither tall nor short, nor particularly muscular. He looked like any ordinary Russian businessman and wouldn't cause much of a stir in the streets of St Petersburg. Not until people heard his name, that is.

"Shall we?" he said, looking at Kozak.

"Shall we what?" Mikhailova said.

"Get going," Mischenko replied and went out to the cars.

Mikhailova could see that Kozak knew nothing more than she did. But it was clearly not a time for asking questions, so she put on Kolya's coat and found a pair of smart shoes that he had grown out of. Then they left the house and got into one of the cars.

"Where are we going, Mamma?" Kolya said. He was trying to remove his shoes.

"Don't know, darling. Don't know," she said, trying to sound unperturbed. "Leave your shoes on." He obeyed reluctantly.

It took them exactly one hour on the E45 and the E14 to get to Östersund. The cars parked outside Stadshotellet and a total of fifteen people got out. Mikhailova felt somewhat more reassured holding Kolya's hand in hers and climbed up the steps to the hotel entrance. It had obviously all been planned in detail. One of the men, who was wearing a more sober outfit, a jacket under a long coat, spoke to the receptionist, who led the party over to a large dining room on the ground floor. It was four in the afternoon and it occurred to Mikhailova that they had just missed the Donald Duck Christmas special on T.V., but she wasn't about to remind Kolya. He was fascinated by all the lit candles and beautiful carpets. He had never come into contact with this kind of luxury.

A large section of the restaurant had been reserved for their group. Mischenko sat at the end of the table and indicated that he wanted Kolya beside him. Mikhailova took a seat next to Kolya and saw Kozak settle a few places further down. There were ten people at the table and three men stationed around the room. She assumed that some had stayed with the cars.

Then the supper was brought in, and the dishes were very different from the food served at the restaurant's Christmas buffet. At first Mikhailova was uncomfortable with the curious but timid glances of the Östersund families dining in the background, but then she realised that Mischenko must have matters under control and that she could relax. It irked her to think of all the food she had prepared at home that would now go to waste, but she was brought back to the present by a question from the boss.

"So how's it going?"

She didn't immediately understand what he was referring to, but it became clear when his eyes turned slowly to Kolya, who was trying to open a lobster using two forks. "Well, I think."

"You think?" Mischenko said in a serious tone. "I'm assuming that things are going better than that."

"Of course," she corrected herself. "He's really, really well."

"He seems happy enough. And he's getting his schooling?"

"Yes."

"She does a good job?" Mischenko said, raising his glass of vodka.

Mikhailova raised hers and toasted back. Took a careful sip of the strong alcohol.

"She's fantastic."

"So are you," Mischenko said softly, without meeting her look.

"Thank you."

He let his eyes wander around the table and whispered to her. "I can see that he is well. Not a day goes by without my worrying and wondering how he is, and it stops me sleeping. But I get regular reports from Sasha, who tells me you're doing a fantastic job."

Mikhailova was amazed. She'd had no idea.

Mischenko carried on. "But I already knew that when you got the job. And now I find, to my delight, that I was right. He will grow into a fine man."

Mikhailova didn't know what to say, she just sat there and soaked up the praise. There were a thousand follow-up questions that had occupied her thoughts every evening for the past three years, but she couldn't bring herself to ask. How much longer were they supposed to go on living here? Had there been any change in the threat that Kolya faced? What was the long-term plan? She knew that Kozak was her link to Mischenko, that he was given all the information they needed, and that that would simply have to do. There were clear limits she was not allowed to overstep, so Kozak had told her.

As the meal went on, the men's conversations grew louder and easier the more they drank. When the cake trolley was wheeled in, Kolya was busy playing with his new Star Wars cards.

"Come here," Mischenko said in a friendly tone, pushing back his chair. He patted his thigh. Kolya stole a quick look at Mikhailova, and she nodded. He got to his feet slowly and took two small steps towards Mischenko, Santa Claus, who had come to them in his black car.

"I'm going to tell you a story," he began, speaking so softly that only the boy and Mikhailova could hear. The other men were noisy and boisterous. "You know that when you were just a tiny newborn baby, you used to cry all night long."

Kolya stared up at the strange man with the snow-white shirt and black jacket.

"You screamed so loud that you kept the whole house awake, night after night. After a few weeks everyone was terribly tired because no-one could sleep. Then suddenly one night you stopped crying, do you know why?"

The boy shook his head.

"We put a dog in your cot."

"A real dog?" Kolya exclaimed. It was the first spontaneous remark he had made all evening.

"A real dog. It lay beside you in your little bed and slept, just like you, all night long. Isn't that fantastic?"

Kolya looked as if he were trying to imagine what the dog was like. He must have wanted to ask what became of him, but before he had time to do so, the man set him down on the floor and raised his glass. "Merry Christmas one and all! May Saint George watch over you and protect you from evil."

The men drank a solemn toast.

Mikhailova looked at Kolya and saw that he was staring straight ahead. He seemed happy, deep in thought, no doubt something to do with the dog and the cot. And perhaps he was trying to work out how Santa Claus could know a story about him when he was newly born.

As the evening drew to a close, Mikhailova was feeling quite tipsy from all the toasts. She stumbled down the steps to the cars and sat in the same seat as before. Kolya fell asleep in her lap on the way back to the cottage. She wondered if the men would be staying and, if so, where they could be accommodated, but she assumed they would leave. After a while, she dozed off, staring out into the dark Jämtland night.

When they arrived back at the cottage, she gathered that they would be driving on. Kozak went in and turned on the lights while she woke Kolya. Mischenko came walking towards them, holding something with a blanket thrown over it. Kolya's tired head was leaning against Mikhailova, he was waiting to go inside and get into bed.

"Mamma, I want to sleep."

Mischenko stopped. He looked into her eyes and, for a moment, she thought that he would slap her, or do something even worse. She steeled herself, feeling the adrenalin washing over her tired brain. Prepared for the pain.

But he didn't hit her. At first Mischenko seemed tense, as though he had something on his mind, then he broke into a smile. "Well of course. Obviously. Mamma . . ." With that, he put what he was carrying on the ground and pulled off the blanket.

Kolya saw what it was before Mikhailova.

"A dog!"

"Your Christmas present," Mischenko said.

A golden retriever puppy in a cage. Kolya was immediately wide awake, jumping up and down.

Mischenko set the cage down on the snow and turned to Mikhailova.

"Merry Christmas then . . . *Mamma* Yulia. Until we meet again."

She put out her hand but was swept into a big hug by Anatoly Mischenko. It lasted for ever.

RÄTANSBYN
Seven months earlier

It was either Mikhailova or Kolya who took the dog out, rarely Kozak. They walked him at least three times a day, all year round. In spring and summer, Boris the dog usually slept in the barn, in a kennel which Kozak had built for him. The reason why Boris became more of an outdoor dog was not because he was particularly fond of nature. It was because his excessive flatulence bothered Kozak to such a degree that he threatened several times to "take the dog and my rifle for a last walk in the woods".

"You don't really mean that, do you?" Mikhailova said. Kolya was racing after Boris down to the lake, while she and Kozak followed at a gentler pace. She wasn't worried for Kolya, the ice had just begun to thaw but the water was shallow until quite far out and the boy would never dare to run along the jetty by himself.

"Sasha?"

"Of course not," Kozak said, shoving his hands into his builders' jacket. "But he does stink to high heaven."

"Well, now we're outdoors." She slipped her arm through his and kissed his clean-shaven cheek. Saturday, and Kozak had done his "weekly scrub" as he liked to put it. It was also the first time for months that he was not going away for the weekend. Family time, how fantastic was that, Mikhailova thought, revelling in the clear blue, admittedly crisp, sky. There was still a little snow here and there in the meadows around the lake but, to her delight, the spring sun had managed to cajole some wood anemones out of the ground. She tried hard not to think about his trips home to what he referred to as his "other family". As if she had not understood his priorities.

Although she knew perfectly well what the situation was, she kept hoping that he would reconsider. That he would make up his own mind as to who he wanted to live with, not because she nagged him or made him feel guilty, not because he had a bad conscience, but because she gave him the feeling that he was loved and he actually wanted to spend the rest of his life with her.

Kolya had already found the key to the small hut by the lake and pulled open the wide wooden doors so that they swung on their hinges in the light breeze. He was busy looking for his fishing rod. There were life jackets, inflatable rings and folding chairs lying all over the place now, but Kozak did not get cross. One of his strengths, which she greatly admired, was his patience and his readiness to take on practical challenges. He would always oblige if it was something he could get to grips with. Kozak knew how to fix just about anything with his hands, but was quite incapable of doing the same with feelings.

She set down her basket and bag on the frozen grass by the outdoor furniture. Boris was sniffing along the water's edge, hoping to find something that winter had left behind.

"Let's see now," Kozak said as he started to help Kolya sort out the mess.

"Do you think they've woken up?" asked the excited boy.

"Why not? We'll soon see." Kozak only smiled at the disorder that had been created in less than a minute in the lakeside hut.

Mikhailova pulled out seating mats, a coffee thermos and some hot chocolate from the rucksack. She had even prepared rye bread sandwiches and baked a honey cake, which she had carefully packed into an ice cream container. She sat down on the bench and poured herself a cup of coffee, enjoying the caress of the sun on her face. The air was still cold, three degrees, but as there was no wind she soon warmed up and it all began to feel quite wonderful. She wasn't sure what gave her more joy, the weather or the fact that the three of them were together. And that they had not had a row for several days. The previous night, Kozak had been unusually considerate, helping with dinner and sitting with Kolya and reading to him until he fell asleep. This behaviour made her suspicious, but she did her best not to worry. Experience had taught her that such moments rarely lasted very long.

Kolya made a few valiant attempts to fish, but the lure kept getting caught in the ice floating around Lake Lill-Maren.

"Can't we go out in the boat?" Kolya asked over and over again, but Kozak only smiled and said: "It's not in the water yet, you know that. And no . . ." He raised his hand in protest. "It's too much of a hassle to do it now. But if you like, I can help you put on a different lure."

"Oh please!" Kolya pleaded in vain.

Kozak sat down on the bench and was handed a mug of steaming hot coffee. He ate a sandwich and stared at the lake with empty eyes. When Boris came over to the table, he shooed him away.

"What are you thinking about?" Mikhailova asked.

"What? Nothing."

"Come on, I can see there's something on your mind." She felt more and more uneasy. The calm before the storm.

"Can't you just enjoy a beautiful day?" Kozak said as he chewed away. "Do you always have to analyse everything to death?"

"I'm sorry. I only . . ." She topped up his coffee.

"I only . . ." he mimicked before taking a few gulps.

Mikhailova sat in silence and poured some hot chocolate for the boy. "Here. Come and have something to drink."

Kolya downed it in one go, standing beside her.

"Some *medovik*?" she said to Kozak, holding out the box.

He shook his head. "You always put too much honey in it."

What could she say? Too much honey in a honey cake. It was her grandmother's recipe, a cake she had grown up with and which Kolya loved. Was she not even any good at baking cakes? She tried to recall the last time Kozak had paid her a compliment. It had been a long time ago. All her life she had been told that she wasn't up to it, a mediocre brain who might just about manage compulsory school but no more than that. Hardly anyone, not even her parents, seemed to expect anything more ambitious of her, and nor did she herself. Not until her seventeenth birthday, when she realised that life after secondary school was only a year away and that she was, against all the odds, nearing the finish line. Two years later she met Pavel, who turned out to be even better than the others at telling her how useless she was and that she need not even bother to think about venturing further afield. For that very reason she had not hesitated when the opportunity arose for her to go to Sweden. And here she was, sitting by a lake in Jämtland on a beautiful spring day, all three of them together for once. And yet her heart was filled with sorrow. It was as if he were determined to destroy her from the inside out, until she was nothing more than an empty shell. She was afraid that the next gust of wind would reduce her body to atoms.

She helped herself to some cake. "I like it. My mother was proud of her cakes. And my dad was fond of them."

"Good for you," Kozak said, standing up. "But I'm not your father." He got out his phone and checked the screen. Went over to the hut and sat down by the doorpost.

Boris came and lay down at Kolya's feet.

She stroked the boy's head and he patted his beloved dog. Mikhailova saw that he was caught up in his own world and had not registered Kozak's spiteful remarks. It was her greatest wish that he might be immune to the tension, that the bubble he and she had created for themselves over the past six years would prove strong enough. The boy seemed to be doing well, and didn't appear to be suffering from his unusual upbringing. Perhaps it was sufficient for her to have arranged such encounters as she could with other children over the years, as they moved through a succession of villages. He rarely complained, seemingly content that she was his substitute mother, friend, provider, his everything. Of course she knew that this would be enough for a seven-year-old, but not for a teenager with completely different needs. When would their lives change? When would Kozak be able to tell them what to expect around the next corner, in the autumn, next year ... The only constant feature of their existence was "Santa Claus", who had arrived on Christmas Eve with his retinue of black S.U.V.s and a boot full of toys and booze. Undoubtedly Kolya had a very unusual perception of Santa Claus, but it was no less romantic for that.

They had lived in four different villages, four cottages which she had never quite had the time to turn into real homes. There was always the imminent threat of a move, that they would have to up sticks with just a few minutes' notice. Two suitcases packed with basic necessities always stood ready in the hallway. Two bags containing all the material possessions she was allowed to become attached to. Therefore it seemed to her unnecessary and pointless to do anything more than a bare minimum to decorate the cottages. They did not belong to them anyway. She had become used to this, and so she built her dreams within herself. And she was brave enough to consign some of these hopes and dreams to her diary.

She watched Kozak sitting there cross-legged with his body folded forward like a jack-knife. He was speaking in heated tones, but she couldn't hear what they were discussing. It reminded her of other conversations he'd had in recent days. Most of the time he had gone out into the barn to talk. Was there something in the offing? Another change to their lives? Is that why he was so short-tempered? All questions. No answers.

Mikhailova took another piece of cake and dipped it in her coffee. It tasted just as it should. She looked at Kolya.

"Shall we play something?"

YTTERHOGDAL

Wednesday, 6 November

"Who's taking me to school tomorrow, Mamma?"

Mikhailova opened Kolya's door and put down the laundry basket. "I'm not really sure, darling." She had a runny nose, a cold she couldn't seem to shake.

"But Pappa is here," Kolya said, "surely he can . . ."

"I . . ." Mikhailova did not know what to say. In recent days Kozak had been so vague, so stressed about something he didn't want to discuss. The previous week he had said that he was going to St Petersburg, before cancelling the trip on the Saturday morning. On Sunday he mentioned going to Stockholm "next weekend". Was that supposed to be this weekend? She got no straight answers. That morning he had gone off to Sveg on some errand. "Got to buy some stuff," he'd said as he left after breakfast.

She'd had to get their second car, an old Toyota Corolla, out of the barn and take Kolya to school, even though she didn't like to drive. Kolya had started school in August and gone into the first year with children who were a year younger than him. He absolutely loved it and didn't want to miss one single minute. Olga had been his teacher ever since he was three, and he spoke Swedish and Russian fluently. He could have gone straight into year two, but he was small for his age and hadn't mixed much with other children and Mikhailova did not want him to fall behind right from the beginning. She needn't have worried about his social skills. It was as if his subconscious had been longing for a normal life all those years, the kind he had never experienced but got to know about through social media and YouTube channels. His favourite programme followed a group of American schoolchildren leading very ordinary lives across many, many episodes, which he watched over and over again.

"We'll see," she said, taking the clean clothes into the bedroom to be folded and put away in their respective drawers. She blew her nose and heard the front door bang.

Kozak looked into the bedroom. "Is he asleep?"

"Go and see for yourself."

Kozak closed the door hard. "I asked if he was asleep."

Mikhailova wanted to point out that he hadn't taken his shoes off, and she had just finished cleaning the floor, but she could see that now was not the right time. She knew exactly how he would react. He would get even more annoyed and probably start slamming doors. "No, he's waiting to hear about tomorrow."

"We're catching the train at 11.18 in the morning."

"The train? Where are we going?"

"Stockholm. We're driving to Östersund."

"But—"

"Just pack the bags."

"Has something happened?" She steadied herself against the chest of drawers, felt sick. Did she have a temperature?

Kozak appeared to calm down. "No, no. We're just going to Stockholm for the weekend. Thought it would be fun to go on a little break."

"Absolutely, but . . ."

Kozak came over to the chest of drawers where she stood feeling dizzy. She still wanted to ask him to take off his shoes but he put his arms around her and kissed her on the mouth. The first kiss for at least a week, maybe two.

"But what about school?"

"He's only in the first year."

"But he really doesn't want to miss even one day."

"I'll call the school when we're on our way." Kozak let go of her and went out of the room.

Mikhailova was left standing there, holding a shirt and feeling

156

confused. Then again, she had been longing to get away. A few days in Stockholm with both Kolya and Kozak felt like a real treat, just what she had been dreaming of. It might help them take a break from the constant bickering. Perhaps even rekindle his feelings for her, make him show some sort of affection again. It had been so long . . .

She folded the shirt carefully and placed it neatly where it belonged.

The next morning, Mikhailova packed a bag for her and Kolya and prepared a substantial picnic of pancakes and meatballs. Hot chocolate in one thermos and coffee in another. She stowed it all into the boot of the car and called to Kolya who was standing by the front door.

"Are you coming?"

She saw Kozak arriving back at the wheel of the Toyota. He parked it behind the barn and walked towards her with a rifle in his hand. There was a resolute look in his eyes.

"Where's Boris?" she asked.

"I thought we'd leave him with Einar."

"Einar? Have you been to Einar and Greta's?"

"I didn't think he would enjoy being in town."

Mikhailova noticed that he was avoiding her eyes.

"But why did you take the rifle with you?"

"Oh, yeah," Kozak called without turning around. "Einar borrowed it. I just got it back."

She stood by the car and let the words sink in. It was true that Kozak had gone hunting with their neighbour a couple of times, but why would he have lent him his rifle? Surely Einar had one of his own.

Kolya came out, looking dejected.

"What's the matter?" she said.

He got into the car and crossed his arms.

Mikhailova crouched down. "Is school the problem?"

Kolya stared straight ahead.

"You'll only be missing a few days. We're going to Stockholm . . . You know all the things they've got there. I've told you about it . . ."

Kolya's eyes wavered, and she saw that he was beginning to relent.

"Museums," she said. "Toy shops."

"What about cinemas?" he asked, turning abruptly to face her.

"Loads," she answered before closing his door and getting into the front seat.

Kozak joined them and switched on the engine. "Stockholm, here we come!" he called out, in a very different tone this time.

She couldn't make him out, his mood was always changing. Glancing back at Kolya, she saw that his expression was also completely different now. He seemed excited. She tried to forget about Boris, to stop analysing everything. He'd be fine with Einar and Greta. The main thing was they were on their way to Stockholm for some adventures of their own.

After they had been driving for about an hour, Kolya said that he needed to pee.

"Can't it wait?" Kozak said.

"No," Kolya answered.

"Well, we're not in that much of a hurry and I need to get petrol anyway."

Östersund was only twenty minutes away and they had plenty of time. Kozak pulled into the Gulf service station in Brunflo. He stopped by the pumps and got out.

"Come on," he said to Kolya, who was struggling to get out of the seatbelt.

"Can you fill up in the meantime?" Kozak asked.

Mikhailova nodded and got out. She watched them walk over towards the warmth of the building. Her nose was running as she put petrol in the car. Would this cold never go away? Returning to the passenger seat, she opened the glove compartment, hoping to find some tissues or a paper roll. She pushed aside the instruction booklet, a torch and some energy biscuits which had been squeezed in. After lifting away some more junk, she came across a thick envelope, which she pulled out. Opening it, she was amazed to find a bundle of pristine banknotes. Her eyes turned instinctively to the petrol station, where she spotted Kolya's hat. Kozak was standing by the checkout.

A huge amount of money . . . what . . .? Her body suddenly stiffened. A rush of adrenalin entered her bloodstream, her brain went into top gear. Why all this money? She ran her thumb over the banknotes, a bundle of five-hundred-kronor notes, at least a hundred of them. Did Kozak take it out for their weekend trip? But why so much, in that case? There was something wrong. A whole string of disaster scenarios involving Kozak and his trips to Russia began to play out in her mind. She thought about his foul mood over the past few weeks and tried to make some sense of it all.

The glass doors slid open and Kolya emerged. Kozak followed a few metres behind, holding a cup of coffee. She quickly stuffed the envelope back into the glove compartment, panicking because she could not remember if it had been lying underneath the instruction booklet. Decided it had. Kolya opened the door. She raised her shoulders, flipped down the sun shade and pretended to be fiddling with something in her eye when Kozak came and sat down in the seat beside her.

"All good?" he asked.

She avoided his look.

"All good," she said, swallowing hard. "Just got something in my eye."

III

INTENSIVE CARE UNIT, NOBEL HOSPITAL

Friday morning, 8 November

"Eva, you take care of the woman and I'll deal with the man!"

Tekla turned to the intubated patient with a knife stuck in his chest. It looked as if it had gone straight into the heart, but with any luck it would have hit the lung instead. She considered pulling it out, but decided to leave it where it was, fully in keeping with the guidelines. A sharp object penetrating a vein or artery anywhere in the body could be fatal, but it could also act like a cork and put a temporary stop to the bloodflow. Someone who just couldn't leave well enough alone might remove the stick or scissors or whatever it happened to be, and the patient would haemorrhage. Tekla hoped that no vessel or, worse still, the heart had been perforated.

Her next instructions were for the nurse beside her: "Call Surgery and tell them we're on our way. And notify surgical backup. And get more staff over here!"

Tekla looked up at the monitor. Damn, a flat line: asystole. She felt the throat: no pulse.

"Cardiac arrest!" She quickly folded back the headboard and started compressions. Not easy, since the knife was in the way. Each time she pressed down on the thorax, the handle bent sharply to one side.

Three I.C.U. nurses came running and Tekla spotted some more further away. She saw that the boy was being looked after.

"This isn't working," Tekla said to one of the nurses. "I've got to go in. Get me a scalpel." It would take too long to snip open the wire threads holding together the ribs that Tekla had prised apart down in the service tunnel fourteen hours earlier. She had to find another point of entry into the ribcage so she could reach the heart.

Tekla asked a nurse to take over the compressions. She went around the bed and saw Elmqvist trying to establish a clear airway in the woman, who was still shaking.

"We have to give Stesolid," Elmqvist said, looking up at Tekla. "And we need more doctors. Get the first on-call over here, I think she's in Room 8." An assistant nurse rushed off to get reinforcements.

"Could you hold here?" Elmqvist asked. Tekla sat down on the floor to help keep the cramping woman's airway open. As Elmqvist injected muscle-relaxing Stesolid into the woman's thigh muscle, Tekla got to her feet again. She heard a shrill scream behind her and suddenly something gripped her thigh. Looking down she saw the boy cling to her leg like a koala bear. She could feel his warm, panting breath. And now the object in his hand was also visible: a gold-coloured helmet. Tekla saw a nurse come running with scalpel and compresses.

"I've got to help your mother now," she pleaded.

The boy held on even harder. Tekla bent down, patted his hair, which was damp with sweat. She recognised both him and the golden mask – she'd seen them in the lift lobby outside the I.C.U. the previous day.

"Hey. Listen to me. I'm going to do everything I can to save your mother. Is that your father, over there?" Tekla gave a discreet nod in the direction of the bed, taking care not to say either "knife" or "heart".

The boy appeared to relax his grip somewhat. Which suggested that he had heard what she said. But there was no reply. In her mind's eye, Tekla could see her father on his deathbed. She remembered how worried he had been for Simon and her, and how she had assured him that she'd look after her brother. Then she heard herself saying the same to the boy:

"I promise to look after you, no matter what happens."

It was as if they were suddenly travelling back in a time capsule, just the two of them. She found herself in her father's hospital room, the colourful drawings on the walls, the whites of her father's eyes gone yellow.

"No matter what happens, do you hear me?"

With the golden mask clenched tightly in his fist, the boy lowered his eyes, as if shutting a visor.

"Tekla!" Elmqvist could be heard calling somewhere in the distance.

Slowly she was brought back to the I.C.U. at the Nobel Hospital and the boy's panic-stricken look. She touched his cheek, wiped away the tears. "Whatever happens." Then she loosened his hold on her and left him to be looked after by an assistant nurse. She went over to the patient.

"Scalpel?"

A nurse handed her the scalpel and Tekla bent down to find a way in between the ribs, underneath the old incision. By now she had the hang of it, and quickly got through the ribs and pushed the lung aside with her hand. Gently felt her way to the heart, making sure that she did not cut herself on the breadknife. She knew exactly how long it was, thanks to the image of the woman holding it up in the air in her mind's eye, but she had no idea how sharp. She searched with great care through the warm mess of blood and lung tissue. At the same time the nurse kept compressing the thorax in a vain attempt to send blood up to the man's brain.

Gray, who was the first on-call, came running. She looked as if she had just woken up.

"What can I do?" she asked.

"I'm trying to find the knife," Tekla said. "Don't know if it's stuck in the heart."

"Why not just pull it out?"

"Not recommended," Tekla said. "It could be stopping the bleeding. But we have to get to Surgery. Has anyone seen Klas Nyström?"

No answer.

Gray made sure that the tube was properly placed and the ventilator settings correct.

Tekla looked down at the floor, where Elmqvist was struggling to help the woman, who was now lying motionless.

"Have the convulsions stopped?" Tekla asked.

"Yes, but we've got to intubate," Elmqvist replied. "Her airway isn't clear."

Tekla felt something hard between her index and middle fingers. She felt her way up towards the ribcage, followed the path of the knife down through the thick cardiac muscle. Running her fingers along the smooth surface of the pericardium, she then located the exit point on the posterior wall.

"The knife goes straight through the heart," she noted.

"So what do we do now?" Gray said.

Tekla ran through the relevant chapter in *Traumatology* and found the passage on penetrating cardiac injuries. "He needs an operation. By a thoracic surgeon."

"In that case it'll have to be the N.S.K.," Gray said.

"Under normal circumstances," Tekla said, pulling her arm out of the man's chest.

"What do you mean?"

Tekla looked over at the boy, who was now standing still with his arms hanging down by his sides. The mask in one hand. An assistant nurse was crouched down with an arm around him. Then Tekla lowered her gaze to the woman, who was being intubated by Elmqvist.

"Tube inserted," Elmqvist said, attaching an Ambu bag and handing it over to a nurse who began squeezing it. "Now all we need is a bed and a ventilator and we've just got ourselves a new patient."

"Who's also a murderer," Tekla heard an assistant nurse behind her mutter under her breath.

"Can't really argue with that," Tekla said. The nurse appeared to regret having said it out loud.

Right then Nyström came walking in. At a faster pace than yesterday. Did that mean that he too had spent the night there? Seemed unlikely, but the alternative would be some overnight accommodation on Ringvägen, which was even more unlikely.

"Haven't you done enough harm already?" he said, standing at the foot of the patient's bed.

"The answer to your question is that we can stop the compressions and turn off the ventilator," Tekla said. "The patient died at 06.45."

"And that's something you decide, just like that?" Nyström said, as if he were speaking to a three-year-old.

"Yes Klas, I decide. You don't need to be a thoracic surgeon or a professor of hepatic surgery to see how hopeless the situation is. The patient already underwent a record number of emergency procedures yesterday, and goodness knows what state his brain was in even before the woman stuck a breadknife in his heart. He had the acidity of a lemon, thanks to both his kidneys and his liver shutting down. And, as a minor detail, the knife runs straight through both the right and the left ventricle. Who'd be capable of saving that heart? Maybe if you were a thoracic surgeon who had the patient all ready and intubated for surgery. And, I regret to have to add: at the N.S.K."

Nyström managed to produce a stiff smile. "No, you're probably right. It doesn't look good for the poor man."

He walked around the bed and with a careful but unambiguous gesture ushered Gray aside. The anaesthetist took a step back and switched off the ventilator while Professor Nyström opened one of the man's eyes and quickly flashed a torch at it. Then he applied his fingers to the patient's throat.

"Time of death 06.47."

The star surgeon left the patient and strode past the boy, ignoring his very existence.

Tekla watched Gray remove the tube from the man's windpipe while the rest of the staff were busy disconnecting monitors and tidying away cables. She took the man's hand in hers. It was still warm. Then she looked over at the boy and saw him pull away from the assistant nurse in a flash, run towards her and, for the second time, grab hold of her thigh as though it were the last living thing on earth. Tekla put her hand on his small shoulder and glanced down at the man's forearm. The tattoo was still there.

Suddenly, something erupted in the pit of her stomach, shot like a rocket past her lungs and wanted out. She felt like screaming "Bloody hell!" but shut her mouth, swallowed hard and knelt down. All the sweat, the whole struggle to save the man had now vanished into a dark pool of blood under his bed. Tekla had done everything in her power, and then some. She had put her career on the line when she resisted Nyström, when she opened up the man's thorax in the service corridor. And then, once she had done her duty as a doctor, to save lives whatever the cost, the rug was pulled from underneath her feet. A knife in the heart. A woman out of nowhere. A disoriented wife? An unhinged psychiatric patient?

She looked straight into the boy's tearfilled eyes. Then she hugged him.

In the background, a bit further away, Elmqvist could be heard instructing her staff: ". . . she's stable, we need a C.V.C. and an arterial catheter, but there's no rush. First I've got to call the police to report a murder."

This has got to be the very definition of chaos, Tekla thought as she looked around her. She quickly established that there were eighteen people in the room. They had got the alarm just before the night staff went off duty. It was precisely during this sleepy limbo that the woman came in and stabbed the man in the heart. His life could not be saved. Now his body was turning cold under a white sheet. Tekla had given the order not to remove the tube from the man's airway, knowing that the police would want everything left untouched.

Three screens surrounded his bed, forming an impregnable wall, with Tekla standing guard at one of the gaps. Now that the worst of the fury and frustration at having lost the injured man were beginning to abate, fatigue was gaining the upper hand. She clung to the fact that she really had saved the man's life. Against all odds. Even so: he was dead. Who was that woman who had suddenly appeared like an angel of death, a messenger from the darkness of night?

"It took eighty milligrammes of Stesolid," Elmqvist said, standing in front of Tekla. The chief anaesthetist removed his gloves and held up the blood gases for her to see. Tekla took the narrow strip.

"That was unexpected."

Elmqvist pulled off her plastic apron. "If you say so."

"Well, do you think a pH of 6.9 seems reasonable?"

"It all depends on what's causing it."

Tekla visualised the blood gas readings without looking at the slip of paper. "She's been having convulsions, so a lactate value of 10 shouldn't have us scratching our heads."

"But now she's sleeping like a log," Elmqvist said.

"What do you think it could be?" Tekla asked.

"Other than the obvious?"

"You mean epilepsy?"

Elmqvist smiled and pushed her fingers through thick, curly hair firmly held in place by a pink hairclip. "If, that is, epilepsy patients are known to get confused and stick knives into their unfaithful spouses?"

"What about an overdose?" Tekla suggested.

"Or a psychotic patient who's overdone their meds," Elmqvist said in a weary tone. She was probably hoping for a straightforward explanation for the woman's cramps.

"Don't agree," Tekla said. "Not with such severe metabolic acidosis and low sodium levels which . . ." Tekla stopped in her tracks. Nyström came back in again, leaning forward slightly with his hands clasped behind his back.

"I'm just going to check on the boy," Tekla said, buying herself some time. "But it doesn't fit with epilepsy either."

"The police should be here any minute now," Elmqvist said. "They asked us not to touch anything. I think you ought to stay until they arrive. And I'm sorry but I do think it was a generalised epileptic seizure."

"I'm not going anywhere," Tekla called out. It had not escaped her notice that Elmqvist was irritated by her reluctance to accept epilepsy as a diagnosis.

The boy stood with his arms hanging by his side, staring blankly at the partition screens. It struck Tekla that his attention was focused on the father, not the mother, who was actually alive. Admittedly, his mother was intubated and had stuck a knife into his father's heart forty-five minutes before, but still. If he was capable of rational thought, he ought to be looking to the living parent. Not the one he had just lost. But Tekla realised that there was nothing natural or rational about the situation. The fact that the boy was in shock was perhaps the only natural or rational thing about it. Or rather, logical. He was going to need all the professional help that healthcare and the community could muster. And Tekla had faith in the system. She trusted that there were kind people ready to step up, just like the woman on the chair beside the boy, who was a model of calm and total commitment.

Carefully, Tekla opened the door to the glass cubicle, intending to slip in and stand by the wall, listening. But the boy swung around, took a few quick steps towards her and flung his small arms about her waist. The plastic mask fell to the floor with a dull thud. Tekla held out her arms and stared helplessly at the social worker, who gestured to Tekla to stay where she was. How long, Tekla wondered, as panic gripped her chest. Through the window she could see Nyström signalling something to her. He evidently wanted her to come out.

Gently Tekla laid her arms around the boy's back. His T-shirt was damp with warm sweat. She stroked his head. His scalp was also moist. Out of the corner of her eye she saw Törnqvist walking around the cubicle. He opened the door.

"Would you come out please."

"Is that a question?"

Törnqvist gave an irritated shake of the head and shut the door.

"I think I have to . . ." Tekla said, but she felt the boy's arms tightening around her waist, like a boa constrictor with its prey.

At last the social worker stepped in. "Listen . . ." Carefully, she took hold of the boy's arm. "The doctor has to do some work. Maybe we can talk to her again later on." She met Tekla's eyes and gave her an encouraging nod. Then she prised open his vicelike grip with the utmost care. Tekla could feel how hard he tried to resist and crouched down. He looked straight at her. She was not prepared for such intimacy. Surely a child in shock is more distant? More confused? His eyes were brown and beseeching.

"I'm going to come back. So you and I can talk some more. Later on I'll tell you everything that's happened. O.K.?"

The boy showed no sign of having taken in what Tekla told him. He kept staring at her with the same intensity. Eventually Tekla stood up and left the glass cubicle. Her phone pinged – a text which she glanced at quickly: Can you talk?

No, not right now.

A while later, Nyström looked in through the sliding doors.

"So that's it, he's dead."

"It's not absolutely certain," Tekla said. "Perhaps you'd better check to be sure. If you like, I can remind you how to establish death. I expect you haven't done that for a while. Your patients never die, do they?"

The professor turned to Törnqvist. "How the hell could you allow a lunatic to charge in and stick a knife into a patient I've just spent the better part of the night saving?"

Tekla couldn't believe her ears. There was so much that was wrong in that one sentence.

"A murder in my hospital," a familiar voice said behind Tekla. She turned to see Carlsson. The C.E.O. was limping. It was barely noticeable, but Tekla saw that one leg did not seem to be following along properly. Behind Carlsson there were two police officers, a man and a woman.

"So glad you could come," Nyström said. In a very different voice, Tekla noted. As if a sound technician had upped his pitch by three tones and used a filter to get rid of all the rasping.

"Did I have a choice?" Carlsson said. "What exactly happened?"

"We don't know," Tekla said. "Only that a completely unknown. woman showed up an hour ago and rammed a knife into the heart of this patient, who we operated on late last night. We're assuming he's her husband."

"And why are you assuming that?" the policewoman behind Carlsson asked. Her colleague went over to the screens and looked in at the dead man. Tekla recognised his silhouette.

"Because of the boy who came with her," Tekla said. "First he shouted 'Mamma' as she assaulted the man. And then 'Pappa' once the knife had been stuck . . . well, where it was stuck."

The woman police officer made some notes in a small booklet and nodded to her colleague, who got out some blue-and-white tape.

"What a bloody waste," Nyström said.

"Meaning?" Carlsson said.

"My patient."

Tekla and Carlsson exchanged looks. The C.E.O. seemed to be considering various possible replies. She finally settled on: "Let the police do their job. We can go and sit down over by the reception."

Carlsson went into an empty doctor's office and Nyström, Törnqvist, Elmqvist and Tekla followed her. Elmqvist closed the door behind them.

"A real mess, this," Carlsson said, sinking into a chair. She brought out what looked like a large white matchbox and helped herself to something black which she popped into her mouth.

"And the only thing I know for certain is that Dr Berg cannot go on working here after all that has happened," Nyström said.

Carlsson's eyes were fixed on the computer screen.

"I don't know what you're talking about."

"The totally disastrous medical decisions she took during the night that I told you about."

Carlsson turned to Nyström.

"Hang on a moment. Have I completely misunderstood all this? Wasn't he alive when he was stabbed through the heart?"

"Yes, but—"

"So you're blaming Tekla for . . . for what? Failing to tackle a crazy woman who appears out of nowhere at six in the morning and sticks a knife into . . . *your* patient?"

"It's not only that—"

Carlsson held up her hand. "We'll deal with this later. Right now we need to focus on the police investigation and find out how the woman is doing. You'll take care of that, will you?"

Elmqvist nodded.

"And you Tekla . . . you should probably go home once you've spoken to the police."

"Maybe."

"No, wait," Carlsson said. "It would be good if you could attend the morning meeting at eight. I'll be talking about the new organisational structure."

Carlsson got to her feet. Tekla couldn't help gloating at Nyström's ill-concealed frustration when he had to make way for the C.E.O. to leave the room.

Out by the nurses' station, Tekla spotted the familiar silhouette again. She had not seen him for six months. At the time they had discussed the metabolites of heroin, morphine and codeine. She walked up to him.

"Alvaro Silva," Tekla said.

"Ah . . . Dr Berg?" the policeman said. "It's been a while."

"How's it going with the heroin?" Tekla said. There had been no reason for her to have any contact with either Superintendent Silva or his nemesis on the heroin market, Victor Umarov. The patriarch was now locked up in Kumla prison, presumably serving a long sentence, but she had no details.

Silva seemed to shrink as he patted the few strands of hair that barely covered his scalp. "It's like dandelions, you know. You have to pull them up by the roots, before the seeds begin to scatter. Otherwise you have them all over the bloody lawn." He smoothed out a fold on the duffel coat that he had draped over one arm, looking pensive. "This town is full of that crap. Somehow it never ends."

Tekla wondered if his foreign accent was more noticeable when he was worked up. "So are you responsible for some sort of drug squad nowadays?"

Silva smiled. "If only. Responsible . . . hmmm, responsibility is such a relative concept in our business. People take it on when it happens to suit their own agenda. Then, once something extends beyond their turf, the commitment rapidly diminishes. This summer one of my colleagues was diagnosed with cancer of the large intestine. What a disaster . . . terrible. Hell, before he found out he was actually thrilled that he'd lost some weight. Thought it had something to do with his diet. Cancer . . . what a sneaky devil."

Tekla waited for him to continue. She glanced over at the policemen who were securing the scene and saw Carlsson disappear out through the exit with Nyström in her wake.

"You mean . . .?"

"I got to take over his duties. But I'm still with Serious Crimes. They say it's temporary . . . who are they trying to fool . . . about the heroin investigation, that is. But, hey . . . I've only got three years to go till I retire. They can always try to pull a fast one on me, but I won't cave in." Silva turned his attention back to Tekla and lit up. "It's lucky I enjoy my work. Don't you agree?"

The social worker was leaving the I.C.U. with the boy, who was resisting her. Tekla wanted to rush over and ask where they were taking him, but she knew she had to accept that it was no longer her concern.

"But what about this . . . alleged murder," Silva said. "The duty officer reported it straight to Serious Crimes."

Tekla was confused.

"In other words . . . that would be me," Silva explained. "Pretty unnecessary, I'd say. Looks like a straightforward case, doesn't it? Manslaughter, surely. Disoriented woman, psychotic, drives a knife into the chest—"

"Well, it's not really my area—"

"No. Quite," Silva cut in.

"But I have some thoughts," Tekla said, determined to focus her attention on the blood gases, which she felt needed further investigation.

"I can just imagine," Silva said, sounding weary. He held up one finger. "And it's precisely those bright ideas that I would like you to keep to yourself. This time I want a quick and painless solution. No protracted labour, so to speak . . . Surely you can come up with a diagnosis that includes the term *psychosis* . . .?

Silva left Tekla and lumbered across to the other police officers. He had no idea just how wrong he would prove to be.

Tekla went over to a computer and logged in. The first test results were coming in. She squinted at the screen, convinced that her eyes were deceiving her, checked to see that she had the right sample identification number. The liver values were all over the place. Now she understood why her brain had gone into overdrive: hyponatremia – it was the low sodium concentration that stood out. Why did the woman have hyponatremia? Then she thought about the boy. His searching eyes were etched in her mind, they had brought something to life.

NOBEL HOSPITAL

Friday morning, 8 November

As Carlsson went up to the podium she saw her husband, Gregor Dabrowski, sit down in the first row next to Collinder. The other seats there were occupied by the division heads and, right at the end, the new C.F.O., af Petersén. The head of communications, Nyrén, was standing by the wall holding her wallet and phone in one hand. She surveyed the room, in which every chair was soon taken. Some twenty doctors were leaning casually against the wall along the stairs.

Microphone in hand, Carlsson looked at her watch. Eight o'clock sharp.

"Good morning. Welcome. Coffee and sandwiches will be coming round. And don't worry, I'm not going to take it out of your salaries."

Carlsson paused for two seconds but heard no laughter and saw no smiles.

"I won't be keeping you too long, but the management team has some important information for you."

Suddenly Carlsson felt a stab in the pit of her stomach and took a deep breath. She pretended that a buzz had alerted her to an incoming call, glanced at her phone and put it down on the table next to the bottle of mineral water. Avoided Nyrén's prying eyes. There was nothing unusual about being in demand if one is the C.E.O. of a hospital. Nor was it surprising that she'd left her phone switched on, that was just like her.

"As you know, there is building work going on here and there at the moment. We regret the inconvenience, and Locum have

177

promised to hurry things up on the ground floor. It's unfortunate that some passages have had to be closed off, but it won't take long."

She looked over at the team from the Department of Medicine. Saw Klein-Borgstedt, Tekla, Sigurdsdottir and the others.

"We're very proud of the fact that work on the intensive care unit was completed before the summer and next week we'll be inaugurating the two new hybrid surgery rooms. Later on you'll be informed about Klas Nyström's liver transplant plans, but . . ."

Once again, Carlsson felt such a sharp pain in her stomach that it almost took her breath away. She had to improvise, create a diversion.

"No, on second thoughts," she managed to utter. "Klas, stand up. Most people here probably know you but . . . let's hear it for the foremost liver surgeon in Sweden, perhaps even in Europe."

Nyström got to his feet in the second row and turned to face the assembly. Scattered, measured applause could be heard. He pushed out his lower lip, revealing his splendid set of large white teeth, and bowed his head in gratitude.

"Yes," Carlsson went on, "it's going to be fantastic to have—"

"Liver transplants," Klein-Borgstedt interrupted, raising her hand. Large bracelets landed with a jangle on her tanned forearm. "Isn't the N.S.K. meant to be dealing with all transplant activities?"

Struggling to maintain her composure, Carlsson shot a look at af Petersén, who did not move a muscle. "Let's not discuss that today, but . . ."

"Have I got that wrong?" Klein-Borgstedt was not going to be put off.

Carlsson's stomach was hurting more and more. She tried a different position but then her intestine began to make itself felt. Was she heading for a nightmare scenario where her insides would explode in front of all the doctors in the hospital?

"Anita," Nyrén broke in, moving forward very slightly. Her body as steady as a birch tree, notwithstanding the high stiletto heels. "It's great that you brought this up, but we promise that we'll get back to you with more details. As I'm sure you've all heard, Klas has been recruited to launch something we know will become a world-leading programme. We're absolutely convinced of that."

Nyrén turned to Carlsson with a smile.

"Correct," Carlsson said, noticing with horror that not only was her stomach playing up, she was also losing all sensation in the fingers holding the microphone. She switched it to the other hand, but that was not much better. What if she dropped the damn thing? She deliberately avoided Gregor's eyes and those of anyone else sitting in the first row by fixing on a vague point right at the back of the room where, by tradition, the psychiatrists were sitting.

"We'd also like to inform you that Göran Collinder has been appointed senior consultant and that Hampus Nordensköld will take over from him as overall head for the red division." Then she added: "It's going to be fantastic." Oh my God, Carlsson thought, what am I saying? She was quite simply losing it. There was nothing fantastic about that reshuffle, except that Hampus would be far easier for her to manipulate than Göran had ever been.

"What about this morning's events? Are we supposed to pretend they never happened?" It was one of the younger doctors sitting in the middle of the room who called out. A woman with dark hair and thick-rimmed spectacles, someone Carlsson had never seen before.

"You mean the drama in the I.C.U.?" Carlsson asked, trying to stay calm.

"Well, for example," the young woman sniped.

"Yes, we've at long last made it into an Agatha Christie thriller: *Murder at the Nobel*," Carlsson said, writing quotation marks in the air.

A ripple ran through the sea of doctors. Clearly it was too soon for everyone to have heard the gossip. Out of the corner of her eye, Carlsson could see Nyrén squirming. She realised that her choice of words may not have been the best.

"Actually . . . I mean there was an incident in the I.C.U. last night which is now completely under control. Nothing to worry about."

"Why would we be worried?" said an older doctor from the Infectious Diseases Department, who was sitting in the fourth row. Several others in the room began talking among themselves.

"Quiet please." Nyrén raised her voice. "Quiet." The auditorium fell silent again. "As Monica just told you, the police have the situation under control." With an unnatural laugh, she added: "You're all accustomed to death and police presence in the I.C.U. You'll be told what happened. In due course."

"Yeah, right, in the evening papers," the infectious diseases specialist said.

"By us," Nyrén clarified, without taking the forced smile off her face.

"There's one part of the renovation you haven't mentioned," Klein-Borgstedt said out loud.

"Oh yes?" Nyrén said, looking relieved by the change of subject.

"What's going on in the rock chamber?"

For the first time that morning, Nyrén seemed at a loss. She turned to Carlsson, who was battling the unstoppable forces at work in her bowels. Carlsson grasped the microphone and straightened up.

"Thanks for raising this, Anita. We were actually planning to keep this as a little surprise for you all, but since you ask . . . We've created a . . . patient hotel. Not so big, but soon ready to welcome its first guest."

"Guest?" Klein-Borgstedt asked, leaning forward so that her long pearl necklace clattered against the backrest of the chair in front of her.

"Yes, we'll be admitting patients from other countries who are going to get a new liver thanks to Klas. And they need somewhere to stay."

As if someone had thrown a match onto a sea of oil, the voices of the doctors flared up again. Several members of the Infectious Diseases Department got up and walked out. A few endocrinologists followed them.

"Yes, I suppose it is about time we call it a day," Carlsson said, sounding dejected. She was barely able to make herself heard. "We'll be keeping you abreast of all new developments. I think we're done for today."

Gradually everyone left the room. Carlsson stayed by the podium and watched the blurred shape that was her husband stand up. She barely noticed af Petersén's presence beside her, but she could not miss the fruity fragrance he was wearing. "You seem to be having a tough time," he said in an obsequious tone of voice.

"What do you mean?"

"The doctors."

"Oh, right."

"What did you think—"

"Nothing."

Her husband came up to the podium. Carlsson avoided his enquiring look. She knew what he was going to say. Af Petersén greeted him politely and then left them to it.

A few metres away, Nyrén coughed discreetly. "I hate to interrupt, but shall we have a word later, Monica?"

"Why not. I just need to eat something. Seem to have skipped breakfast."

"Of course," Nyrén said sympathetically. "I'll be in my office." Tekla was the only person left apart from Carlsson and Gregor. She was sitting in the first row.

"Tekla. Did you want something?"

"No, I . . . or rather . . ." Tekla looked at Gregor.

"This is my husband, Gregor Dabrowski."

"I don't want to disturb you." She was about to leave when Gregor came forward and held out his hand.

"Not at all. I've heard so much about you."

"Have you?" Tekla sounded surprised.

"Well look—" Carlsson began, but her husband cut in.

"How do you feel, darling?" Gregor asked.

"What do you mean? This is not the time to . . ." Carlsson nodded in Tekla's direction.

"Yes it is. It is the time."

"What are you talking about?" Carlsson snapped.

"You're not well, darling," Gregor continued in a calm voice. "Am I right, Tekla? You can see it too."

Tekla stood there quietly, looking at her C.E.O.

"It's alright Tekla," Carlsson said. "You can leave now."

"No," Gregor said firmly. "Stay."

"I just have a bit of stomach pain," Carlsson said eventually, sitting down. She didn't have the strength to argue. She was overcome by fatigue.

"You look as if you've lost some weight," Tekla said cautiously.

"Of course she has," Gregor said.

"Have you changed your diet?" Tekla asked.

Carlsson stared into space. Her right hand was completely numb. She ran through a list of possible causes for her symptoms. Was it just a straightforward panic attack? But surely they wouldn't last so long? She was perfectly calm now.

"No."

"You haven't?"

"I've got this dreadful gastritis, that's all it is. Probably ought to do a course of Losec."

"You need to see someone," Gregor said. "Can't you help her, Tekla? She trusts you, I know that."

"Me?" Tekla looked embarrassed. "I think that—"

"I'll call Ersta," Carlsson said, getting up. She felt a wave of dizziness. She couldn't see either Tekla or Gregor clearly, but she wasn't going to mention that. She would have to consult the gastroenterologists at Ersta as soon as they could give her an appointment. Gregor held out a yellow bag for her. "But there's something else you could help me with, Tekla."

"What?"

"I know that the doctors have enormous respect for you. They listen to you."

"No, I don't think that's true, I—"

"Yes they do. They certainly do. If you could try and generate some goodwill on my behalf, I'm pretty sure I'd be able to fix the financial aspects of the renovation work."

"I'll see what I can do," Tekla said.

"Good." Carlsson brushed away the yellow bag proffered by Gregor. "Sometimes I wonder if you know me at all? Sweet liquorice? Me?!"

NOBEL HOSPITAL
Friday, 8 November

Tekla filled the refrigerator with the bright blue cans. One hundred and eighty milligrammes of caffeine. The equivalent of about two medium-sized cups of coffee. That meant she could cut her coffee intake to about eight cups a day. Apart from messing up her stomach, it didn't even boost her energy levels that much. But above all: she had reduced her amphetamine bomb consumption by two thirds. Her dealer had mixed feelings about that.

"Thirsty?" someone behind her asked.

Tekla turned. There was no way she could hide what she was doing from Klein-Borgstedt. "I know, not terribly good for me but—"

"Please don't feel you have to justify yourself to me. I've been smoking three cigarillos a day since I turned eighteen and was finally allowed to leave the vicarage. It was such a relief never to have to set foot on those creaking floors again, my father would have disowned me if he'd known about my sinful vices. Those small poison sticks have become a reminder of the strict upbringing I had, and I've never felt like giving them up. They bring me luck and remind me of my free will." Klein-Borgstedt came in and sat down in Tekla's chair. "So what did you think of that spectacle? Quite entertaining, if you ask me. Things are really shaping up. Or, rather, degenerating."

Tekla gently closed the door to the fridge. She put the last box on top of her clothes locker.

"But I gather you don't intend to get involved in this whole mess," Tekla said.

"My dear, you're not very good at concealing your anger."

"Anger?"

"Tekla, I'll tell you what my motto has always been. Or rather, my guiding principle."

Tekla shook her head. In her chest she felt the same sorrow she had when her father, on his deathbed, had begun to share with her the wisdom he had gleaned in the course of his life. In less eloquent terms, naturally.

"Choose your battles carefully. Avoid the hopeless cases. First you do a thorough calculation – and I know your supercomputer of a brain is doing that every second anyway – and if you reach the conclusion that your chance of victory is less than about two per cent . . . pull out right from the start. Throw yourself into another battle."

Klein-Borgstedt pressed her narrow lips together. Tekla could only guess at the exclusive brand of lipstick she wore. Probably something she'd found in Paris as early as the '70s.

"You know that I've never been afraid to take on a challenge. Eighteen years as trade union representative in this fine hospital. You were hardly . . . well yes, of course you were, but you can't have been very old when I fought for our first collective agreement after the turn of the millennium."

"So you're saying you don't give a damn that the management wants to privatise the whole lot?" Tekla sighed.

Klein-Borgstedt placed her bony hand on Tekla's. It was cool but not dry.

"The good thing is I'm leaving early, but I'm not retiring with any bitter feelings. Do you know why?"

"Nope."

"Because there are fantastic doctors like you and Ragna. There aren't many of you. You swim in a muddy pond where the visibility is bad and the smell rank, but you do so with elegance. I have hope."

Tekla thought back to what Carlsson's husband had said: "Monica trusts you." She must not betray this trust.

"I don't suppose there's any way of persuading you to stay on?"

Klein-Borgstedt's broad smile revealed a glittering gold tooth at the back of her mouth.

Tekla checked her phone. "Have to go to the I.C.U."

"Don't you think you ought to let that go?"

Tekla could feel the boy's arms around her waist. The next image she called up was the woman's resolute look as she raised the knife. Tekla held on to it for a few seconds. Turned it a bit and saw the boy a few metres behind his mother. Tekla was standing in front of the bed with the man, the father, about to be stabbed in the heart. Was there anyone who could uncover the truth behind their story? Tekla couldn't help feeling a bond with the woman. What had pushed her to relinquish what she held most dear in life and throw herself with such force straight at the precipice?

"I really should go," Tekla said.

"If you have to, you have to. Certainly if you happen to be Tekla Berg. So good luck then," Klein-Borgstedt said. "Let me know if you want to discuss any interesting cases. And promise you'll be at my party on Friday. Everybody's coming."

"I'll do my best."

"I have one piece of advice if you do come."

"What?"

"Never ask another doctor how much they earn. Not even if you're a bit tipsy."

"How come?"

"Their salary is the second last thing they'll want to tell you about."

"What's the last one, then?"

"If they've ever made any mistakes."

Tekla got a can of energy drink out of the fridge and left Klein-Borgstedt in her office. She wasn't sure that "everybody's coming" would prove all that persuasive.

INTENSIVE CARE UNIT, NOBEL HOSPITAL
Friday, 8 November

A more orderly chaos reigned in the intensive care unit than a few hours earlier. Nowak was busy with a spinal tap that seemed anything but straightforward. Gray had at last been able to go home and sleep. Tekla saw several policemen behind the screens, probably technicians securing the crime scene. But no sign of Silva and no sign of Elmqvist.

"Are you looking for someone?" asked an assistant nurse who was carrying four small white boxes.

"Eva."

"They're out there, in the conference room. We're trying to follow police orders." The nurse rolled her eyes. "Have to move some of the patients to other rooms. But there are no available spaces."

Tekla went up to Nowak and whispered in his ear: "Raise the bed, your angle's all wrong." Then she headed for the common area outside the I.C.U. The shortage of intensive care beds in the county seemed to have become the norm. But it was quite unacceptable to send those patients off to ordinary wards. The police would have to adapt their investigation to the circumstances.

She passed the staff coffee room, took out her Lypsyl tube and washed down a bomb with half a can of energy drink. It had the advantage of being so sweet that it covered the bitter taste of the amphetamine. She opened the door and there were Silva, Elmqvist, Törnqvist and two I.C.U. staff she'd never seen before, sitting around an oval table. How come Törnqvist with the nose was there and she hadn't been invited? She got the explanation right away.

"Haven't you gone off to get some sleep?"

Tekla saw the surprise in Elmqvist's eyes. But there was also a hint of distance in her look which Tekla didn't like. She ignored it and chose an empty chair across the table from Silva, which looked less uncomfortable than the others in the room. She briefly wondered if she had messed up during the night, and then forgotten all about it because she was so tired. Nothing came to mind. She wiped her face with the flat of her hand. Did she have food or something stuck to her cheek? Impossible, she hadn't eaten. But her headache was making itself felt. The effects of the bomb hadn't kicked in yet.

"What do the tests show? Is she still intubated?"

Elmqvist shot a look at her two I.C.U. colleagues. Perhaps she considered asking Tekla to leave, then dropped the idea. "Complete liver failure. Hyponatremia. High blood lipids." Elmqvist pulled up the lab results on the large screen on the wall.

Tekla ran swiftly through the list. "Disastrous. So what do we think?"

"*We* in the I.C.U. believe that she suffers from liver failure from an unknown cause," Elmqvist said. The emphasis on the "we" had not escaped Tekla's notice. Another sign that she was distancing herself. What was going on? Tekla tried to stay calm.

"She's probably poisoned herself with something which has left her confused," Eva said. "And resulted in cramps."

"Paracetamol?" Tekla asked, scanning the list.

"That's not on there yet but yes, one possibility is that she's stuffed herself full of Alvedon. As well as everything else between heaven and earth."

"Drugs?"

"Nothing on the urine dipstick," said one of the junior doctors, who sported a well-trimmed carrot red beard. "Negative for benzodiazepines, opioids and amphetamines."

Something gave Tekla the idea that Silva was observing her as the drugs were mentioned. No doubt she was just being paranoid.

"E.C.G.?"

"No changes. So probably not an overdose of psychotropics,"

Elmqvist said, sounding tetchy. Tekla assumed that they'd already been through all this in the I.C.U. and were irritated at having to repeat themselves now that she had joined them.

"But who is she?" Tekla asked.

Silva cleared his throat. "We've not been able to find any proof of identity so far."

"Nothing?" Tekla said.

"No wallet, no bag, no phone."

"But surely there ought to be something somewhere?"

Silva nodded slowly. "You're absolutely right. There *ought* to be. But where?"

"Strange," Tekla said. "And no report that our psychiatrists are missing a patient?"

Elmqvist exchanged a quick look with doctor redbeard. "We've not actually . . . got around to checking that yet. But . . . thanks for reminding us Tekla. Though I must say she doesn't look like a psychiatric patient."

"And why would her son be with her if she was?" Silva said.

"Maybe she'd been allowed out for a few days," Tekla said, seeing the boy in her mind. "What'll become of him now?"

"The boy? He'll probably be looked after by social services for the time being . . . Maybe in temporary accommodation."

"Could you find out where?" Tekla said.

"Why?" Elmqvist asked.

"Why? So I can . . . see for myself how it's going."

Silva rose to his feet and turned to Elmqvist. "In any case, we're leaving the medical side of things to you. And all we can do is note that the woman was disoriented and appeared to be in . . . shall we say a psychotic state. Is it safe to assume as much?"

"It's conceivable," Elmqvist said.

"The technicians should be finished out there soon. Then you can transfer him to Forensic Medicine." Silva began walking towards the door.

"It just doesn't add up," Tekla said.

"What doesn't add up?" Elmqvist said in a noticeably weary voice.

"The whole thing. Abrupt liver failure with completely crazy test results. Cramps. And, from what I saw immediately before she collapsed, she wasn't confused. Just determined. Something had a sudden effect. Something that affected the blood supply to the brain. Did you check her heart? What do the cardiac markers look like?"

"They're high, but that doesn't mean anything. Cramps can make them go up . . ."

"What about a brain scan?"

"Obviously we've done one. Completely normal."

Tekla had a sudden thought. "And how come I'm not being heard as a witness?" She stood up but was stopped by Elmqvist.

"Tekla!"

"Yes?"

"Go home and get some sleep."

Tekla reached into her pocket and rolled the Lypsyl tube between her fingers. "Later."

"No, now."

"By the way, have you alerted the transplant surgeons?" Tekla said.

"No, why would I?"

"With a liver failure like this?"

"Not on the cards, I don't think."

"Why not?"

"We don't even have her identity."

"Well, get hold of it. And of course you have to talk to the specialists. It takes planning to get hold of a liver."

Elmqvist smiled and shook her head. "Go home and go to bed, Tekla."

Tekla walked off. Going to bed now was about the last thing on her mind. She spotted Silva over by the staff toilets.

"Wait!" She ran over to the policeman. Silva's drab off-the-peg

190

shirt looked as if it might burst under the pressure of his bulging stomach when he pushed aside his duffel coat. "What's the matter?"

"You've got to talk to the boy."

"And what makes you think I don't already have someone on the job?"

"Gut feeling. You seem terribly keen to wind this case up on the double."

Silva mopped his receding hairline. "I don't know about your bosses here at the hospital—"

"Fat, spineless creatures, only interested in the bottom line."

". . . but my immediate superior is expecting a full report on the heroin market in Stockholm by the first of December. And I haven't even opened a Word file yet."

"So you don't have time for this. I get it. But surely you're not the only policeman in town?"

"I don't think you realise quite how few of us there are now."

"But I can help."

Tekla did not understand why Silva looked at her with such a pained expression. "You're offering to help? With what?"

"Anything you say. Let me—"

Silva had his hand on the door to the toilet. "I really need to—"

"So you are talking to the boy?"

"We're talking to the boy."

"I don't believe you," Tekla said, turning away. "The only way to get anything done is to do it yourself." She heard Silva mutter something before he shut the toilet door behind him.

Nowak came lumbering along.

"Thanks."

"What for?" Tekla said.

"You were right. I got the angle wrong. The spinal tap worked out fine."

SÖDERMALM AND VASASTAN, STOCKHOLM

Friday evening, 8 November

Tekla stripped off her black jeans and kicked them away in frustration so that they landed on top of the plastic orange shade of the floor lamp. In their place she picked out a dark grey pair from a pile of clothes on the carpet. The crotch needed mending, but they had a narrower waist. She wiped her damp forehead and the small of her back with a T-shirt – the half hour she'd spent under a hot shower had opened every pore in her body and left her covered in sweat. Exhausted, Tekla let herself fall back onto the bed while putting on her trousers. Her knickers ended up pinched between her buttocks, which irritated her, so she yanked them out. Banished the idea of finding something sexier since no-one would be seeing her in her underwear anyway. She squirmed back and forth. These jeans were also too loose. Her hip bones chafed against the belt which was pulled tight to the last notch. There was something about those test results she had checked twenty-five times that evening, something abnormal. She was deeply disappointed that her brain was letting her down by not flagging whatever it was she was searching for. Perhaps it would be worth upping her amphetamine intake.

She stood up, then had to bend over immediately so as not to faint. One look in the cracked mirror, the only piece of furniture she knew for certain came from her maternal grandmother's home in Östersund. Tekla did not like what she saw: her bra strap hung loose on one shoulder – she tightened it – and the trousers were much too wide for her skinny thighs. As for her hair . . . She ruffled the short fringe, did not get the desired effect, went to the bathroom and squeezed a large blob of shaving foam into the palm of her hand. She smeared it into her hair, which she then flattened into a sleek side parting. There, she thought, now I look like a certain German dictator, all I need is the moustache. Hopeless case. But it did the job. And smelled good. Reminded her of her father, his methodical, firm way with his razor.

She checked the time. She still had forty-five minutes. Right away she began to sweat. It was a different type of perspiration, in awkward places, the kind that smelled and made her palms and the soles of her feet tingle. Should she shake hands? Or would there be air-kissing? Why had Klein-Borgstedt not told her? Tekla pulled the bar stool over to the kitchen island and pushed away a half-full bowl of noodles. Took the lid off the coffee tin and ripped open the packet. About twenty white bags the size of peas spilled out onto the bottom of the aluminium container. Whoever had packaged the amphetamine had twisted one end of the toilet paper into a horn that stuck out. Tekla took two balls and threw them into her mouth after pouring tepid coffee into a large mug. Four big gulps masked most of the bitter taste when the paper quickly dissolved in her mouth.

She swallowed and brought up Simon's number on her phone. Tekla only had three favourites in her contact list: Simon, Sigurdsdottir and the home for dementia care in Nyhammar. After eight rings, it went through to voicemail. She hung up, finished her coffee and went back to the bedroom. The small of her back was beginning to feel less damp. Digging around with her foot on the floor, she looked for a top to wear. Tried on four different ones before settling for a black blouse with wide lapels and a winding pattern of small holes down the back. She didn't bother to look at herself in the mirror. She knew that nothing really fitted her skinny body, that every piece of clothing looked as if it had been draped over some bony frame.

Half an hour to go. She could have done with hearing Simon's cheerful voice to take her mind off the ordeal before her, listening to him talk about that Spanish therapist he was trying to chat up at the rehab centre. Apparently she had the most enormous breasts, which fascinated him no end. She even considered calling Nyhammar, but what would be the point? She wouldn't be able to speak to her mother, at best she might get to hear Gun-Britt or Anna-Stina or one of the other women with hyphenated names on the staff tell her how good Karin had been and how she had "eaten up all her food at dinner". Tekla remembered the day she had been to see her that summer. A quick visit, five hours spent talking to an elderly demented person who sat staring out of the window at a pine forest twenty metres away, as if she were watching a glorious sunset over a lake. The smiling lips, the complete absence of tension in a face that had been ravaged by wrinkles and worry for so many years but had now shed all the pain, as if a mask that was no longer needed had at last been removed. She was in that other world, one that would seem like an extended eternity to her loved ones. All Tekla could do was to sit there asking her mother all those questions she should have asked long ago and which would now never be answered.

Her phone rang.

"Are you up for it?"

"Can I call off sick?" Tekla asked. She was holding a lipstick which was at least five years old.

"Certainly not." Sigurdsdottir was laughing. "It's going to be absolutely fine. He's incredibly nice and super—"

". . . intellectual," Tekla cut in. "You've told me that a thousand times. I still can't see what's so fabulous about going on a date with Einstein." She put the lipstick back in the cupboard.

"Pull yourself together."

"I have to leave."

"Call when . . . no. Don't call. There won't be time for that," Sigurdsdottir chuckled, hanging up with a cheery "big hug".

Tekla didn't want hugs. Didn't want to wear this transparent blouse. She would have liked to put on sweatpants and a hoodie and curl up on the sofa with her computer, searching through articles on kidney failure and hyponatremia. At the same time, she was reluctant to be seen for the loner she really was. Why was this world

194

designed for couples? Why should someone who chooses to live alone be defined as a loser? A victim. Tekla didn't see herself as a victim, she had countless relationships with doctors and nurses, she just didn't have sex with them. Wasn't that enough? When would people understand that she didn't need their pity?

Elmqvist's attitude earlier that day had irritated her. She decided to clear both her and Silva with his laid-back mañana attitude from her mind. Back to the present. Back to so-called normality. Back to getting all dolled up.

Ignoring the dirty dishes in the sink, she went to the kitchen island and poured herself another large cup of coffee. Thirty seconds in the microwave. As she drank, two letters on the counter top caught her eye. They had already been opened, and she needed no reminder of the account number of the private dementia care home and the unpaid bill for October. She thought about her bank balance. Worryingly low so early in the month. There was definitely not enough there to cover her own expenses as well as the other bill, the one that was lying underneath: the considerably higher amount she owed the rehab clinic on the Costa del Sol.

Out in the hallway she put on her thick down jacket and a woolly hat. She could hear Sigurdsdottir's voice in her head: "Don't you have something a bit less ... wintery?" No she did not. And if you're as skinny as a pretzel stick and feel cold from the end of August to the beginning of May, those are the only clothes that work. And some furlined boots as well. By the time the door slammed shut, she was already halfway down the stairs. With one word echoing in her mind: normal. What was today's normal? Back in Edsåsdalen, her father's drinking and smoking would probably have been considered normal, since he was definitely not in a minority. In A. & E. at the Nobel Hospital, laddish, loutish non-communication among colleagues was normal, in other words: you would certainly be in good company if you acted the way doctors did in the year 1936. Not much progress on that front. So what actually amounted to normal behaviour these days? Where did she fit in on a bell curve?

It had already been dark for several hours. This early in November, Tekla would only see daylight on the rare occasions when she had a day off. It had been snowing in the morning, but since then the temperature had risen to half a degree above zero. The delicate snowflakes had turned into ice-cold droplets that fell on the left side of Tekla's face as she walked across Skanstullsbron Bridge. The occasional e-scooter came wobbling past on the way to join in the Friday night fun at Södermalm. Soon it would be time to lock them up for winter. Just as well, Tekla thought, remembering two ugly lower arm fractures she had taken care of in A. & E. in the past forty-eight hours alone. She had been tempted to send a photograph to one of the papers to kickstart a debate about banning e-scooters in town.

After a slippery twenty-minute walk, Tekla came within sight of Götgatspuckeln, which was already in full-on party mode. Crowds of people behind the steamed-up windows of restaurants and cafés. She took a right into Hökens gata. Omnipollos Hatt, a place where she had actually felt relaxed sharing a pizza with Sigurdsdottir two weeks earlier, was absolutely packed. She turned left before the Södra Theatre and continued along the pedestrian walkway to the Katarinahissen lift. It was raining harder now and Tekla pulled her hood as far forward as it would go to cover her face.

Once she was inside Gondolen, she saw how badly she was shaking. No idea if it was due to a slight excess of coffee and amphetamines, or a paralysing fear of the nightmare ahead. Walking down the steps to the cloakroom, she passed well-dressed couples, who took no notice of her, they probably thought she was a staff member who had gone out for a smoke.

An elderly pair were handing their elegant overcoats to the young female assistant, who had not yet deigned to look at Tekla. She was trying to see into the restaurant, past the head waiter who was pressing buttons on a screen in front of him. Tekla had tunnel vision. Could hear Sigurdsdottir saying: "It's going to be absolutely fine." Some hope. It would all go to hell. There was nothing good about this. Other than the fact that she'd actually made it here. And managed to dress in something she hadn't bought from Stadium. She'd almost put on some lipstick. Nearly given some thought to the underwear she had on. Was this being normal? She pushed the pocket of her down jacket back in, waggled her phone back and forth a few times. The cloakroom girl had finished putting away the smart coats and now caught sight of the far-too-thick down jacket two metres away.

Tekla spun round and made for the lift lobby. Jogged down the stairs and started walking towards Gamla Stan. Should she text Sigurdsdottir? Couldn't be bothered. Kept walking, passed the terminal for the Djurgården ferries, along the quayside by the Royal Palace and across Strömbron Bridge towards Kungsträdgården, where there was nobody about. Music spilled out of the warmly lit entrance to the Operakällaren restaurant over on the left.

Her phone rang. It was bound to be Sigurdsdottir; she didn't want to answer but had a look anyway. *Magnus*. She declined the call. Instead, Tekla rang the hospital switchboard and asked to be put through to the I.C.U. She turned left onto Hamngatan and passed a Roma woman outside the N.K. department store's main entrance. Once again, the boy's face came to mind. She wondered how he was doing.

She wanted to turn her thoughts to something more pleasant, so as usual she conjured up memories of Simon, from the days when he was still working and had his own money. She remembered the time they had gone to buy a new bed at IKEA. He was as excited as a seven-year-old over the "great big squishy mattress" he'd found at half price. They celebrated by treating themselves to a large plate of meatballs each, with potatoes and cranberries. Simon splurged and they had a foam rocket with chocolate and coconut to go with their coffee. That was two years ago. Now she could imagine him gesticulating with his long fingers, on which he wore those silver rings. A skull, a winding snake and an "S". He seemed happy in spite of the hollow cheeks and sparse stubble that had made him look like a junkie. She had been less concerned about his addiction when she last saw him – it was the shaking that really worried her. He had to hold his coffee with both hands. Then there was the cigarette he'd dropped on the floor. Taking all that together with his mood swings, irritability and wavering, she could not help thinking about their mother's condition. Did Simon have the same genetic makeup?

Tekla was approaching the corner of Sankt Eriksgatan and Fleminggatan. Stopped by the front door. The code was in the right compartment, it just had to be associated with the right person. It had become much easier to "sort" images since she stopped taking sleeping pills that summer. They had been replaced by other "soporifics", a strategy she had read about on the net. After keying in the code, she walked up two flights of stairs and rang the doorbell. The creaking of the parquet floor could be heard all the way out on the landing.

"Tekla?"

"Could you call and say that I got sick?"

Sigurdsdottir was holding a glass of red wine that, judging by the colour of her teeth and her partially unbuttoned blouse, must have been at least her fifth. Surely not, she was pregnant, after all.

"What . . ." Sigurdsdottir shut her mouth and tilted her head to one side. "Sweetie. Was it too difficult?"

"Sort of."

"But did you go there?" Sigurdsdottir's husband Bjarni appeared behind her. He also had dark purple lips.

"Come on in, Tekla."

"Yes, darling, come in," Sigurdsdottir said, with nothing but kindness in her voice.

"No, I'm going home."

Bjarni laughed. "But why come here then you silly girl?"

"Needed to walk a bit anyway," Tekla said, thinking about her nightly routine. She had another five kilometres to do before she could go to bed, her own little sleeping draught, a ten-kilometre evening stroll.

Sigurdsdottir reached for Tekla's hand on the doorknob.

"Sure?"

"Sure."

"O.K. I'll call him and say that you'll take a rain check."

Tekla wanted to protest, but Sigurdsdottir beat her to it.

"Don't think I'm going to give up so easily." Tekla's Icelandic friend broke into a broad, sparkling smile.

"O.K.," Tekla said, zipping up her jacket. "Enjoy your evening."

"Take it easy, Tekla," Sigurdsdottir called after her. "See you tomorrow."

Saturday morning, 9 November

It turned out to be a bad night for Tekla. She had found it impossible to unwind, thoughts crowded her brain and the long evening walk to tire her out had had pretty much the opposite effect. Lying awake half the night, she had instead tried ploughing through articles on liver failure and hyponatremia. All the more difficult then to get up when her alarm went off. After an ice-cold shower, two bombs and two cups of coffee, she did manage to march across Skanstullsbron and get to work on time. It was a relatively quiet morning in A. & E. at the Nobel. Tekla counted only twenty-eight patients on the screen. She would normally have put that down to bad weather but no, it was quite a beautiful and clear November morning.

"Who's here?" Tekla asked.

"Ragna, Tariq and two junior doctors," Viola replied, her arms piled high with yellow blankets.

Tekla gave her a hand. "Where to?" She looked around – she could relax, there was no sign of Moussawi.

"A. & E.," Viola said and smiled in gratitude.

Tekla helped the assistant nurse and then went in search of Sigurdsdottir, who was in one of the suture rooms stitching up the forehead of an eighty-year-old woman who had fainted and hit her head on a washbasin.

Leaning over Sigurdsdottir's shoulder, Tekla whispered: "I can smell Rioja."

Sigurdsdottir pushed her away with a friendly nudge of the elbow. "Come on. Can't be that bad. But I think I could do with a coffee after this."

"Absolutely," Tekla said. "Let me know if you'd like me to hold those tweezers for you. That hand looks a bit shaky."

"Get lost," Sigurdsdottir said with a smile. "You've got to explain what happened yesterday. But you don't have to worry, he'll give you a second chance."

"Too bad." With that, Tekla went back to the reception area. She asked the head nurse which patient she wanted her to take on, and was directed to a four-year-old with abdominal pains. But first she checked to see how the I.C.U. patient was doing. She sank onto a chair. The liver results had deteriorated, she was still intubated and still in hyponatremia. She walked over to the cubicle and shook hands with the four-year-old's mother.

"Tekla Berg. Emergency doctor. Shall we have a look at that tummy?" She sat down on a stool next to the boy, whose name was Axel. He had a slightly flat nose, a wide forehead and questioning eyes.

"Not much fun being here on a Saturday?"

The boy first gave Tekla a frightened look and then turned to his mother, who put a hand on his head. "Let's see if this nice doctor can't magic away your stomach ache."

"Can you point with your finger to where it hurts?"

The boy immediately stuck out his index finger like a laser sword and pointed to his navel.

"Here? Not anywhere else?" Tekla asked.

The boy shook his head.

"How long have you had this pain?"

"Since last night," the mother said.

"Does your tummy often hurt?"

The mother waited for her child to say something, but the boy did not answer. "Axel does tend to get a little constipated."

"Have you been to the toilet these past few days?"

The mother shrugged. "I don't know. He was with his father until yesterday. He hasn't been this morning, though."

"I'm just going to feel you gently," Tekla said, looking straight at the child. Then she put her hand on his stomach, far away from the spot that hurt. The boy smiled.

"I know," Tekla said, laughing. "I keep ice cubes in my pocket to play with before I touch little boys' tummies." She carefully palpated the child's abdomen, which was soft. He showed no reaction whatsoever.

"And it doesn't hurt when you pee?"

He shook his head.

Tekla felt confident. "I don't think there's any monster in that stomach of yours." The boy's eyes opened wide. "I think it's a big poo that wants to come out."

Tekla got up. "We'll run a few simple tests including a urine sample if that's O.K. Then you can probably go home again after an hour or so. Will that be alright?"

The mother's face lit up as she took Tekla's place on the stool. "I told you, didn't I? A superdoctor, don't you think?"

The boy stared at Tekla as if she were suddenly wearing a green outfit with a red cape. That reminded her that she wanted to find the boy with the gold mask – she'd have to get hold of the address of the foster family.

After leaving the cubicle, she attended to two more patients. An elderly woman with diarrhoea and acute liver failure who had spent the night in A. & E. because there was no bed for her, and a young man with a painful neck and a high temperature. Since he had been in Ghana two weeks earlier, he was subjected to a full battery of tests with a focus on malaria.

She spotted Moussawi by one of the computers and considered making herself scarce, but he had already seen her, so she settled down next to the alpha male from Baghdad.

"Any exciting cases?"

Moussawi folded his large hands in his lap and swivelled around to face her. Even though they were on better terms now since the Umarov business in the summer, Tekla was still on her guard when it came to the most self-satisfied doctor at the clinic, a man with a big, fragile ego whom it was best not to confront. But he was strong and willing to help carry things.

"My friend," Moussawi said. "How's everything?"

"Anything in particular bothering you today ... *my friend*?" Tekla knew that attack was the best form of defence with him. She had learned that he could not stand weak doctors, especially women.

"The opinion of a good colleague never bothers me."

"And this is where I'm supposed to ask who that good colleague might be?"

"Only if you're a fighter who wants to win."

Win what, Tekla asked herself. His approval? She could live without that.

Moussawi leaned forward on his chair. It was as if he could sniff out her lack of confidence. She felt the sweat stinging in her hairline.

"When I was going to get married, my future father-in-law rang me two days before the wedding. I was obviously apprehensive; when your father-in-law wants to see you, your legs start to shake."

"An old Iraqi saying?"

Moussawi waved his hand in the air. Unsure what that was supposed to mean, Tekla began to fidget. She wasn't in the mood for any folklore.

"He wanted us to meet in a café. I put on a jacket and tie and even went to the barber. We had a coffee together. Strong coffee. Really strong. I remember being incredibly tense."

Tekla had a hard time imagining him looking nervous, but it was possible, maybe even conceivable, that a younger Moussawi might have been capable of some degree of apprehension.

"He said to me: 'Tariq, my daughter is the second most beautiful woman in the world. Never forget that. And never ask who the most beautiful is.'"

"Did he mean his own wife?"

"Up to you if you feel like asking who's the best."

Tekla stood up. "I'll think about it."

"You know who the junior doctors go to when they have a difficult case?"

"No."

Moussawi patted his own chest.

You bet, Tekla thought. No way do they consult you, your assessments are so random they might as well be tossing a coin.

"I'm off to the I.C.U. for a while, if that's O.K.?"

"No catastrophe here."

"Not when the best doctor at the clinic is on site," she quipped.

"Precisely." There was no hint of irony in Moussawi's reply.

Tekla shook her head, she knew he'd never ask for help even if disaster were to strike. She left the emergency unit and took the shortcut round the back of the building to the I.C.U. Had she managed to stand her ground in that trial of strength? She was quite pleased with herself, her new tactic was probably the only one that worked: refusing to submit to or shy away from Moussawi and his in-your-face manner. Not that she really cared what he thought, but it was better to avoid getting into his bad books since she knew what he was capable of when he had someone on his black list. She hurried on. The building work around the entrance had divided the hospital into two parts. She took a bomb out of the Lypsyl tube and swallowed it with some water from a patient toilet by the library.

"So you really don't have a life?" Elmqvist sighed. She was sitting in the middle of the office and hardly raised her eyes from the screen.

Tekla sat down next to her. "This is my life."

"But not mine," Elmqvist said, running the cursor around the screen. "I can't face any extra stuff today, Tekla. After the rounds I'm going home. Do you realise this is my fourth Saturday in a row."

"Has the man been taken away for forensic autopsy?"

"Why do you ask?"

"Well has he?"

"The transport company couldn't come yesterday. So the body is down in Pathology. They're taking it to Forensic Medicine on Monday."

"I saw that her liver is worse."

"You said it." Elmqvist reached for a pear in a bowl. "There aren't even any apples here," she complained, biting into the bruised fruit. "You certainly don't get to see three-digit liver scores every day."

"And she didn't test positive for paracetamol or any other drugs, I see. What about the abdominal C.T. scan?"

"No cirrhosis and nothing in the bile ducts."

"The abdomen is completely clear, in other words?"

"On radiological evidence, yes." Elmqvist was being slowly drawn along by Tekla's doggedness, whether she liked it or not.

"No news on her identity? We still don't know who either of them are?"

"The police haven't come up with anything yet. No psychiatric patient has absconded."

"Have you thought about mushrooms?" Tekla asked.

"We've tested for amatoxin and destroying angel and a few other delicacies, but we've not had any results back yet. Saturday . . . But we have nothing by way of a medical history, nobody we can talk to. The woman didn't have any mushrooms in her pockets, in any case. We have no witnesses to tell us anything."

Tekla's thoughts went back to the boy. She wondered if any-one had been able to speak to him. "But you're treating it as if it were mushroom poisoning?"

"Yes," Elmqvist said through a mouthful of pear. "She's been given large volumes of fluid since yesterday and we'll probably need to go for dialysis, her kidneys are about to give up. We've even tried antidotes, silibinin and benzylpenicilline. And she's had acetylcysteine."

"Have you tried using pyridoxine?"

Elmqvist looked in fascination at Tekla. "No, we don't think she's eaten any false morels."

Tekla was about to object, but feared she might get thrown out if she made too much of a nuisance of herself.

"Then surely you ought to begin dialysis? Or liver dialysis?"

"Well yes, but we'd like to bounce it off the liver doctors."

"Hepatitis and H.I.V.?"

Eva groaned. "Negative. But high immunoglobuline levels."

"So you're thinking autoimmune hepatitis?"

"We don't have the antibodies yet, but yes. We've started cortisone."

Tekla read the fourth chapter of Donaldson's *Textbook of Hepatology* from 2007. "But ten per cent don't have any antibodies. So would you still look on it as autoimmune hepatitis?"

"We're not there yet, but—"

"It can't be right."

"What's wrong now?" Elmqvist said without even bothering to hide her exasperation.

"Those elevated transaminases are still lingering. And the convulsions. How does that fit in?"

"We're going to do an E.E.G. tomorrow, the physiology lab is closed today so—"

"But you've put her on the waiting list."

"For the time being."

"What do you mean, for the time being?"

Elmqvist was looking over Tekla's shoulder. "In about thirty seconds we'll have the final verdict."

Tekla turned to see Nyström arriving with Törnqvist hot on his heels. The professor stopped in front of Elmqvist's desk. He did not dignify Tekla with so much as a glance. There it was again, that lump in her stomach. She saw images of her father in his hospital bed. The panic she felt at not having enough time to ask any questions during his brief moments of consciousness. Her frustration when he lapsed back into oblivion.

"Aha, is our liver still living?"

Tekla rolled her eyes. Wondered how many times he had bored his poor students with that one.

"Yes, the *woman* is still alive," Elmqvist said and stood up. Together they walked over to the bed where the patient lay intubated. A nurse who had been sitting got to her feet when the doctors approached.

Tekla followed them. Törnqvist glanced casually in her direction. Maybe they had decided that the best way to deal with the "house mouse", as Nyström had called her, was to ignore her.

"I saw the test results," Nyström said. "Looks pretty dire. And no identity."

"So far," Elmqvist said.

"So far," Nyström repeated under his breath. "There's not an awful lot of time left for this liver to acquire an identity."

"What do you mean?" Tekla shot in.

The doctors at the Department of Medicine in Östersund had told her in no uncertain terms that her father's liver could not be saved. His illness was fatal. No point in protesting. But a young woman with a child? Then and now.

Törnqvist raised his hand like a bouncer outside a club in Stureplan. Tekla pushed it away and went round and stood next to Elmqvist along one side of the bed. Nyström signalled to Törnqvist to calm down.

"Are you some kind of a joke?" Nyström asked in a silky smooth voice while polishing his glasses on his red-and-white checked shirt.

"What do you mean about the liver not having so much time?" Tekla repeated. "Surely she's on the hot list? Have you found one?"

Slowly Nyström put on his spectacles and looked around the room, as if the lenses had been dirty before. He smiled. "I took her off the hot list half an hour ago."

"You can't do that," Tekla said.

"Oh yes," Törnqvist said. "I rang the coordinator myself."

"What the hell are you saying? A young woman with total liver failure, of course she must have a new liver." Tekla saw the boy's worried eyes in front of her.

"She doesn't have an identity," Nyström admonished. "She could be a junkie, some Polish mushroom picker who ate a poisonous specimen in a drunken stupor . . . I'd say she looks pretty neglected. What do you think, Olof?"

"No doubt about that," he said, fawning. He would never dare to contradict the leader of his sect.

"And?" Tekla said. "In her current condition it's obviously not going to be possible to send her to Warsaw for a transplant."

"Exactly," Nyström said. "You do seem to be learning . . . Katla, was that your name?"

Tekla ignored the jibes. He was only trying to provoke her. She breathed deeply a few times and turned to Elmqvist.

"We know from the C.T. scan that she doesn't have cirrhosis. And alcohol . . ."

Tekla tried to stay calm. Her brain didn't work so well when she let Nyström get in behind her frontal bone. She had to stick to facts. "Haven't you run a C.D.T. test to exclude alcoholism?"

Elmqvist nodded. "But it hasn't come back yet."

"I got the impression that the husband might also have been inclined to drink a little too much," Nyström went on, as if he really wanted to see how far he could push Tekla.

She took a deep breath. "There's no reason to deny this patient a liver. But seeing that our surgeons here at the Nobel Hospital are too scared to operate on patients in such a poor condition, I suppose we'll have to contact the N.S.K."

The room fell silent. This had clearly hit the mark.

"I wouldn't do that if I were you," Nyström said in a far more restrained tone.

"I do what's best for the patient," she said and walked off. "And you know that patients can hear what you say, even when they're sedated!" she yelled, startling Nowak, who was sitting by another patient.

208

On her way out of the I.C.U., Tekla ran into Superintendent Silva. "Good morning."

"Not particularly." Tekla had intended to walk right past him but then changed her mind. "Can we talk?"

"Absolutely. I could do with another coffee."

They went to the staff room, where three nurses were sitting on a black leather sofa, each with her phone. A large T.V. screen was showing the morning news without the sound. Tekla got out two black cups and pressed a button on the machine, which rattled and shook as it ground the coffee beans. They sat down by a table some distance from the group on the sofa. Tekla sipped her coffee. She also pulled a can of energy drink out of her pocket and downed it in one.

"Breakfast?" Silva was fascinated.

"Topping up," she said. "What about you? You don't look all that great either."

Silva seemed to be trying to remember what he had done the night before. Maybe there were some gaps due to a surfeit of cheap Chilean red?

"I got a call from my boss at seven o'clock in the evening."

"Is that usual?"

"It happens. But last night it really annoyed me. I was just cooking a nice steak for myself and my son. His girlfriend loves . . ." Silva realised what he was saying and took a deep breath. "The boss asked me to give this case priority over my report on the heroin market."

"You mean the woman here in the I.C.U.?"

"*Sí, claro.*"

"Well that's good news," Tekla said. "The report not being so terribly urgent any longer. Since you told me that it stressed you out."

"They've brought someone in for the preliminary investigation, and I'm supposed to be in charge."

"Which you don't want?"

"I don't like it when my superiors set priorities for me."

"There's also something else getting on your nerves, though."

"What makes you think that?" Silva asked.

"Gut feeling."

"You and your gut feeling." Silva drank some coffee. "Although I do know all about that from last summer. But yes, I have a suspicion that someone's been leaning on my boss. Because it's not like her to go changing plans like this. I know that she's keen to have that report. Don't we all love bad bosses telling us what to do. Especially when they've got their bloody priorities all wrong."

He undid a button on his white shirt. Silva's forehead shone with sweat under the harsh light from the ceiling.

"So there's nothing for it but to get to work," he went on. "But this *murder* . . . The doctor out there told me you thought it was mushroom poisoning. Can mushrooms mess up your brain so badly that you stick a knife into your husband's chest?"

Tekla's mind had already moved on. Her brain was overheating from the intense activity. Every single cell that could generate ideas was busy working on the enigma of the woman. How could she be given a new liver? She suddenly thought of a patient who might be able to provide some answers.

"Unlikely. Not that I've seen all that many cases . . ."

They stood there, each absorbed by their own thoughts about mushrooms.

"But what was it you wanted to talk about?" Silva eventually asked.

"Where are you planning to start?"

"You mean with the woman?"

Tekla nodded, trying to keep track of her parallel lines of thought.

"We obviously have to find out who she is," Silva began. "Neither the man nor the woman had a phone or a wallet. Quite bizarre. She didn't even have a payment card. There's got to be one somewhere. Or a bus pass. How else did she get to the hospital?"

"Maybe she lives nearby."

"So then we'll go on to dental records and fingerprints. We've got a whole team working that angle." Silva paused for thought. "But no phone. How many people live without a mobile phone these days?"

Tekla thought about her mother, who had never learned their home telephone number. And that was long before dementia set in.

"Far too few," she said. Silva nodded. "So you're going to try and solve the case?"

"Do I have a choice?"

"One can put more or less effort into doing a job."

"Not as far as I'm concerned," Silva said. "And not you either."

Tekla remembered that there was something else she needed help with. "Could you get me the number of the temporary foster home?"

Silva looked at Tekla, seemed about to make a comment, but changed his mind. Then he nodded. "I'll see what I can do."

SÖDERMALM, STOCKHOLM
Saturday, 9 November

"Would you like some coffee?" said the man who had introduced himself as Andrus Gudaitis.

"Yes please," Tekla replied, taking off her trainers in the yellow hallway. She was wearing thick tights, sweatpants and a Helly Hansen pullover, and had worried on the way over that it might not be suitable to turn up for morning coffee looking like some exercise junky. But she soon relaxed when she saw how Andrus was dressed. His greying hair stood out in all directions, his collarless shirt was buttoned up wrong and his jeans had seen better days. And he was barefoot. She spared a thought for Silva, grateful that he had taken it upon himself to bend the rules and give her the family's address and telephone number.

"It's so nice of you to come," Andrus said.

"I'm sorry to bother you on a Saturday." She took off her jacket and, out of the corner of her eye, saw somebody enter the large sitting room.

The boy paused a few seconds in the pool of sunlight that came streaming in through the tall windows of the turn-of-the-century building. Tekla had a strange sense of déjà vu, an image she had seen before but couldn't place. Before she could work it out, he marched straight across the creaking parquet floor and flung his arms around her. For about a second Tekla was just as overwhelmed as she had been at the hospital, and then she wrapped her arms around him. He was not as sweaty this time. She ran her fingers through his thick hair. He kept his hold on her and didn't look up.

A woman who introduced herself as Jennifer Holmgren-Gudaitis arrived carrying a tray with a large cafetiere, three rattling, gold-rimmed cups and a jam roll. She set it down on a low coffee table. Andrus tidied away some books, pencils and a tablet.

"You've got a lovely home," Tekla said, in an effort to sound normal.

"Thanks," Jennifer said. "It's an old rental contract that I took over a thousand years ago. Otherwise we could never afford to live here, it's just about the most expensive part of Söder."

"I can imagine."

"Who's that?" A young voice was heard behind Tekla. She turned to see a blond girl of about five. She had turquoise paint on her face and was dressed in a panda suit that was unbuttoned to the waist. A tiara was set askew in her tousled hair.

"This is Tekla. She's here to talk to Yoda."

"Yoda?" Tekla mouthed to Jennifer.

"We're calling him Yoda for now." Jennifer picked up the boy's mask from the coffee table and twisted and turned it, as if it were an archaeological find that she had trouble placing.

"That's not Yoda," Tekla said. "Surely it's Iron Man?"

The boy released his vice-like grip on Tekla and looked up at her face.

"Isn't it?" she said.

He nodded carefully.

"Have you been able to talk to . . . Yoda?" Tekla said.

Jennifer shook her head. "No, he hasn't said anything . . . yet." She smiled and set out the cups at both ends of the table.

Carefully Tekla drew the boy with her to the sofa and sat down. He remained standing by the armrest but kept a firm grip on her hand, beginning to look a little less fearful.

Tekla continued as she had begun.

"Do you like the Avengers?"

He nodded at once. No need to think. There were no filters when it came to superheroes. It was obvious from his quick response that he understood Swedish perfectly.

213

"Cool. So do I. My favourite is Thor. What about you?" Tekla remembered the names of all the characters in the films. Not that she was a particular fan but, for some reason, Sigurdsdottir was obsessed with the whole Marvel universe and had dragged Tekla along to see four of the films. Tekla liked Star Wars, but Marvel . . . there was simply too much of everything.

The boy pointed to the mask on the table.

"Iron Man. Well I suppose he really is the coolest, he's the leader after all, but I don't think he has quite enough muscles. Have you seen 'Endgame'?"

The boy shook his head mournfully.

"But you do understand Swedish?"

Andrus came and sat down discreetly, careful not to disturb the interplay between Tekla and Yoda. There was an atmosphere of tense anticipation in the room, as if Tekla were slowly managing to persuade a tiger cub to follow her gentle instructions.

"I think you do," Tekla said. "And you seem to have come to a lovely place here with Andrus and Jennifer. Do you have your own bed?"

The boy looked back and forth between the host family and her. Tekla noticed that he had dark rings under his eyes.

"Are you finding it a bit hard to sleep?" Tekla enquired softly.

"I sat with you last night," Jennifer said. "Until you fell asleep."

"Isn't that nice?" Tekla said, reaching for the coffee. The small girl climbed into her mother's lap and took a large piece of the jam roll. Jennifer deftly caught the falling crumbs without taking her gaze off Tekla and the boy.

"How many children do you have?"

The mother held up one finger.

"And a dog," Andrus added. "But he's getting old. Where's Oliver?"

"He's sleeping . . ." The girl shoved half a slice of the cake into her small mouth. ". . . in the kitchen."

"Isn't it nice to have a dog?" Tekla said, holding the boy's warm, moist hand. She thought that the emergency foster family seemed really great. Anyone would feel safe in the reassuring atmosphere of this old apartment. There was everything the boy needed. Easy, affectionate and effortless companionship and a girl to play with.

"Do you like Star Wars?" Tekla said.

The boy tightened his hold on her hand. Waited nervously for her to carry on. Tekla saw that he looked worried.

"My favourites are the old films. The ones with Yoda, Luke and Han Solo. How about you?"

The boy looked pensive. This was an important question which had to be considered with care. He loosened his grip for a second now that he'd found himself in a familiar world. Who had watched Star Wars with him? Who had bought him that mask? Tekla wondered if he was thinking about his father, the patient whom she had done her utmost to save before his mother murdered him, right in front of Tekla's eyes. And above all: right in front of *the boy's* eyes. How does one come to terms with something like that? Was he a loving and attentive father? The kind that actually sits down on the floor and plays with his child without a phone in his hand? Was he a father with crazy ideas, like building an igloo outside when it had snowed, or a raft which then capsized amid howls of laughter? But above all: was he a kind father, a father who was not aggressive, one who provided a calm and secure life for his child?

"I know," Tekla said, accepting a piece of the jam roll. "I bet you like 'Return of the Jedi' with those cute teddy bears."

A tentative smile crept across his lips and remained there for the time being. Jennifer gave Tekla a look of gratitude and happiness. Tekla's thoughts went to the boy's mother. Who was she? Was she as gentle and calm as Jennifer appeared to be? Did she have a good relationship with her son? Maybe she was the one who had a childish liking for Star Wars and Marvel? The idea appealed to Tekla, perhaps it was mother and son who played games all day and read science fiction stories by the light of an orange lamp at night?

"And how do you like the more recent films?"

The boy shrugged. He swallowed hard.

"You don't?" Tekla said. "I think they're still pretty good."

Something had obviously cropped up in the boy's mind. Once again he tightened his grip on her hand. Then suddenly, with a broad Norrland accent, he said:

"The old man is evil."

Tekla tried not to show her surprise. She sensed Jennifer and Andrus completely motionless in the background, like two stone pillars. A lorry could be heard reversing below the windows. And the sound of the dog's unclipped claws against the kitchen floor a few metres away.

Were there any other elderly characters in Star Wars, apart from Yoda?

"Do you mean the Emperor?" Tekla asked.

"The old man is mean," the boy repeated, and looked up at her. A plastic bowl fell to the floor in the kitchen. The girl had followed the dog there.

None of this prevented Tekla from giving her full attention to what the boy had just said and to the fact that he had such a strong Norrland accent. Was he still speaking about Star Wars? Was he referring to Emperor Palpatine? Or thinking about a real, living person? There was a fear in his eyes that had not been there before, and she could feel it too.

Tekla had some more coffee and a piece of cake and tried to talk to the boy, but he didn't say another word. Eventually he sat down in an armchair and watched Tekla, while carefully eating some of the jam roll. Gradually the anxiety seemed to disappear from his eyes and his body language eased up. Tekla did not want to push him any further. After a while he seemed tired and went and sat next to the girl, who had started building something huge out of Lego. Every so often he handed her a brick, which she added to the tower she was making. But his mind was elsewhere. He stared absently at the carpet or the Lego. He appeared to be thinking about something.

After a while, Tekla got up and walked out into the hall. Jennifer went with her.

"I don't want to disturb him," Tekla said in a low voice. "He seems tired now. It's lovely that he's playing so well with your daughter."

"I don't think he likes Palpatine though," Jennifer said.

Tekla gave it some thought. In her mind, she saw the frightened look in the boy's eyes.

"Do you think he really was talking about Palpatine?"

"Well . . . isn't that what he said?"

"No," Tekla said. "It was 'the old man' . . . Admittedly we were speaking about Star Wars, but I wonder—"

"What do you think he could have been referring to?"

"No idea," Tekla said, trying to shake off her uncomfortable feeling. "But I'm very glad he's here with you."

She thanked them for coffee and left the apartment after promising that she'd be back. Out in Swedenborgsgatan she felt sick. She set off for Mariatorget, still intrigued by what might have been going around in the boy's head. Had he suddenly remembered his mother stabbing his father? No wonder he had nightmares and stared vacantly at the carpet. But there was something else, something that had nothing to do with the dramatic events at the hospital. She saw the man before her again, lying there with a knife driven into his heart. Tekla quickened her pace, furious once again. Could she ever forgive herself for failing to prevent the woman from killing her husband? She tried to be rational: she had never been good at sports, never done any martial arts, never hit anyone. How could she possibly have tackled a woman wielding a knife? The nausea was getting worse, damn that jam roll. She had to get back to the hospital. She had a meeting today that she did not want to miss.

Tekla had never given much thought to the end of her life, but with her father lying on his deathbed she had promised herself one thing: she would not die before Simon, he'd never be able to manage on his own. If anything unexpected were to happen, he would simply have to join her on the next level. They might have to do a Brothers Lionheart.

"Hades."

"What?"

She realised that she had been thinking out loud. "Nothing."

The autopsy technician didn't seem bothered. He held his pass against the card reader and the door opened. "You do realise it's Saturday?"

"I took a chance. I didn't actually know that you guys work at weekends."

"People don't stop dying just because it's Friday 5 p.m., you know," the man said. According to his badge he was called Leif. As he shuffled off down the corridor, Tekla felt somehow cold and tried to dismiss the feeling that she had reached the realm of the underworld. She had been aware that there was another floor beneath the service corridors and changing rooms but not that Pathology was down there. She only found out when she called the switchboard. She had not been ferried across the Styx, but still had trouble finding the place, which was rather out of the way. If Leif was indeed Hades, watching over the dead, where was the three-headed guard-dog Cerberus?

"Are there no colleagues here today for you to have coffee with?" she said.

"We always take turns at weekends." Leif went over to a room whose glass windows gave onto the large, deserted autopsy room. He sat down at an ordinary table with a soup plate and two open cans of Coca-Cola on it. "We don't do autopsies at the weekend. We only receive the bodies for storage."

Tekla welcomed the scent of tobacco in the office. Infinitely preferable to the cold, metallic smell outside. Even though she was breathing through her mouth, she was already feeling sick. No amount of chlorine could cover up the stench of iron in blood coming from the autopsy room. Leif lit a cigarette that had been lying on the table next to the plate. Tekla smiled.

"A sense of freedom."

Leif took a deep drag. "What?"

"Nothing."

"What did you want?"

Tekla stopped herself asking Leif if he washed that enormous beard when he came home after a day spent hunched over the corpses. Took a deep breath to overcome her nausea.

"I had a patient who died this week. Thought I'd come down and have a look at the body."

"When was it sent here?"

"Yesterday."

Leif skilfully balanced his glowing cigarette on the rim of the plate and got to his feet. He had to brace himself against the table to lever his large belly off the chair. "Let's have a look." He walked slowly past Tekla and turned right. She held her breath and followed him. The spotlights shone on four empty, gleaming steel tables in the autopsy room. There were no corpses to be seen. The grey floor tiles were spotless, no sign of blood, hair or fragments of skull.

"Are you coming?" Leif was standing by an open metal door. He coughed up a mouthful of dead cilia.

"Sorry. A bout of nostalgia for my student days," Tekla explained.

Leif looked a tiny bit less forbidding. "Where did you go to med school?"

"Umeå." Tekla stopped outside the cold room. "I did some moon-lighting in pathology. Opening up corpses and doing some simple autopsies. Good money."

Suddenly Leif looked alarmed.

"What's the matter?" Tekla said.

"Are you a surgeon?"

"God no."

Leif walked into the cold room. "What was the name of your patient?"

"A man. Unknown identity. From the I.C.U." She looked at the rectangular aluminium plates along the wall. Each with a large handle and a number. Tekla counted twelve of them.

Leif stopped. "Oh, I see. Why didn't you say so right away?" He turned back towards the door. "It's going to Forensic."

"Can't I just have a quick look?"

"No way. The police have sealed the body bag."

"Please," Tekla pleaded.

"Even if you were to produce a twenty-year-old bottle of whisky, it wouldn't make any difference."

Tekla hung back, looking at the wall of cold storage compartments, as if she could see straight through the metal and black rubber to glean some clues.

"Come along now," Leif said from the doorway, sounding matter-of-fact.

Tekla felt the cold all the way to her bones. She followed Hades on stiff legs.

The evening shift had taken over in A. & E. Tekla spotted Nordensköld chatting with some of the nurses outside one of the patient rooms.

"Tekla!"

She couldn't be bothered to smile, but she did stop. "Yes?"

"Where have you been?"

"Why do you ask?"

"I got here half an hour ago but I haven't seen you around. There are patients waiting."

"How come *you're* here on a Saturday?"

"You. Haven't. Answered."

"And. You're. Talking. Funny," Tekla said. "But now I really need to get to work on some patients."

"You can't just come and go as you wish when you're on duty, you know."

"What are you going to do about it? How about some new surveillance routine? A G.P.S. that'll allow you to loaf around at home watching Netflix while keeping tabs on us. Maybe you ought to get changed and go and look after some patients yourself. Or have you forgotten how to do that?"

Nordensköld's hand shot out and grabbed Tekla's tunic. She was so stunned she forgot all the clever comments she'd been cooking up in her head.

Nordensköld immediately realised what he had done and let go of her top. He looked around quickly. Had anyone seen him?

Tekla leaned forward and whispered: "You can chill. I won't tell the boss. But if I were you, I'd try to keep that aggression in check. Imagine if you'd done that to Tariq."

Nordensköld seemed lost for words and turned to go. Tekla watched him disappear over to the other secretariat. She stepped aside for a transport trolley and noted that there were patients lined up against both walls in this part of A. & E. Moussawi was filling a mug at one of the washbasins.

"What the hell is Nordensköld doing here on a Saturday?" she asked.

Slowly Moussawi drank the water and then wiped his mouth carefully with a paper towel.

"He has every right to be here, surely. It's good when the boss makes his presence felt."

Tekla studied Moussawi, trying to see if there was any irony in what he had just said.

"Listen . . ." She bit her lip and left the fawning Moussawi to his devices. She couldn't bear to think what he sounded like when he was actually speaking to Nordensköld. Disgusted and disappointed but not surprised, she approached the cubicle where Klein-Borgstedt was busy dictating a patient report.

"Are you on the night shift?"

Klein-Borgstedt held up a bony finger, nodded and went on speaking into her recorder.

Tekla waited outside the cubicle. Her phone rang. *Magnus*. She wasn't quite sure what was different today, but she decided to answer.

"Hi."

"Well I never!" Lundgren sounded elated. "Cancel the search party. Tekla's been found. I thought you were dead."

"I've been extremely busy."

"I understand," Lundgren said in a tone that helped to put Tekla in a slightly better mood. "Just wanted to check that you're O.K."

"It's fine. Just a lot going on at work."

"That's the way you like it, isn't it?"

Normally she would have answered yes. But she was not so convinced today.

"What about you?" She remembered what Sigurdsdottir had told her: *Do at least try to seem interested. It gives men the feeling that you're aware of their existence.*

"Alright, a bit bored. This workplace rehab really isn't my thing. But I'm told I have to go step by step. I just wonder how long this bloody ladder is and when I'll be allowed to get going again for real. But I'm well, thanks. Would love to meet up."

"Magnus, I . . ." Tekla thought about the disaster at Gondolen. "Let's talk some other time. I've got to work."

"Oh well . . . but I'm glad you at least picked up."

"I promise to mend my ways," Tekla said and hung up. She knew it was a lie. And she had heard the disappointment in his voice. Why did he persist, why didn't he give up? There were thousands of hot women he could have, without any effort whatsoever.

"Done," Klein-Borgstedt said, coming out of the cubicle. "I sent home that boy you examined."

"Oh, thank you," Tekla said. "You needn't have bothered."

"The test results had been in for several hours."

Tekla was ashamed. No-one should have to take over her patients because she was off on other business. Especially not Klein-Borgstedt. "And were they normal?"

"Yes, everything was fine. I also thought it was constipation. And I spoke to the mother for a while. She's pregnant, and I told her about linkage analysis."

"She's pregnant?"

"Only seven weeks. She was feeling sick and explained why, so to speak. In any case, since the boy suffers from skeletal dysplasia and she's about forty, I thought I'd explain linkage analysis to her. That they don't have to go for amniocentesis."

"Ah. How kind of you," Tekla said. "Thanks for taking care of that."

"No worries. How are things with you?"

"There's a limit to how happy one can be when a guy like Hampus gets promoted to boss."

Klein-Borgstedt straightened a gold earring. She had a tan which seemed unlikely, given the time of year. Tekla assumed it was the result of an early autumn week at their place on the Costa del Sol.

"Ignore him."

"Easy for you to say."

Klein-Borgstedt nodded. "I understand. But try not to let useless bosses get to you. Do your thing. That's more than enough."

"Right now, my toughest challenge is to get that idiot Klas Nyström to put our I.C.U. patient on the hot list for a liver transplant. She needs one as soon as possible."

"And?"

"Her identity is unknown."

"So?"

"Klas is assuming that she's a junkie and doesn't deserve a new liver."

"That's outrageous," Klein-Borgstedt exclaimed in disgust.

"You said it."

"It's up to you to insist," Klein-Borgstedt said, pursing her lips like a stern schoolmistress. "It's blindingly obvious that one can't deny the woman a new liver on the mere suspicion that she's a drug addict. Especially since there's no evidence of that. One must, on the contrary, assume that she's *not* an addict, treat her acute illness and hope that she'll survive the aftercare in her home country. She doesn't exactly look as if she's from Somalia, I imagine that they have health services in Poland or the Baltic states or wherever she's from?"

"Absolutely." Tekla could feel her mood improving, thanks to Klein-Borgstedt.

Klein-Borgstedt looked pensive. "But I'm not really surprised. It's fully in line with Klas Nyström's plan for the hospital to have a unit for active euthanasia."

Tekla did not know whether to laugh or cry.

"You're not serious."

"Unfortunately, yes. But listen, I've got to take care of some patients. Let's talk later. We'll have to try and come up with something that will get the professor to change his mind."

Tekla thought of suggesting her strategy involving the N.S.K., but decided against it. For the moment it was enough to have Klein-Borgstedt "try and come up with something".

When Tekla's shift was over, she saw that she had a text from Lundgren: If you feel that way inclined, we could do a movie and a glass of wine tonight. Give me a shout. I have no plans. Tekla did not feel like giving him a shout or seeing any action films, for that matter. Instead, she was going to check on a patient she had been wanting to see since she arrived that morning, but had not had time for.

She had her seventh energy drink of the day and washed down two balls of amphetamine. She swallowed, walked down the long corridor past Gynaecology and the secretariat until she reached a part of the hospital which she rarely visited. Only if there was a cardiac arrest alarm. She took the lift up to the Orthopaedics Department, K 81. She asked someone in the nurses' office to direct her to the man injured in the car accident.

"Room 8," one of the nurses said without taking her eyes off her phone.

Tekla thanked her and went to Room 8. It was a double room. One of the beds was unoccupied. The place was silent and cool, with one of the windows ajar. The strip lighting was switched off, and the only illumination came from the reading lamp on the patient's over-bed table. Tekla tiptoed over to the bed, thinking it would be best to leave him to sleep, but just as she was turning to leave he opened his eyes. She was startled, because it looked as if they had been shut on purpose and he had been pretending to be asleep. Now he stared straight at her. For the moment he was lying completely still, as if his entire body were paralysed and he could only communicate with eyes.

"I'm sorry I woke you up," she said in Swedish.

"English, please," the man said with a strong accent.

"Oh, sorry," Tekla replied, switching to English. "I didn't realise you were asleep."

"Don't worry. Now I'm awake." The man smiled. He was of indeterminate age, tall – probably about one metre eighty-five – with a sinewy body. Tekla guessed he was at least seventy. Snow-white hair and quite a lot of wrinkles.

"I'm an emergency doctor and my name is Tekla Berg. I was one of the people who took care of you and the other injured man when you were admitted to A. & E. Do you think you could tell me a bit about what happened?"

The man gestured to Tekla to take a seat on a chair by the window. She sat down and leaned forward. He radiated such calm that Tekla felt quite relaxed.

"The police have already asked me all that."

"Alright," Tekla said, happy to note that Silva was doing his job. "But did you know the other man?"

"No," the old man said briefly. "I only happened to be at the same bus stop."

"I see," Tekla said. "Such bad luck. But, then again . . ." She looked down at the cast on his arm and his bandaged head. His legs were not in plaster. "It could have been a whole lot worse."

"I know. Nine lives." The man smiled and looked up at the ceiling.

"Where are you from?"

"Serbia."

"I see. And do you live in Sweden?" Tekla knew that the man had a temporary identification number.

"No. Tourist. I'm here to look at your beautiful churches."

"Exciting." Tekla would have liked to enquire further into his background, but that obviously had nothing to do with his medical condition. She stood up.

"I expect you'll be taken to the geriatrics unit soon. You won't be here all that much longer."

The man placed a hand on his chest and nodded in gratitude. It almost looked like a religious gesture.

"You get a good rest now."

"No problems," he said, holding out his hand. Tekla grasped it and was astonished to find it large and warm but also sweaty. Even more moist than her own hand. "Thank you for coming to see me."

Tekla released the hand and went towards the door. "So you had never seen the man who was run over before? Are you staying nearby?"

"No," the man said. "I'd been visiting a friend."

Tekla left it at that.

THE NATIONAL MUSEUM
Sunday morning, 10 November

"We need to spend more time out in the archipelago next summer," Gregor said.

Carlsson fished out a piece of Turkish pepper salt liquorice and bit into it. She was still suffering from the nausea that had overcome her two days earlier at the Friday meeting. Looking up at one of the funnels on the ancient steamship, a legitimate fear ran through her body like a cold stream. The last thing she needed now was to have to vomit on a boat that was bobbing up and down.

"Absolutely. But it's a bit cold for that at the moment. And you know how Stephanie feels about it. I don't suppose she'll be that keen, especially now."

"I said next summer. Why are you always so confrontational?" Gregor did up another button on his oilskin jacket. The damp, ice-cold wind came blasting in from Lilla Värtan across Strömbron before turning right past the Grand Hôtel. "And what do you mean, especially now?"

"Haven't you seen what a fuss they're making of her?"

Gregor shook his head. "Why don't we try and get a table for brunch on the verandah instead?"

Carlsson ground the liquorice between her teeth so hard that her jaw ached, and popped in another two pieces. "I'm not hungry." She would have liked to get out her phone and make a few calls, but abstained – she wanted them to have some quality time together without work intruding. "Am I being aggressive? Surely not. I even brought you your breakfast in bed."

"How come you're never hungry anymore?" Gregor asked, puffing at his e-cigarette. "You need to get that stomach checked."

"If you stop nagging me." Carlsson refrained from telling him how ridiculous she thought it looked. A grown man sucking on a large dummy. It was something he had evidently picked up from his publisher friends in London, along with the stereotypical wardrobe consisting of checked shirts, woolly cardigans and expensive tweed jackets from Harrods.

"One thing that really annoys me is the way Ludwig af Petersén thinks he can decide which research groups I should be keeping on at the hospital. Bloody bean counter."

She could have kicked herself, there she was talking about work again. She should be able to keep it at bay.

They stepped off the ferry and wandered in silence along Strömkajen, past the Lydmar Hotel and up the steps to the entrance of the National Museum. Why did she feel as if she were wearing a suit of armour from the Royal Armoury? Getting herself up that short flight of stairs suddenly seemed an impossible challenge. She wondered if Stephanie would have the same weight problems as she did. Her daughter had put on quite a bit after the baby. Hadn't she? God, they saw so little of each other, was it all her fault? Carlsson stopped in the entrance hall and tried to concentrate on the newly renovated murals by Carl Larsson, but ended up having to struggle not to faint.

"Can't wait to see Midvinterblot in a new light," Gregor said, putting away his e-cigarette. "Natural light – the daylight in which he actually painted it – I'm sure that'll get us closer to the essence of what he wanted to express. Shall we leave our coats?"

They went on down the stairs to the beautifully refurbished vaults in the basement. Carlsson led the way to one of the cupboards at the far end, where she began to shrug off her fur coat. Just as she was stuffing it into the locker, she heard a voice behind her:

"Monica Carlsson, long time no see."

She looked around. Niclas Oljelind, a fellow student from her days at the Stockholm School of Economics.

"Niclas!"

"This is Gunilla, my wife."

Carlsson shook a bony hand wearing so many rings that you could have gilded a whole dinner service with the molten precious metal. She had seen the woman before, but could not place her.

"Nice to meet you," Gregor said, extending his hand to Oljelind.

Carlsson should be saying something about their crazy student union days or Oljelind's enormous property in Östergötland. She might also hint at the great time they had in Torekov that summer eighteen years ago when the two of them had an affair, as Gregor probably knew deep down inside. Instead, it required all her strength merely to stay upright, and she only managed it by leaning discreetly on Gregor. Carlsson tried hard to say something about Oljelind not looking one day older, but her tongue had gone numb, as if she had just swallowed a glass of dental anaesthetic.

Oljelind's stiff smile seemed to have got stuck in an unnatural expression and he turned to his anorectic wife.

"Well, there are a few pictures we want to check out that have been put up since our last visit. It was good to see you, Monica. Let's do dinner sometime soon so we can catch up."

The Oljelinds slipped away, but Carlsson knew that within a week all the members of Idun would know that Monica Carlsson looked "very sick indeed". Was it breast cancer? That's where she'd met Gunilla in the spring, at the exclusive Idun club for successful women in the community. Under normal circumstances she would have remembered immediately, and could have mentioned some topic the club had discussed.

She staggered over to their locker and got out the bag of Turkish pepper liquorice.

"How are you feeling?"

"I just need a glass of water. And some coffee. Feeling a bit dizzy."

"We don't have to stay here, darling. You aren't looking too good."

"And what do you think you look like?" Carlsson spat. She closed the locker. "Come on now."

They headed for the staircase, but Carlsson soon realised that it was an impossible challenge.

"My hip is a bit sore. Can we take the lift?"

"Of course. Remind me, what does he do?" Gregor said.

Carlsson breathed deeply, tried to overcome her nausea.

"Oljelind," Gregor gently elaborated.

"He's the C.E.O. of Korefors. The third largest forestry company in Sweden, with a turnover of twenty billion."

"Gosh you're well-informed. Not all that surprising, maybe, considering . . ."

Carlsson ignored the comment.

"Hence the wife's diamonds," Gregor added.

"Hence financial independence," Carlsson said, leaving the lift. "They live in a manor house."

"You seem to know each other well."

With difficulty, Carlsson made her way to the cafeteria. "Is that a question?"

"An observation. It looked as if you were caught off guard. Is there something I ought to know?"

Carlsson ignored her husband's jealousy. "I'm married to you now. Right?"

"Absolutely. But it wouldn't hurt to know the background."

"Are you planning to write my biography?"

"Not until you're appointed C.E.O. at the N.S.K. But why not, perhaps it's something we at the office ought to consider."

Carlsson smiled and took a tray. She scanned the shelves. Nothing but buns of different kinds and overpriced shrimp sandwiches and tuna salads. Over by the coffee she spotted what she was looking for, some glass jars with sweets. Carlsson opened the lid to one of them and began putting salmiac liquorice coins onto a plate.

"Wonderful that we all have our little vices," Gregor said, holding out his Visa card.

They sat down. "Darling, I don't want to nag—"

"Well don't in that case."

"But when your health is at stake, I'm going to insist."

Carlsson removed some of the chewy liquorice stuck in her teeth. "I *will* go and get some tests done."

"You do realise that you've lost ten kilos?"

"Twelve."

"And you're eating very little. Is this some kind of diet you're on?"

"Can we talk about something else?" Carlsson had spent all weekend trying to work out a way to discredit af Petersén. On the one hand she couldn't care less what the board thought, but her more calculating side could see that she would have to play her cards right even if her objective mattered more than how she got there.

Suddenly the cup she was holding began to shake. It felt as if she were looking at someone else's hand. She heard the china bang hard against the wooden table and then bounce onto the less forgiving stone floor, where it broke in two.

"Oops," Gregor said, getting to his feet. He rushed over to the cashier and returned with his hands full of napkins. Carlsson stared at the spot between her legs, where the shards lay. She tried to bend forward but her body refused to obey. Her hands were numb, as if chained to the armrests.

"Monica?" She heard Gregor's voice somewhere above her head. She felt like throwing up. She needed air. She tried to get to her feet, yanked herself up off the chair, placed her paralysed hands on the table and pressed down. A rushing sound rang through her ears and then it began to snow. Black flakes fell from the top of her field of vision onto a post-apocalyptic landscape, the aftermath of a nuclear war. The last thing she knew was that her tailbone had made contact with a very hard surface.

When Carlsson came to, she found herself lying on something soft and warm. Seeing a person dressed in paramedic's uniform made her realise what had happened. She tried to feel if she had wet herself, but didn't want to put her hand between her legs. Chose to lie perfectly still. After all, she was wearing black trousers. It wouldn't necessarily show.

The paramedic squatted down. "You fainted."

"Yes, thanks, I gathered that."

"Are you hurting anywhere?" The man could not have been older than twenty. Slightly spiky hair, clean-shaven, with a gold ring in one ear.

"Don't know. Haven't checked."

"Your blood pressure is a bit low. 100 over 50. Do you usually have low blood pressure?"

"I don't know." Carlsson made a move to get up. The young man took her hand.

"Can you remember having a pain in your chest or palpitations before you passed out? We're going to do an E.C.G."

Carlsson turned to Gregor on her other side. He looked worried.

"How are you, darling?"

"Just help me get up. And no, no chest pains. Not before and not now."

Carlsson looked around. She saw that they were still in the cafeteria of the National Museum. Surprisingly few people around, and, above all, no sign of Oljelind and his botoxed wife.

"How long have I been out?"

"I don't know," Gregor said. "Maybe a quarter of an hour. The staff helped us. They were very kind."

"We should send them some flowers."

"Would you sit down on the stretcher again?" the paramedic said. "We're planning to take you to the N.S.K. Your husband told us that you work at the Nobel Hospital." Another ambulance crew member, a woman of about fifty, was folding away the blood pressure cuff.

Carlsson got out her phone.

"What are you doing?" Gregor asked, but she ignored him.

"Pontus!" Carlsson said. "Could you do something for me? Yes, I'm fine, and I realise it's the weekend, but I need to ask you for a favour. Yes, now. You know, I help you, you help me – don't think I need say any more to convince you to sacrifice a few hours on a Sunday?"

232

SÖDERMALM, STOCKHOLM
Sunday morning, 10 November

Sixteen coffins on every shift. As many as die from septicaemia on any given day in Sweden. The past and the present. Tekla left the safe, dull asphalt of Gullmarsplan and set off down towards the motorcycle club in the park by the roundabout. Not many people knew that the red house, the club's premises, had been a home for gravediggers during the nineteenth-century cholera epidemics. They had to dig sixteen graves a day, a positively inhuman task involving a great deal of what are today considered unsocial working hours. During a few months in 1834, the year of death, people dropped like flies. Tekla zipped up her windbreaker, pulled on her gloves and, in her head, scrolled through the Wikipedia page she had read two years earlier. She crossed the frozen lawn in order to ponder the city's historic past and also, to an extent, to admire it. Her trainers slipped on the treacherous spots where the damp had turned to ice. The temperature had dropped overnight to two degrees below zero.

She quickly passed Sthlm 01, an architectural blunder from the early '90s that looked completely out of place at Skanstullsbron.

Tekla had not had her fill of coffee that morning. That much became obvious when she overreacted to a motor scooter running a red light by the pedestrian crossing. She swallowed an energy drink on her way past Fryshuset. The Hammarby Sjöstad area had not really woken up yet so early on a Sunday morning. While her fellow citizens would no doubt describe the autumn as "quite amazingly beautiful", Tekla enjoyed it in her own unconventional way. Rather than admiring the changing colours of the leaves, she sought out the housefronts, the shiny electric cars and the dry pavements. Walked faster in an attempt to loosen up her body, which had stiffened overnight. She drew her hand over a black tiled façade and marvelled that someone had been bold enough to make a house that dark. An enormous chestnut tree had shed its yellow leaves all over the pavement and the gutter was dotted with conkers. All at once, a 1997 article from *Science Illustrated* appeared in her mind's eye. Her brain had associated the brightly coloured leaves with facts about chlorophyll breakdown and the way rich nitrogen and magnesium shelter from the cold by hiding close to the tree trunk, giving the xanthophyll a chance to show off its yellow pigment. There was nothing Tekla could do about it, and it happened more and more frequently. Knowledge she had not even been searching for would pop out of different compartments in her mind, but it didn't bother her all that much. As long as it didn't affect her sleep, she took it to mean that her brain had been updated. A tremendous asset when she was dealing with patients.

She ran through the woman's symptoms for the hundredth time. Her X-rays and lab tests. Tried to put her finger on the error, because there was one, she could feel it in her bones. But first there were a few practical matters she could deal with before she discovered where the problem lay. One of them would involve some classic divide-and-rule.

Her phone rang. The dementia care home. She answered.

"Tekla Berg, are you Karin's daughter?"

"Yes, what's happened?"

"Karin has had a cough and a temperature these past few days. We wanted to inform you that our duty doctor has put her on antibiotics."

"I see." Tekla felt like asking which antibiotics, but kept her mouth shut.

The woman was still on the line.

"Is there something . . . else?" Tekla said and swallowed a lot of saliva so as not to choke.

"Yes . . . Karin asked after you yesterday."

Tekla stopped – she was at the end of Luma Allé. "Did she?" Tekla remembered her mother the last time she went to see her. She had been mumbling. Uttered a few words – "Nice. Nice. Lovely. Lovely" – but that was all. Nothing to suggest that she was aware of Tekla's presence. She did not look her in the eyes or in any way indicate that she saw her daughter sitting there, waiting. Waiting for contact. Waiting for the answers that had never come, because the questions were never asked. It was too late for all that now.

"Thanks for calling." Tekla hung up on Elsa-Britt. That's right, that was her name. Tekla knew that the right thing to do would be to rent a car and drive up. Right now. It was her only free day in two weeks. So what was holding her back? She ought to go. Get a car and go and see her mother in hospital, if only for an hour. Maybe call Simon when she was there.

Tekla went into a café and ordered a large coffee to go. A man her own age was wiping fog off his glasses. For a microsecond, she wished he were her boyfriend, or husband. The mere thought gave her whole body a pleasant feeling of warmth. The fellow stumbled on his way to the checkout. She realised just how fine the line was, that it was up to her to define what was normal.

Who was the woman? Why was it so difficult to uncover her identity? A name and a personal identification number were all that stood between her and a new liver. Who might be expected to know more about her?

Tekla crossed Hammarby Sjöstad and Henriksdalshamnen, walked by Fåfängan and weaved her way through the Viking Line ferry terminal towards the Fotografiska Museum. As she was passing Restaurant Patricia, she had a brainwave. She would call Sigurdsdottir's husband Bjarni, a gastric surgeon at the N.S.K. He would be bound to know someone who could give her a second opinion on a liver transplant.

Suddenly the nerve endings connected and Tekla knew which of the lab results had set the alarm bells ringing: the blood fats. How come a patient with liver failure had such high blood lipids? Tekla turned and set off in the opposite direction. She had to get to the Nobel Hospital. Then she thought back to the conversation with the care home. She looked at her watch: half past two, too late to make it to Ludvika, it would have to be another day. She walked faster and took out two bombs. With luck, no-one would see her at the hospital and be able to remark on the fact that she didn't have a life. But then again: they would be absolutely right.

THE NATIONAL MUSEUM AND ERSTA HOSPITAL
Sunday morning, 10 November

The ambulance door was pulled shut.

"And it's O.K. to just do this?" Gregor asked.

"I can."

"So I see. But what if somebody at work finds out how you use the community's resources?"

Carlsson grasped her husband's hand. "What do you mean? It's much quicker to go to Ersta than the N.S.K. from here. Who cares what people think? It's my workplace and nobody will know. Besides, I don't trust public healthcare. There's no real incentive to do a decent job."

"You realise you're talking about your own doctors at the Nobel?"

"That's exactly why I'm introducing some pretty radical changes, as soon as possible. So everyone has a carrot dangling in front of them."

The ambulance driver's voice could be heard from the front seat: "Are you all comfortable back there?"

"All good, thanks," Carlsson called out. "And please close the hatch."

The ambulance rolled past the Grand Hôtel and on to an emergency gastroscopy to be performed by senior consultant Pontus Rågsjö in the Surgical Department at Ersta.

"If you want something, then you have to go and get it," Carlsson said with a smile. "I'm not letting the state decide for me. One has to be allowed to take care of oneself. And that also applies to healthcare. Pontus left the public sector because he was the best in his field but was given no encouragement. Besides, I don't have time for this during the week. My diary's full. Might just as well get it sorted. You've been on at me to check out my stomach, after all. So now I'll have a gastroscopy and we'll see if it's a stomach ulcer."

Carlsson felt strangely elated. Her fainting fit had given her head a good shake and helped her come up with a plan for how she was going to get at af Petersén.

When the ambulance reached Ersta, Carlsson was wheeled into the operating theatre, where Pontus Rågsjö was waiting. He put on a plastic apron and nodded at a young nurse who came in. Carlsson heard him say: "Five milligrammes. Then we'll see if we need more."

"There's nothing wrong with my hearing," Carlsson said. "Besides, I happen to be a doctor. I can handle medical information."

Rågsjö walked up to the stretcher and put his hand on Carlsson's arm. His face was tanned, with thin, pale lines radiating out from his eyes towards the temples. Carlsson knew that Rågsjö and his eighteen-years-younger third wife spent a large part of the year in Morocco.

"Right now, you're the patient. Do we agree? I had to skip my tennis today. That's not a problem, but let's not drag this out any longer than necessary."

"You might as well do that colonoscopy while you're at it, since I'm lying here anyway?"

"Let's first see if we find something on the gastroscopy. I'll take some tissue samples too."

"I don't know too much about all those cancer markers, but I trust you."

"And then I'll send you for a capsule endoscopy during the week and a C.T. scan of your thorax and abdomen, that way we'll have soon checked out the whole of your intestines. Only leaves the colon."

"Can we do the scan today?"

Pontus smiled and nodded to his nurse. "We'll see. You said that you've lost twelve kilos, but you haven't had any diarrhoea?"

"No."

"And you haven't been constipated either?" Pontus palpated Carlsson's stomach as he spoke.

238

"No more than usual."

"And your appetite hasn't changed?"

"Not significantly. I don't always have time for lunch, but I still make sure that I eat something."

"But you're getting stomach pains from time to time, you said."

"I can't tell you exactly when they happen, just that they've been worse this last week."

"I'll test the gallbladder and liver too, of course. Could be gallstones."

"Let's hope," Carlsson said. "I don't have time for any more fainting fits."

"It's probably the gallbladder," Pontus said as he picked up the long optical fibre tube he was going to push down into Carlsson's stomach.

NOBEL HOSPITAL

Sunday morning, 10 November

Tekla did not have a car, though it would have been a good excuse for getting to the hospital before everyone else in the mornings. Apparently, the car park was always full by half past seven. Nor was she like many other of her penny-pinching colleagues, who deliberately skipped breakfast at home in order to munch a free sandwich and boiled egg on the ward before the day started. Yet Tekla was always the first to arrive on the ninth floor, often before seven.

"Good morning," Sigurdsdottir said as she glanced into Tekla's room. "When did you get here, for heaven's sake?"

Tekla would have been happy to lie, but not to Sigurdsdottir. "About an hour ago."

"What are you doing at work at six on a Monday?"

Tekla tapped her temple. "It's gnawing away in here. I can't access the patient files at home."

Sigurdsdottir sat down on a chair. "You have heard of sleeping tablets?"

Tekla wasn't about to tell Sigurdsdottir how many drugs she'd already swallowed. "Things are a bit out of the ordinary now."

Sigurdsdottir smiled and laid her thin hand on Tekla's shoulder. "Who are you trying to fool, my dear?" Then the Icelandic doctor made a fruitless effort to stand up.

Tekla pulled her card out of the computer and helped her friend to her feet. "It's the morning meeting soon. Shall we grab a coffee first?"

"I'll treat you to that and a sticky bun at Pressbyrån," Sigurdsdottir suggested as she wandered over towards the lift lobby.

*

240

"We need a bigger conference room," Carlsson said as she walked over and sat down at one end of the oval table. She had to steady herself against the top and seemed to be struggling to get her body into a sitting position. Tekla thought she looked even more tired than the other day. Her face was grey-brown. A drabber version of a sun tan. Nyrén was standing just behind her, clutching her laptop and shiny mobile phone, as usual. She had chosen an extra tight and figure-hugging dark grey suit for the first morning meeting of the week. It put Tekla in mind of T.V. series about glamorous lawyers.

"Today is a big day," Carlsson continued. "Locum called yesterday evening and gave us the green light." She looked up at Emma. Had they rehearsed this?

"Yes indeed ... And the timing is perfect, because our first patient is arriving at Bromma Airport from the U.S.A. as we speak," Emma continued.

"Everything we say here now stays in this room. Is that understood?" Carlsson said, deadly serious.

Only Klein-Borgstedt dared to speak up.

"Is Donald Trump flying in, or why all the hush-hush?"

"Even better," Carlsson said. "We're expecting a patient who's going to get his third liver."

"But why here and not in the U.S.A.?" Klein-Borgstedt asked. "Seems a bit risky."

"Because they don't dare," Carlsson answered. She was enjoying this. "He's frail, and he has cardiac insufficiency and renal failure."

"So why would *we* be doing it, in that case?" Klein-Borgstedt's irritation was unmistakable.

"Because Klas Nyström was involved in the patient's second liver transplant and knows him well. He'll be our first client ... patient," Carlsson corrected herself.

Tekla wanted to make a sarcastic remark about how they might as well sell the Nobel Hospital to Coca-Cola, but bit her tongue. Picking up an energy drink and taking a swig straight from the can,

she tried to refrain from making any comments, despite the irresist-
ible force welling up inside her.

"The simple fact is that the patient *could* be given another liver in
Los Angeles but, thanks to Klas' contacts with Donald Bigoti, we've
arranged it so that we get to take over the patient from U.C.L.A."

"Completely crazy," Tekla said, recognising that her mouth had
just opened of its own accord. Frustration had got the better of her.

"What was that, Tekla?" Carlsson asked. Twenty-eight pairs of
eyes stared at the long side of the table.

Tekla put down her energy drink. "I said, completely crazy.
Why would we risk taking on such a sick patient? He has cirrhosis
of the liver, I presume. What if Klas fails? What if the patient dies
on the operating table? And why should our taxpayers' money go
towards..." She paused for a few long seconds. "...ah yes, of course,
he's obviously paying his own way. And handsomely, what's more."

Nyrén looked nervously at Carlsson, as if she felt that she needed to
reprimand the specialist doctor with the short, nondescript hairstyle,
or give her a real going over in front of the assembled company.

Carlsson raised her hand a little from the table. "We hear what
you're saying, Tekla. Everyone's entitled to their opinion. But I think
we can discuss this a little more later, you and I... separately. Now
we need to focus on taking care of the patient."

Tekla got up and pushed past some interns who were staring
wide-eyed at her, the brave doctor who dared to defy the hospital
C.E.O. She could see that Carlsson didn't actually look all that angry.
Probably still on a high from the whole situation. No doubt she
would be receiving the patient herself. God, how pathetic, Tekla
thought. Lucky she had more important things on her mind. She set
out for the I.C.U.

Tekla was walking alongside her colleague, who was wheeling an
ultrasound machine before her.

It was not long before Elmqvist answered. "Mushrooms. We
should have had the results this weekend, but now testing has been

outsourced to a private laboratory in Kista. Complete bloody lunacy," Elmqvist hissed as she stopped by the intubated woman. She plugged in the ultrasound and shook the tube of gel feverishly in front of her. "Bloody Hell!" Elmqvist turned to the nurse who was standing on the other side of the patient, next to the syringe pumps. "Can you be a dear and fetch a new one?" The nurse nodded and disappeared.

"Probably none left. No doubt they have to be bought from China, some new supplier . . . But first procurement, delays, toing and froing, and then some new firm with different subcontractors, different shippers and a brand that nobody's heard of . . ."

"And the mushroom test?" Tekla reminded her, even though she would have been happy to hear more from a kindred spirit complaining about the covert privatisation of the hospital.

"I'm sorry," Elmqvist said. "Both amatoxin and psilocybin."

"Wow. Death Cap *and* Liberty Cap. What a delicious fricassee."

Tekla could picture the Liberty Cap. A modest-looking little fungus, similar to many others. Belonged to the group of psychedelic mushrooms, in other words those that can cause confusion and hallucinations. "That could explain the disorientation," she went on.

"You mean she could have been psychotic and therefore stabbed her husband in the chest?" Elmqvist gave Tekla an amused look.

"You think?"

"Well, why not? But no smoke without fire."

"You mean she probably wanted to murder her husband anyhow but then the mushrooms got rid of her inhibitions so that she . . . what, dared do it?"

"Something like that," Elmqvist said, as she was handed a tube of mint-blue gel and squirted a thick strand onto the ultrasound probe. She drew aside the sheet which covered the woman's body and began her examination of the lungs and heart. Tekla noted the small spots on the patient's torso. "What's that?"

"Don't know," Elmqvist said. "She has them in patches here and there. Maybe a rash from the antibiotics."

Tekla memorised the spots. She read the values off the monitor beside the bed. "Has her blood pressure been this bad the whole time?"

"Despite large doses of noradrenaline, yes," Elmqvist said. "We can't seem to get it any higher. Her pulse is 130, as you can see. And she's hardly peeing at all. We put her on dialysis this morning."

"Yes, she was looking pretty ropey already yesterday, when I was . . ."

Elmqvist stopped short.

"Were you here yesterday?"

"Kind of . . ." Tekla bit her lip. "I just dropped by. Wanted to see how she was getting on. But it's not looking too good."

"Is it you she's after?" Elmqvist said.

"Who?" Tekla asked in confusion.

Elmqvist nodded at a point behind Tekla's shoulder. Tekla turned and saw Carlsson waving.

"I think so. But one last question, is she still off the transplant list? Now that you know it's mushrooms and her liver tests are completely off the rails. She's going to—"

"Die within forty-eight hours if she doesn't get a new liver, I know," Elmqvist said. "But no, she's not on the list. Maybe Monica's the person you should be trying to persuade."

"And how do you explain the high blood fats?" Tekla asked. She was grasping at straws. She took hold of the woman's hand, it was ice cold and swollen. Like one of the dolls used for practising heart massage. Her ring had been cut away.

"I can't," Elmqvist said.

Tekla went over to Carlsson. As she walked, she considered different causes of high blood fat levels, but none seemed the obvious answer. The patient also had diabetes. Was this something new or a consequence of the liver failure? She had to dig deeper in her memory bank.

"Come," the C.E.O. said and limped out of the I.C.U. Tekla saw no chance of escape, so she followed obediently. "Is there something you want to say to me?"

"Apart from what I said at the morning meeting? No."

Ominously, Carlsson cocked her head to one side. Tekla felt completely transparent. "I appreciate your saying what you think at our meetings. Look at Anita, she's someone who speaks her mind, and I know you're friends. But you contacted the liver section at the N.S.K. without consulting either me or Klas."

"I don't agree that the woman shouldn't have a new liver just because her identity's unknown."

"But don't ever go behind my back. Do you hear me?"

"What's done is done."

Carlsson steadied herself on a washbasin in the corridor.

"What's wrong?" Tekla asked.

Carlsson pinched her eyes shut, breathing heavily. "Nothing."

"Do you need to sit down?"

"Absolutely not," Carlsson said angrily, her blood pressure seemed to be under control again. She stared at Tekla. "I told the division head at the N.S.K.'s transplant section that we wouldn't be needing their services."

Carlsson leaned forward. Tekla thought she caught a whiff of keto breath.

"Get hold of that woman's identity and Klas will probably change his mind. But you're not to go behind my back again. Do you hear me?" Carlsson turned and walked towards the exit.

Tekla got out her mobile to look up the causes of high blood fats. She had a feeling that it wasn't only mushrooms. She wiped the sweat from her forehead as Carlsson vanished through the exit. Maybe they could avoid the need for a transplant if she could establish what the patient was suffering from. Or discover her identity. But, for that, the police would need to get a move on. Then she saw that she had two new messages. One from an unknown number.

We'll take the patient and put her on the top priority list if you can fix transport. Bjarni.

Tekla weighed the options. Would Elmqvist agree to the patient being spirited off to the N.S.K.? She was so unassuming and her sole concern was the patient, even though she was inclined to moan a fair bit along the way. But what would the implications be for Tekla herself, apart from the small matter of Carlsson sacking her?

The other message was from Silva. He wrote that he would come to the I.C.U. at nine. Tekla looked around. No police as yet.

She wrote an answer to Bjarni:

Can we have a word around lunchtime? I have an idea.

As far as she could see, there were three ways to save the woman.

First: find out who she was, thereby showing Nyström that she was not an addict. There was nothing to suggest she was, and Tekla certainly did not believe it.

Secondly: discover what she was actually suffering from. It wasn't just the mushroom poisoning that had caused her liver to fail, she was convinced of that.

Thirdly: defy Carlsson's express orders and risk her career by moving the patient to the N.S.K. so they could give her a new liver.

Just as she was starting to puzzle over those spots on the woman, which looked like nothing Tekla had ever seen before, the pager in her pocket screeched. She took it out.

"G04"

"G04," she called out to a nurse holding a bag of Ringer Acetate. "Where's G04?"

"No idea," the nurse said.

Tekla ran over to the nurses' station, grabbed a telephone and called the switchboard.

"Tekla Berg, doctor on call. I've had an alarm about a cardiac arrest in G04. Where's that?"

"It's the new annex," the telephonist said.

NOBEL HOSPITAL PATIENT HOTEL

Sunday morning, 10 November

Tekla saw the anaesthetists' emergency kick scooter come racing along from the right, but she was closer to the annex and – this time, at least – would win the race.

It did actually say Go4 on a blue sign next to the large wooden door. Above the entrance, in English, she read:

THE NOBEL HOSPITAL PATIENT HOTEL.

Tekla could not help feeling curious as she took the beautiful, timbered staircase down to the old hall dug into the bedrock. She remembered the tour she had been given when she started work at the Nobel's A. & E. department. A medical secretary, who had since retired, had shown her and three other new recruits the space where, during the war, an underground hospital had been installed with an operating theatre, a small intensive care unit and a decontamination station in case of chemical attack. Patients could be brought in by rail through the entrance down by Årstaviken, and the entire facility could be self-sufficient for two weeks. Tekla recalled the white-painted, lumpy stone walls with dreary strip lighting in the ceiling. Now it had been transformed into something totally different. It was clear that Carlsson had pushed the boat out.

"Where is it?" she heard Gray panting behind her.

"No idea," Tekla said to the duty anaesthetist, with whom she had worked well during the recent incident in the service tunnels. The only question was whether she would once again have to open up the thorax to do heart massage. Her hands were almost cramping at the mere thought of it.

As they came down the stairs, the lighting was pleasantly subdued.

A warm red colour on the walls, beautiful sofas in pale wood and brown leather on a glossy floor made of some dark green, expensive-looking stone. They passed what looked like a boutique hotel reception, where a man in a suit pointed them in the right direction.

Further along the corridor a man and a woman in dark suits were gesticulating.

"In here," the woman said in a broad southern American accent, as she helped to hold the glass door open.

They came into a large room with a sofa suite, beige wall-to-wall carpeting and dimmed spotlights in the ceiling. Straight ahead, a top-to-bottom glass wall, in which another door stood open, showing the way into a second room. In its middle was a hospital bed with an infusion stand on either side, and behind it an enormous abstract green and yellow painting. Tekla could smell toast, or perhaps pizza?

"When did he flake out?" Gray asked, running to the head of the bed.

A woman in a black blouse and tight jeans was carrying out chest compressions, counting aloud in English. She did not seem to understand that the question was addressed to her. Carlsson was sitting in a large armchair next to a glass table, staring fixedly ahead. She was speechless.

Tekla turned to one of the guards, who had followed them in. In English, she asked him: "When did he stop breathing?"

"Just . . . like five minutes ago."

Tekla stepped forward and took over the compressions from the woman, who smelled strongly of sweat.

"I'm intubating," Gray said.

Tekla compressed the man's ribcage. He was tall and had clearly been strong before age and alcoholism had taken their toll on his muscles. She had no difficulty in forcing his ribs against the vertebral column. Five to ten centimetres deep. The heart had to be squeezed together to pump out the blood to his oxygen-starved brain.

"Ready. Tube in place," Gray said out loud.

Tekla looked around. Who could take over the compressions?

She called to the guards – they did at least have the necessary muscles. One of them took off his jacket and began to roll up his sleeves.

"What's going on?" another familiar voice could be heard saying. Nyström came and stood next to Tekla. "What the . . .?"

"He's intubated and we're doing C.P.R.," Tekla answered. "Can someone please get us a defibrillator?"

The anaesthetic nurse ran to fetch the portable device and started connecting the electrodes.

"Could you?" Tekla asked The Hulk, who took over the compressions. "Not too fast," she corrected him, taking a step back. The muscle man would probably be able to keep going for hours. She listened to the lungs. "That sounds good."

The nurse had got the electrodes in place and now turned on the defibrillator, which immediately gave out a mechanical order: "Stand clear. Analysing. Do not defibrillate."

"Continue with the compressions," Tekla instructed the guard in English.

"What do you mean?" Nyström asked. "Aren't we going to defibrillate?"

For a split second, Tekla enjoyed seeing the world-famous surgeon reveal his ignorance of cardiology.

"You don't defibrillate an asystole."

"But—"

"I need an ultrasound machine," Tekla interrupted. "Is there one down here?"

When she did not get an answer, she went on:

"No defibrillator and no ultrasound. Don't you have any medical equipment down here?"

Tekla looked at Carlsson, who seemed to have regained some of her strength. The hospital C.E.O. got up, but had to steady herself against the wall.

"Go find an ultrasound machine," Tekla said to the first on-call, who had just crept in unnoticed, having probably had trouble locating the place. She turned and left.

"We'll give adrenalin," Tekla said. "I don't suppose we can get a blood gas test?"

"So what do we do?" Nyström asked. Without his underling by his side, the professor seemed somewhat bewildered. Tekla almost felt sorry for him.

"He has liver failure, right?" Tekla asked, looking at the patient's swollen belly.

"Yes, but he wasn't in a confused state during the flight," Nyström said.

"Who was in charge of the patient during transportation?"

"A doctor from U.C.L.A., but he's checked in at the Sheraton. It all looked stable, as I understood it," Nyström said, clutching awkwardly at his chin. Tekla noticed that he had just had his hair cut. He had no doubt also prepared some new classical music for the operating theatre. "He's going to need E.C.M.O."

"You're joking?" Tekla said.

"We'll take him for E.C.M.O. at the N.S.K.," Nyström repeated, "so they can stabilise him and do a coronary angiogram. He's having a heart attack, I'm sure of it."

"He'd never make it," Tekla protested.

Carlsson cleared her throat and took Tekla aside.

"You want that woman up there to have a new liver."

"What's that go to do with it?"

"If you can manage to get this man to that E.C.M.O. machine alive, then I'll see to it that Klas operates on your patient as soon as possible."

Tekla weighed the impossible – and totally bizarre, never mind unethical and medically repugnant – offer. To get the American patient to Solna ought only to be a logistical problem. But then what, since there was no way he would survive it? Old, suffering from liver disease and presumably with calcified coronary arteries. He would die, as surely as Tekla's father had that sad afternoon in Östersund. And E.C.M.O. hadn't even been invented then.

"But he'll die, either on the angiography table or in theatre."

"Just see to it that he gets there," Carlsson gasped, miserable and pale. Tekla would have liked to hear some more about her tests, but it would have to wait.

A look at the muscular bodyguard told her that he needed to be relieved. Maybe the bulges under that jacket were mostly steroid-induced, after all.

She turned to the anaesthetic nurse: "Can you fetch a L.U.C.A.S.? That way we'll get some stable, mechanical compressions during transport."

"Transport?" Gray asked.

"To the N.S.K.," Tekla said.

"You're kidding me."

"Just get the L.U.C.A.S., will you?" Tekla said, feeling as though she had sold her moral compass to the devil.

NOBEL HOSPITAL
Sunday, 10 November

If somebody had told Tekla during her training that the greater part of a doctor's day was spent solving logistical and administrative tasks, she would probably have considered dropping out. The purely medical steps she took down there in the patient hotel below the Nobel Hospital were things she could have done in her sleep. What came next was a project management epic in five acts. The L.U.C.A.S. had to be located. Gray had to be persuaded to stay behind after her night shift, to take care of the patient's airway during transportation. Tekla needed to come along, but there were rules about how many were allowed in the ambulance. On top of that, the E.C.M.O. team at the N.S.K. had to be forewarned, and persuaded to take on a hopeless case – once again Carlsson had to call her opposite number there – and finally Tekla had the American entourage to contend with. In the end she had to yell at the woman in the black blouse, the patient's agent, telling her that the N.S.K. was a respectable hospital, perfectly capable of performing coronary angioplasty.

Three hours and four energy drinks later, Tekla was back at the Nobel Hospital. The American patient had been moved to the E.C.M.O. unit at the N.S.K., but his prognosis was poor, to say the least. The blood gas test they had managed to perform before their departure for the N.S.K. had shown a lactate level of ten. All the patient's organs were in a state of hypoxia, including his heart, which would probably also have to be replaced if he was to survive. After all, Tekla thought, he can afford it. They would only need to ring the right people, who could oblige with a new heart.

She stopped outside the newsagents' in the entrance as it dawned on her how hungry she was.

"Two boiled ones with fried onion," Tekla said to the young woman at the cash desk, "and a Pucko." She gobbled up the two hot dogs and washed them down with the cold chocolate milk, before setting off for the I.C.U.

"I'd like you to check this out," Nowak said as she entered, in his familiar restrained, rather measured manner. Tekla wondered if he ever got worked up.

They walked towards patient number five in the unit. A nurse was busy giving the woman a bed bath. Tekla noted that Silva was waiting by her bedside together with a male colleague.

"At least her intestines are functioning," Tekla observed.

"Clostridium bacteria," Nowak said.

"That too?"

"And Klebsiella in the blood."

"Is there anything she doesn't have?" Tekla asked.

"A healthy liver," Nowak answered, looking pleased with himself.

Tekla saw that the spots on the body had become worse.

"How is she?" Silva asked.

"Her liver's totally shot," Tekla said. "But you've got something to tell us?"

Silva pulled up a shiny metal stool and sat down. Tekla thought he looked pale.

"No hits in any register. D.N.A., fingerprints . . . and we've checked dental records with all the clinics we were able to get hold of here in the southern suburbs."

Tekla saw the nurse turn back to the woman. She had bigger spots on her trunk and some of them were like blisters. The nodular, vesicular lesions, reddish in colour, had even spread to her face. Nowak helped to hold the tube in place in the woman's lungs.

"And no credit card or anything else to go on?"

"Nothing. Not even any keys or a travel card."

"But she must have had something with her?"

"We assume so. We're looking through all the C.C.T.V. footage from the hospital, to see if she stopped off somewhere, but it takes time."

"Not exactly good news," Tekla said.

"I'm keeping that till last," Silva said.

Tekla ran through all the causes of pemphigus, the formation of blisters on the skin. She scrolled through Derm Web, the largest database for skin diseases. It was three years since she had last looked at it, but all she needed was an energy drink to perk her up a little and she'd probably be able to come up with a diagnosis.

"Thirsty?" Nowak asked. Tekla could see how inappropriate it was to be drinking here and now.

"Sorry."

"No problem. But you were muttering something about pemphigus."

"I was?"

"Yes."

Disconcerting as it was for her not to be conscious of her own behaviour, Tekla had no time to dwell on that. Images began to emerge. Familial benign pemphigus. Pemphigoid. Bullous dermatosis. Erythema multiforme. Behcet's disease. There were twenty-two illustrations in the list. Each had several illnesses linked to it, but none that would fit with liver disease, high sugar levels and high blood fats. There was something wrong with the overall clinical picture. Could the woman be suffering from more than one condition at once?

"How do you interpret the blisters? They weren't that big this morning," Tekla asked.

"Pemphigoid," Nowak answered.

Tekla leaned closer to the patient's face. "That doesn't seem right."

"What doesn't?"

"Two things, actually."

"Such as?"

"First, why should she develop pemphigoid all of a sudden?"

"Her immune system isn't exactly healthy, with that liver."

"True. But that's not pemphigoid."

"It isn't?"

"There's no liquid in the blisters, if you look carefully. They're more like a raised, flat rash. And it's worst on the face."

"Yes, but . . ."

"In any case, it's not pemphigoid."

Nowak gave a slight shrug. He was not the most prominent doctor at the hospital and seemed to buy her argument.

"We've asked the dermatologists to come and take a look."

"Good," Tekla said. "But I think I can crack it before then. I've just got to look through a few more images." Nowak opened his mouth, probably about to say something about her being welcome to use the computer, but she turned to Silva, who had been given a mug of water by the nurse, and asked: "And the good news?"

"On the one hand, we now have a good description of the car."

"Which car?"

"The one from the hit-and-run. A white estate, probably a Škoda."

Tekla had completely forgotten that the man and the older man from K 81 had been run over.

"What's your thinking?" she asked.

"We have to take a broad view. Both men had been hit by a car, after all."

"I'll say."

"Tekla saved the life of the younger one," Nowak added.

"Fat use that was," Tekla said bitterly.

"We need to identify the driver. Apart from anything else, it might give us a clue to the men's backgrounds."

"And the boy?"

"I gather you've seen him."

Tekla looked up. "So . . .?"

"Nothing. I just happen to know," Silva said. "And I'm assuming you'll tell me if anything came up."

"Of course."

Tekla avoided Silva's searching eyes and looked once more at the woman's face covered in small nodules. More than anything, it looked like leprosy, except that that wasn't exactly an illness one developed overnight.

"And on the other hand?"

"What other hand?" Silva asked.

"Just before, you said 'On the one hand'. Was there something more?"

"*Ah, bueno.* We have a witness, a hospital employee who says he saw the woman with the boy in the lift as early as Thursday. She seemed in a state of confusion then too."

"Then too?"

"Well, we said she was most probably disoriented by the mushrooms and the liver failure when she attacked the man, didn't we?"

Tekla wanted to object, but held her silence.

"We're going to try to get hold of C.C.T.V. footage from the central hallway to see where they headed next. We've also got people going around the wards trying to find out if she was spotted anywhere else. I still don't buy the idea that she had neither handbag nor mobile phone."

Tekla closed her eyes and tried to conjure up an image in her mind. Where had she seen a skin rash like that before?

SOPHIA HEMMET HOSPITAL
Monday morning, 11 November

He was said to be the best in Stockholm. According to Pontus Rågsjö, who wrote the referral, for what that was worth. The views of a gastric surgeon at the Ersta Foundation were not, however, sufficient for Carlsson. She rang the head of the Nobel Hospital's own Neurological Clinic and asked for advice.

"Best of all the Greeks in town," was the answer she got.

"And by what standard does that make him a good recommendation?" she asked.

The answer came quickly: "The Greeks are the best neurologists and Christos is their God," the clinic head said with a laugh.

That was good enough for her. But she was distinctly unhappy about having to sit and wait on a red, lumpy sofa and stare at some flowery curtains. Or listen to the old man in the leather chair two metres away as he noisily sucked and chewed on his Läkerol pastilles. A pile of Sköna Hem interior decorating magazines lay on the table before her. The last thing she needed was any tips in that department. She straightened the patterned woollen skirt which she had chosen to wear that day. A mistake as it turned out. The temperature was meant to be below zero. And in the neurologist's waiting room at the Sophia Hemmet Hospital, saving on the heating was clearly not a priority.

Gregor texted that he wanted to come to offer support. NOT necessary, Carlsson answered, and brought out the only form of salt liquorice she had found in the cafeteria: Marabou black. Why was Gregor making all this fuss? The man with the Läkerol was making such loud noises that she debated telling him as much. She broke off

257

three squares of the chocolate at a time and had her mouth full when Nyrén called.

Carlsson turned away but raised her voice.

"Yes?" she managed to say.

The man in the leather chair looked up from his thick book in irritation as Nyrén said: "I'm sorry to disturb, I know that you—"

"What?" Carlsson interrupted. "I'm going in soon, so tell me."

"Apologies. Well, you see . . ."

Carlsson wanted to shout at her head of communications to get a grip, but her mouth was stuffed full of chocolate.

"I just wanted to tell you that the patient –" Nyrén lowered her voice to a whisper – ". . . didn't make it."

Carlsson swallowed. "He died?"

"Unfortunately."

The door outside the recess where she was sitting opened and a middle-aged woman in a wheelchair came out.

"Shit!" Carlsson said.

The old gentleman cleared his throat and stared fixedly at her. A doctor in a white coat and checked shirt with thinning hair emerged. "Monica Carlsson?"

"I'll have to call you back," Carlsson said. "You must stop the press from finding out about this."

"But how am I supposed to . . ."

"By doing your job, for example," Carlsson said, ending Nyrén's call. She knew that only she could stop the news leaking from the N.S.K., but it would have to wait ten minutes. A neurological examination could hardly take longer than that. She braced herself against the sofa's armrest and avoided the inquisitive gaze of the elderly snob – from his dress and bearing she assumed he must be from the posh district of Östermalm. She hoped he was afflicted with some kind of malignant brain tumour.

"Hello," she said, taking the neurologist's outstretched hand. It was knobbly and cool. She went into the room and was about to sit down on the only chair when she heard the man's voice behind her:

"May be just as well if you sit on the bed right away. I see you're having a little trouble walking."

"Shall I sit or lie down?"

"Sitting will be fine. I'm Christos Papadopoulos."

"Monica Carlsson. Thanks for seeing me so quickly."

Carlsson was having trouble determining the man's age. He was lean and pale, as if he hadn't left his room for several years. His hair was black, with silver streaks that clambered up his sideburns towards the few remaining wisps that adorned his bald pate. Maybe he was only around forty but had begun to lose his hair at an early age.

"Pontus and I have a good working relationship on cases like this one."

"Cases like this one?"

Doctor Papadopoulos unbuttoned his coat and reached for a small notepad.

"Once he has excluded gastroenterological causes for symptoms like those he described. And, by the same token, I exclude neurological illnesses and then refer to him."

"Sounds sensible."

"And do I understand correctly that you don't want to be treated in your own hospital."

"So you know who I am?"

Papadopoulos took a pen from his breast pocket. He was very careful in his movements. He looked frail, his skin almost translucent. Carlsson thought back to her studies and tried to fish out some exciting diagnoses, but most of her medical knowledge had been replaced by financial graphs and diagrams.

"Diffuse symptoms from the hands, but also an unsteady gait, as I can see."

"That's right," Carlsson said, trying to focus on being a patient. If nothing else, she could speed things up by being cooperative. There was something fish-like about the Greek doctor which she found off-putting. She shuddered.

"No symptoms affecting the eyes or the hearing?"

"Not apart from my husband's snoring at night, no."

As Papadopoulos slowly wrote down his observations, Carlsson could see that his handwriting slanted steeply. At first, the lower temperature in the room had been welcome, but soon she began to shiver.

"And you've lost weight, but Pontus found no signs of either cancer or any inflammatory intestinal illness. He'd taken a very large number . . ."

There was a ring on Carlsson's mobile.

"Hello?" she answered. Nyrén was breathing heavily.

Papadopoulos got to his feet and picked up a reflex hammer. He seemed to accept the situation and began to tap Carlsson's knees and Achilles' tendons with it.

"I'll call back in five minutes."

"You have to call the N.S.K.'s C.E.O.," Nyrén said between gasps.

"Tell me more," Carlsson said guardedly, nodding at Papadopoulos to indicate that he could go ahead and shine his light into her eyes.

"Their communications director rang to say that several evening papers and also a T.V. channel are camped out in their entrance lobby."

"Tell them to wait. I'll call in five minutes."

"Ludwig is also on at me. What shall I say?"

Carlsson hung up on Nyrén and saw that Gregor had sent her two text messages. She ignored them. And she certainly didn't want to hear anything more about the suntanned af Petersén and his crusade against her leadership of the hospital. She was pretty sure she knew what he was after, it was blindingly obvious. If he thought he could out-manoeuvre her just because she was a woman who would eventually buckle under period pains or menopausal anxiety, he was mistaken. He had no idea what he was letting himself in for.

"And your memory and concentration aren't affected?" Papadopoulos asked.

"I haven't come to see you about dementia, have I?" Carlsson said, and she heard how harsh it sounded. "The answer is no."

Doctor Papadopoulos hummed and hawed and made notes. His thin veins shone through, especially on his forehead and the backs of his hands. Her physical aversion grew stronger by the minute. Would she end up vomiting into his crotch?

"So what do you think?"

The doctor mumbled to himself, scribbled away and circled Carlsson, as if she were an interesting insect he had never seen before.

"What. Do. You. Think?" she said, a little more loudly.

"Too early to say. Can you lie down?"

With considerable effort, Carlsson heaved her heavy legs up onto the bed. She left her shoes on, feeling anything but comfortable when the fish-doctor came over with his long tentacle-like fingers splayed. He palpated her stomach, examined her every joint and continued to test her reflexes by hitting her elbows and wrists with his hammer, until he said in a serious tone:

"You can sit up now."

She got up. "Are you done?"

No answer. She had time to see that Gregor had texted her again.

"Can you do this?" Papadopoulos said, slowly moving his index finger in a wide arc to the tip of his nose. Carlsson knew what he was doing, once upon a time she had actually learned how to perform these tests for neurological status. He continued through the repertoire, the Romberg, the Grasset, heel-to-toe and all the nystagmus exercises that were to be found in the neurological textbooks.

"Now I must—"

Carlsson was interrupted by the door opening.

"Hi Mamma."

She turned and found herself staring at a younger version of herself. Except in modern clothes and not quite as overweight as she had been at that age.

"Stephanie, what are you doing—"

"Would you mind waiting a while?" Papadopoulos said, cutting in, but Stephanie Carlsson smiled broadly, went up to her mother and gave her a hug.

"I felt I ought to be with you. Pappa called and told me you were coming here."

"I would appreciate it if you—"

"I'm staying," Stephanie interrupted him.

Papadopoulos shrank back instinctively, jotting something down in his notebook instead.

"But sweetie, aren't you working?"

"Hellooo, Mamma, wakey-wakey, I'm still on maternity leave with Zoe."

"Ah, is that so? I didn't know."

"Yes, you did. I told you last week, but I think that there's a little too much on a certain hospital boss' plate right now. Isn't that so, Doctor?"

"You mean me?" Papadopoulos asked in surprise.

"Aren't you a doctor?"

"Yes—"

"Good," Stephanie said, taking off her fur coat and putting it on Papadopoulos' desk. "So how's my Mamma?"

Carlsson didn't bother to argue with her daughter. She knew who would win.

"Hellooo? Is it anything serious?" Stephanie repeated.

"Yes, well . . ." Papadopoulos cleared his throat.

"Is it?"

"No, I mean, we don't know yet. We have to do a lumbar puncture and get some samples."

Carlsson shivered. "A lumbar puncture?"

"I think we need to do that in order to—"

"So that's a yes, Mamma. How bad can it be? I'll hold your hand."

Carlsson would have preferred to avoid that procedure, but she knew that the neurology guru was right, they had to rule out all dangerous neurological conditions.

"And then we'll have to get you appointments for an M.R.I. and an E.E.G."

"When will that be?" Stephanie asked, brushing her fluffy hair out of her face. Carlsson wanted to ask her not to use so much perfume, but she would never listen.

"In the next few weeks."

"I don't think so," Stephanie said before Carlsson even had time to open her mouth. "We might as well get it done today. Isn't that right, Mamma?"

Carlsson didn't know where to put herself. Stephanie ground on: "You know that my mother is the C.E.O. of a hospital, right? She can't very well run back and forth doing tests whenever it suits you."

Papadopoulos looked towards the door, as if he wanted either to run away or call for his secretary to come to his aid.

"I don't know . . ."

"But I do," Stephanie said forcefully. "You'll write 'very urgent' in the referral, that it's something which needs to be done today. Right?"

Carlsson tried to smile at her resourceful daughter. She could see how Stephanie had become so successful as a project manager in the telecoms field.

"I'll see what I can do," Papadopoulos said, walking over to his computer. "But we'll certainly exclude everything that could have a neurological cause."

"Shall we go and get a coffee in the meantime?" Stephanie said, picking up her coat. "Let us know when we can do that lumbar puncture."

Carlsson let her daughter lead her out and sit her down in the waiting room.

"I'll go and get two coffees, so you can have a bit of a rest."

Carlsson didn't need to rest. She knew exactly what needed to be done and got out her mobile.

"Hanna Parida, please. It's Monica Carlsson. Tell her it's urgent."

The medical secretary in the N.S.K. management office put her on hold. After a few minutes, she heard a voice.

"Monica. I'm glad you called."

"We have a situation on our hands."

"No kidding," Hanna Parida said calmly. Carlsson could picture her counterpart smirking into the receiver on the far side of town. "We have every media channel here on the premises and we're wondering what to do."

"It's very important that nobody finds out what's happened. So a bit of discretion please."

"The fact that there's an American multi-millionaire in town isn't exactly a secret," Parida said. Carlsson had never before heard her so soft-spoken. It annoyed the hell out of her.

"No, of course, I realise that. But they don't know that he came to get a new liver."

"His third."

Carlsson clenched her fist and managed to contain her anger.

"Yes, his third."

"I hardly need to say what I think of the whole business."

"No, sweet of you," Carlsson said, gagging briefly.

"But . . . I could see my way to doing you a favour, just this once."

Carlsson tried to lower both her shoulders and her heart rate, which was about to run away with her.

"I imagine that it won't come cheap."

Parida allowed herself an artificial pause and gave a little cough.

"Apologies. I have a bit of a cold."

"Poor you."

"But I have a suggestion as to what you can do for me in exchange."

Carlsson felt her jaws lock in a clamp-like grip.

"Let's hear it."

NOBEL HOSPITAL
Monday, 11 November

Tekla stopped by a patient toilet near the X-ray department. She took out her tube of Lypsyl, hesitated for a second, shook out two bombs and swallowed them with lukewarm water. She stood outside the door, leaning against the cold wall, and contemplated a portrait of Professor Göran Runge, chief physician for seventeen years during the '80s and '90s. He looked good-natured sitting at his large, white desk with his typical, imposing 1980s steel-frame spectacles. On the wall behind him hung a large painting representing a field hospital from the previous century.

About ten men between the ages of thirty and fifty walked by. Several wearing leather jackets, almost all of them in jeans. Tekla smiled. They could only be plain-clothes officers. This was confirmed by the police badge she spotted on a belt when the man wearing it reached back for his tin of snus. Tekla went in the opposite direction, taking the stairs down to the patient library. She was five minutes early.

She nodded to the librarian by the counter and passed the shelves of detective stories. Her phone rang: it was the dementia care home. Tekla felt obliged to answer, though she didn't want to.

"Yes?"

"Is that Tekla Berg?"

Tekla stopped by the public computers and leaned against a chair. This part of the library was empty – she wouldn't have to leave if she were to break down.

"Yes."

"I just wanted to let you know that Karin's condition worsened this morning, so we've transferred her to the hospital."

"Worsened in what way?" Through the windows overlooking the corridor, Tekla could see Silva walking along.

"She had trouble breathing and developed a fever. She was shaking so badly."

"Sepsis and pneumonia," Tekla said to herself.

"What was that?"

"Nothing. Good that you transferred her."

Silva came into the library. Tekla's eyes met his.

"Was there anything else?"

The woman appeared to hesitate. "We . . . I just want you to know that Karin's asked after you several times in the last few days."

Tekla pointed to an empty sofa group in the corner of the library. Silva went over to it and took off his windcheater.

"Oh, O.K . . . Good to know."

"It probably wouldn't be a bad thing for you to—"

"Come up and visit her," Tekla cut in. "I understand. But I have to go now." She ended the call and walked over to the superintendent.

"Why did you want to meet here?" she asked, sitting down facing him on the sofa. He put his mobile on the pinewood table in front of him.

"It's sensitive."

"What is?"

"The investigation into the man and the woman."

"Don't forget the son," Tekla said. She was going to call later in the day to see how he was getting on.

"And the boy," Silva added. Tekla saw that he had not shaved that day. A grey layer covered his cheeks, making him look older. She wondered if he dyed his sparse hair darker.

"We managed to get hold of some C.C.T.V. images from the central hallway. It seems she was already in the hospital by Thursday lunchtime."

In her mind's eye, Tekla saw what time it had been when she admitted the traffic accident victim to A. & E.: 12.31.

"She went into Pressbyrån and bought some microwave food,

266

disappeared up to one of the wards and then returned to the central hallway two hours later. The whole time, hand-in-hand with the boy. Then she took the stairs down to the service tunnels. That was late on Thursday evening. Then she reappears via the same stairs early Friday morning, just ten minutes before she rushes into the I.C.U. and stabs the man in the heart."

"So she never left the hospital?" Tekla asked in surprise.

"Not so far as we know. She wasn't wearing any outdoor clothes on Friday morning. And she had no bag with her."

"So you think that she slept in . . . what, the basement?"

"Maybe. That's what we're assuming. We're still looking for her belongings."

"And the search is being carried out by plain-clothes officers?"

Silva nodded. "They're getting help from some cleaners who saw the woman in a lift."

Tekla ran different scenarios through her head. "But why sensitive? You said it was a sensitive investigation."

Silva stared at the glossy tabletop before him. Nodded pensively. "I'm worried."

"About what you might find in the cellar?"

"About what lies behind the murder."

"So you no longer think it's just a psychopathic woman who was jealous of her husband?"

"That would of course be the simplest explanation. And the most obvious."

"But?"

"When your bosses start to meddle and say 'you can have all the resources you need', and at the same time act as if it's just any old investigation, well then, it's often a bigger deal than first appears. You hardly need your gut to tell you that."

"But what do you think might be behind it all?"

"I've honestly no idea. But I'm grateful to you for trying to get us as much medical information as possible."

Tekla cursed the situation she found herself in – she was being pulled in so many directions. She ought really to march straight out, take a taxi to Stockholm's Central Station and get on a train to Falun Hospital.

"I'm doing what I can."

"Good," Silva said. "I'll be in touch if we find anything in the service tunnels."

"Oops," Tekla said as her phone rang. "God's calling."

"Best take it, so you don't end up in hell."

Tekla got up and left the library.

"Can you come to my office?" Carlsson said.

"Now?"

"Yes."

"I'm on my way."

Tekla aimed for the east wing and texted Sigurdsdottir: Can we meet in half an hour? Need your input.

By now, Tekla knew the routine. Carlsson's secretary, the over-eager, slightly muddle-brained Fredrik Franck, held up his hand, asked Tekla to wait by the door, then knocked and announced "Tekla Berg is here" in a loud voice, at which Carlsson called out: "Yes!"

"She'll see you now," Franck said, backing towards his ergonomic chair.

Carlsson was at her desk. Already from a distance, Tekla could see that there was something different about the C.E.O. Tekla sat down opposite her. This time, she wasn't as dazzled by the fantastic view over the rooftops of the Rosenlund area. She waited, tried not to stare as Carlsson struggled with a bag of liquorice cars. Either her hands were refusing to obey, or the plastic was very thick. She let go of it.

"What the hell," Carlsson said, apparently looking for something on the tabletop.

"Can I help . . . ?"

"Where were we?" Carlsson asked.

"You rang and told me to come."

"Oh yes. Well . . ."

There was another knock on the door.

"Klas Nyström," Franck's falsetto voice could be heard saying.

"Yes!" Carlsson called out.

Nyström came in, pulled up a chair for himself and sat down near Carlsson.

"Excellent," Carlsson said. "Yes, excellent—"

"I'm not giving the woman a new liver," Nyström said with a serious expression. Tekla was still fixated on Carlsson's strange behaviour. Confusion and muscle weakness. What was happening to her?

"How did you get on at the neurologist's?" Tekla asked.

"Well," Carlsson said. "Nothing on the M.R.I. or the E.E.G."

"They ran other tests too, I assume?" Tekla asked.

"Yes, I'll get the results tomorrow."

Tekla saw how an unhealthy-looking weariness had settled around Carlsson's mouth. There was a marked stiffness in the lip muscles.

"No objections?" Nyström said from the side.

Tekla realised that she was fighting on two fronts and began to deploy her forces. "You bet there are. You will be giving the woman a new liver. You just don't know it yet."

"I'm sorry?"

Carlsson tried to get up but found it difficult, something was wrong with the coordination between her arms, her hands and the tabletop.

"Are you alright?" Tekla asked. She could hear huffing from Nyström, but her main concern was to make it around the table in time in case Carlsson were to fall. The risk of that seemed imminent.

"You'll have to continue this dicussion somewhere else," Carlsson said when she did eventually manage to get to her feet.

"Shouldn't you lie down?" Tekla suggested. "You look pale."

"Not at all," Carlsson protested. She wanted to say something more, but her mouth wasn't responding, so she walked away and stood by the window, looking towards the horizon. "You can go now."

*

Tekla met Sigurdsdottir outside the chemistry lab.

"Don't get up," Tekla said as she sank down. "I need your advice."

"O.K., so no small talk. Shame. Shoot."

"Klas isn't going to operate on that woman."

"What? Why not? What does Monica say?"

"She seems to be leaving the decision to him."

"But you've spoken to Bjarni? He said he could help you."

"I know. But that seems to have been blocked. By the powers that be, I guess."

"Bugger." Sigurdsdottir shifted in her chair to accommodate her stomach.

"Are you O.K.?" Tekla asked.

"Absolutely. I just have to pee all the time. My 'bugger' was directed at all the power politics." Sigurdsdottir gave Tekla a sly look. "But you've already got another plan, haven't you?"

"I was thinking of asking you to contact the media."

"Me? Why not you?"

"It would make it too easy for Monica to sack me."

"But you're happy to put my head on the block?"

"You're going on maternity leave. You'll be gone for a year. At least."

"One and a half."

"And by then everyone will have forgotten all about it."

Sigurdsdottir patted her stomach. Her belly button stood out under the tight hospital shirt. "You cunning devil."

"God, I'm going to miss you," Tekla said. "Imagine having to lunch with Tariq or Hampus every day for a year and a half. Total nightmare."

"You can always call your buddy the hospital C.E.O. for a cosy coffee break."

"Only if I want to have liquorice for lunch."

Tekla felt incredibly low at the thought of Sigurdsdottir going away.

"Are you up for it?" she asked quietly.

"Not on your life!" was Sigurdsdottir's determined answer. And then in a whispered exhalation: "But for you, of course!"

There was another call on Tekla's mobile.

"We've found a bag," Silva said.

Tekla jumped up. Then sat down again when the blood plummeted into her trainers.

"And?"

"There are car keys and money. A lot of money."

"So who is she then?" Tekla asked.

"There were no identity documents. No driving licence, no passport, no credit cards. Nothing."

"Well, what then? Some car keys and a couple of thousand kronor?"

"More."

"How much?"

"One hundred thousand in cash."

"Wow."

"So now we're looking for the car in the car parks and down on Ringvägen. Speak later."

Silva hung up. Something was swirling around before Tekla's eyes like an annoying moth.

"What?" Sigurdsdottir asked.

Tekla repeated what Silva had said, but her thoughts were elsewhere. The chase was on and they had picked up a trail. She wasn't about to let go. She felt they were very close.

"Tekla?"

"Wait."

Tekla picked up an energy drink and downed it in one. Then she got to her feet. She skipped three times and slapped herself in the face.

"I've got it!"

"What are you talking about, Tekla?"

"I know now what's wrong with her!"

"What?"

"Dioxin! It's clearly dioxin poisoning!"

"Dioxin? Why would she have dioxin in her body?"

Tekla began to speed through the articles she had read over the years about dioxin. There weren't many, she had to deepen her knowledge. But Sigurdsdottir was right.

"Yes, why should she have been poisoned with dioxin?" Tekla burst out. "And the big question . . . Who the hell is she?"

NOBEL HOSPITAL
Monday, 11 November

Tekla ran all the way up the stairs to the I.C.U. Much to her annoyance, she had to catch her breath before being able to make herself understood by Elmqvist, who was waiting patiently outside one of the meeting rooms.

"Di . . . ox . . . in," Tekla managed to stammer.

"What do you mean?"

"The woman has dioxin poisoning."

Elmqvist looked more tired than impressed. "And how did you work that out?"

"Look . . ." Tekla picked up a desk-pad to fan her sweaty forehead. "The rash on her face. That's chloracne. Looks like nothing else. It's not pemphigoid at all . . ."

"Wait," Elmqvist said, knocking on the glass pane facing the corridor.

Silva appeared with a new assistant. He opened the glass door. "What's up?"

"Tekla has a theory," Elmqvist said. "You may as well hear it straight from her."

Tekla immediately felt less sure of herself. She hadn't prepared for a panel debate. "Dioxin," she finally said and continued to read the 2007 article from *Toxicology*. "The skin rash is something called chloracne. The same thing the Ukrainian president Viktor Yushchenko got when he was poisoned."

"Dioxin?" Silva repeated as he unbuttoned his wet windcheater. He took off his cap, which also looked soaked. "Why would she have been poisoned with dioxin? What is it even?"

"A chemical compound that belongs to the dangerous group of polychlorinated dibenzodioxins. The formula is C-4—"

"I think what Alvaro meant was . . . what does it do to the body?" Elmqvist interrupted. "And where does it come from?"

"But don't you understand?" a frustrated Tekla said.

"I think you need to explain, not all of us know everything there is to know about dioxins off by heart," Elmqvist said, blinking meaningfully at Tekla.

"Chloracne, cystic rashes which primarily affect the face and trunk. Just like the woman out there. But it's also associated with high blood fats, especially cholesterol. And diabetes. There was something wrong with her blood count," Tekla said, scanning the lab list once more in her head. She pointed into the air. "See?"

"What do you mean, see what?" Silva asked.

"In the lab list."

Silva looked at Elmqvist as if Tekla were hallucinating.

Elmqvist clarified: "Sometimes our dear Tekla seems to carry an awful lot in her head. Nothing to worry about. Just listening to her conclusions is usually the way to go."

Bloody hell, Tekla thought. She really needed to tone down her behaviour.

"Bleeding disorders, the confusion before the seizures set in . . . It all fits."

Elmqvist smiled at the young doctor before her. "I love you and all your theories. But this time I really think you're barking up the wrong tree. You're forgetting one detail."

"I don't think so," Tekla said.

"Yes, you are, because we've found both fly agaric and hallucinogenic mushrooms in her blood. She has liver failure caused by mushroom poisoning."

"That too," Tekla said, continuing to fan herself with the desk-pad.

"Does one have to isolate the patient if it's dioxin?" Silva interrupted.

"Surely you're not saying . . .?" Elmqvist threw out her hands in resignation.

"It *is* dioxin poisoning," Tekla said. "Why don't you trust me?" She was excited. Maybe they could save the patient now. Perhaps push even harder for a liver transplant.

Elmqvist reflected. "And how do we confirm that?"

Tekla leafed through the article from the British security services. "We take tissue samples and send them to Umeå for analysis."

"Let's do it, then," Elmqvist said and got up. "Jesus, Tekla, why do we always end up like this when you're on a case?"

Tekla didn't understand what Elmqvist meant, but she followed her over to the patient area to contact the Umeå special laboratory. Silva followed them there.

"How about we go outside for a breath of fresh air?" he asked.

"I first have to . . ."

"I think you really do want some fresh air," Silva said.

It finally dawned on Tekla that he was referring to more than just having a smoke. They went round to the back of the building. Silva brought out a blue packet of Memphis and offered her one.

"No thanks," Tekla said, suppressing an urge to offer him a bomb from her Lypsyl tube. They had to keep close to the grey façade, so the ice-cold rain wouldn't reach their feet. Every now and then, a gust of wind flung in a few drops. She was freezing.

"We found the car."

"Great!" Tekla said. Her phone rang: Lundgren. She declined the call and wrote a message. Call you in a little while.

Eventually Silva managed to light a cigarette and took two quick puffs. Tekla inhaled his smoke and saw her father before her, lugging freshly chopped wood into the big house. Naked from the waist up, twigs and leaves stuck to his sweaty stomach. A green cap with the factory's sun-bleached logo. Cigarette in the corner of his mouth. Tekla walking behind him and picking up the logs he'd dropped.

"It had been in a crash. Blood on the front," Silva said.

"Seriously? But that means—"

"And the make of car fits with the eyewitness accounts from the hit-and-run. A Škoda, so . . ."

"Does this mean the woman ran over her husband?" Tekla quickly sketched out a timeline in her head. The man was admitted on Thursday morning and the woman stabbed him in the chest on Friday morning. One day. Tekla thought about the boy. Was he in the car? Had he seen his own mother run down his father? What had led to these brutal events?

"Obviously we have to let the forensic technicians work it all out, but that's what it looks like. We're in the process of confirming the blood on the front of the car is a match, and that will take a bit of time."

"So you're saying she was capable of driving on Thursday morning and tried to run over her husband and then, when she stuck a knife into his heart less than twenty-four hours later, she was completely befuddled by mushrooms and dioxin? Could the first have been an accident? Did she just happen to crash into him, and then later on become psychotic?"

Tekla now had the sequence of events clearly laid out in her head. Confusion after ingesting psilocybin and amatoxin could definitely be right.

"The effect of the neurotoxin in Liberty Cap kicks in one to four hours after consumption. Liver failure as a result of Death Cap comes within twenty-four hours."

"Are you trying to say that, from a purely medical point of view, this could make sense?" Silva inhaled his nicotine in the casual way of someone with a twenty-year smoking habit. Nothing special. No great enjoyment. Just basic routine and a need to be a tiny bit more alert.

"Yes, it could. But I still don't understand . . . Why would she stick a knife in him? Did she start off trying to murder him with the car and then—"

"Finish him off?" Silva said. "There are many possibilities. You have no idea what lengths abused women will go to. I've seen axes to the head and bloodbaths in bed. If a woman is mistreated over many years, a huge amount of aggression builds up, and it can find brutal expression. But how are we going to find out what happened before the accident? Is there any chance that she might come to, so we can question her?"

They stood in silence for a few seconds. Tekla stared at the wet carpet of leaf detritus on the pavement. Her whole body shook.

"But you said she had cash in the bag."

"And not a little, either."

"If this was a domestic drama, and she was trying to run over her husband . . . why would she have all that money on her?"

"Could they belong to some criminal network, maybe smugglers or something drug-related—"

"With a small boy who speaks with a Norrland accent in tow?"

"Yes, intriguing to say the least." Silva straightened the chain around his neck, the electric guitar dropped down among his chest hairs.

"And did you think they looked like criminals?" Tekla wondered. "He was wearing normal jeans and rough work boots – the ones with reinforced caps that building workers use. And not much in the way of gang tattoos."

"Maybe they really are berry pickers."

"With one hundred thousand in cash?"

"Perhaps there's a lot of money to be made picking berries, what do I know?" Silva said, giving a little shrug. "Better than a cop's salary, I'll bet. I wouldn't mind a spot of coffee."

It didn't make any sense. "Why not a construction worker?" Tekla had the boy's pleading eyes in front of her the whole time. There was something more personal behind all this than a fight over money from berry-picking or smuggling drugs. You don't stab the father of your child in the heart unless he's done something dreadful to the boy. But he had been examined by a doctor, there was no sign of violence, fractures or other physical abuse.

"We need D.N.A. from the man," Silva said. "To compare with

D.N.A. from the Škoda, like I said. But it'll take time, since he's presumably still in Forensics."

"I'd guess so," Tekla said, pulling open the steel door. "A Škoda, you said?"

Silva shook his head in disgust. "Actually, I never told you anything. Should have kept my mouth shut."

"It's not hard to go out and check the car park, the bit the police have sealed off."

"True," Silva said as he stepped into the warmth. "But you're not going to do that."

"Because?"

"It's raining."

Tekla smiled at the crafty policeman and noticed that her trousers were soaked.

NOBEL HOSPITAL AND SÖDERMALM, STOCKHOLM
Monday afternoon, 11 November

Since the dioxin breakthrough, Tekla had been finding it difficult to concentrate, more obsessed than ever with finding out who the woman was. She was unlikely to wake up from her hepatic coma, they would only be able to talk to her if she were to receive a new liver.

Things were relatively calm in A. & E. Two registrars were wrestling with the influx of cases and seemed to have the situation under control. Moussawi was keeping an eye on the stock market via his telephone and gave Tekla an absent-minded nod as she passed the doctors' office. Walking towards the vending machines in the patients' waiting room to buy an energy drink, she reflected on all that had happened. Obviously, more than anything else, she really ought to be in Falun by now. To have spoken to the doctors and checked what treatment they were giving her mother. It had to be right. There were cures for pneumonia and sepsis, but only if you administered the right drugs at the right time. So what was stopping her? She threw away the can, went back to Moussawi and asked if she could leave early.

"No problem," he said with a casual look in the direction of one of the registrars. "They're slaving away, nothing to worry about."

The changing room was quiet. Tekla put on a fresh pair of trousers and was just about to go back up to A. & E. when Sigurdsdottir came in.

"Hi. What are you doing here?" Tekla asked. She took a sideways glance at her phone. There was a message from Lundgren. Call when you can/feel like it. Tekla ignored it. She'd chosen the head-in-the-sand approach.

Sigurdsdottir lowered herself onto a bench. "I've done you a big favour."

Tekla sat next to her. "For real? That's great."

"So now you owe me."

"Tell me what you want."

"A new brain. I'll have one like yours, please."

Tekla smiled. "I'll give you something really nice. Promise."

"It'll be . . ." Sigurdsdottir's mobile let out a loud electric guitar riff. "Yes, I will turn it down, I just don't know how. Hello?"

Tekla noted the change in tone.

"I see. O.K. Of course. I'm on my way." She hung up. "That didn't take long."

"Who was it?"

"Our little emperor."

"Hampus? What did he want?"

Sigurdsdottir levered herself to her feet. "We'll see."

"Are you heading there now?"

"It should be you going to the guillotine."

"I know," Tekla said, following Sigurdsdottir to the door. "I owe you a brain."

"Or a head on a silver platter. See you in eighteen months."

Tekla hurried up to the main entrance and jumped into a taxi. She continued to sift through articles on dioxin. It should take no longer than twenty-four hours to have the tissue samples analysed, provided they could be sent up to Umeå quickly. And the fallout from the piece in the media should put pressure on Carlsson to release the woman to the N.S.K. for a transplant. By now, Tekla was beginning to understand where the hospital C.E.O.'s Achilles heel was. It was well concealed, but what it amounted to was vanity and pride. The last thing that Carlsson wanted was to lose face before the media. And least of all if it put the N.S.K. in a better light. So either she would let the patient go to the N.S.K. or she would overrule Nyström and force him to do the job himself at the Nobel. Just so long as her own condition didn't deteriorate. She really hadn't looked her best.

"Card?" the taxi driver asked as he pulled up.

Tekla paid and got out. She thought about her mother's vacant eyes. Wondered if she would recognise her only daughter. She took the stairs up and rang the doorbell.

"Tekla?" Jennifer said in surprise. The foster mother was wearing dark green corduroy trousers, a simple blouse and flat shoes. She looked as if she were going somewhere.

"Yes, I'm sorry to just pop in like this but I . . ."

"Come in," Jennifer said. "Andrus is out with Agnes, so it's just me and Yoda at home."

"Are you sure?" Tekla said, looking down at Jennifer's shoes.

"Oh yes, don't worry, it's not a problem, I'm going to something later this evening. I was just sitting around surfing the net a bit."

Tekla closed the door and removed her wet shoes. She hung her jacket next to a leopard skin print coat that she assumed belonged to Agnes. The apartment was darker than last time. Maybe due to the rain outside or because only a few of the table lamps were lit.

"Where is he?" Tekla whispered.

Jennifer pointed in the direction of the children's room.

"How's it going?"

Jennifer sat down at the dining-room table and closed her laptop. She looked tired. "So-so. He's not talking. Most of the time he plays with the Lego that Andrus bought. Star Wars." She summoned up a strained smile.

"Is he crying?"

"At night. I went in and lay down beside him. Then he fell asleep again."

"Nightmares." Tekla tidied her wet hair, patting down a few unruly tufts.

"Presumably."

Tekla paused. Something remarkable struck her: had she just talked about a child's nightmares, and during her last visit managed to get the boy to speak after a trauma? It didn't fit her image of herself, she who had never had contact with children, made no effort to play with her colleagues' kids at some party or other, never squatted down and chatted to them about superhero films.

"May I go in and see him?"

"By all means do. I'm sure he'll be happy to see you."

Tekla got to her feet and realised that she was nervous. She had an impulse that she should go and tell him that his mother had died. But then persuaded herself that that wouldn't happen. She'd see to it that the woman got a new liver, even if she had to carry out the operation herself. She swore by all that was holy, on her father's grave, that she would do everything she could to save the woman and see her hug her son again.

Tekla walked into the spacious room, with a big round mat in a warm, yellow colour in the centre of the parquet flooring. Two beds stood at an angle in one corner, one of them a bunk bed. There were Elsa Beskow illustrations on the walls. A large, square bookcase with slime-yellow drawers, some of them half open, with dolls' hair, a plastic snake and a Spiderman costume spilling out.

The boy was sitting in the middle of the mat, wearing red tracksuit bottoms and a striped jersey.

"Hi," Tekla said, sitting cross-legged beside him.

The boy looked up from the grey Lego pieces. Tekla saw several figures she recognised from the Star Wars universe. He glanced up shyly a few more times, then continued to assemble the parts of the spaceship.

"May I help?"

The boy nodded carefully. Tekla knew that he understood Swedish perfectly, which tended to discredit the theory of the Polish berry pickers. Why would a seven- or eight-year-old child understand Swedish if he had Polish or Russian parents, whether they picked berries or smuggled cocaine? Were his parents quite simply Swedish?

"What are you making, a Starfighter or a spaceship?"

The boy looked up at Tekla, non-plussed.

"That's not what it's called, is it? God, how embarrassing."

"The *Millennium Falcon*," the boy said.

"It was on the tip of my tongue," Tekla burst out. "*Millennium Falcon*. That's Han Solo's ship? I remember when they play chess with the hologram pieces at a round table. And then . . . whoosh, off at the speed of light." Tekla sketched a quick movement with the Lego model up towards the stucco ceiling.

The boy smiled cautiously.

"But there's still quite a lot left to build," she said. "Isn't there?"

He didn't answer. They sat and put pieces together in silence for a few minutes.

"Do you like hot chocolate?"

He nodded, without letting go of the pieces.

"Me too. Shall we ask Jennifer if she has any chocolate?"

The boy nodded again.

Tekla weighed her options. She took a chance. "Were . . . were you in the car when Mamma drove into Pappa?"

The boy continued to assemble his Lego. As if he had not heard or understood the question. Tekla knew nothing about child psychology, had no idea what you called the defence mechanisms of a child in shock.

"You don't have to answer, I just . . ."

Suddenly, the boy jumped up and threw himself onto Tekla's lap. She dropped the Lego and let his little body burrow into her arms. He held her tightly around the neck.

"There, there," she said and patted him on the head. She had to loosen his sturdy grip around her throat a little, so as not to suffocate. "It must have been horrible. But I'll make sure Mamma gets better." The boy was in fact quite big, heavier than she had expected. How old was he? A large six-year-old, or a small nine-year-old? Anything in-between was also possible. She hugged him back.

The boy carefully relaxed his embrace and looked at Tekla, his face now just ten centimetres from hers. She felt his moist breath against her mouth.

"Is she going to die?"

As good as it was, there was still something strange about his Swedish. Perfect pronunciation, but there was an accent underneath the Norrland dialect which she couldn't quite place. Was he bilingual? Did his parents come from different countries?

"No. She's not going to die. I promise!" Tekla said. "Don't think any more about it. Now let's go and see if we can find some chocolate." Tekla reminded herself of her earlier promise, to save the woman's life. This time, she would not fail.

She lifted the boy up and put him down on the floor. Hand in hand they went out towards the kitchen.

"We fancy some chocolate," Tekla said, giving Jennifer a wink.

"Of course," she said, getting up.

At that moment, Tekla's phone rang. It was Sigurdsdottir.

"Can I call back a bit later?"

"Just wanted you to know what's happened."

Tekla took a few steps out into the hallway.

"What?"

"Monica was admitted to A. & E. in some sort of shock. She's in Infectious Diseases."

"Really?" Tekla exclaimed, and immediately began racking her brains to see what she might have missed.

"Hot chocolate for you too, Tekla?" she heard a voice behind her.

"And one other thing, could you take over my shift this evening, I don't feel so hot," Sigurdsdottir asked.

"Sure thing. No problem. I'll call back in a little while," Tekla said and hung up. Carlsson in shock. What could that mean? Something which Tekla had not identified? She debated whether to rush to the hospital or drink hot chocolate with the boy and Jennifer. It would normally have been an easy decision, the hospital would come first. But something in Tekla had changed during the past week. Something had been awakened, something she had not felt before.

NOBEL HOSPITAL

Monday evening, 11 November

When Tekla got back to the hospital, she hurried to change and went up to A. & E. Moussawi came out of the main emergency room wearing an apron covered in blood.

"Anything exciting?" she asked. "I'm standing in for Ragna."

"Where on earth do they recruit the junior doctors from these days?" Moussawi asked, pulling off his apron.

"So the patient died?" Tekla asked.

"No, but the idiot in there may not survive very long in this department."

"O.K.," Tekla said, resisting the urge to lay a soothing hand on Moussawi's shoulder. He was perfectly capable of tearing a strip off her in public. "But aren't you done for the day?"

"You deal with that walking calamity in there," Moussawi said and left the department.

Tekla saw a poor, dejected junior doctor with a well-groomed beard and leaden look come out of the emergency room followed by Cassandra, a nurse she recognised, and one of her colleagues. Cassandra washed her hands and angrily snatched up some paper towels.

"How did it go in there?" Tekla asked.

"Bloody circus."

"Do you mean the senior doctor or the junior?"

Cassandra stared at Tekla. "Both. What a shitty way to treat your younger colleagues! Even when they do mess up, there's no need to humiliate them in front of everyone – including patients and their families."

The department was a shambles, twenty-two patients had yet to be seen and three alarms were going off at the same time. Tekla joined Hassan in Room 2, where he seemed reasonably in control of his patient with liver failure and sepsis.

"Don't forget to do a diagnostic tap of that abdominal fluid," Tekla reminded him, after guiding the young trainee through an ultrasound. The patient was ashen, their blood pressure down and body temperature low. Tekla found herself thinking of her mother in Falun but decided to push that anxiety to the back of her mind by attending to two hip fractures, a nasty burns case and a patient with cystic fibrosis who had been admitted for respiratory support.

Thirty-five minutes later, Tekla had managed to deal with a few knotty cases which Moussawi had been leaving to stew, probably because he had no time for "elderly multi-afflicted shipwrecks", as he liked to call them. She had also helped another doctor with her treatment of a young man whose cardiac insufficiency had worsened.

"Remember to take a good alcohol anamnesis," Tekla said. "One forgets how common alcoholism is."

Her phone rang. Unknown number.

"Tekla Berg."

"It's Emma Nyrén."

"How's Monica doing?"

"That's not why I'm calling. I think we need to meet."

"Because?"

"I think you know."

"No I don't."

"Have you read the evening papers?"

"Every now and then."

"I think you know what I'm talking about. Monica and I want to see you."

Normally, Carlsson herself would have called, so she was either too unwell or her head of communications was acting on her own initiative – though she probably didn't have the guts for that.

"Where shall we meet?"

"Come to I 23."

"Infectious Diseases. Is that where Monica is?"

"I'll see you there in half an hour."

Tekla put away her phone and noticed that Cassandra was standing there, waiting for her.

"Sorry."

"A traffic accident in Room 1."

"Now?"

"Yes."

Tekla's thoughts immediately switched to the hit-and-run victim. Would the next twenty-four hours involve open heart massage or some equally delightful procedure? How many energy drinks did she have in her pocket? Only two. She took one out and drank it while receiving the ambulance crew's report. The patient did not look too badly injured.

"Sixteen-year-old woman riding an e-scooter with a friend. They were hit by a lorry."

Tekla looked at the girl's face. She was pretty, her make-up had run from the tears, but there was no sign of blood. "Any damage to the head?"

"No," the ambulance nurse said and began to undo the straps around the girl's ribcage. "As far as we can tell, only the knee injury."

"But you put on a neck brace because—"

"To be on the safe side. There's quite severe trauma, after all."

Tekla helped to lift the patient across to the stretcher.

"Ow!" she shouted out as they moved over her right leg, which was immobilised in a vacuum mattress.

"Have you given her anything?"

"2.5 milligrammes of morphine I.V." The ambulance nurse patted the young patient's forehead. "And next time, maybe don't give some friend a lift against the traffic flow on Sveavägen, right?"

The young woman grimaced and looked shamefaced.

"Do we know her name?" Tekla asked.

"Tell the doctor, so she'll know you can breathe!" the ambulance nurse called out as she left.

"Kattis."

Tekla began her examination from top to toe.

"Can you please open wide, Kattis? Good. Any pain here in your neck? No . . .? Good."

She picked up her stethoscope and listened to the lungs. No damage to the thorax. It felt good to be examining a patient and delaying the meeting with Emma Nyrén for a while. But as soon as her brain reminded her of the woman up there in the I.C.U. with the failing liver, Tekla felt the pressure building.

As she got close to the knee, Tekla noted that the patient's entire body stiffened.

"Is it broken?" Kattis suddenly asked.

Tekla cautiously loosened the vacuum mattress.

"I think we need more morphine."

The nurse went over to the refrigerator to get some.

"Five milligrammes I.V., please."

She turned to the young woman.

"You were lucky. But your knee's busted."

Tekla tried to hold back the superlatives. The chances were they might not even be able to save the lower leg. There was an open fracture, just below the knee.

"I'm going to see if there's any damage to the blood vessels and the nerves. But you'll have to be operated on today."

By the time the young woman was on her way to Surgery, Tekla was already a quarter of an hour late. She saw Nyrén's upright figure waiting outside I 23.

"We did say half an hour."

"The patient comes first," Tekla replied. She was just about to go into the ward when Nyrén stepped in front of her.

"Just so you know. She's very worked up."

"I've seen it before."

"I mean *very* worked up."

"O.K.," Tekla said, stepping around the head of communications. She made her way to Carlsson's room, one of four singles in the unit. There was a man standing outside whom Tekla did not recognise. He was wearing a tight jacket, jeans and a pale pink shirt.

"Tekla," he said, breaking into a dazzling white smile. The pink shirt signalled business degree rather than the medical profession, it could never belong to a doctor. "Ludwig af Petersén. C.F.O."

"Is she that valuable?" Tekla said.

"How do you mean . . .?"

"Just kidding."

The man with the salmon shirt smiled again. At least he had a slight sense of humour.

"Is Monica in there?"

"Yes, but Emma and I would like to have a word with you afterwards," af Petersén said. Tekla saw that there was a hard edge behind the initial affability.

Carlsson was lying in bed, her hands clasped. It looked as if she had just passed away. The only things missing were the burning candle and a prayer book. She opened her eyes as Tekla stood by her bed.

"You've gone too far this time," Carlsson said in a weak but clear voice.

"How are you feeling?"

Carlsson tried to raise herself from her pillow, but gave up. "What the hell were you thinking when you asked Ragna to contact the media?"

Tekla stood still. What had happened? Sigurdsdottir would never have told on her. How did Carlsson and her sidekicks find out?

"Don't blame it on Ragna."

"I get that too. She'd never have dared do anything so stupid on her own. She's just your puppet."

Carlsson grasped Tekla's forearm. Then she turned and looked over at the door, where Nyrén was standing to attention.

"Please get out."

Nyrén left the room.

"You're playing for high stakes, Tekla. Those vultures out there want me to sacrifice you. It's your good fortune that I have this little infection to deal with. But as soon as I'm back on my feet, you and I have to speak. I need you to do something for me." Tekla noticed how hot Carlsson's hand was. At the same time, her face was pale, glistening as if someone had poured cooking oil over her.

"Let's see what comes of all this. But for now, you'll have to face the inquisition out there. For appearances' sake."

Hearing these surprisingly mild words, Tekla couldn't help but feel privileged. By rights, Carlsson should be sacking her on the spot. She had gone behind her back again, but been given a respite, been spared. There was no telling how long the grace period would last, but still. They had clearly established some measure of trust, which was now paying dividends. But Tekla couldn't drop poor Sigurdsdottir in it.

"Let Ragna be."

"She's off on maternity leave so there won't be any problems," Carlsson said.

"Hope you get better soon."

"It's just an infection. The doctors here know what they're doing."

"When it comes to infections, yes," Tekla said, sounding sceptical. There was something about the lab results that didn't add up.

"Go out to the wolves now," Carlsson said.

"Just one last question," Tekla asked. "How did you manage to hush up the fact that the American patient died at the N.S.K.? I figured Hanna Parida would have had a field day feeding all that to the media."

Carlsson slowly turned her pale face towards Tekla. "Mum's the word, right?"

"Absolutely."

"I'm going to let Hanna have Paediatric Oncology at the N.S.K."

"But I thought you weren't prepared to give up any research. Isn't that exactly what the economists out there want you to do? Why are you accommodating them?"

"It's all about controlling the narrative. I'm the C.E.O., I decide when things are done and why. And I decided that Hanna gets Oncology if she can keep her mouth shut."

"You scratch my back, I scratch yours," Tekla said.

"What else is there?" Carlsson said with a cautious smile.

Tekla left the hospital C.E.O.

"Let's try and find a room," Nyrén said as Tekla emerged. She looked around. Tekla suspected that she'd never set foot in any of the wards. The head of communications seemed to suffer from an intense fear of bacteria.

"I don't think anyone's listening in," Tekla said, sitting down on the armrest of one of the chairs in the corridor.

"Now that Monica's sick, I'm the acting hospital C.E.O.," af Petersén began.

"It's not as though she's lost her wits," Tekla countered.

Nyrén and af Petersén exchanged a quick, knowing glance. "No, but right now we need to let her be a patient and, from what I understand, you and she have developed a special relationship."

Tekla could not stop herself smiling. "Have we indeed? Is that common knowledge in central admin, or what?"

Af Petersén ignored the jibe. "It's very reassuring to have Monica looked after by our professional doctors, including yourself, Tekla. But . . . and we'd appreciate it if you'd let us know if you notice Monica starting to behave strangely. If she's contemplating anything radical . . ."

"Radical? How do you mean?"

"It's in everyone's interest for Monica to get well as soon as possible but we don't want her holding back any of her wisdom."

"So you want me to spy on her? What did you say your job title was? Head of which branch of the Stasi?" Tekla got up.

"We think you understand that we want what's best for the

hospital, Tekla," af Petersén's voice could be heard behind her. Did she detect a trace of desperation there?

Tekla's mobile rang. Unknown number. She rarely answered those, but today she didn't want to miss anything that might be relevant to the woman in the I.C.U.

"Tekla Berg?"

"Yes, that's me."

"I'm Kristina Olsson and I'm calling from A. & E. at Falun Hospital."

Tekla froze.

"Hello?"

"I'm still here," she managed to say.

"Well, I'm a doctor here and I just wanted to tell you that we've admitted your mother, who's been transferred from her residential home. She's been having trouble breathing, and also a temperature these last few days. We suspect she has pneumonia. So we're now giving her antibio—"

"What was the C.R.P.?" Tekla broke in.

"Err . . . C.R.P. at 325."

"And the creatinine?"

"It was probably high . . . just a moment . . . it's 180. We're also giving her—"

"Ringer. I understand. Has she had Cefotaxime?"

"Yes."

"And anything for atypical bacteria?"

"I haven't had time to check with our infectious diseases consultant yet, but maybe we should do that."

"Give her Avelox too. She's had mycoplasma before."

"It sounds like you work in healthcare," the doctor said.

"At the Nobel Hospital in Stockholm."

"We'll look after your mother and give her the best possible care. But if her condition were to worsen—"

"You won't put her in Intensive Care," Tekla interrupted. "I understand. You've written a limitation of treatment protocol on the basis that she has serious dementia because of her Huntington's."

"But we'll do everything else, just not intubate her."

"I know," Tekla said. "Which ward is she going to?"

"Department 23."

"O.K.," Tekla said. "Thanks for calling."

She ended the call, wondering where it would be quickest for her to rent a car. Everything else could wait. She knew where it was all heading.

NOBEL HOSPITAL

Monday evening, 11 November

Tekla scanned the area outside A. & E. but there was no police car to be seen. Around her, people were shaking the rain off their umbrellas and hurrying into the warmth. November was showing off its worst side. Tekla was just about to turn back when a car about twenty metres away hooted, then flashed its headlights. She couldn't see the driver but she took a chance, yanking open the door and diving into the passenger seat. Despite the short distance, she was already soaked from head to toe.

"Thought you had a police car."

Silva chuckled. "I see – no, it's been a long time since I went on patrol. And they were hard, uncomfortable cars. No thanks."

This car did indeed have nice seats. It smelled of tobacco and aftershave and she noticed that the superintendent was even wearing a jacket and a freshly ironed shirt.

"What make is this? It looks old."

"Citroën BX. Once it dies on me, I'll quit driving."

It was warm and cosy in the car. For the first time that day, Tekla felt she could relax. All she was missing was a bomb for her headaches. What would Silva say if he saw her Lypsyl? She got out an energy drink and took a few sips.

"I thought it would be better to talk outside the hospital," Silva said. He peered out through the rain, leaning forward to try to look up at the hospital roof, as if he were expecting a helicopter to land.

"I don't think they can hear us from here," Tekla said.

Silva opened a sachet of chewing gum and popped three into his mouth.

"You'd be surprised."

"About what?"

Silva held up his blue cigarette packet. "Do you mind?"

"Go ahead."

He pushed in the cigarette lighter on the old French dashboard. Ten seconds later, a fiery red circle lit up the darkness, which Silva held to the tip of his cigarette. "Do you know where dioxin comes from?"

"Well ... industry. Chemicals which factories release into the natural environment, fat-soluble. I imagine we absorb them through fish, for example?" Tekla had not had time to do much research on dioxin, but she quickly ran through the half page on toxicology in the textbook they had read in medical school.

"To get that chlor ... those blisters in the face you were talking about ..."

"Chloracne. Tissue samples were sent to Umeå today."

"Chloracne – you'd have to eat a few tonnes of dioxin-contaminated fish that have been swimming around inside a seriously polluted factory."

"And ...?"

"I mentioned your suspicions to my boss, which wasn't perhaps such a clever idea."

Tekla's fingers were itching to get at that Lypsyl in her pocket. "You're speaking in riddles. My friend Ragna always accuses me of that. I'm beginning to understand why it irritates her."

"So presumably ... if it really is chloracne and the tests do show high levels of dioxin, then ... well, we'll have to assume that somebody tried to poison her."

"With dioxin?"

"Nobody in Sweden has access to such large volumes of dioxin."

"Not in Sweden, you say?"

"Not in Sweden, no," Silva said, taking a deep puff.

Tekla tried to get her thoughts into some kind of order. They shot off in different directions but kept coming back with one over-arching question: when would the woman get a new liver? Tekla had, after all, promised the boy that his mother would survive. Now wasn't the time to worry about the source of the dioxin, and besides, she knew too little about it. "So, what, somebody from abroad might have tried to poison her?"

Silva punched the steering wheel gently with his clenched fist in a restrained gesture of aggression.

"Well, they've got the N.O.D. involved anyway." He was angry. He didn't want to hand the investigation over to the security police.

Tekla thought back to that summer, when the burns victim from Söder Tower had been suspected of being a terrorist. "We know all about them, don't we?"

"Anyhow, they're coming to the hospital. Maybe this evening. But I was thinking . . ." There was something Silva seemed reluctant to say.

"I've got to get back to the I.C.U., so if you . . ."

"Would it be O.K. for me to call you sort of unofficially every now and then, do you think?"

"You mean privately?" Tekla asked.

"Not privately, more that . . . I'm sure you understand. I don't want Rebecka Nilsén to know what I'm up to."

"You want to continue investigating the woman's identity but you're afraid that the N.O.D. will see you off."

Silva looked relieved. He took another deep drag on his cigarette.

"I don't understand why you can't work together," Tekla said. "Why all these barriers between you?"

Silva just shook his head in resignation. His body language said it all. It was evidently a law of nature.

Once Tekla was back inside the hospital, she called Infectious Diseases at Falun Hospital. After a few minutes, she got to speak to the nurse who was responsible for her mother.

"Tekla Berg, Karin's daughter."

"Hi. It's good that you called," a calm voice said in a broad Dalarna accent.

"How's my mother getting on?"

"She opened her eyes this evening and managed to swallow a few mouthfuls of water."

"So it sounds like she's feeling a little better?"

The nurse didn't reply, someone in the background interrupted her. "Yes, hello, sorry. Karin is feeling a bit better, like I said, but we think it would be very good if somebody from the family could come and visit her."

Tekla sent a bitter thought off to her mother's brother, Uncle Bertil, who had broken off all contact with his sister more than twenty years earlier. So the family that was supposed to "come and visit" consisted solely of Tekla and Simon.

"I know. I really will try to come up."

"Well you never know, after all."

Tekla heard what the nurse was trying to tell her, but chose to interpret the situation to suit her current needs.

"True, but it sounds like she's stable right now, doesn't it?"

"We'll take it one hour at a time," the nurse said, finishing the call.

Tekla kept walking up to the I.C.U. So far, no sign of any plain-clothes N.O.D. security police officers. Everything was calm, the evening lighting subdued. Tekla didn't bother to look for the I.C.U. doctor in charge but went straight to the woman's room. No decision seemed to have been taken on the degree of isolation; the sign simply said "Isolated. Infectious." Tekla put on a mask and plastic clothes. A nurse sitting in the room was wearing far more kit, a face shield and yellow boots.

"Hi. I'm Tekla Berg from A. & E."

"You'd best put on some more P.P.E."

"Really?" Tekla asked as she walked up to the woman. "Do you have any idea what she's been infected with? Dioxin isn't exactly transmitted through the air from person to person."

The nurse was getting to her feet but sat down again. "No, we don't know anything. But we're all very unhappy."

"Why?"

"Because *we*, who are supposed to look after her, aren't being told anything. Is it radioactive or what?"

Tekla gave a laugh. "Not at all. She's only a danger to herself. How's it going?"

The nurse laid her phone aside on the windowsill. "No urine production. We've put her on continuous dialysis. And liver dialysis too, but it's not having any effect."

Tekla lifted the sheet and saw how the blisters had spread down to the breasts and arms. The face was covered in grey-brown spots. They were small to medium-large with a reddish base. Some appeared to be filled with liquid, but for the rest it looked as if someone had poured a sandy slush over her face and it had then hardened.

Tekla stroked the woman's pimpled cheek. Who was she? Why had she been subjected to this? Her thoughts drifted to the boy again. Might he also have dioxin in him? But in that case, he too would be sick. And the dead man, had he too been poisoned? Tekla could probably leave that to the N.O.D. people. She saw that the woman's eyes were sunken – dried out – while at the same time her hands were swollen because of the low albumin levels. She was caught in a vicious circle and there was only one way out: a new liver.

"And the blood gases?"

"The pH has been parked around 7.1 and lactate between seven and ten."

"Not compatible with life." Tekla could see what was happening: nothing. And it stressed her enormously. They had reached deadlock, with Carlsson laid up in Infectious Diseases, incapacitated and under Nyström's control. The article in the evening newspaper had lit a fire which Carlsson's smarmy head of communications had unfortunately managed to put out. Tekla had not got the conflagration she needed. Now there was only one thing to do.

"Let's keep our fingers crossed," Tekla said and left the room. The adrenalin was in full flow, she wanted to snatch up the nearest scalpel and dig that sick liver out. She spotted Elmqvist's frizzy hair over in one of the glass cubicles. Tekla slipped into the sterilisation room, which happened to be empty just then. A sliding door slowly closed. Two large dishwashers, a long aluminium counter and masses of healthcare equipment. Tekla took out her mobile.

"I'm sorry I'm calling so late."

"No problem," Bjarni said.

"The woman who needs a new liver, she's not doing too well."

"So I heard. Our transplant surgeons have offered to take her on, but it's been vetoed by the powers that be. I don't really know what's happened."

"But I do. And it doesn't matter, we can't let them kill her off. She needs the liver now."

"So what do you want me to do, Tekla?"

"If I fix transport for tomorrow morning, can you make sure there's a surgeon there to receive her?"

"But we need a new liver, you can't just take out the old one and—"

"She can have half of mine."

"What did you say?"

"She can have half of my liver. Or a lobe or two or whatever's needed. I've checked, we're the same blood group."

Bjarni let out some strange little sounds, a mixture of sneezes and laughs. "You're crazy, Tekla."

"Not at all. I'll manage fine on half a liver."

"But that's not how one does it, she has to have a whole one."

"I know. But if she gets none at all, she'll die. So better one lobe than nothing. Then we can continue hunting for a new liver later on, once we know who she is and we can show those idiots up there that she's not a junkie."

"I don't know . . ."

"Yes you do. I just need you to find a surgeon who can operate on her. And on me."

"You *are* crazy, Tekla."

"Sure. I am crazy, let's just agree on that, but will you do it?"

"O.K."

"Great. Tell Ragna I'll call tomorrow to check how she is." Tekla hung up and sneaked out of Intensive Care. She needed to go home and rest, if she was to undergo the small matter of a liver operation the following day. She had already established that Nowak would be happy to transport the woman. And Elmqvist wouldn't be working tomorrow, so she couldn't scupper their plan. A rescue mission. She just needed to recharge her batteries.

SÖDERMALM, STOCKHOLM

Monday evening, 11 November

Tekla was still sweating after her hot shower when the doorbell rang. It was ten at night, she hadn't had time to eat and wanted nothing more than to get into bed as quickly as possible, perhaps read some articles about dioxin, then round off the day with a bomb and two Stilnoct. Could it be a neighbour? She considered ignoring the doorbell when she heard the annoying sound again. She pulled on a hoodie and her checked pyjama bottoms and opened the door.

"Magnus?"

"Doughnuts instead of a bedtime sandwich?" He held out a bag from 7-Eleven. "Actually, the most you eat is like coffee filters, right?" He broke into his warm smile, free of any undertone or accusation.

Before Tekla had time to be angry or disappointed, her heart conquered her head as a wave of positive energy unexpectedly washed over her.

"Sure. Come in." It was too late to think about underwear or ruffled hair. If he chose to appear like this, out of the blue, he had only himself to blame.

"Coffee or tea?"

"Tea, please," Lundgren said. "I can't sleep if I drink coffee after eight. Getting old."

Tekla put on a pair of IKEA down slippers and switched on the kettle.

Lundgren was tactful enough not to take a look around the untidy apartment. He sat on a bar stool in the kitchen, took off his wet cap and ran his fingers through his thick mane a few times.

"Your hair's grown," Tekla said, setting out two cups. She was surprised to feel so happy over an unexpected visit. Doubly so that it was Lundgren who gave her that joy.

"When I'd finished my rehab, I was put on administrative duties, so I didn't have to be quite so commando for a bit." He sucked in his stomach and ran his hand over his denim shirt. "The only problem is all the bloody weight you put on if you don't move. All this workplace rehab's a bugger, it should come with a free gym membership."

Tekla patted her own flat stomach. "Luckily I have an active job."

"I don't think you need worry, even if you did sit around doing nothing for the rest of your life you wouldn't get fat."

Tekla thought about her mother's stick-like legs. Her father's bloated belly contained mostly liquid, but the rest of his body had also been skinny. She got out two mint tea bags and poured boiling water over them. "Not too fancy, I'm afraid."

"Perfect," Lundgren said, placing the doughnuts on a chopping board, after discreetly removing a few old cheese rinds.

"I'm sorry I didn't—"

"No problem," Lundgren interrupted. "Honestly, no problem."

"I just want to say—"

"That you've been ignoring my calls. I know. And I get it. That's you. Tekla. And that's what everyone likes about you. That you do your own thing. Integrity and all that."

Tekla fiddled nervously with a teabag and swallowed heavily. Those were big words to be contending with on an ordinary weekday evening. Why didn't he just meet up with some friends, go out into the bars and restaurants on Stureplan and get it together with some busty blonde? At the same time, she couldn't help wondering how she would feel if she found out that that was exactly what he had done. If for once she were honest with herself, she'd like nothing more than to go off on that weekend trip with Lundgren. She hadn't had sex for . . . my God.

"So you're feeling . . . well?" she finally asked.

"Everything's fine. I got rid of the colostomy bag some months ago. They shut down my gut, as they put it. I thought it sounded so funny, shut down . . . And you can live without a spleen, can't you?"

Tekla wondered what the scar would look like after a liver operation. How long would she be out of action? And would there be a job for her to come back to, after what she was about to do? Presumably not. She would have to look for work as a locum in Norway in the spring.

"Yes, you don't need one. It just means that when you're older, you have to get a pneumococcal vaccination."

"I am old," Lundgren joked, with a liberating burst of laughter. "That means I can eat as many doughnuts as I like. Here."

Tekla took a warm one and wiped the sugar from her lips.

"And you? How's it going at the hospital?"

Strangely enough she didn't feel like telling him about any medical cases, but she still found herself saying: "Same same. Lots to do. And right now, one case which really has me interested."

"I can imagine. And Simon?"

Tekla felt a weight like a bag of sand on her shoulders. Simon. Her mother. Falun.

"He's well. Still in Spain in rehab."

"Sounds nice. Why don't you go down there and chill out in the sun for a bit?"

"You think I look pale?"

"Yes."

Tekla punched his shoulder. "Bastard."

"Ouch!"

They laughed. Tekla wanted to tell him about her mother, about the row with Klas Nyström and the N.O.D.'s involvement in the case. She wanted to bring Lundgren up-to-date on everything. But the urge just to feel normal for once proved stronger than anything else. She took a large gulp of tea and a sugary bite of her doughnut and relaxed her shoulders slightly.

"Let's go sit on the sofa? Maybe check out a series?"

NOBEL HOSPITAL
Tuesday morning, 12 November

Tekla fastened the velcro strip on the lead apron. Her thoughts went to the *Chernobyl* T.V. series, which she and Lundgren had started the night before. "They're prepping an older patient with chest pains who I was looking after in casualty just now. Usually takes a few minutes." She had a hollow feeling in the pit of her stomach. Not surprising, given that she'd been fasting since the previous evening.

Silva took off his black, shiny coat and pulled at his sweaty shirt. "How can you lot keep so many balls in the air at the same time?"

"You lot?" Tekla asked, wrestling with her lead thyroid collar. She felt as if she were about to choke.

"You doctors. You're a strange breed."

Tekla had never considered that before. Did doctors share common characteristics? She took out an energy drink but remembered that she was meant to be fasting and put it back in her pocket. How was this going to go, Tekla wondered. She already had a headache and not the faintest idea when the operation would take place. In all likelihood she had a long and painful day before her.

Silva's phone rang just as a large door slid open and a nurse in a lead apron looked out. "Five minutes. We're just putting out the sterile cloths."

"Good," Tekla said.

Silva sounded irritated: "I see. No. If you must. We're in . . . X-ray, something called Lab G 9." He put away his phone. "Overbearing fucking cow."

"What?" Tekla wasn't surprised to hear him swear, it suited him admirably, she'd just never heard him so unfiltered before.

"You'll see."

"Do you have any more information about the woman?" Tekla asked. At the same time she made a mental check list of everything that had to fall into place throughout the day: Nowak, the ambulance, the transplant surgeon at the N.S.K.

Silva stroked his unshaven cheek. "It might be better if you focus on the medical side of things."

"Tell me."

"I've already given you far too much information which you shouldn't—"

"If you were sure about where to draw the line you probably wouldn't be here," Tekla said.

Silva hesitated. "But you understand that what I'm telling you has to remain—"

"Between us," Tekla interrupted him. "I wasn't born yesterday."

"No, that's for sure."

"So, what have you found?"

"The blood on the front of the Škoda was the man's. The car was a rental, from Hertz."

"A rental, what does that tell us?"

"Anyone's guess."

The nurse stuck out her head. "Should we be giving her anything beforehand?"

"Just three milligrammes of Stesolid," Tekla replied without having to think. "You also have to check the man for dioxin," she said to Silva.

"That has come up, but we have to see if we can get tissue samples. I hope Forensics haven't got rid of the body."

Another door opened. Tekla immediately recognised the colourful policewoman from the N.O.D.

"Well, what a delightful surprise," Rebecka Nilsén said, proffering her hand to Tekla. Nilsén also introduced a younger colleague. "Alba Linnander, also from the N.O.D."

"Alvaro," Nilsén continued, in a much more serious tone.

"Rebecka," Silva replied, without meeting her eyes.

Even though she had so much else on her mind, Tekla could not help feeling intrigued. Was there a hint of a personal relationship between them? A love affair?

"We're nearly done," the nurse said through the sliding door.

"O.K., I have to be there when they go in."

"Go in where?" Nilsén asked. She was wearing a yellow-and-black patterned skirt, an elegant, short jacket and a glossy blouse. If Tekla hadn't already known better, she would have guessed she was a cultural journalist or something similar.

"A subacute coronary angiogram, S.T.-elevation myocardial infarction and . . ." Tekla realised that what she had said was incomprehensible. "An eighty-year-old woman with acute heart failure. I'm only there to see that it doesn't stop altogether during the intervention."

"Jesus," Nilsén said, sounding as if she meant it. "Hope it goes well. My old mother had atrial fibrillation."

"*That's* a different condition," Tekla said, and bit her lip for the second time. Linnander, whose manner was a little more formal than Nilsén's, and who didn't appear to be particulary impressed by medical terms, whispered something in Nilsén's ear.

"Absolutely," Nilsén said. "We'll leave you to your patients. And all the rest will be handled by us together with Superintendent Silva."

"Tekla is very closely involved in everything that concerns the woman with the dioxin poisoning and—"

"Hold on," Nilsén interrupted, lowering her voice. "We don't know that dioxin is in any way relevant to the case. You mustn't go around talking about it."

"But it *is* dioxin," Tekla said, hearing the sliding door open behind her.

"Are you coming, Tekla?" the X-ray nurse said.

Tekla raised a hand. "One second." She turned to Nilsén. "Have the results from Umeå come back yet?"

"You stick to your patients and Alba and I will look after the dioxin side of things. From now, that's the N.O.D.'s responsibility, no-one else's." Nilsén's not-so-subtle message to Silva did not pass Tekla by. The battle lines were drawn in no uncertain terms. "We've put two guards on the patient up there. And we sent tissue samples from the man she killed."

"Guards? What are you talking about?" Tekla burst out.

Alba made as if to break in but Nilsén held up her hand. "Alvaro will no longer be part of this investigation."

Tekla was utterly fed up with the constant turf wars, especially now that she'd managed to get Silva on her side.

"I'm not letting this go," Silva said out loud as he walked towards the door. He swore when he couldn't find the button to open it.

"Tekla!" the X-ray nurse said.

"I have to . . ."

"Of course," Nilsén said. "Don't worry about Alvaro, he can be like that sometimes."

Tekla did not answer but followed the nurse through to the operating theatre. The elderly woman had been suffering from two constrictions, which had now been opened up with angioplasty. Tekla could therefore forget about this case, the one unstable patient in A. & E. that morning, and concentrate on her own project. Nowak had promised to take time off after lunch and Tekla had found an ambulance nurse who was willing to help with the transport. The official story was that he was borrowing the ambulance in order to wash it. Tekla had promised to be his personal doctor for ever to thank him for all the trouble. By this stage, she owed quite a lot of people. That left only one challenge – the operating team at the N.S.K. According to Bjarni, everything would be ready and Tekla need not worry. Hanna Parida would sanction anything that might cause trouble for Carlsson. An operating theatre with a full team would be no problem.

Tekla would have to rely on the fact that all who were involved had their own reasons for helping out: favours given or favours owed, she didn't mind which, so long as the patient got a new liver that day.

She had a dizzy spell in the lift going up to the I.C.U., when it sunk in whose liver the woman was actually going to get. Or at least half of it. She had taken a long shower and scrubbed herself more thoroughly than ever in preparation for the operation. The results of the tests which she had taken on herself had been fine, apart from a slightly low blood count, which was hardly a surprise. She needed a more balanced diet. That would have to wait until after the operation, when she would need to take good care of what was left of her liver. The only thing she worried about was the potential effect of her amphetamine consumption on the anaesthesia. She had increased her intake recently, though she couldn't take any today, obviously, because she was fasting. She felt tired and sluggish, and her headaches were getting worse by the hour. What if her blood pressure suddenly dropped while she was being anaesthetised? Would she have the courage to tell the anaesthetist about the bombs? No, that would be too embarrassing. Then again, the patient was key: she must not take any risks when it came to her.

Nyström and Nowak were standing outside the entrance to the I.C.U. Tekla was determined to ignore them but they appeared to be discussing something serious.

"Tekla," Nyström said. There was an unfamiliar note of respect in his tone. "Have you heard about Monica?"

"What's happened?"

"She's here," Nowak said.

"In Intensive Care?"

"She was transferred this morning because her blood pressure was falling. We've done everything we can."

Tekla wanted to walk straight in to the hospital C.E.O. to ask how she was, but Nyström took her by the arm. "She's been asking after you."

"Let go of me, then."

Nyström maintained his grip. "She's very fragile. You'll have to choose your words with care."

Tekla pulled herself loose. She pushed open the doors to the

I.C.U. and continued along the corridor. She heard Nyström and Nowak following her. "Where?"

"Room 1," Nowak said. "But you can relax. We have the situation under control. This is the I.C.U., after all."

Tekla went over to Room 1 and put on a plastic apron and gloves in the airlock. She had the gravest doubts about the ability of all these super-specialists to think outside the box. After all, Carlsson had been to see both gastro experts and neurological gurus, and not one of them had been able to work out what was wrong with her.

"How goes it?" Tekla asked as she stood by Carlsson's bedside.

Carlsson struggled to open her eyes and seemed to have trouble focusing on Tekla's voice. "Things . . . could be better."

Tekla read the blood pressure off the screen. She turned to Nowak. "You have to increase the noradrenaline."

"We're doing that," he said.

"It'll be alright," Tekla said to Carlsson. "It's septic shock, but you're getting the right treatment." Tekla could hear herself saying the words, but at the same time felt there was something wrong with the whole picture. Low blood pressure, despite the right antibiotics and fluids. Something was pecking away behind Tekla's frontal bone. But there were too many plates spinning for her to be able to see everything clearly.

"I hope so. Gregor . . ."

"Yes, Gregor. Where's her husband? Have you called?"

"He's on his way," Nowak answered. Tekla stole a look at Nyström, who was anxiously wringing his hands.

"The woman . . ." Carlsson said. Her lips were dry and cracked, her face ashen, worse than before.

"Don't worry," Tekla said.

Carlsson managed to rustle up a discreet smile. "Not . . . me . . . worrying. You . . ."

"Yes, but it doesn't—"

"Klas will operate."

"What?" Nyström burst out.

"You're to give her . . . a new . . . liver."

"But didn't we say that—" Nyström tried.

"I'm still in charge."

"Yes, but—"

"Just do it!" Carlsson hissed.

Tekla felt overwhelming gratitude towards Carlsson for indirectly backing her by finally siding with the patient. At the same time, warning bells were ringing. Nyström would never find a new liver in time, nor would he accept Tekla's donating half hers.

Nyström stormed out of the room. Carlsson waved to Tekla to bend down.

"Don't trust Ludwig."

"Which Ludwig?"

"Af Petersén. He's a snake. He's trying to tell me how I should run my hospital."

"O.K.," Tekla replied, not sure what to do with that information, given the circumstances.

Carlsson turned her face away and closed her eyes.

Bloody hell, Tekla thought. Was Carlsson going to die? What impact would that have on the balance of power in the hospital? There was something not quite right about the septicemia diagnosis, wasn't there? It had to do with the lab list, that much she knew. And something that someone said about Carlsson. Or that she had done. Tekla had to concentrate, but that was impossible without either amphetamine or caffeine in her system. Gastro, neuro, an infection and now the I.C.U. How come none of these specialists were capable of looking beyond their own little patch?

But first she had to save the woman. She thought about the boy. How would she explain to him that he had lost both his parents? She couldn't let that happen. The woman had to be saved, come what may. If only Sigurdsdottir wasn't so pregnant. Tekla could have done with the support of her best friend to stop herself going to pieces.

NOBEL HOSPITAL AND N.S.K. HOSPITAL
Tuesday, 12 November

Tekla stood in the hall, waiting for the ambulance. Nowak was on his way down with the woman. Bjarni had messaged that the operating theatre would soon be ready to receive them. The anaesthetist had asked if Tekla had fasted for the operation, which she could unhappily confirm. She was finding it hard to concentrate on her various concerns: Nyström's annoying presence, Carlsson's illness, her mother in Falun Hospital, Lundgren, Simon's absence . . . Her brain was on fire, it was more than enough for a complete meltdown. Amphetamine would have allowed her to put some order into her thoughts. Just so long as her body could take the anaesthesia . . .

The doors to the arrival hall opened and an ambulance drove in. At the same time, Nowak appeared, accompanied by a junior nurse from the I.C.U., who was wheeling a bed with a portable respirator.

"Her pressure's falling," he said, fidgeting with the monitoring equipment. The paramedic and his colleague immediately helped to get the patient over onto the ambulance stretcher.

"But she'll make it?" Tekla asked nervously.

"She's unstable," Nowak answered. "I've just started an adrenalin drip."

Tekla was dreading the operation. Both for herself and for the patient. "They'll have to fill her up with more blood before they start," she said.

Nowak didn't answer, he was too busy installing the patient in the ambulance. After a few intense minutes, everything was ready for departure.

"So where do I sit?" Tekla asked.

"You'll probably have to take a taxi," the paramedic said. The vehicle was undeniably full.

"O.K., but . . ."

"We have the situation under control," Nowak said.

"I know," Tekla answered. "Thanks for doing this."

"You helped me with the lumbar puncture."

Tekla smiled. "A big favour, that."

"A favour's a favour. See you at the N.S.K.," Nowak said, pulling the sliding doors shut.

Tekla hurried out to the A. & E. reception and on to the hospital entrance. Outside, there was a line of waiting taxis. She hopped into one and leaned forward.

"N.S.K. Quickly please."

The driver pressed a few buttons and drove off. Not fast enough, but Tekla used the time to try and sort her thoughts. She considered taking a bomb, but restrained herself, enduring the pain in her head.

Twenty-one minutes later, the taxi stopped outside the main entrance to the N.S.K. Tekla jumped out and grabbed her mobile. She called Bjarni and was given directions to the operating theatre. She had never been to the N.S.K. before – it looked as if you needed a drone to find your way. The entrance hall was enormous, with steel and glass everywhere.

Tekla broke into a run. She was sweating and had the taste of blood in her mouth. She tried ringing Nowak, but there was no answer, so she asked at the desk for directions to Surgery.

She felt both hungry and nauseous at the same time. How the hell was she going to cope with an operation, she wondered? A glucose drip would be necessary. The anaesthetists would understand, it was all a bit ad hoc after all. But why wasn't Nowak picking up? They should have arrived by now.

She took the elevators up to the right floor. Glass, glass and still more glass everywhere. How did they manage when it was sunny outside and not overcast like today?

"Where's Surgery?" she asked a nurse dressed in blue, who

showed the way to the next corridor. Tekla jogged on. She wondered how many bags of blood she would need during the operation. Two seemed reasonable. As far as she could recall, a liver operation caused a fair amount of bleeding.

Tekla stopped and looked down at the motorway. The heavy traffic advanced slowly, like a train rolling along. She called Nowak again and this time he answered.

"Where are you?" Tekla asked. She could hear the noise of traffic in the background.

"We had complications . . ."

"What do you mean?" Tekla wasn't sure if she'd heard right.

"She had a cardiac arrest," Nowak shouted.

"What are you talking about?"

"A cardiac arrest. The woman's heart stopped."

"I know what a cardiac arrest is but . . . where are you?"

"We're on Centralbron Bridge."

"Centralbron! What the hell are you doing there, you're meant to . . ."

"She's dead," Nowak yelled. Tekla had never heard him raise his voice before.

"What do you mean, dead? Cardiac arrest, you said, all you have to do is—"

"Listen, Tekla," Nowak cut in through the noise of the traffic. "She began to bleed in the tube, I sucked and sucked but it wouldn't stop. She must have lost two litres just like that, and it all ended up in the lungs. We've been doing C.P.R. for a quarter of an hour but it's no good. Asystole. She's dead."

"You've got to keep going!" Tekla shouted, so loudly that several passers-by stopped. "Bring her here so they can operate with L.U.C.A.S."

"No, Tekla. It's over. She's dead."

Nowak hung up. Tekla closed her eyes. She thought of her father, tried to retain an image of him sitting by the kitchen table and smiling. When he was still alive and well.

STOCKHOLM
Tuesday, 12 November

Sleet, like an ice-cold shower curtain, whipped across Tekla's face. She had borrowed a rescue jacket from the Nobel A. & E. before jumping into the taxi, but it didn't protect her head. Walking over Solnabron Bridge, she balanced right on the outer edge of the pavement to avoid being impaled by open umbrellas. She pulled the zipper up to her chin and stepped straight into a puddle by a street crossing. It didn't matter. Nothing mattered right now.

As if in a trance, Tekla continued past Sankt Eriksplan and on towards Fridhelmsplan. The transparent snowflakes did not survive long after landing on the wet asphalt. Tekla put her hands over her ears to shut out the squeaking sound of the windscreen wipers on the cars creeping by on Fleminggatan. She tried to think of something positive, her warm bed, but that was soon supplanted by her mother, ill in hospital. She tried with Simon on a beach, but all that came to mind was her conversation with Nowak, when he'd confirmed the woman's death.

Tekla turned right by the Norrmalmsgallerian shopping centre and briefly considered going inside for the warmth, but she wanted to feel the pain in her frozen feet, to have the snow lash against her face. She would have gladly plunged her hand into a meat grinder. She needed to experience a greater agony than the woman had when she fell to the floor with convulsive cramps. Down on Norr Mälarstrand she got confused and had to concentrate to be able to see the map before her. The quickest way was for her to cross the street and walk into Rålambshovsparken. In the distance, a solitary person could be seen taking a dog for a walk. Apart from that, nobody was braving the biting wind. Flecks of foam ran across the waves over to the left on Riddarfjärden. Tekla took shelter up against one of the concrete bridge supports. Debated whether she should just head home and go to bed. Or call Lundgren – it had been wonderful to fall asleep on his knee while they watched old episodes of *The Wire*, which he had never seen. But nothing seemed to hold any meaning at the moment. And the worst was still to come: having to tell the boy that he had now lost both his parents.

Tekla continued up to Västerbron Bridge. The wind was blowing so hard from the side that she imagined herself being thrown over the parapet and down into the black water. At the far end of the bridge, she turned left, avoiding the gusts of wind by taking to the back streets. With each step, her feet hurt a little more, which gave her strength. She was sweating as well now, an ice-cold damp layer settled over her skin as she made her shivering way between families with prams and couples heading towards one or other of the many restaurants in the district. It occurred to Tekla that she ought to be famished, but more from a logical analysis of how long it had been since she last ate than any physical sensation.

At Zinkensdamm, she nevertheless went into the Co-op and wandered around aimlessly for a few minutes before picking up three energy drinks and a chocolate wafer. Standing at the sweet counter, she couldn't help but smile when she imagined Carlsson stuffing herself with liquorice monkeys.

Tekla paid and paused inside the swing doors. Her feet were slowly thawing out, making them ache even more. One energy drink, half the chocolate wafer and then another energy drink helped to boost the surge of adrenalin from the pain. Passers-by stared at her, perhaps wondering if she was a mental patient who had escaped from hospital.

She crumpled up the receipt and rolled it between the palms of her hands. Then flicked it away and left the shop.

The Zinkensdamm sports ground lay empty, awaiting the right temperature for the start of the bandy season in a few weeks' time.

Tekla had never worn a pair of skates, not after seeing Simon fall and break his wrist. No ice sports for her, thank you very much, it was like water, only with a different consistency.

On her way up the steps to the Nobel Hospital, she felt a definite tightness across her chest. For a brief moment she wondered if it might be a heart attack, but then dismissed that as illogical. As soon as she started to taste blood in her mouth, everything felt better. Because she was so hopelessly unfit, some airsacs in her lungs had burst. An oddly reassuring thought.

Tekla arrived just in time for the change of shift up in the I.C.U. Evening was turning to night. Lengthy handover reports and careful notes on A4 paper with preprinted headings. She had popped two bombs into her mouth in the lift but not yet swallowed. The paper was beginning to dissolve, releasing a bitter taste.

"Well, look who's here," Elmqvist said, glancing up.

Tekla was unsure what she was referring to. The mere fact of her presence, or "look who's here" as in "Piotr told me what happened".

"How is she?" Tekla managed to say, picking up her third energy drink and draining it greedily. "How's she feeling?"

"Who?"

"Monica, of course."

"Tekla, shouldn't you go home and get some rest? It's been a tough day."

"Holding back your answer isn't going to make it any better."

Elmqvist got to her feet and left the night duty doctor with the nurses. Tekla followed, and the doors slid silently shut behind them. "She's intubated and her blood pressure is dreadful."

Tekla pulled off the drenched rescue jacket and let it fall to the floor. The caffeine and amphetamine were beginning to take effect, the molecules landing on thirsty receptors, her brain finally starting to function. Tekla saw lab lists before her. Carlsson's sodium had been low and her potassium high a few days ago. The values had only got worse.

"Are you giving her antibiotics?"

"Of course. And we've added something to cover atypical bacteria."

"Good." The thought of Nowak's failed rescue attempts on Centralbron still haunted her. She used her anger to heighten her concentration on Carlsson's condition. It was as if more and more generators supplying her brain were being switched on. She continued her scrutiny of the morning's lab results. Relatively low infection parameters, and no growth in any of the blood cultures, so far. It might take time, but the overall picture didn't suggest a normal septic shock. She tried to understand what the insistent bird pecking away inside her skull wanted. It was something that Tekla was searching for, something she had heard or seen.

Her phone rang. Tekla was just about to decline the call when she saw that it was from Falun Hospital.

"I've just got to take this." She hurried over to the doctors' office and closed the door. "Yes?"

"Is that Tekla Berg, daughter of Karin Berg?"

"Yes."

"I'm Ulf Granlund, the physician in charge of Ward 4, where Karin was a patient."

Tekla heard the past tense, *was*.

"I'm afraid I have bad news."

Tekla tried to say something, but it was as if a sock had been rammed down her throat.

"Hello, are you still there?"

"Yes . . ."

"Unfortunately, I have to tell you that Karin passed away an hour ago."

"I see . . ."

"Yes, her condition deteriorated during the afternoon and we gave her more and more oxygen but her lungs were very tired."

"She had pneumonia. I'm a doctor."

"That's right, of course, the nurses told me. Well in that case you know that Karin was in a very fragile state."

She hadn't been all that fragile when she'd ruled the family with an iron hand throughout Tekla's childhood. Nor did she show much weakness when she made Tekla stay in her room a whole day, at the age of twelve, after she had destroyed the washing machine by trying to clean her gym shoes in it.

"Yes . . ."

"She was unconscious for the last hour. We gave her morphine and other drugs so that she wouldn't suffer."

"Scopolamine."

"Among other things."

Tekla wanted to ask why they hadn't called earlier, but knew that she might not have answered. In any case, she couldn't have got up there in time. And even if she had, what good would it have done?

Apart from allowing them that all-important last farewell.

One that should have taken place several days ago, when her mother was admitted to hospital. Or when the first symptoms of Huntington's made themselves known.

"So what happens now?" Tekla asked.

"Is there anyone who wants to come to say goodbye?"

"No."

"In that case she'll be taken to the mortuary and—"

"I know. And then we have to arrange the undertakers." Tekla could hear how testy she sounded. Ulf Granlund from Falun had been nothing but friendly and informative.

"So . . . well I guess there's nothing more."

"Thanks for letting me know." Tekla ended the call with the doctor from Falun. She stared at her phone. Wondered if she should ring Simon. But what would she say? She wasn't up to it. She made as if to go back to Elmqvist, but suddenly everything was hazy, there was a buzzing in her ears and the room began to tilt to one side. She sank down by the wall, about to faint, but somehow the blood got to her brain. She saw her mother before her, smiling. A cigarette in one hand, waving to Tekla. Why was she looking so happy? That had almost never happened. Tekla tried to fight back the tears, pinched

318

her own arm until it hurt. Then she braced herself against the floor, got up and checked to make sure that nobody had seen her. The corridor was empty. She went through to join Elmqvist.

"Anything on X-ray?"

"Are you alright?" Elmqvist asked, taking off her plastic apron.

"X-ray?"

"I hear you, Tekla, but how are you feeling? You look very pale, has something happened?"

"Just the fact that, in barely a week, a man has been murdered by his wife, who has died from dioxin poisoning, and now our C.E.O. is hospitalised with fulminant shock."

"I know all that, but are you sure there's nothing else?"

"What did the X-rays show?" Tekla repeated.

"Nothing apart from a minor infiltrate in one lung," Elmqvist said, reluctantly relinquishing her focus on Tekla. "But you don't need to worry. We have the situation under control. In fact we—"

"No."

"What do you mean, no?"

"You do not. Don't take it personally, but you haven't a clue what's going on."

"Excuse me?" Elmqvist said, taking a step back. "I've spent the whole week working like a dog on your liver patient, who you quite literally kidnapped with Piotr while I wasn't here. I've reported the breach and I've also rung Göran."

"Good," Tekla said.

"Good?"

"Do what you feel you have to. I only have one interest now: to save Monica."

"O.K., Tekla. You're going too far now. It's one thing for you and Piotr to go behind my back, that will have consequences, but I'm not going to stand here and be insulted—"

"The stomach pains!" Tekla exclaimed.

"What are you talking about?"

"The X-rays didn't show anything, nor did the tests from Ersta."

"And? Can't you just let this go and trust my competence as a senior emergency physician?"

"No."

Elmqvist took a deep breath.

"You're being very trying now, Tekla."

Elmqvist had no idea how trying she could be. This was only the beginning. "The neurologist couldn't understand her various symptoms either, what with muscle weakness and numbness in her hands."

"If you have some theory, then I'd be grateful if you could just . . ."

"Wait," Tekla said. She saw all the vital parameters before her. Carlsson's history of diffuse symptoms, all the examinations that had revealed nothing other than low blood pressure and strange, unexpected levels of electrolytes. At last, the various mental images began to fall into place and present themselves to Tekla as a beautiful painting.

"Is there a fly in here?" Elmqvist asked. "Or is your blood sugar low?"

Tekla's eyes met Elmqvist's as she realised what she had been doing. She lowered her hand. "No, no. Blood sugar, you said . . ." She could picture all the shelves of sweets at the Co-op. Carlsson's constant munching of liquorice. And it always had to be salt liquorice, she turned her nose up at sweet liquorice.

"I know!" The canvas finally lay ready before her. And it was beautiful.

"What?"

"Addison's disease!"

Elmqvist gave a start.

"Monica has Addison's disease, for heaven's sake. You have to give her cortisone, quickly. It all adds up: the fact that she eats liquorice – it's to compensate for subclinical Addison's, which has got worse these last weeks. It explains the low sodium and the high potassium values. Then she's admitted with an infection, which has now tipped her into severe shock. She's massively short of cortisone! I knew it was something to do with the lab lists."

320

Elmqvist nodded and stared straight ahead. "You're right."

"Give her cortisone!"

Elmqvist hurried to a nurse. "Get two hundred milligrammes of Solu-Cortef ready and administer it to Room 1."

Tekla's mind began to freewheel, to live a life of its own. She felt strong, exhilarated. Her failure to prevent the woman's death had pushed her to the bottom of an abyss. The walk through the city had got her to start living again. With some energy drink and bombs to top it off. Carlsson would survive. But it was too late for the man and the woman, both of the boy's parents were dead. Despite all of Tekla's efforts. But she wasn't going to give up – she would find out why the woman had been poisoned with dioxin. If only for the boy's sake. She wanted him to grow up knowing what had happened to his parents.

Elmqvist returned. "All is forgiven, Tekla. You're fantastic. The way you connected the liquorice with . . ."

"Wait!" Tekla said.

"Have I got that wrong?"

"Not at all. Monica has Addison's, I'd bet my licence on that. But I've just remembered something else. I bought sweets at the Co-op."

"And so?"

Tekla was thinking of the receipt, and associating it with the one she had seen in A. & E. that Thursday. The man had only had one thing in his pocket: a till receipt. She enlarged it, read it from memory. Two litres of milk, a loaf of rye bread and a packet of macaroni. But most important of all: the address. It came from a Tempo store in Rätansbyn.

"I'm going to Jämtland."

"You are?" Elmqvist said. "This winter, you mean?"

"No, this evening."

"This evening?"

Should she go alone? There was one person she might consider asking.

"Is this anything to do with the woman who died?"

"Yes."

"You know that both Alvaro Silva and Rebecka What's-her-name from the N.O.D. will be mad as hell if you go off without telling them."

"Do I look as if I could care less?"

Elmqvist stared at Tekla for a few long seconds. "You *are* crazy." She began to laugh.

IV

TRAVELLING TO STOCKHOLM

Wednesday, 6 November

"Are we there yet?"

Mikhailova took Kolya's hand, it was sticky with chocolate and sweat. She looked at the clock above the toilet. "Another half hour. Do you want me to finish reading?"

Kolya had his eyes glued to the window. He kept wiping the condensation away with his hand. "Will we see the Globen arena?"

She knew why he asked. Kozak had mentioned that the man who wrote the music for the Star Wars films had once held a concert there.

In fact, Kolya's hand wasn't sweaty. It was Mikhailova herself who was hot all over and worried. She couldn't get the wad of bank notes in the glove compartment of the car out of her mind. Kozak's evasive look when she finally plucked up the courage to ask where the money came from. "Just forget it," was all he had said. Forget it . . . how could she? They had always had plenty of money, but no large sums like that, they hadn't needed them. Her body had gone into standby mode, a state of heightened focus. She was confused, but sensed a threat, a heavy feeling that things weren't as they should be.

She tried to dismiss her apprehensions. "Sasha?"

Kozak looked up from his phone and leaned across the aisle. "Yes?"

"Will we be passing Globen on the way in to Stockholm?"

He smiled, just as he did when he told her about cities he had passed through, museums he had visited, concerts he had attended; that warm, caring smile that made the troubled furrows in his brow disappear, those close-set eyes open up. She subsided into his warmth, just for a few seconds.

"Sadly. It's to the south of the city. We'll be coming in from the north."

At the same time: the smile didn't seem genuine.

She reached for his hand, but a conductor was just about to go by and the moment passed. Kozak was back on his phone. The creases in his forehead were back again, the thick veins snaking up from his temples and vanishing into the thin strands of hair on top of his head. "A hairy chest is to compensate for what one's missing up on top," he had joked the first time they'd had sex. He'd had more hair and fewer wrinkles then. "I've also heard it said that thinning hair goes with high testosterone levels." She was pulled along by his charm. But that was then. Mikhailova said to the boy, "No, unfortunately we won't see Globen, but we'll see masses of other buildings."

Kolya seemed not to hear. He turned his head this way and that when he saw some new building or a cool car on the motorway, which ran parallel to the railway tracks. He had been doing that ever since they'd left Östersund Station in the morning.

Mikhailova buttoned up her chequered flannel shirt and tucked it into her jeans. She felt cold. Regretted not having put on long underwear. They were the only ones on the train who looked to be dressed for a hike in the woods – they were, it might appear, heading in the wrong direction. That didn't bother her. It was ages since she'd last worn anything other than outdoor clothes. She blushed at the thought of the leather thongs with stay-ups and knee-high boots that had been such an important part of her outfits in the bars. Another life. Another time.

"One of the things we have to go and see is an old ship which sank in . . ." She couldn't remember when. "Several hundred years ago. It was loaded with way too many cannons, so when the wind blew from the side it capsized."

Kolya looked at her. "Did anybody die?"

"Yes, many, I think. And the ship went under, but after a while they raised it, hundreds of years later. And by then it was all dark and rotten. But it's been fixed."

326

"Are we going to go and see it?"

"Absolutely. And we can go by boat, right in the middle of town."

Kolya looked excited. He peered out of the window again. In his lap he had his favourite mask, a replica of Iron Man's, which he occasionally opened up and then closed again.

They were approaching the capital. Mikhailova tied the laces of her hiking boots and felt Kozak's coarse hand grasp her wrist across the aisle. At first with determination, then he relaxed his grip. "No hurry."

She met his sad look. "Do you know when I was here last?"

He shook his head.

"Kolya was one. We were looking for our first house in Norrland."

"That's not right. We were in—"

"Göteborg? I knew you'd say that. We've only been to Göteborg once, when you thought that our cover had been blown. You wanted us to take that boat." Kozak made a dampening gesture. The meaning was clear: don't talk so loudly, even if people here don't speak Russian.

"And as for Copenhagen," she insisted, "the other day you said I'd been there, but I haven't." That was important, because he was often saying things like that. Maintaining that she had been present somewhere and done something, whereas in fact he'd forgotten that he'd experienced it all by himself. As if he were completely unaware that she wasn't always with him on his trips.

Kozak looked angry, more than anything. As if it were her fault that she hadn't accompanied him. As if he'd ever invited her to come with him when he travelled to Moscow, Helsinki, Frankfurt or Riga. As if he'd ever asked if she'd like to go on her own, if only just for a weekend, to Stockholm, check in to a hotel and simply stroll around town, incognito, to enjoy a bit of city life. She'd been to Östersund on her own three times, but just for the day. She'd never taken a hot bath in a hotel, never rested her head freshly bathed on a down pillow, never eaten a buffet breakfast and taken a discreet look at the businessmen and women with their suits and financial newspapers. She'd lived through Kozak's experiences. At first she enjoyed his vivid descriptions of all the trips. But the days when she was able to feel happy for his sake were gone. Not that she really missed all of that, she was perfectly satisfied living in the countryside with Kolya. She knew that she'd never been a city girl, not really. It was Neverova who had drawn out that other side, the fleeting pleasures, the things which were not actually her. The only thing missing during the six years in Sweden had been any real closeness with Kozak. On so many levels.

He let go of her arm but she was quick to capture his hand. It was rough. She stroked the scars on the back with her thumb, let the tips of her fingers bury themselves in his chapped palm. He pulled his hand away and left her alone with her dreams of a life that was no longer real.

"Does he live in town, your . . . colleague?"

"In a house. Close to town," Kozak said without looking up from his mobile.

She was happy about that. Close to town meant no more than a few stops on the underground before she and Kolya were at Stockholm's Central Station. From there she knew it was only a half-hour walk to Djurgården Park and Gamla Stan. She had read that on the internet.

They passed Arlanda Airport and, after another ten minutes, the city began to pile up outside the window, larger and larger buildings, fewer and fewer green areas. The train slowed and Kolya kneeled on his seat.

"No shoes," she said, firmly guiding his boots down onto the floor. He stood up.

"Is that the Royal Palace?"

"Sasha?" she asked, pointing out a large brick tower topped with golden crowns.

"No, that's the city hall," he replied disinterestedly, rising to his feet in unison with the other travellers. Trolley cases were lifted down, their handles pulled out. Mikhailova brought down her and Kolya's luggage, a large bag with XXL written on it.

328

The train rolled into Stockholm's Central Station and Kolya pushed his way to the doors.

"Wait for us," Mikhailova called out. She realised she sounded rattled. There was obviously no way he could disappear while the train was still moving. But the station was big, she knew, and Kozak looked weary. On edge and at the same time tired, his thoughts elsewhere.

The train stopped and Mikhailova wanted to shout to Kolya again but stopped herself. She recalled what Kozak had said the night before. "Keep a low profile. Try to stay calm, even if you feel panicked." Why had he said that? He never had when they were in Östersund or Umeå, after all. Was the capital more dangerous? Or had something changed? She thought again of the bundle of bank notes in the glove compartment. Where had it come from? And what did he need so much money for? She left the bag for Kozak and hurried after Kolya, who had eagerly jumped down onto the platform. "You mustn't run away."

"Hurry up then. We have to—"

"We have to wait for Sasha."

Kozak followed them, the buttons on his black sports jacket casually undone and his sweater rucked up by the strap of his bag. His hairy stomach showed. Mikhailova went up to him and pulled the sweater down. Tried to kiss him on the cheek, but he pushed her away.

"Not now." He seemed to be searching for someone further away. "We're supposed to meet at the main entrance."

Mikhailova followed him. They passed a few fast food outlets near the entrance before rushing through the large central hall and on to the station exit. Mikhailova had to drag Kolya along because he wanted to stop and look in each shop. There were tempting smells drifting through the door of a café and hot air coming out of a flower shop. An electronics store blazed with light. Kolya tore himself loose and stopped by the brightly lit windows, staring in.

She realised what he had caught sight of. "Great, aren't they?"

He nodded. Then she acted on impulse, as if she didn't know how many more chances she would have. She went into the shop. In faultless Swedish she asked: "The orange headphones. How much are they?"

"Two hundred and ninety-nine."

"I'll have them, please." Mikhailova took out a five-hundred kronor note while the young man in the shop went to fetch Kolya's first ever headphones. At last he would be able to listen to his film music in peace, without an irritated Kozak asking him to turn the volume down.

They left the shop. "I'll hide them for the time being. O.K.?" A delighted Kolya nodded. They continued to make their way out of the station's central hall.

It was raining in the street. The word "chaos" did not even begin to describe Mikhailova's impression of all the taxis, people and luggage. As she emerged through the swing doors, she imagined that she would be met with a terrible sight: Kozak with his wife. She got it into her head that he would be standing there, embracing his wife, who had for some reason suddenly appeared. He had never shown Mikhailova any pictures of his son, but she knew he resembled his father, that much he had told her. Apparently the daughter was more like her mother, lighter in both colouring and mood. Maybe all three would be there. Was the money for his wife? But if so, where did it come from?

"Yulia!"

He was standing and talking to an elderly man next to a white station wagon. Kolya was pulling her this way and that, he would probably have vanished had she not been holding on to him.

"Where did you get to?" Kozak snapped.

She ignored him and held out her hand.

"Yulia."

The old man grasped it with both his hands. Like a priest, but there was no robe or collar to be seen.

"I've heard a lot about you."

330

He had? She remembered her surprise that Christmas supper three years earlier, when Anatoly Mischenko told her that Kozak had praised the wise and caring way she had with Kolya. Why did he never say things like that to her face? Why did three years have to go by between compliments, why did they have to come to her second-hand?

The man before her was wearing a shiny grey suit. It seemed to have been bought long ago, whereas the rough shoes and the overcoat were clearly more recent acquisitions. Her first impression was that there was something not quite right about him, as though he were a cut-out doll that has been put together so carelessly that the different parts don't really fit. There was also the way in which he had said "a lot", with an undertone she was not sure she had understood. Was he in fact saying: "I've heard from Sasha that you're very demanding, that you don't follow orders?"

The man turned his attention to the boy. Mikhailova noticed that his facial expression changed, sharpened, that his eyes narrowed.

"I'm Spiro Lazarov," he said to the boy. Kolya did his best to look the man in the eye, as they had practised before he went to sleep the night before.

Mikhailova gave a start. The man spoke fluent Russian, but Spiro was no Russian name. Who was he, Kozak's so-called business colleague? Why did he wear such strange clothes and why did he make her feel so uncomfortable and vulnerable? Why was he greeting Kolya so formally? His tone had shifted, and the look on his face too. She felt like leaving and checking in to a hotel with Kolya, asking Kozak for a few days on their own in Stockholm, but a hand against the base of her spine gave her a clear signal to get into the white Škoda.

STOCKHOLM
Wednesday, 6 November

Mikhailova sat in the back seat with Kolya. She began to feel calmer as the car started moving and the men launched into a discussion about Teslas, the latest Trump scandal, and Swedish football, something about how weak the league was. The elderly man appeared to be an ordinary, rather dull person. Her anxiety began to subside, but it didn't altogether disappear. She and Kolya huddled together and pointed at things through the window.

"Look! Ships in the middle of town. And how about that round building? And all these cars! And water, there's so much water everywhere." They drove into a tunnel that lead them up a long uphill stretch. Then came another canal and water on both sides of the road. Suddenly the boy burst out: "Globen!"

"Yes, look," Mikhailova said. "Look," she repeated, this time to herself, and she heard the sorrow in her voice. She had never been to a concert, and she wondered if Kozak would ever take her to one. The boy stretched across her thighs to be able to see Globen through the other window as they turned off at Gullmarsplan and continued down through the next tunnel and on to Huddingevägen.

"Was the trip O.K.?" the man asked. He sounded off-hand, like a driver who collects people from the station and takes them to their hotel, someone who feels obliged to ask at least one question out of politeness. Could he be a professional chauffeur? She wondered how old he was. His hair was as white as snow, neatly combed with a parting.

"Absolutely," she said. "We have high expectations here in the back." She saw the man and Kozak exchange looks. How well did they actually know each other? She had never heard Kozak mention him, not that he ever gave very detailed accounts of his trips. And she preferred not to know since she presumed that he was mostly at home in St Petersburg with his family.

"And you, Kolya? What do you want to do in Stockholm?"

"See the cannons."

"Cannons?" the man said in his deep bass. "Are there cannons in Stockholm? I didn't know that."

"The Vasa Museum," Mikhailova explained.

"I got that," the old man said sharply. She must ask Kozak later how long they were staying, he hadn't given her an answer to that. But when she had packed for "a few days" the night before, he had given her a nod of confirmation.

They passed Örby and the Stockholmsmässan exhibition centre before the man swung right towards Stuvsta. There were three or four more turns before he parked in the driveway of a large single-storey house next to a piece of woodland. Mikhailova got out and immediately noticed that the noise didn't stop even though the engine had been turned off. After a few seconds, she realised that there had to be a motorway nearby.

The old man left his guests to carry in their own cases and kept his shoes on when he entered the house. Mikhailova took off her hiking boots, after helping Kolya remove his outerwear. The house looked so neat and tidy, she was very keen for them not to make a mess. The boy walked carefully into the dark entrance hall and followed the sounds to a kitchen where Kozak and Lazarov were already pouring glasses of beer. Mikhailova followed just behind. The house was large, at least four times the size of the biggest of the four places they had rented in Jämtland. But it was so empty, there was so little furniture. She was fascinated by the enormous windows in the living room and the open fireplace, where she longed to light a fire. She was freezing, in part because she was so tired.

"There's a pool!" Kolya shouted from the doorway at the end of the room. Had he even been in a house with a pool before?

Mikhailova followed him, and there was indeed a swimming pool, one flight of stairs down, about eight metres long. She looked around but couldn't see a sauna, which was what she really needed. They'd had one in their previous house, her favourite, where there was even an old baking oven. But sadly there seemed little prospect of any sauna that evening. Nor was there anything to show that the pool had been used recently, unless you could count a large bathing costume hanging on a hook.

"Can we swim?"

"We'll have to ask Spiro after we've eaten."

"No, now!"

"Kolya."

The boy fell silent. She squatted down.

"Do you remember what we talked about? It's so important that you do as I say and don't make any scenes." Kolya seemed to be listening. "You have to try to be like all the others." She changed to Swedish. "Can you do that? Can you be like the other Swedish children?"

He nodded.

"Good. And if I'm not there?"

He didn't seem to understand. She spelled it out, this time in Russian: "What will you do if I disappear?"

The boy looked slowly up at her. She saw the fear in his eyes. This was the worst part of it, the thing she absolutely did not want to do, but which she knew was a part of her assignment, their reality. "Kolya, what will you do if I disappear and some Swede has to take care of you? The police, for example. What are you supposed to do then? What did we say?"

"Nothing."

"What do you mean, nothing?"

"I keep quiet."

"And if they ask you what your name is, what do you say then?"

He looked confused.

"Kolya, what do you say then? Nothing. Never say what your name is. Whatever happens."

She felt the tears in her eyes but controlled herself. It was brutal on him, but at the same time it was vital that he should know what to do if something were to happen.

"Good," she said, wrapping her arms around Kolya's little body. It suddenly felt so incredibly small. As if he had shrunk, as if he were not the big seven-year-old she loved more than anything in the whole world. Now the tears came and she allowed them to flow for a few seconds. Then she let go of him. "We need to eat – then we'll swim."

They went back to the kitchen. The old man had taken off his jacket and rolled up his shirtsleeves. "Do you want to help?" he asked the boy. "I guess you know how to slice an onion?"

Mikhailova wanted to object, she felt uncomfortable leaving Kolya, but Kozak spoke first.

"Of course. That way, we can settle in." Kozak knocked back his glass of beer and nodded to her to follow him. Despite her misgivings, she left Kolya. They found their way to the sleeping quarters, a separate corridor with four bedrooms in a row, forming a horseshoe facing the woodland. No garden furniture to be seen, no swings, no barbecue. Kozak carried their bags into one of the rooms.

"Have you been here before?" she wondered.

"Why do you ask?"

"You seem to know the house."

Kozak ignored her. Just as he always did when he didn't want to answer her questions. He unpacked his clothes and put them in a cupboard, hanging up a shirt and then holding out an envelope. "You must only use cash."

She took the money, four five-hundred-kronor notes. Not even a tenth of the bundle from the glove compartment. What was he going to do with the rest? She wanted to ask, but he would only feed her lies.

"I know."

Mikhailova didn't feel like unpacking. She wanted to throw herself into that pool and then take a hot shower. Most of all she wanted Kozak, but she saw from his distant manner that they wouldn't be

having sex that evening. He would stay up with the older man, whoever he was, and drink both beer and vodka, and then go to sleep
several hours after her. And by that stage the boy would in all likelihood already have come in to her, had his first nightmare and lain
down close by her side. Kozak would give her a telling-off when they
woke up in the morning, somehow make it her fault that Kolya was
so insecure. She hadn't given him a sheltered upbringing, she hadn't
"done her job", as he would say. As if it were a job. Raising a child,
wasn't that the whole meaning of life? How could that ever be called
a job? Not even when, as a two-year-old, he'd had such bad diarrhoea
that he was barely able to swallow any of the soup she fed him with a
teaspoon during three long nights. Nor when he had his first bout of
flu and was delirious with fever and she sat up with him all night in
their cottage – not once had she thought it was a burden. She looked
at Kozak. He was sitting on the bed with his back to her. Scrolling on
his phone, as if waiting for some important message which never
came.

"Is it her you're messaging?"

He didn't answer. They had been here so many times before that
all words seemed empty. Silence had taken the place of the very
harshest ones and, when it came to silence, he was her master. But
she felt stronger than usual, unafraid of the consequences, willing to
stand her ground.

"You're never going to leave her, are you?"

She saw him raise his head from his mobile. Recognised the tension in his neck, it was so obvious and quick when it came. He
sighed, presumably intending to demonstrate yet again his mastery
of silence.

She repeated. "Are you?"

"I heard what you said."

"But you don't want to answer?"

"You already seem to have decided on the answer. Why would I
bother?"

"Every time you tell me it's your last trip home. Why wouldn't I believe you? What else can it mean, other than that you're leaving her? How else am I supposed to interpret those words ... last trip home. You're never going to make that last trip, are you?"

"Make of it what you will." He was still sitting with his back to her.

Mikhailova found strength in the hug she had given Kolya just before. She had already shed her tears once that evening and was feeling unusually combative. Did she have to accept this assignment as something that was going to last for ever? That was not what she had been told six years before, when she left her parents and accepted the job in a country she didn't even know had a king or a football star called Zlatan. She had always done as she was told by the men in authority around her, had always fallen in line, at school, at home, when she worked as an escort, and now in the dark forests of Jämtland. When would she get to decide for herself?

"I want you to leave her."

"I know you do."

"And?"

Kozak put his phone on the bedside table and turned around. She saw the irritation, it was clearly visible around his mouth, which became a little crooked. "I will leave her. I promise."

She wanted to believe him. She heard his words and saw how little they matched the look in his eyes. She wanted it so badly, she made up her mind, she hoped against hope, she chose to believe him.

"Is that true?" She crept onto the bed and tried to kiss him but he jumped to his feet.

"Time to eat." He left the room.

She fell onto her back and looked up at the white ceiling. She wanted to believe him. Clung to the thought that all would be well. She would eat, they would swim in the pool, she would have a good night's sleep, they would see the city tomorrow. She so wanted it all to be O.K. But deep inside she knew that it wouldn't be.

In spite of it all, she woke up with the impression that this was what a hotel pillow must feel like. She had been dreaming that she and Kozak were having sex in a train compartment. Mikhailova lay completely still for a while and enjoyed his snoring. She also liked having Kolya lie on her other side and the fact that Kozak had not got out of bed when the boy came in during the night. He had perhaps been too drunk, but that did not detract from the joy she felt. She couldn't recall the last time the three of them had slept in the same bed.

"Good morning," the old man said when Kozak and Mikhailova came into the kitchen. "Sleep well?"

"I did, as a matter of fact," she said and she heard how impertinent it sounded.

The old man was frying eggs and had lined up juice, yoghurt and muesli on a kitchen counter.

"Help yourselves," he said and walked towards the hall. He was wearing the same rough shoes and suit as the day before.

"Aren't you going to eat with us?" Mikhailova asked, mostly out of politeness.

"I've already had breakfast." He put on his jacket and gloves and went out.

Mikhailova poured yoghurt into a bowl. Kolya tried to spread butter onto a slice of dark bread, but she stepped in to stop him making a mess. She heard the car drive off.

"I wonder where he's going."

Kozak helped himself to coffee and sat down at the dining table.

She had to get her own coffee, warming up some milk in the micro-wave while she was at it.

"Is it O.K. if we go into town today?" she asked, trying not to sound too hopeful. If he said no, at least they'd have the swimming pool and the garden to keep them amused.

Kozak finished his coffee and went to fill up.

"Is it O.K.—"

"We'll see," he interrupted. "Maybe." He left the room.

She could live with a maybe; with a bit of effort she might in due course be able to turn it into a yes. Kolya looked at her. She saw his disappointment, but just let it hang over the breakfast table, like the familiar companion it had become over the years.

"He did say maybe. Don't forget that." She patted his dark hair, but he knocked away her hand. They ate in silence. Then she cleared away their breakfast and tidied and cleaned up the kitchen, just as she was expected to. She noted that the few groceries in the refriger-ator had been bought recently, during the last few days. In the larder there were only potatoes, a bag of onions and some tins of tomatoes. She put two and two together. The man was renting the house, it def-initely wasn't his home. Or he was always travelling, just like Kozak, and the house was for occasional visits. But why was it so big? Did other people use it too? She thought about the years in St Petersburg, the places where she and the other girls had lived. There had always been a man who kept an eye on them, like a circus director watches over his animals. Was that Lazarov's role in all this? A person who guarded others in his power? Would she be bold enough to ask Kozak who he really was?

Kolya was sitting on the floor of his room holding the new head-phones. It was smaller than theirs, with a beige wall-to-wall carpet, a single bed, a desk, two lamps and an empty wardrobe, and probably hadn't been occupied for many years. It felt abandoned and smelled of old dust.

"Would you like to listen to something?"

He nodded. She brought out her mobile. Her favourite music

from before. Timeless tunes that never died. And she had also created a file with John Williams' film music. "Shall we start with 'Jurassic Park'?"

The boy nodded again and eagerly put his headphones on while Mikhailova pressed play. The French horns were loud enough for her to hear them as well, so she lowered the volume a bit and lay down on her back. The fitted carpet smelled old, but was comfortable to lie on. She curled around the boy's body like a cheese doodle. He rested against her stomach. She could have lain there for ever.

Mikhailova was woken up by Kozak knocking at the door.

"Lunch."

"That was quick," she said, tidying her hair. Kolya was still listening to music, now in his bed. "I fell asleep."

"It's ready," Kozak said abruptly, leaving the door open as he walked away. There was a smell of food, and it seemed delicious.

"Are you coming?" she said, removing Kolya's headphones. They went to the kitchen. She could see through the large living-room windows that it had begun to snow lightly. Kozak or Lazarov had lit a fire in the hearth. She reflected that life was long, the Vasa Museum would still be there tomorrow and the prospect of spending time together ought to be enough for them.

The table had been laid in the kitchen with two candles burning. It looked very cosy.

"Smells wonderful. What are we having?"

"My grandmother's meat stew."

"With mushrooms, I see," she said, thinking back to autumns outside St Petersburg. "I love them!"

"Alexander told me."

So they had actually talked about such personal things? She remembered going out into the forest with her grandmother and afterwards sitting in the kitchen, watching the old lady clean their haul, her fingers covered in earth, while the saucepans on the stove simmered away. The smell of mushrooms throughout the house. "Maybe not one of Kolya's favourites, though."

The old man put boiled potatoes and salad on the table, a bottle of Fanta for Kolya and beer for the grown-ups. "I know. That's why you're getting lamb sausages instead." The man brought over a frying pan with some nicely browned sausages for Kolya.

The boy's face lit up. They *were* his favourite.

Mikhailova nodded gratefully to Kozak, who sat down, looking more cheerful. She immediately felt hungry and fell on the rich meat casserole. Kolya was more interested in the Fanta, which he drank in large gulps. They rarely had soft drinks at home in Jämtland. He managed to pick his way through half a sausage. Lazarov lit a cigarette and had some beer. He didn't seem very hungry either.

"So you like T.V. series?" he asked.

Kolya didn't seem to understand the question. Mikhailova elaborated. "You like Star Wars and Avengers, don't you?"

The boy nodded shyly. She saw the stains on his white T-shirt. She would have to do some laundry.

"And cannons," Lazarov added.

"Will we see the ship today?" Kolya asked.

"Maybe. If we have time," Kozak answered. Mikhailova told herself again that she could live with a maybe. She was a patient person. Hope was her friend. She had always made a virtue of being able to wait her turn and not being presumptuous or helping herself at the expense of others. But Kozak was being unfair, he was taking advantage of her good nature. Had he ever agreed to anything she'd asked for?

She was feeling full now. Kolya had eaten two potatoes, some cucumber and almost the whole of the sausage. Kozak's plate was clean. He lit a cigarette, and Lazarov did too.

"How about a little walk?" the old man asked. "I need to buy some more cigarettes before she arrives."

Kozak got up from the table.

"Where are you going?" Mikhailova asked, with an uncomfortable feeling in the pit of her stomach. As so often when Kozak went away, as always when she was left behind. She could cope with it, but fundamentally she didn't like being on her own. And who was this "she" who was apparently on her way?

"To the centre of Stuvsta, just five minutes from here," Lazarov said. "We won't be long."

The men left their plates on the table and went out into the hall. As a matter of routine, Mikhailova began to clear the table, but then stopped and decided to do it later. At some point she had to give priority to Kolya and that swim.

"Shall we go for a dip?"

Kolya brightened up.

"You can swim naked," she added, feeling a sudden stab of pain in her stomach followed by nausea. She wondered if it might be her period but that didn't seem right.

Kolya began to take off his clothes and she picked them up. "Go to the toilet first and I'll just put some stuff in the washing machine."

The boy rushed away to the bedrooms. Mikhailova fetched some dirty clothes and went to the other part of the house, where she had seen that there was a garage. The laundry room was probably somewhere over there. She found the large double garage, which was cool and smelled of oil. The next door led to the laundry, but there was neither washing detergent nor fabric softener there. She went back to the garage and looked through the cupboards, which were empty. She continued the search and saw some low lockers near the garage entrance. She opened them to find four large drums on a shelf. She read the label: "Hydrofluoric Acid". An icy sensation shot straight through her stomach like a sword. She swallowed another sick feeling. Hydrofluoric acid, she knew very well what that was used for. She remembered the intensive training she and Kozak had undergone before they took on their assignment. A lot of weapons drills but also some theory. She recalled the "lesson" when they were taught the easiest way to get rid of a body. It was important to use plastic tubs, because the acid dissolved all biological material, including enamel – like on a bathtub.

The old man with his menacing, sarcastic manner.

The empty house.

Hydrofluoric acid.

She realised what was about to happen. The big question was whether Kozak was on the man's side or ... Yes, of course, there wasn't an ounce of doubt in her mind. His unfriendly behaviour, his edginess during the journey here. The money in the car; he'd sold them out, made a pact with the devil. But who were they planning to kill? Kolya? Her? Both of them?

They had gone to Stuvsta to buy cigarettes. How long might they be away? At most, half an hour. She launched herself out of the garage, found Kolya waiting in his room, completely naked.

"Quick, darling. Put your clothes back on again."

"But we were going to . . ."

She paused for a moment. Had to take some deep breaths and think. Was she being paranoid? Could the acid be for something else? No, she'd been wearing blinkers, hadn't realised what was going on. Hadn't wanted to see, but Kozak's aggressiveness, his inability to look her in the eye, the money and the peculiar journey to Stockholm . . . it had all been there right in front of her. But the truth was too painful to grasp.

"Don't fuss. Now's not the time . . ." She squatted down. "I'm sorry. But we have to get away from here. It's not safe."

The boy began to get dressed. "Put on your blue over-trousers and boots," she shouted, running into her room and snatching her things together. When she was on the point of leaving the bedroom, a thought struck her: a weapon. Did Kozak have a pistol? She searched through his suitcase, among his clothes. Nothing. Then she found his sports bag, in which he normally kept his gym shoes and training gear. She tore it open and stared down at a mass of bundles of bank notes. At least fifty. Huge sums.

She was absolutely convinced. Kozak had been bought. She was alone. And they had no time to waste. She took the bag with the money, her own clothes in a carrier bag, and ran to find the keys for the Škoda.

STUVSTA, STOCKHOLM
Thursday, 7 November

"Why?" she suddenly screamed. Kolya squeezed his Iron Man mask as hard as he could and stared down between his legs.

"I'm sorry," she said, leaving her hand on his thigh.

Mikhailova had found the keys to the Škoda. The engine was running. The street empty. Not a soul to be seen on a Thursday in the middle of the day. The people of Stuvsta were at work, their children in school. Nobody had any inkling of the terrible deed that was being prepared in the garage of the house by the woodland between Stuvsta and Älvsjö.

Last night was the first time in ages that she had felt what it might be like to live a normal life, if only for a fleeting moment, with a cup of tea in her hand. After she and Kozak had finished arguing, before he joined the old man in the kitchen to start boozing, he had asked her if she wanted anything. "A cup of tea," she had said. Kozak went and fetched them one each and they sat in the living room with Kolya on a leather sofa listening to music. Could it have been five minutes? Ten at the most. But Kozak had been there. Thoughtful, a little edgy, holding his cup, yet a real presence. He had often been like that in the beginning, when they came to Sweden, when they first went to live in Jämtland, when they had that pioneer spirit, alone against the rest of the world. The nervous months before they realised that life wasn't going to be one long flight, a battle for survival. Kozak found his first construction job near Östersund and had to leave for work first thing in the morning. When he came home in the evenings, she would pamper him for a few hours, massage those aching hands unaccustomed to physical work in the cold. So why? What had happened?

344

How had they ended up here? When had Kozak stopped caring about the boy's fate and hers?

"Shall we go?" Kolya asked.

"Absolutely." She rolled out of the driveway of the brick house. Found her way along the street they had come down the day before. She followed the signs to the southbound motorway. Things felt a little better now. They were secure in the white Škoda, leaving the catastrophe behind them. Would she really never see him again? Never get an answer to *why*? How much money might there be in the bag? Fifty thousand? A few hundred thousand max. Was that worth six years of their lives together? Had his words yesterday been a lie? "I will leave her. I promise."

It was a lie. He and the old man had already made their plans. Spiro, as he called himself.

She drove out onto the motorway. The signs said Södertälje.

But who was he? A hired assassin who was going to dispose of her body. A former member of the security services?

She looked at Kolya. All of a sudden, the penny finally dropped. A penny that had got stuck in the machine. It was the boy they were after. Obviously the old man had been sent by the other *organizatsiya*, the whole point was to get rid of Kolya. She was incidental, collateral damage to cover their tracks. And obviously the old man wouldn't just give up when he found the house empty. They would pursue her, wherever she fled. They would track her down, there was no doubt about it.

A fury bubbled up inside her, a violent rage which was primarily aimed at Kozak. He had stolen a large chapter of her life, enticed her with empty promises about leaving his family, that they would get married, spend the rest of their days together. But he had never meant to keep his promises. And now this.

She left the motorway at Kungens Kurva. A long turn towards Skärholmen, another exit. She passed IKEA on the left-hand side and followed the road signs back towards Stockholm. Out on the motorway again, she accelerated.

"Where are we going?" Kolya asked. "I'm hungry."

"Yes, you didn't eat that much."

She felt another shaft of pain in her midriff, followed by a wave of nausea. She had to get to a toilet soon. Her hands tightened on the steering wheel, her pulse rose. She stole a look at Kolya. Could she leave him somewhere with some trustworthy person? But there was nobody. She was the only one who could protect him. He was wearing his seatbelt, there was an airbag, he was clearly safe, they were in a new car.

She passed the house, wondering if the two men had got back. Probably not. She slowed down, followed the road to the town centre. Five minutes away, the old man had said. They'd probably had a beer somewhere. She thought about waiting for them. Stopped the car and weighed her options.

Then she spotted them. They were walking along the pavement. She saw the commuter train station in the distance. Both men were smoking and seemed deep in conversation as they approached a bus stop. She put the car into gear, saw no other traffic on the road. Pressed the accelerator and the car started to roll forwards.

"Shut your eyes!" she shouted.

"Why?"

"Just shut them!" she repeated and stepped hard on the accelerator.

Barely twenty metres from the men she drove up onto the pavement, the car bounced, then she saw them look up, Kozak begin to move to the right, she followed him, the rear wheels bumping against the pavement and the next second the front of the car struck his body.

Mikhailova moved her foot from the accelerator to the brake, the car skidded sideways and hit the old man. She knew that she'd run over Kozak, but she was unsure about Lazarov.

STOCKHOLM

Thursday, 7 November

She breathed heavily, her heart pounding in her ribcage. The bodies lay on the pavement by the bus shelter. It was an almost peaceful scene, as if two people waiting for the bus had decided to lie down and rest for a while. Or like the moments in a war film following a sudden gas attack.

Then Mikhailova saw something she had not reckoned with, a person on the other side of the road. A jogger with white earphones, which he pulled out as he slowed his steps. How much had he seen? The man already had a phone pressed to his ear, probably calling the ambulance service and the police. He looked in Mikhailova's direction, but it was too far for him to be able to see her face. Wasn't it? She felt an impulse to run the jogger over as well, but calmed herself down. She had done what she needed to do: the men were dead, they would no longer be able to come after her.

She was just about to drive off when she saw the old man move. He rolled over from his stomach onto his back. The jogger crossed the road to help. Mikhailova began to reverse when she heard sirens in the distance. There must have been an ambulance somewhere in the vicinity – they had responded incredibly quickly. What the hell should she do? Surely Kozak must be dead, there was no way he could have survived. She had heard his body being torn to shreds under the chassis. The impact was brutal and merciless. The old man would likely not survive either.

She put the car into gear and drove off, saw the ambulance in her rear-view mirror and then remembered that she wasn't alone in the car. Her mind cleared, like a blocked ear popping when a plane lands.

347

"What happened?" Kolya asked, staring at her. She braked, put the car on the verge. A bus went by in the opposite direction. She stole a look in the mirror, the bus was waved past by the ambulance crew, who were bringing out a stretcher and a large orange bag.

"Nothing," Mikhailova said, feeling the boy's head. No bumps, no soreness in the neck. "Did you close your eyes, like I said?"

"Yes. But why did we crash?"

"I went the wrong way. But we're O.K. We'll get going now. Are you sure you're not hurting anywhere?"

The boy pushed away her hand and fiddled with his superhero mask. "I'm hungry."

"I know. We'll find something."

Mikhailova saw the ambulance crew a few hundred metres away. They were huddled around the two men. A police car appeared from the opposite direction, the sirens were turned off as it pulled up. She started to drive away. At first she didn't understand what was holding her back, she should be making her escape, should be afraid of the police, who might catch sight of her. But somewhere in her over-heated brain the analytical processor developed during her training six years earlier was at work: she wanted to make sure the men were dead. It was pointless to flee if they survived and were able to con-tinue chasing her. They came to a bend in the road. She could no longer see the ambulance. Her stomach was in uproar, she really had to hold back in order to stop her guts from emptying out, she needed to get to a toilet. And now the nausea was getting worse. Water, she had to drink something.

Mikhailova stopped the car in a garage driveway. Searched the seat-back pockets behind her. She was in luck. An unopened bottle of mineral water. The boy didn't want any, but Mikhailova drank. She felt better, leaned her head back and closed her eyes. A decision had to be taken. She tried to draw a red line from where it had all begun to where they were now sitting.

"There's just one more thing," she said, edging out of the drive-way. She turned the car.

"What? What are we doing?" Kolya asked.

She felt alive, not in the least paralysed. And she knew why. She opened her window and gulped in some fresh air. Tried to breathe so the sickness would go away, but it didn't work. Her mind was made up. She wouldn't let anything put Kolya's future at risk.

"There's something I have to finish off," she answered. "Then we can go for a little outing, just the two of us. I promise."

She saw the yellow vehicle far away. The police car had left, the ambulance crew were shutting the rear doors and getting in. She followed.

On Huddingevägen, the ambulance's sirens were turned on. Mikhailova followed as closely as she dared. It didn't take long to drive the short distance in to the city. She got her bearings again at Gullmarsplan, near Globen, recognising the bridge that led towards the centre of town, took a left turn which was not allowed but which she decided to risk. There were no police nearby. The ambulance moved into the bus lane. She followed. At last, it appeared to have reached its goal, braking at some red lights, turning left again, up a hill and waiting by some large doors which were pushed open. To the left, a staff parking area. Mikhailova stopped the car.

The boy was listless, tired and uninterested, he had run out of energy. "It's a good thing you brought your mask with you. In case we have to hide," she said.

"Why would we have to hide?" Kolya asked, looking at her with big eyes.

"Only joking. There's just this one thing we have to do, then we'll be on our way." Now she felt a tightening across the chest when she breathed deeply. The seatbelt must have compressed her ribs on impact. Had she broken something? She looked at Kolya. He did not seem to be feeling any pain, and that was all that mattered.

She saw the sign saying "A. & E." Held Kolya tightly by the hand, increasingly worried as she suffered more and more from nausea and stomach pains. Despite the discomfort and nervousness that just about paralysed her, she had to finish what she'd started. Doing nothing was not an option. She had to bring it to a close, make sure that neither Kozak nor the old man could pursue either her or Kolya. Ever again. Then they could find themselves a quiet corner of the world and rebuild their lives. New lives. Far, far away.

"Can I play on your phone?"

She picked it up and turned the sound on so Kolya could play. Stayed sitting in the car and tried to compose herself, delaying the inevitable.

"Just for a little while."

Kolya took the mobile from her and quickly clicked his way into his game. He bent his head over the phone and was soon lost in a world of his own. Mikhailova resisted an urge to stroke the boy's hair. Two doctors walked past. They didn't look in her direction, absorbed by an intense discussion about something. Maybe a complicated case, some course of treatment they couldn't agree on.

"Now you're doing it again, Mamma."

Mikhailova looked at Kolya, whose eyes were fixed on the game.

"Doing what?"

"Talking to yourself. About Pappa."

"I wasn't talking about him, was I?"

"O.K. But you were talking out loud."

"So what did I say?"

"Something about you showing him."

She wanted to laugh at the absurdity of the situation, but it was all she could do to focus her eyes on the clock. Her vision kept blurring.

"Forget it," Kolya said.

"No, I'm glad you told me. I'm a bit tired. Maybe I sometimes talk to myself when I get like that."

"Funny."

"Yes, perhaps it is a bit funny."

She remained in the car for a few more minutes. She had been on her own for such long periods. Did she talk to herself? Maybe she did.

"We have to go in now," she said and stepped out of the car.

Kolya followed reluctantly. Mikhailova took the boy's hand. Had to concentrate on getting her pulse and breathing down. The glass doors slid apart and they walked in to the A. & E. reception at the Nobel Hospital.

V

DRIVING NORTH
Tuesday night, 12 November

"Are you hungry?" Lundgren asked and lowered the volume. The knocking sounds from the back of the car could be heard again, as if something was loose.

"How far do we have left to go?" was Tekla's reply.

"However far it is, you can't drive all night on an empty stomach," Lundgren said calmly.

"But seriously, how much further?"

"Don't ask me. You're the navigator."

Tekla got out her mobile and enlarged the map. "Like about another twenty kilometres to Bollnäs." She looked out and saw that it was still raining, as it had been for two and a half hours. The lights of the oncoming cars helpfully lit up Route 83, but she could only guess at Hälsingland's rolling hills out there in the compact darkness.

Tekla saw that the petrol gauge was near to empty. She took the last energy drink out of her jacket pocket and opened it. Held it out for Lundgren.

"Thanks, but that kind of stuff gives me the jitters."

Tekla swigged from the tin. "At most a bit of tachycardia."

Lundgren looked in the rear-view mirror. Smiled.

"Are you sure you don't want me to drive?" Tekla asked.

"A subtle way of saying that I'm a lousy driver. Once we stop. It'll be fun to see how *you* get on."

"I grew up in Jämtland. It's not as though there were any night buses to go home on after a party in the middle of winter," Tekla said and finished off the can, her seventh that day.

Lundgren was tailgating an articulated lorry, as he had done the whole way since Gävle. Tekla wondered if he was being careful, had difficulty seeing in the dark or just found it hard to concentrate while they were talking. She had expected an entirely different driving style from a policeman.

"All good," Lundgren said. "I know why you're so irritated."

"I don't want to talk about work." Tekla was not going to tell Lundgren about her mother's death. She didn't want to let those thoughts in. Even calling Simon would be too much. She needed to get away from the city, from all the dying. All she wanted was to feel a little of the Norrland cold for a few hours. And to hear Lundgren talk about nothing in particular.

"Agreed," Lundgren said, putting the volume up again. "Forever Young" by Alphaville. "You don't have enough Eighties music in your life." He started singing along.

"But I'm finding it hard to come to terms with the thought that the man whose life I saved got stabbed in the heart by a woman who also died before I could get her a new liver. What are the odds of that? That I should fail to save two patients in such a short period of time?"

"You haven't failed. I know you well enough to know you did everything that could be done, and then some."

"Do you know me?" Tekla asked bitterly.

"Actually, I think I do."

Tekla unbuttoned her thick down jacket. She thought about Klas Nyström and shifted in her seat. One of her legs had fallen asleep. She also thought about the message from Silva, which she had been ignoring. She might as well throw her phone out of the car window, she wasn't going to answer anyway if somebody called. She had told Nordensköld that she needed a few days' overtime leave, because her mother was unwell, which not even he could dismiss.

"I must say, I'm very grateful you've tagged along," Tekla said.

"I hate workplace rehab. It was an easy choice to take a few extra days off. Besides, you did agree to go away for the weekend with me."

Tekla knew very well what she had agreed to. A trip to Jämtland probably wasn't what Lundgren had had in mind.

"Sorry."

"This is at least as good."

Tekla tried to change the subject.

"What vintage is this luxury limo?"

A road sign revealed that they would soon be getting to Bollnäs. Lundgren stretched his back. "Two thousand and nine."

"Feels like it could have a heart attack any moment."

Lundgren turned off at a petrol station.

"Would you like something that'll make you less irritable?"

"I'll come in with you." Tekla opened the car door and immediately had to do up her jacket again. "Oh Jesus ... Childhood memories."

"There's no such thing as bad weather, only ..." Lundgren answered, unscrewing the petrol cap and beginning to fill up.

With help from the gusting wind, the rain reached far in under the roof, but not quite as far as Tekla, who was cursing her choice of footwear. She was aware that her brain was clamouring for attention. Like a skipping vinyl record, her thoughts kept jumping back to the woman in the mortuary cold room. Had Leif had time to carry out the autopsy? Tekla had asked him to pull out all the stops, but she didn't know if he had it in him.

When Lundgren had finished, he ambled off towards the warm light of the service area shop. He was large, but had lost several kilos since his knife wound that summer. And he walked a little more carefully, as if he were afraid of slipping. He had aged several years in a matter of months.

As she followed, Tekla tried to warm up by swinging her arms against the cold.

"You mentioned childhood memories. Were your autumns this freezing?" Lundgren asked.

"Feels more like late summer. There was never really an autumn. From crimson leaves straight to whiteout."

"That sounds wonderful, in a way. To skip the autumn slush, I mean."

Lundgren went to the cash desk and asked Tekla if she wanted anything. Her eyes roamed aimlessly across the shelves of sweets.

"Three energy drinks and a large coffee," she replied.

"Something to go with that?"

Tekla shook her head. Lundgren had bought a cling-filmed chicken curry wrap. They sat down by the entrance. Lundgren got out two headache tablets and took them with his coffee.

"You still have your headache?"

"It's not too bad," Lundgren answered.

Tekla sat and fidgeted with her ribbed coffee cup, debating whether to call. Annoyed by her own indecision. "I'm so glad you came along."

Lundgren smiled and changed his position on the chair. He looked uncomfortable on all furniture, he was always a little too big. "I'd much rather take a road trip to Jämtland with you than sit at home and wait for a winter that never comes."

"What does your boss say?"

"What do you think? Is there such a thing as a decent boss?"

Tekla thought about Nordensköld and swallowed a sick feeling. "You have a point. I've never known anyone to be entirely happy with theirs. Seems to be some kind of law of nature."

"To hell with bosses. As long as I'm able to hang with Tekla Berg, just the two of us." He took a large bite of his wrap and continued with his mouth full. "At a fancy dinner like this in the middle of . . . Hälsingland . . . Is it Hälsingland we're in?" Lundgren smiled. Tekla felt herself warm from the inside out.

"It's certainly nice that you're here," she said.

"The pleasure is on my side," Lundgren said in very poor English, tearing the last of the paper off his wrap. The curry sauce ran out onto the white tray. "I like playing detectives with you."

"It could get quite exciting." She sipped some of her luke-warm coffee. "Not such a bad idea to have a policeman along."

"I'll be keeping a low profile."

"We'll see," Tekla said. Only now did she notice how freezing cold her feet had become. She looked down at the dirty Stan Smith shoes, noted Lundgren's heavy boots, and then contemplated the darkness outside the petrol station. She made up her mind and took out her phone. After four rings, a gravelly voice answered.

"Hi, it's Tekla Berg here. Sorry I'm calling so late—"

"It's . . . half past two."

"Oh my God, has it got that late?" Tekla went on. "But you're awake?" She could picture how the autopsy technician must have pulled off the mask he wore because of his sleep apnea. He coughed hard and breathed heavily for a few long seconds.

"I am now."

"Good. I wonder if you've had time to do an autopsy on the woman?"

"You'll have to call tomorrow. I can't . . ."

"No."

"What do you mean, no?"

"You're no longer sleeping, so you may as well tell me. I have to know. It can't wait until tomorrow."

"Tekla Berg, you said . . . what's the name of your boss?"

"Hampus Nordensköld, I can text you his mobile number so you can call and wake him up. But I don't think you'll be able to get me sacked for this. No point in trying to scare me with that. I'm totally immune to threats of dismissal. You can ask me to buy you a bottle of whisky instead, as a thank you. That would be a much friendlier attitude."

Leif seemed to deliberate.

"I did the autopsy yesterday evening, and missed dinner as a result. The lady wife was not happy."

"I can buy her something nice too."

"The histology report isn't ready yet, of course, but—"

"What did you find?"

"No cardiovascular problems apart from some fluid in the

pericardium. Brain, nothing. Lungs filled with fluid, just like the rest of the body."

"Her albumin was low, so that makes sense," Tekla interjected.

"The liver was swollen and inflamed through and through. It'll be interesting to see what the pathologist has to say. The gut was oedematous, but no sign of earlier operations or any tumour. I'd say that the most striking thing was extensive endometriosis."

Tekla's eyes fastened on Lundgren, who was wiping curry from the corners of his mouth.

"Really?"

"Yes, she wouldn't have found it easy to get pregnant," Leif said.

"But she's had a child, hasn't she?" Tekla asked.

"Hard to say," Leif replied. "Certainly not a caesarian. And considering all the pelvic adhesions and the severe endometriosis, I'd be surprised if she'd ever been pregnant."

Tekla looked right through Lundgren, all the way to the Nobel Hospital and the small boy's searching eyes.

"But you're not certain?"

"No . . . but probably not."

"Probably never been pregnant, is that what you're saying?"

"That's right."

Tekla thanked Leif for his help and tucked away her phone.

"What?" Lundgren asked, putting down the mess of cornbread, bright yellow sauce and wilting iceberg lettuce.

"Nothing," Tekla said. "Just a strange piece of the puzzle that I have to try and fit in. I'll tell you later." There was no need to tell Lundgren everything, his mere presence was already more than enough. Eventually she would let him have all the details of the drama at the Nobel Hospital, the dioxin, the mushrooms, the woman and the man . . . She had given him a brief summary, but right now she just wanted to enjoy some time together with a man she found so attractive, yet was afraid to let into her life. They finished their coffee break and walked back to the car.

Lundgren handed Tekla the keys. "Are your tyres studded?" she said.

"Should they be?" Lundgren asked, with an equal measure of childlike curiosity and sudden consternation in his eyes.

A Stockholmer through and through, Tekla thought, wearily shaking her head as she sat down behind the steering wheel to take the night shift into the nation's heart.

BROMMA, STOCKHOLM
Tuesday evening, 12 November

There was a sour smell. Some old milk packet, perhaps, or a forgotten piece of cheese. Silva glanced at the kitchen clock. It was too late to start sorting out the chaos. He opened the refrigerator and stared into what felt like his own innermost void. He considered going down to the pizzeria but decided he couldn't be bothered. He didn't want to see anyone. Brommaplan was like a small village where everybody knew everything about everyone else, at least those who had lived there for a while. There was a piece of meat hiding under a plate. Silva wondered how long it had been there. When did meat turn dangerous? Should he fry it up again? He cut it into strips which he arranged on two slices of rye crisp with French mustard. There was half a bottle of Casillero del Diablo in the refrigerator door. He found a glass that was passably clean, sank onto a kitchen chair, pushed aside some old newspapers and magazines and poured himself some wine. Knocked it back, cold with a touch of acidity. Helped himself to another glass. Or should he call Agneta, who lived three floors up? They stopped seeing each other several years ago, but he hadn't spotted her with anyone else. No, that would feel like taking out a year-old piece of meat, vacuum packed to be sure, but nevertheless way past its use-by date.

He tried to concentrate on his work, the only constant in his life. Apart from Paolo, of course. Silva needed no papers. No to-do lists on his phone. In his head he ran through what he knew so far about the case at the Nobel Hospital. To his intense irritation, he realised that there were gaps in the story. A crazy woman comes to the hospital together with her son, gets lost down in the cellars and then reappears in Intensive Care where she sticks a knife into her husband's heart. She herself then collapses, is put on a respirator for a few days and . . . dies. *Puta madre*, what's going on? And she had been poisoned with dioxin. The question was whether the husband had also been poisoned. It would take another day or two to find that out, if indeed he managed to tease the information out of the N.O.D., which ought to be feasible. Would it have been the same people who poisoned the wife?

But above all: who were these people? How did the little boy fit into the story? Was he quite simply their son? Had they run a D.N.A. test on him? Probably not. There were so many loose threads.

He drank half the glass and got to his feet. Realised how tired he was, how his body felt heavy, as if he was wearing one of those divers' suits from two centuries ago. He turned on the light in the living room, saw that the chaos extended even there. But who was going to complain? His son? He was just as messy. Lotta perhaps, Paolo's girlfriend, she seemed very tidy. Silva switched on his Pioneer stereo set from 1992 and put on George Benson's "Breezin'". He needed to pump a little positive energy into his weary veins. He went back to the kitchen and took a bite of the meat. Tough as leather, and cold, but it didn't taste too bad, maybe because the French mustard killed all the bacteria. The clean, clear tones of Benson's guitar filled the apartment.

His phone rang. He turned down the music.

"*Hijo.*"

"Hi Dad. How's life?"

"I'm tired. You? What are you up to?"

"We're going to the cinema."

"Sounds as if you're walking in the middle of the motorway."

"Sergels Torg."

"You and Lotta?"

"Yep."

"Say hi and smother her with kisses from me."

Silence at the other end of the line.

"Was there anything in particular you wanted?" Silva asked.

"Not at all, just wanted to check how you were."

"Any reason why I shouldn't be fine?"

"No, no, it's just that . . ."

"What?"

"You looked so tired the last time we saw each other."

"That's work for you. You'll understand when you grow up." He knew immediately that the remark was gratuitous, the sort that would put Paolo in a bad mood. "Surely there's nothing wrong with being tired?"

"Of course not. But perhaps you ought to be taking better care of yourself."

"How does one do that?"

"Maybe cut back on the booze. Maybe get some more exercise and not just sit there all day long."

Silva took a defiant mouthful of wine. "I walk more than most of my colleagues at work."

"For sure. It's up to you what you do with your body. I'm only saying . . ."

"I appreciate your concern. *Claro*. But you don't have to worry. Do you know what age *abuela* lived to?"

"Didn't she die before I was born?" Paolo said with a laugh.

"She was old when she had me."

"That's no age today. Way below the average for Swedes."

"She was Chilean. And it was many years ago."

"I know. But you live in Sweden now. Perhaps you should also reduce your meat consumption? Have you heard about greenhouse gasses and meat production? It accounts for fifteen per cent of the world's emissions."

"That's just theories though, isn't it?"

"O.K., Dad," Paolo sighed. "You decide for yourself what you want with your life. I guess it's too late to teach an old dog new tricks. Let's speak tomorrow. We're going in to see the movie now."

Did that imply that he was an old dog?

"I'm sorry, *hijo*. I didn't mean . . ."

"I know."

"Enjoy the film."

"Chat later."

Paolo hung up. Silva needed something stronger. He got out a new glass and filled it with ice. Then he found a near-empty bottle of Pisco Sour and helped himself to the last dregs before slumping down on the leather sofa in the living room. His calls with his son always left him with mixed feelings. It made him proud that Paolo was so independent, so driven and full of ambition. Environmentally aware and conscious of his diet, politically engaged – even if he was too much of a centrist for Silva's own tastes – mindful and informed. Perhaps it was just that it reminded him how old he was, of how he himself had once been equally naïve and curious about life. That was many years back, and here he was now, sitting in an apartment on Brommaplan. Nothing wrong with the neighbourhood as such, he was just so bloody alone. And he could see himself growing increasingly bitter. It wasn't him. Ought not to be him. He still had one third of his life ahead of him, why not make something of it? Oddly enough, he came to think of Rebecka Nilsén.

He took a large gulp of the drink. Turned his mind back to the case. There was no doubt that the presence of that doctor, who was so on the ball, was a good thing. She was the one who'd worked out that it was dioxin. Then what about the till receipt she'd been talking about? Did that mean he had to get in touch with some surly colleagues from Norrland, just to enquire about a chit from a cash register? He had to follow up all leads, for example that old man who came in from the accident in Stuvsta. For that, he needed more help, so he would have to talk to his boss about it. On the other hand, the N.O.D. now appeared to have taken over the investigation, simply because there was dioxin involved. He wondered who was handling the biochemical side of things? He had an idea who it might be, but it would need to be confirmed. Would he be cheeky enough to call his one contact at the N.O.D.? He took a large mouthful of the Pisco and at last felt his body beginning to relax. A few gulps more. He turned the volume up. George Benson and his funky band were pounding through the loudspeakers, all he needed now was for that dreadful man with young children to ring the doorbell and complain. He couldn't face any more rows today.

He found the number, drained the last drops of Chile's national drink and dialled. The familiar voice answered after two rings.

RÄTANSBYN

Wednesday morning, 13 November

From time to time, Tekla heard a mixture of throat clearing and lip smacking from the back seat and felt the car rock as Lundgren changed position. Then silence again. Every half hour she started the engine and turned the heating up as high as it would go. It took a few minutes for the warmth to spread through the car. Lundgren didn't wake up once, and he seemed to be making his noises in his sleep. He was lying on his side under a grey emergency blanket with the rear seats folded flat. Tekla found herself dozing pleasantly, probably deeply enough for it to count as sleep. She knew all about spending the night in cars in parking lots from her teenage years; older friends, nocturnal adventures with quite a lot of moonshine, clumsy boys who pulled their caps down to hide the pimples on their foreheads.

"Is it still night?" Lundgren suddenly asked.

Tekla turned in her reclined front seat. "It's seven. An hour to go."

"God it's cold."

Tekla switched the engine on again. "There's no such thing as bad weather . . ."

"Just crappy cars, is that it? I have to pee," Lundgren said. Tekla stepped out and opened the back of the car. Lundgren slid to his feet, his joints stiff from the night and his eyes blind in the Jämtland darkness. He took out his mobile and turned on the torch. "I'll go behind the shop."

Tekla saw him walk carefully round the corner of the square box of a shop. He limped more now that he was tired, the injuries from that summer clearly caused him pain.

Two simple lamps lit up the green sign which said Tempo in

white letters. Apart from the even sound of the engine, the area lay in complete silence. During the last hours of the night, Tekla had been able to count exactly three cars passing by on Route 315, ten metres away.

For a few cold minutes, as she waited for Lundgren to empty his bladder, Tekla turned her face up to the pristine snowflakes as they fell. It was November, and even though the temperature had slipped to a few degrees below zero, there was still a risk that warmer days would melt away the snow cover before winter set in and protected it for good. She tried to see through the compact darkness out there, remembered that they had passed by water on both sides of the road just before they reached the shop three hours earlier. A neck of land, something that Nordensköld and Moussawi had probably never even heard of, but as much a part of Tekla's childhood as a climbing frame or a bicycle with training wheels. It was a common feature back home in the forests around Edsåsdalen, the perfect location for a log cabin from which one could fish as well as hunt. Wide open. Light from both sides. Freedom. The darkness did not yield to her eyes, but it did clear the way for something she had not felt for so long. A kind of liberating calm. Her head was beginning to ache again, since her brain had received no caffeine from either coffee or energy drink, but she didn't care. She welcomed the pressure across her temples, decided that she could force away the pain, send it off into the darkness, not allow any more stress in. Was it really that simple? A snowflake landed right in the middle of one of her eyelids. It tickled a little, and made her think how glad she and Simon used to be when they woke up and their father called to them from the kitchen: "I see snow!"

"There we are," Lundgren's slightly more cheerful voice could be heard a few metres away. "That's the sacred relics frozen off."

"Whatever," Tekla said, shaking her head at the male inanity. As if every man had the British Crown Jewels between his legs. They got into the car and Tekla watched as Lundgren tried to smooth down his hair, which was standing on end.

"Just in case you meet some hot chick up here," Tekla said, fascinated.

"You never know . . ." Lundgren said, giving up. "Although I do actually already have one sitting right beside me."

Please don't let's have any emotional displays now, Tekla thought, feeling uncomfortable, but she was saved by Lundgren's phone going off. He checked it briefly but seemed uninterested. Tekla looked at her own mobile and saw that the battery had run out during the cold night hours. Useless. She plugged the charger into the cigarette lighter.

"Did you manage to get any sleep?"

"Yes indeed," Lundgren said. "I'm just a bit hungry now."

"You didn't eat much at the petrol station."

"Neither would you have, if you'd tasted that yellow gunge."

They sat looking at their mobiles while the Ford spewed its ethanol out into the last hour of the Jämtland night. To check her bearings, Tekla studied a map in her head and saw that Rätansbyn was indeed in Jämtland, very close to Härjedalen, and that they had left Hälsingland not all that long ago. By now, her phone had recharged sufficiently for her to receive Silva's call.

"Tekla."

"Are you at work or—"

"Not today."

"O.K.," Silva said. "I thought I'd update you a bit on what's going on. Can we meet?"

"That'll probably be tricky, unless you happen to be passing through Jämtland."

"Jämtland?"

"A friend and I thought we'd follow up on that receipt thing from Tempo."

"What are you talking about? What do you mean, Jämtland? Have you gone completely crazy?"

"Not in the least, but I have someone beside me who would sometimes match that description." Lundgren acknowledged the compliment with a crooked smile.

"You're not to go playing police," Silva said. "I've already contacted Östersund."

"Good, that means more sharp minds."

"Tekla, I—"

"Can't stop me. You can always try, but I'm quite—"

"Stubborn," Silva cut in. "You don't need to remind me."

"You wanted to tell me something."

"Yes, we have the results of the tests done in Umeå for the woman. High levels of dioxin, you were right."

"So what happens now?"

"I suspect they've enlisted a group from N.O.D., called C.B.R.N.-E."

"Which is?"

"They deal with biochemical weapons and a few other top secret things. Nerds with too much authority and far too little to do."

"Sounds advanced."

"Not especially," Silva said testily. "In practice it's just a couple of guys who swallowed a chemistry textbook. Swots from high school."

"Judging by your patronising tone, I take it you don't expect to be invited to their Christmas party?"

"Rebecka has barred me from the investigation."

"But you're going to ignore that because you're as stubborn as me."

"That would be a slight exaggeration, but . . ."

"And who has access to dioxin?" Tekla asked.

"Nobody in Sweden. That's why the N.O.D. are going to have to get in touch with their partners abroad."

Tekla fell silent. Her mind was buzzing. She thought about Sardor and Victor Umarov, whose connections to Russia she had vaguely understood, but there were other countries that were not above attacking individuals on foreign soil. Her thoughts went to Israel, the U.S.A., Iran and China. And they probably weren't the only ones.

"That seems complicated," she finally said. "My main concern is finding out who the woman and the man were. I just want to help the boy."

"I know," Silva said. "But you mustn't pass yourself off as police or get up to any other nonsense."

Tekla wanted to tell him about Lundgren, but saw that it could cause a major row.

"No chance."

Silva went on: "I'm going to dig a little deeper into the accident they were brought in from at Stuvsta. The N.O.D. have taken over here at the Nobel but the accident is still our patch. I thought I'd be a bit naughty and—"

"Probably best you don't tell me."

"No, you're absolutely right."

"Are you at the Nobel now?" Tekla looked at the dashboard. "It's nearly eight o'clock."

"I'm sitting in the entrance having a coffee. Why do you ask?"

"You're up bright and early. Will you be able to get hold of any information, do you think?" Tekla asked.

"The advantage of having worked in the same city for as long as I have is you get to know one or two people. I've invited many colleagues to share good Chilean meat."

"You know someone at the N.O.D.?"

"Possibly."

Tekla was about to hang up when she remembered one detail. "Check out the other patient who was admitted."

"What other patient?"

"The old man who was hit by the same car. He said he came from Serbia. He was in Orthopaedics with concussion and a broken forearm."

"Oh yes. I've been meaning to get on to that. But first I have a long list of things I must do today."

Silva cut the call. Tekla looked through the window, she could just make out the contours of a house beyond the parking area. It was eight o'clock and the day was finally dawning. Could it have been the man who poisoned the woman with dioxin? And if so, why? A crime of passion? Were they involved in something criminal? That seemed

371

unlikely, judging by their clothes. None of it made sense. She lowered the volume on the radio and, at that moment, a car drew up next to the Ford and a woman got out. She went over to the shop entrance to open up.

"Time to have breakfast?" Tekla said.

"And play detectives," Lundgren replied, forming his swollen fingers into a pistol.

"You promised you'd keep a low profile."

"Promise."

"Not only for my sake. You could lose your job if you—"

"I know," Lundgren said. "I'm just here as your friend."

NOBEL HOSPITAL
Wednesday morning, 13 November

His duffel coat was heavy with damp and there was a smell of old sheep in the small lift. Silva avoided the looks from the people in white, but couldn't help noticing how they turned away from him, as if he were a tramp they were afraid of touching. The lift finally stopped and all the doctors and nurses got out. He took off his duffel coat in the small space for putting on those blue shoe covers and debated whether to hang it on the back of a chair. In the end, he decided to carry it in one hand and went into the reception where he had been so many times during the last week. He was looking for the woman with the frizzy hair and the dark support stockings, the only doctor he had seen in Intensive Care wearing a dress. And a doctor's coat. He found her outside the staff room, where some sort of meeting had apparently been taking place. Most of them came walking at a leisurely pace, each with a white mug in their hand. He caught her eye and it was clear that she wasn't particularly happy to see him.

"Doctor Elmqvist."

"Eva. Surnames make it so formal."

Silva could never get used to that. It simply didn't sound right, addressing a doctor by their first name. He couldn't imagine his father doing it when he went to have his prostate checked out each year in Santiago.

"I was actually planning to bother Tekla Berg, but I heard this morning that she's taken a few days off."

Silva kept up with Elmqvist as she set off for the large I.C.U. reception area. "I see. So then you thought that I might be able to help you instead?"

"Just briefly. I know you have a lot to do."

"Don't worry. It's not that bad. I only need to look after three wrecks who've had liver transplants, arrange a replacement for a colleague who's at home with a sick child and was meant to be on the night shift, argue with the other hospitals in town who are refusing to come up with beds, some brilliant new directive from on high, and then I'll probably . . . no, I guess I can forget about that . . ." She spread her hands in a theatrical gesture. "I'd planned to have lunch with an old classmate from Obstetrics, but I guess it'll end up being a cup of hot chocolate in the coffee room at around one. But apart from that I have oceans of time for policemen."

"I'm really sorry, but I just wondered if you took any samples from the man who was here."

Elmqvist looked surprised.

Silva elaborated. "The man who was stabbed in the heart. Do you know if you took any tissue samples to test him for dioxin?"

Elmqvist looked as if he had asked the way to some forbidden Inca temple. "Why would we have done that? We didn't suspect that he had been poisoned, did we?"

"Not then, maybe, when he was brought in injured from the road accident. But later, when it turned out that the woman had been poisoned."

Elmqvist scratched her scalp. "You'll have to ask the forensics guys about that. I have no idea what's going on there." She turned away and seemed to be looking for someone.

"Do you have a name?" Silva asked.

"In Forensics? No." Then a thought struck Elmqvist. "I thought that other officer was in charge of the investigation."

"Rebecka, yes, but . . ."

"Listen, I honestly can't be bothered with any police turf wars today."

"There is absolutely no problem here, I promise you."

Elmqvist looked down at Silva's loafers. "You promise?"

"Yes."

"And I don't believe you. You know, now I really have to . . ."

"I understand. Sorry for bothering you."

Silva was fairly confident that he'd be able to dig up a contact at the Institute of Forensic Medicine in Solna. He had been there many times over the years. He left the I.C.U. and took off the blue shoe covers. Just then, the doors to the department slid slowly open and he saw none other than his chief antagonist walking straight towards him.

"Alvaro," Nilsén said. "I didn't know you were such an early bird. A headache? Upset stomach?"

Silva was tongue-tied, cursing himself for not having prepared something punchy to say in case he ran up against his tormentor. Instead, he burst into forced and completely unnatural laughter that died out when they found themselves standing in the way of some blue-clad staff coming into Intensive Care. They had to take a few steps back. Nilsén's sidekick Linnander seemed put out.

"So, what's happened?" Nilsén asked.

"Forgive me, but your clothes . . ."

"What about them?" Nilsén asked, pulling a little at her white coat with black patches.

"Is that real cow?"

"Very funny," Nilsén said, looking offended.

"Where do you get them all from? Can you guys at the N.O.D. really afford to spend so much time shopping? I suppose it does explain your lousy clearance rates."

Nilsén smiled and scraped a little at Silva's shirt. "Let me know if you want some advice on taste. Or at least the name of a dry-cleaner."

Silva looked down and saw the wine stain. He adjusted his jacket so it didn't show.

"But seriously," Nilsén said in a harder tone, "what are you doing here? Looking for a lost cat? Because you have understood, haven't you, that the dioxin investigation is none of your business? I've told Umeå that they're not to give out information to anyone but me."

"Who's in charge of this at your shop?"

"Didn't you hear?" Linnander asked.

"Oh, I see," Silva said, trying to stay calm. "The trainee . . ."

Linnander took a hasty step forward but Nilsén held up her hand. "Now then, easy." She turned her back to her younger colleague and lowered her voice. "Time to withdraw, Alvaro. This is no longer your case."

Silva shook his head and began to walk away. "That remains to be seen."

"No. Nothing remains to be seen. I guess I'll just have to call your boss, so it's man to man. Maybe that's the only thing that works with you."

Silva ignored Nilsén and walked on to the nearest stairwell. He tried to focus on the case. On the woman and the man. He would call Forensics and then try to get some information about the old man who was injured in the traffic accident in Stuvsta. He needed to go back to the hit-and-run and understand more about what had happened. The only good thing about this morning was the increased resources he had been given for that very purpose. That had allowed him to send out two patrols to knock on doors near the incident. But later he had a lunchtime meeting which might perhaps disperse some of the clouds surrounding the N.O.D.'s mysterious ways.

RÄTANSBYN
Wednesday morning, 13 November

"Good morning," Tekla said and, as she came into the warmth, she realised how frozen her feet were. They were already starting to ache in the shop entrance.

"Good morning," answered the woman they had seen opening up. She was stacking a shelf with packets of broth. Around forty, plump, she had slightly wavy hair with a crooked side-parting. Her cheeks were chubby, her thighs stocky, and she was the very picture of robust good health. Tekla felt like a tramp who had spent the night in a doorway. Luckily Lundgren was there to balance them out.

In her mind, Tekla read the receipt she'd seen in the emergency room. "We'd like to ask you about some customers of yours."

The woman continued setting out dark blue packets of herbs, salt and soy sauce. Glancing at Lundgren, who had gone to choose things from the bread shelves, she said: "You don't look like police."

Tekla smiled. "No, we're doctors from the Nobel Hospital."

"That's a bit unusual."

Hearing her slightly cool tone, Tekla decided it would be wise to rewind. "Rätansbyn's just by the border with Jämtland, isn't it?"

"That's right." The woman picked up the empty cardboard box and walked towards the storeroom beyond the refrigerated counter. Tekla followed.

"I'm from Edsåsdalen."

The woman stopped. "You don't sound like it."

"Oh yes I do, once I've been home for a while it . . ."

The woman brightened. "Perhaps a bit now."

377

"We've driven through the night and we're quite tired. Do you have coffee?"

"I'm sure we can fix that," the woman said, leaving Tekla to pick up ten energy drinks and a few Daim chocolate bars. The woman returned with two cups of coffee. "Milk?"

"Not for me," Tekla said. "Magnus? Milk?"

"A splash, please," Lundgren answered.

The woman took a new packet from the refrigerated counter and poured. "But you take it black, of course." Tekla sensed a shift in the woman's look, a sudden meeting of minds. "But boiled coffee is best of all." Then she went over to the tills and continued with her preparations for the day.

Tekla savoured both the coffee and the woman's down-to-earth manner, which seemed so familiar. "We work at the emergency clinic and two of our patients unfortunately died this week, in rather dramatic circumstances."

"I see, that sounds serious," the woman said. She sounded as if she meant it.

"We think they came from around here."

For the first time, the woman stopped what she was doing. She put down the cigarette packets she was busy loading into the plexiglass container above the cash desk.

"Oh no, really?"

"The man was in this shop exactly two weeks ago, buying rye bread, semi-skimmed milk and macaroni."

The woman seemed to be searching her memory. Tekla didn't doubt for one second that she remembered all her customers' shopping lists. How many could there be in a week? A hundred or so?

"Two weeks ago, you said?"

"Friday two weeks ago, yes. A man in his forties. He may have had a little boy with him."

"And comes from Bulgaria?" the woman asked.

Tekla saw that Lundgren had stopped by the shelf with the sweets and was listening, though he was trying not to look too interested. "Well yes, that could be right. If he said so. Unfortunately, he's dead."

"Oh my God. Dear Lord. And the boy . . .?"

"No, he's alive. But unfortunately, the woman also died."

"How awful. What happened . . . No, I mustn't ask. We become far too nosy here . . ." The woman seemed to be having difficulty containing herself. Tekla felt very sorry for her, she appeared genuinely shocked by what had happened. Lundgren sat down on a low bench by the entrance and drank his coffee.

"We're trying to work out who they were. Did you talk to them much?"

"No, or rather . . . I only saw the man maybe three times since they moved here."

"Moved here? When roughly was that?"

"Well it wasn't him who told me, it was her. She would come in about once a week. I asked her, when was it, maybe a year or so ago? She said that they'd moved here to Rätansbyn from Svenstavik."

"Where's that?"

"Forty kilometres north of here, just follow the E45 . . ."

Tekla unrolled the map in her mind. "And here in Rätansbyn, where did they live?"

"I'm not sure, but I think Per-Arne down at the camping site might know. He has tabs on most people in the area, he hunts and moves around a lot."

"Per-Arne?"

"Flovik. He's the manager of Rätans Camping."

"Thank you." Tekla looked at Lundgren and nodded that they were ready. He staggered to his feet and put their shopping on the conveyor belt.

"Where's the camping site?"

The woman smiled. "Hard to miss. Take a right on the road."

"Just one last question," Tekla said. "Did you notice anything out of the ordinary about this family?"

"Well . . . no, I'm not sure what it might be. Except that she, the mother, seemed to have a particularly good way with the boy. Their Swedish was excellent, so of course I wondered what they were doing here."

"Did you ask?"

"No. I assumed they were berry pickers. Or that the husband worked cash in hand as a labourer. There are masses of Poles, Bulgarians and Albanians on sites all the way over to Östersund."

"But you said that they might be from Bulgaria?"

"Yes."

Lundgren paid and they said thank you for all the help. "Delicious coffee," Tekla said before leaving, and she was about to close the door when the woman asked: "What did your parents do in Edsåsdalen?"

"Dad worked at the factory, but he's no longer alive. Mamma . . ." Tekla's eyes met those of the woman.

"I understand," she replied.

Tekla said nothing, leaving the shop. The woman perhaps imagined that her mother had calloused hands, deep furrows in her face from the pain of having raised so many children, cooked so much food, washed so many rag rugs . . . But that wasn't true. The only images Tekla could conjure up were of her mother on a chair in the kitchen with a long cigarillo in her hand.

When they emerged, day had broken and the snow was falling more heavily. Tekla and Lundgren had to brush a centimetre-thick layer of new snow off the car.

"A true detective, no less," Lundgren said. Tekla caught his searching look and felt herself blushing. "Couldn't have done it better myself," he added, knocking the snow off the brush. They sat down in the front seat. Tekla drove carefully out from the parking area, tested the brakes and confirmed her suspicion that it would have been good to have had studded tyres.

"Bulgarians," Tekla said. "What do you think?"

"I'm not sure," Lundgren answered. "I know that there are many Thais who pick berries and mushrooms, and there must be people from other countries as well, but Bulgarians . . . I'd be more inclined to link them to organised crime and the cities."

"Your department."

"We've launched some raids where I know Bulgarians were involved."

Tekla's thoughts went off in different directions. Organised crime didn't fit the picture she had of the family. She drove at snail's pace along the lake road and saw that the woman had been right. It was only a few hundred metres to the camping site. They stopped before a low house with closed shutters. A pickup truck was parked there, with a ladder propped against the cargo bed. Tekla got out of the car. A dog came walking around the house, a Labrador which approached and calmly sniffed at Tekla. She held out her hand to introduce herself.

A short man appeared through the whirling snow. He was wearing an open jacket and a dark shirt which strained across a large belly.

"Do you have any beds free?" Tekla joked, to break the ice.

"Certainly do, but you'll have to manage without heating."

Tekla gave her name and explained why they were there. "The woman in Tempo said that you might have known the couple."

The man opened the front door of the pickup and waved the dog in. It slunk aboard with ease and lay on the floor. "Can't really say that I knew them. They came by once to swim here at the camping site. I haven't seen them since."

"But you know where they live?"

The man pushed back his lined cap. "Why do you ask?"

"We were told that you know who lives in the area."

He waited for Tekla to continue and she added: "Because you hunt."

"We'd like to see their house," Lundgren said.

"But they're not there," Per-Arne Flovik replied curtly.

"We know, but . . ."

The man looked sceptical. As if he suspected that there was something dubious about their errand.

"We've cleared it with the police," Lundgren chipped in. That seemed to reassure Flovik, who finally showed them on a map how to get to the house.

"Nice white lie," Tekla said as they drove away from Rätans Camping.

"What?"

"Cleared it with the police."

"You have to let me help, just a little," Lundgren said and smiled. Then Tekla saw how he squinted at the windscreen.

"How's the headache going?" she replied.

"It won't let up. Don't know what it is. Perhaps I'm just tired."

Tekla followed Flovik's directions and drove along Route 315 towards Överturingen, almost missing the turning north. The road was narrow, they would have to back out again if they encountered any vehicle larger than an estate car. And it was a long way to Lake Stortjärnen. The forest never seemed to end. "Who chooses to live this far from civilisation?"

"Someone who doesn't need broadband?"

"Or who doesn't want to be disturbed."

"I think it's mostly to do with money," Lundgren said. "Imagine how cheap it must be to rent a house here."

The forest opened up into a glade. Tekla stopped and brought out her phone. "No coverage. But the distance is about right."

"And he said the first house on the right. Must be this one."

Tekla drove off the road and rolled to a halt in front of the low, black single-storey house. There was a smaller building to the right, maybe a garage, but if so then only for one car. And a shed further away towards the forest, which looked on the point of collapse. No footprints in the blanket of snow, which had grown to several centimetres thick. Tekla nearly slipped a few times in her trainers. She peered in through a window.

"A living room with old furniture. Neat and tidy." She went right around the house, looked into a bedroom with two separate beds, each in its own corner. Like when older people give up sleeping together. Dark bedcovers. No clothes on chairs or the floor. Nothing to suggest that anyone was living there.

They met at the front of the house. "It feels as if nobody's lived here for a while," Tekla said. As she turned to Lundgren, she saw him falter. "Are you O.K.?"

Lundgren walked to the car, opened the door and sat down in the front seat. "I'm fine. Just a drop in blood pressure."

"You look pale. Are you sure?"

"I could maybe use a piece of your chocolate bar, if you think you can spare some," he joked.

Tekla brought out the Daim and an energy drink. "Are you really sure you don't want some?"

Lundgren shook his head. He preferred his bottle of mineral water. "So, what do we do now?"

"I don't think we're going to get much further here." Tekla closed the door, brushed snow off the seat and tried to start the engine. She looked anxiously at Lundgren when she heard it coughing.

"Ethanol," he said. "Can be a bit tricky in the cold."

She tried once more. This time, the engine started.

"Lucky."

Lundgren did not seem worried. He looked out at the forest.

"The wind's come up," Tekla said.

"Yes, isn't it lovely?"

"What do you mean, lovely? It can get bloody cold, bloody quickly."

"Yes, but it reminds me of skiing up in the mountains."

"Well, if that's what it makes you think of." She looked out. "Just a second." Tekla opened the door and headed for the forest, past the garage, past an old water pump. She continued over untouched snow, planting her feet firmly with each step, feeling the soft but uneven ground, perhaps heather or moss. She came to a large spruce fir whose branches hung barely half a metre above the ground and formed a dry hut which extended to the roots. Tekla found a way in between two metre-long boughs and finally reached the trunk. She ran her hands along the rough surface, picked at a hardened strand of resin. Smelled her fingers and closed her eyes. Then she went back to the car.

"What were you doing?" Lundgren asked.

"Feeling something uneven. Back home, everything's so smooth. So sterile and hard."

Tekla turned the car and drove along the same road they had taken before. It was snowing more heavily now, and the windscreen wipers had to work hard.

"You look happier," Lundgren said.

"Do I?"

"It's probably the forest."

They sat there, each lost in their own world. As usual, Tekla had something buzzing around above her head, calling for attention, a detail, some information she hadn't let in to the warmth. She thought about the room with two beds. Two oldies. She recalled what Silva had said about going back to the scene of the accident. Tekla thought about the old man who'd had the misfortune to be standing at the bus stop when the woman tried to run over her husband. Collateral damage. She thought back to when she had visited him, how taciturn he'd been, just saying that he was in Sweden to visit churches, that he was from Serbia. Tekla saw him before her, lying there with the sheet covering everything except his arms and hands. She couldn't see anything noteworthy. No rings on his fingers. No jewellery around his neck. Nothing that could give her a clue as to who he was. But his neighbour. There had been another man in the room, with a broken hip. Newly operated on. Perhaps he could provide some more information on the old man from Serbia with an interest in churches.

KUNGSHOLMEN, STOCKHOLM
Wednesday, 13 November

There was steam on the windows. Silva was surprised at how many people were out having coffee on Kungsholmen in the middle of a working Wednesday.

"An extra strong cappuccino and a –" Silva knew he shouldn't, but continued anyway – ". . . one of those things with the nougat filling." The barista, a young man of about twenty-five with a thin ponytail and pimply forehead, answered in English and put a cup in the machine which then began to hiss and rumble.

Silva took the warm cup with the elegant heart-shaped foam topping and walked into the room beyond the bar. Lone men with laptops wearing large, noise-cancelling headphones, but also a group of youngsters who were actually carrying on a conversation. He was just about to turn back when he saw her at a table, partly hidden away to the left.

"*Hola*," he said and started to unwind his scarf. The woman tried to get up but was squeezed in between chair and table. "Don't get up." He bent down and gave her a kiss on the cheek. Silva pulled out a chair and sat down close to the woman he had shared a bed with at least five times.

"Why did you suggest meeting so close to home?" she said in an irritated tone.

Silva took a sip of his coffee and smiled. "I thought you lived in Vällingby, but maybe you've moved?"

Beata Ernryd smirked and shook her head. "You know what I mean."

"Ah, to your office . . ."

Ernryd spread her hands on the table. Silva noted that she still painted her fingernails black, a detail which for some reason he loved.

"So how are things at work?" Silva continued.

"I know why you want to meet up, even though it's two years since the last time."

"*Mentirosa*. It's not been that long, has it?"

"Åbo, October two years ago. The conference hotel in Nådendal. I remember what you said: that you hadn't had anybody since me. As if that were something positive, as if I wanted a eunuch." Ernryd clasped her hands in front of her.

Silva remembered the golden room, the décor looking as if it hadn't been updated since 1984. And more than anything he remembered the fantastic spa where they'd had sex in a sauna.

"Well, nobody forced you to come here today," Silva said, taking a bite out of the brittle pastry. He tried not to look too self-confident, knew very well that integrity was important to Ernryd and she didn't want him to take anything for granted. Some nougat leaked out and stuck to his chin. Before he could pick up his napkin, Ernryd caught the goo with her middle finger, stopping him from doing it himself. She slowly scooped up the creamy filling and then languidly sucked it off her finger while gazing into his eyes. Silva noticed how he blushed and instinctively wanted to look around – was anyone watching them? But he didn't move.

"You had a question?" Ernryd continued, licking her finger clean.

"Yes . . ." Silva had lost the thread. His mind was in his apartment, had he tidied it up? Changed the bedsheets? But then again, she was probably just teasing him. She was married, would never risk going home with him like this in broad daylight. How old were her children? They would have left home by now. Weren't they about ten when the two of them started their relationship a decade ago?

"The dioxin from the woman at the Nobel Hospital. Can you tell me more?"

"Without getting the sack, you mean?"

"Oh come on, you know that whatever you say here will stay—"

"Bullshit. You're going to use it in your little battle with Rebecka Nilsén. Do you think I'm an idiot?"

"Quite the opposite. Which is exactly why I hope you can trust me when I say that—"

"It doesn't matter anyhow," Ernryd continued. "I don't report to her."

"How many of you are there at C.B.R.N.-E.?"

"Four. And we have a very keen boss these days."

Silva finished his coffee and tried to catch Ernryd's hand. She drew it back and smiled. "This isn't going anywhere, just so you're aware."

"*Claro*, I know. You're married."

"I was the last time, too. But I have somebody else now."

"So you're divorced?"

"Not at all, he earns way too much money for that. I can put up with having sex with him every six months. No, the arrangement works just fine. The kids are grown up, manage on their own. And Torsten's always travelling for work. Perfect opportunity for me to get myself a real man, and he's seven years younger."

Silva was angered by his gut reaction, a wave of jealousy. It was irrational and illogical, and yet he couldn't help it. But he was there for something else.

"Do you think we could talk about the case? Just a bit . . ."

Ernryd drank some of her coffee. She seemed to be appeased by his hangdog eyes and pleading voice. "What do you want to know?"

"Have you had the results from the man's tissue samples?"

She nodded.

"And?"

"Him too."

"He also had dioxin in him?"

She nodded carefully. "Sky high levels. He wouldn't have survived more than a few days."

"But got a knife in the heart instead and didn't have time to develop any symptoms," Silva muttered, seeing Elmqvist's frizzy hair before him. Perhaps he could tell her and Tekla, after all.

"What?" Ernryd asked.

"Nothing. He died before there were any signs of ... dioxin poisoning."

"I see," Ernryd said, glancing at her phone. Then she sat up and said: "Remember you didn't hear any of this from me."

"I swear on my son's grave."

"Is your son dead?"

"It's a figure of speech."

Ernryd shook her head and smiled. "You can't imagine what this has set in motion."

"What do you mean?"

"The National Police Commissioner, the whole shebang. After all, dioxin poisoning's something you only hear about at conferences in London and Washington, but now global terrorism has kind of found its way to little old Sweden."

"Terrorism?"

Ernryd laid her hand on Silva's. "You're so naïve. What else are we meant to call it? You do realise it's not a case of some chemistry teacher in the suburbs preparing a little surprise for his friends? There's nobody in Sweden who can handle this kind of stuff."

"So who do you lot think's behind it?"

"That's the ten-thousand-kronor question." Ernryd glanced at her phone, as if she had to hurry back to work any second.

"What other authorities are involved?" Silva asked.

"Which ones aren't?" Ernryd answered rhetorically. "Everybody wants to be part of it and have their say, and at the same time it's all meant to be kept secret." She snorted.

"I can imagine it's politically delicate."

"Delicate doesn't begin to describe it. We know that the dioxin probably comes from our friendly neighbours to the east and that the F.S.B. likely has a finger in the pie. At the same time, we can't communicate with them, it's much too sensitive. So we have to go via other security services, who may have some information, and then try to piece the puzzle together."

"But who can I talk to who knows where the dioxin comes from?"

Ernryd looked Silva straight in the eye. "Do you have another old fuck-buddy who happens to be in charge at the N.O.D.?"

Silva was disgusted by her language. He too had a coarse tongue, and no difficulties with young people who swore. But in this particular situation, he wished that Ernryd would maintain the mystique and play the game the way he wanted it played.

"If you mean Rebecka Nilsén, that was a very long time ago."

"Not so long ago that she's no longer interested," Ernryd said. "That's the kind of thing we women can sense."

RÄTANSBYN TO YTTERHOGDAL

Wednesday, 13 November

"What?"

"Nothing," Tekla said and smiled. She reduced her speed as she approached a bend in the road, knowing full well that an elk or a roe deer could come charging out. Tekla had always thought that roe deer looked so lost, a little bewildered, in some ways naïve. Maybe they were a little scatterbrained. Not like the elk, which was calm and level-headed. But once an elk had built up some speed, it was not as agile as a deer. And Tekla had seen what an elk could do to a car, even as big a car as a Volvo estate, and even if the elk was a yearling and not yet fully grown. She slowed down even more.

"Go on, tell me, you're sitting there smiling to yourself," Lundgren insisted.

Tekla glanced at Lundgren's face. It was the opposite of her own. Where Tekla had inherited her mother's high cheekbones, the skin taut across her slightly sunken cheeks, Lundgren's on the other hand looked healthily plump. That, together with his shamelessly positive temperament, meant that he radiated life.

"I just noticed what beautiful features you have."

Lundgren took Tekla's hand in his. She let it rest there for a few long seconds, then pretended that she needed it to lower the temperature in the car.

They were driving back to Rätansbyn, where a rubbish lorry was in the process of emptying the bins. An elderly lady came walking along the edge of the road in the opposite direction.

Tekla stopped at Tempo for the second time and got out. The

wind immediately found its way in via her bare neck and she pulled her jacket tight around her to stay warm.

The shop was quiet. There were all of three customers in there, each most likely over eighty years old, wandering around filling up their baskets. Another staff member was standing by the boxes of vegetables, a woman, maybe ten years younger than the one they had been talking to earlier. She had short black hair, clearly marked eyebrows which almost looked tattooed and was heavily pregnant, possibly past her thirty-fifth week.

"Hi!" At first Tekla seemed impatient, but she relaxed when the woman from that morning emerged from the beer and soft drinks aisle and she realised that she wouldn't have to repeat their whole story for the benefit of the newcomer.

"I see, didn't you get anywhere with Per-Arne?"

The other woman eyed Tekla and Lundgren with curiosity.

"No problem, he did help us, but the house was empty. We don't think they've been living there for a while."

"Who are you looking for?" the pregnant woman with the plucked eyebrows asked. She looked in the best of health.

"That family, you know, the Bulgarians, the one with the little boy and the husband who works in construction," the other woman said.

"They're not Bulgarian," the woman with the eyebrows said.

"Aren't they? That's what she told me, the woman . . ."

"They're Russian."

"How do you know that?" Tekla asked, eager to hear more.

"I studied Russian in high school. I wanted to apply to the Armed Forces Interpreters' School."

Tekla now had another piece of the puzzle. Somehow, intuitively, it felt more logical.

"Do you know where they've been living lately?" Tekla asked.

"They moved to Ytterhogdal about a month ago."

"Oh, O.K.," woman number one said, slightly offended. As if

there were a competition as to who was better informed about the people who came and went in the shop.

"Do you know where, exactly?"

The pregnant woman stopped what she was doing and altered her stance, rocking lightly back and forth. "Yes. They're renting my third cousins' house."

"Which third cousins?" the first woman said. The battle for information was on, laid bare on the red plastic flooring.

"Jan-Erik and Ann-Kristin. They've gone to New Zealand for a year."

"Ah. Well, in that case," the woman said, turning away, as if she wanted to demonstrate with her whole body that she was certainly not going to offer any more help.

"Is that to the south?" Tekla asked, although she actually knew the answer: Ytterhogdal was forty-three kilometres away.

"About half an hour," the woman with the eyebrows said. "But why do you want to get hold of them?"

"Maria, you really shouldn't . . ." her colleague interrupted, clearly not wanting to give up. Maybe she was the woman's boss.

"It's O.K.," Tekla said. "We've had them as patients and there are some questions we'd like to have answered."

Maria looked confused, so Tekla tried to put her on the right track. "No, we know, we're not the police but . . ."

"We just take a bit of extra responsibility for our patients," Lundgren said. He knew exactly how to reassure even the most suspicious of people.

"I can show you where it is," Maria said.

Tekla was tempted by the offer. It sounded like a difficult place to find. At the same time . . .

"That won't be necessary," Tekla said, staring at the pregnant belly.

"Oh I see," the woman said. "No, don't worry. I'm not due for another month, and besides I don't have that much to do here. I'm only working half days anyhow. Gunilla can manage fine without me for a few hours. Can't you? I'll be back before the afternoon coffee break."

"So you're going to take off just like that?" Gunilla called out from beyond the refrigerated counter.

"Come on, Gunilla. You're just jealous because you're not getting time off."

Gunilla emerged from her hiding place. She stared at Maria, who could clearly stand up for herself.

"Not that I can stop you anyway, it'd be the first time if so." She turned. "You obstinate little . . ."

"Honestly, it really isn't necessary," Tekla said. "We can wait till you're off work. Or come back another day."

Maria went up to Tekla. "I'm *very happy* to come along." Her painted eyebrows had shot up at least two centimetres. Tekla could see that it might be stifling to have to spend all day in a small shop with a control freak like Gunilla.

Lundgren came forward. "That's kind of you. How long do you think we'd be, not more than two hours there and back?"

"It'll take whatever time it takes," Maria said, her mind seemingly already made up. She went to the back of the shop and returned with a jacket in her hand. "I'll put this to charge in the meantime." She took her phone out of her pocket and plugged it in behind the tills. "So. Nice to be able to relax a bit," she said and went out.

They left the shop and got into the car. The snow was falling more heavily.

"What names!" Lundgren said as they rolled through the countryside.

"You mean Gunilla?" the woman asked from where she sat in the front seat.

"No, all the villages. Ytterhogdal. Very exotic. But while we're on the subject of names, you're Maria, right?"

"Yes."

"Is this your first child?" Tekla asked, driving even more carefully now that they had such a precious load.

Maria had put on a woolly hat with earflaps and a bobble. "Yes, very exciting." She shifted slightly in her seat.

"Do you need more space?"

"Not at all," Maria said cheerily. "Everything's uncomfortable anyhow, but it's going really well. The biggest problem is I haven't been able to pee so much these last days."

Tekla thought that the woman looked like a forest nymph, almond-shaped eyes and dark features. She must have Sami blood. Very beautiful.

"Just say the word," Tekla replied.

She accelerated. The road was better now, even if it was snowing more heavily. She glanced at Maria, who was peering out through the windscreen.

"Headache?"

"Don't you think it's unusually bright outside?"

"Not particularly."

"My eyes are stinging. I should have brought my sunglasses."

Tekla thought Maria sounded strained when she spoke. She struggled to breathe between words.

"Are you feeling alright?"

Maria stretched back in her seat. "Maybe I just need a little air." She pressed the window down a few centimetres and gasped for oxygen.

Maria was breathing heavily. "Perhaps I'm getting a bit of a cold. I had a feeling I was coming down with something. But I'm sure it'll pass."

They followed Route 296 and kept left at the turning for the E45. After half an hour, the road bore left, became narrower and more covered in snow. No car seemed to have been along there all day, or else the snowfall had already wiped out the tyre tracks. Every now and then they caught a glimpse of a lake on the right-hand side.

"That's Lake Norra Trollsjötjärnen," Maria said, pointing to where Tekla was to turn left, up into the forest. Now the road became worse. There was already a thick layer of snow and Tekla was having great difficulty seeing the edge of the road.

394

"Do you have studded tyres?" Maria asked.

"Unfortunately not."

"This could get interesting, in that case," Maria said, still in a calm and confident voice. She had grown up here. Was neither surprised nor impressed by the weather.

Tekla drove carefully for another quarter of an hour on twisting roads that never seemed to end. She knew that their Ford Focus was not the best choice for this trip.

"You'll see it soon, on the right-hand side," Maria said.

"What?" Lundgren asked from the back seat.

"Ytterbytjärn, where they live."

"Why so far into the woods?" Tekla asked.

"My cousins? They're a bit different," Maria said and smiled.

A few hundred metres further on they reached a turning off. A long slope down to a little lake, a small clump of trees and some kind of mound, like a rock that had slid down but not quite plopped into the water. Tekla only saw the house when they were almost there. It was snowing heavily and the car somehow slid down the hill, through the thick snow cover – she was afraid it would skid off the gravel road. The trees on both sides looked threatening. She stopped the car next to a tractor standing in front of what appeared to be a small barn, and turned off the engine. No neighbours, no houses for several kilometres around. Perfect for somebody who for some reason was seeking seclusion.

"Do you want to stay here?" Tekla asked Maria, who looked up at her. She was bright red in the face.

"How are you feeling?"

"I don't know if I can get out. Not sure what's wrong with me. Maybe I really am getting flu."

"I can take a look by myself. Or are you coming, Magnus?"

As Tekla stepped out of the car, Silva rang. She shut the door.

"Yes? The signal is terrible." Tekla saw that the phone battery was rapidly running down in the cold. The little symbol in the top right corner was shining red. She cursed.

Silva's voice came and went but Tekla was able to make out what he was saying. "Just wanted to update you." Tekla glanced at Maria, who was breathing heavily in the front seat. She was constantly shifting in her seat, as if she were looking for pockets of oxygen in the car.

"What?" Tekla asked.

"The man also had dioxin in . . ."

"The man was also poisoned with dioxin, is that what you're saying?"

"Yes, and . . ."

"I can't hear you," Tekla said. She waited a long while but the call had finally died. She knocked on the car window and called out: "I'll be right back."

The visibility was dreadful, she could just distinguish the lake a hundred metres further down the slope. The snowfall was different now, the wind was blowing and it was as if the skies were pitching it in from the side. Tekla went up to the door and knocked. The windows were dark. She leaned over a rusty railing and tried to look in, but the windows were frosted up and she couldn't see.

She went round the back. The snow lay twenty centimetres deep and was building by the minute. When she came back to the car, she saw to her dismay that Maria's condition had worsened. She opened the door.

"We have to get you to a hospital, you look pale and sick."

"No . . . I . . ." Maria was struggling to get out and seemed about to faint from sheer exertion. Tekla helped her to her feet and made sure that Maria buttoned up her jacket with the hood over her head. The snow soon settled over them like an extra blanket.

Lundgren got out of the back seat. "What's going on?"

Tekla stared at the heavily pregnant woman. "Don't know. But . . ." Tekla realised that she had been wearing blinkers, focusing on one single thing: finding the cottage. The woman was ill. Was she about to give birth? Or was it something worse?

Maria took some deep breaths.

Tekla tried to think. What could have happened? Was it a

pulmonary embolism? They had after all been sitting still in a car, she was pregnant, which meant a heightened risk of blood clots . . . "Are you wearing support stockings?" she shouted through the wind.

"No."

Tekla got out her phone again. "No coverage. I can't see anything for the snow." She sat down in the front seat and, for the first time in her life, tried pressing "Emergency".

"Emergency Services, how can I help you?"

"I have a woman here who's not feeling well, she's in late-stage pregnancy."

"And where are you?"

"I'm not altogether sure, I have no coverage, but like an hour from Ytterhogdal, by Norra Ytterbytjärnen . . ."

"In which week is—"

The call was interrupted. Tekla stared at the screen. Black.

"Useless fucking battery." She tore open the car door again. "Not working. The battery died."

"Here," Lundgren said, taking out his phone.

"Do you have coverage?"

Lundgren looked at the screen. "No. But I can try walking around a bit and see if I get some."

Hell, Tekla thought. Had Emergency Services understood where they were? They had presumably registered the G.P.S. signal, or how did it work?

"Do that. Call Emergency Services when you can and tell them it's urgent." Lundgren left the car and tramped up the hill.

"I'm freezing . . ." Maria said, looking as if she were going to pass out any second.

"Or sepsis," Tekla said to herself. She helped Maria to the back seat, so that she wouldn't lose any body heat.

Lundgren came back after a few minutes.

"They're going to try to get here. But they have to plough the road first. She said it could take an hour or even two. Possibly more."

"That's too long," Tekla said. "Damn."

"So what do we do?" Lundgren asked.

Tekla thought fast. She could see that it was snowing more and more. "We have to get her into the house so she can lie down."

Tekla considered whether they should throw themselves into the car and drive away. But it was perhaps two hours to Sveg and more than three to Östersund, the nearest hospital with halfway decent services. If they even managed to get up the hill without studded tyres.

"Wait here."

Tekla went back to the door and tore at the handle, but it was locked. She tried to find a window that had been left ajar, or an unlocked back door. Nothing. On one of the short sides of the house she saw a frosted window, presumably the bathroom. She hurried over to the barn, found a shovel and an old crate, and nearly slipped and fell on her way back around the house again. She stood on the crate, smashed the window with the spade, shovelled away the splinters and got the bathroom window open.

Tekla sped through the house, noting that the heating was on, and ripped open the front door. Maria took a few faltering steps into the hallway, where a Spiderman jacket was hanging on a hook. She continued into the living room and turned, just had time to give Tekla a worried look before her eyes rolled up to the ceiling and she collapsed, as if somebody had just pulled every bone out of her body. Her skin alone was not enough to keep all that flesh and blood upright.

Maria hit the carpet with a nasty thud and then began to shake.

Wednesday, 13 November

"Pontonjärsgatan, please."

The taxi driver rolled slowly down the hill towards Ringvägen.

The man took out a painkiller he had been given at the hospital and swallowed it dry. The tablet got stuck on the back of his palate and dissolved slowly. He wondered if medicines were also absorbed through the mucous membranes there, or if they had to end up in the stomach. Details. Facts. He knew how to stay young. Or at least how to keep the brain alive by constantly exposing it to challenges. The slow decay of his body, on the other hand, worked to his advantage, a natural disguise which allayed suspicion. An old man, harmless.

He went through the bag his colleague had left him that morning. She had been there, in the ward, only a few hours after the car accident. And had covered up all the tracks at the house, since he was incapacitated by concussion and morphine. The bag contained equipment, more information, tickets.

The street on Kungsholmen was close to a large park. He paid in cash and waited until the taxi had gone. Then he took the short walk around the corner to Baltzar von Platens gata. The area was dead. And probably not just because it was a Wednesday and the drabbest of drab rainy days of the year. He saw no restaurants or shops. It must be a purely residential neighbourhood, not one he was familiar with. He rang the doorbell at the street entrance.

"Yes?" a rasping voice came through after a few seconds.

"Enok Hillerström?"

The person on the entryphone cleared his throat. "Yes, why?"

"My name's Janos Eckhart. I've just moved in but unfortunately I've forgotten the door code. And I also need to get into the laundry room. Could I come by and borrow the key?"

After a few seconds' hesitation, a buzzing could be heard from the door, which then opened.

The man looked at the board with the residents' names and then walked up one floor. Felt his body aching, as stiff as it was back home after a double session of *systema*. He had lost a lot of strength during his stay in hospital. However hard he tried to persuade himself otherwise, growing old was hell.

An elderly gentleman was standing in the doorway, looking through the narrow opening, the chain still attached.

The man arrived at the top of the stairs and said "Hello!", trying to breathe calmly. "I'm sorry to disturb you. I've just signed the paperwork but the broker forgot to give me the door code."

"I didn't know anyone had sold," Hillerström said. "But then I've been in hospital . . ."

The man put his hand through the crack in the doorway. "Janos Eckhart," he said. "I'm afraid I've not managed to learn much Swedish yet, my wife complains but . . ."

Hillerström closed the door and unhooked the chain. "It's easier like this," he said and proffered his hand.

"I couldn't come in and take a look around, could I? It's always interesting to get to know one's neighbours."

"Yes of course, that's fine."

"If I'm not bothering you, like I said."

"No, I don't really have anything on at the moment. Some coffee?"

"That would be excellent," he said and followed Hillerström into the apartment. They were probably about the same age. He closed the door but kept his gloves on. Noted that a rag rug ran all the way towards the kitchen on the left. "So you live alone?" He had recovered his breath now and felt he had the situation under control once more.

"All alone. Don't need anything bigger," Hillerström said, turning on the kettle. He had quite a limp as he went to get two cups from the cupboard. "Take a pew."

"Thanks," the man said as he sat down. "Really kind of you. I just wanted to come by and check on my new purchase."

Hillerström placed two cups on their saucers. The kettle switch snapped. He sprinkled two teaspoons of powdered coffee into each cup and filled them with hot water. Then he sat down at the kitchen table. "Who did you buy from?"

"Bengtsson on the first floor."

"Bengtsson?" Hillerström said in surprise. "I had no idea they were looking to sell. A big apartment. Three rooms, kitchen and bathroom, right?"

"Yes," the man said. "Perfect for me and the wife."

"Well, one never knows what's going on in people's minds," Hillerström said to himself.

"True enough," the man said. He saw that Hillerström was searching for his spectacles, which he had on a string around his neck. "Is it O.K. if I take a glass of water?"

"No problem," Hillerström answered.

The man got up and went over to the sink, where he had seen the stand with the kitchen knives. Hillerström was sitting with his back to him. The man turned the tap on and took out a knife, a bread knife. He changed it for the next one, a smooth meat knife that looked new.

"Do you have any help, home care service or anything like that?"

"Me? No," Hillerström said, chuckling. "I manage just fine on my own. Besides, home care service isn't exactly given away. Many people are fooled into thinking that everything in the community is free."

"But medical care doesn't cost much here in Sweden."

"No, that's probably true. Well, I guess I'll be getting a bill some time soon. Because I had my hip operated on just recently. It took a week, pretty much on the dot, with four days in geriatric rehab. It's terrible how creaky one gets in old age, the physio asked me if I'd been a football player, apparently I was as stiff as a board. I've been given a programme to follow and then I'm supposed to get in touch with the health centre, assuming they have time for me."

"One week since your operation."

"Yes."

"One week since the accident," the man said pensively.

"Which accident?"

"You don't recognise me, do you?" the man asked.

"Should I?" Hillerström was having a bit of trouble in opening the new tin of sweeteners.

"No, it's not so easy when one's half blind."

"I'm sorry?"

"You seem to me to be both blind and retarded."

Hillerström put down the sweeteners and started to turn, but was gripped by a sudden coughing fit.

"We shared a room in the orthopaedics ward at the Nobel Hospital after we'd both been operated on."

"Did we –" Hillerström stifled his cough – "share a room?"

"Yes."

"Ah well, no I don't remember that."

"No you don't. But that's not good enough for me. I can't take any risks . . ."

"I did get a lot of morphine, so . . ." It seemed to take a few seconds for the words to reach Hillerström's brain. "What do you mean, what isn't good enough . . .?"

The man calmly walked over to Hillerström and leaned forward.

"You ought to know better than to let strangers into your home."

With a huge effort, Enok Hillerström spun around. The man looked straight into his hazel eyes. A mixture of fear and surprise.

"Who are you . . .?"

But before Hillerström could finish his life's last sentence, the man who had introduced himself as Janos Eckhart cut open his carotid artery, and his windpipe filled with blood.

"Unfortunately I can't take any risks. I know I was given morphine myself, and when they drug you like that, you tend to talk too much. Did I say what my real name is, for example?"

Hillerström did not appear to hear him, he was struggling in vain to understand what had happened to his throat.

It was strange, the man thought. People become so confused when they're about to die. He had seen it many times. How illogically they behaved. And how pathetic they looked. Wetting and soiling themselves in sheer terror. Sadly, when death caught them by surprise, they were unable to maintain any semblance of dignity. Enok Hillerström was no exception. He lost his balance, fell onto the floor and fumbled at his throat, which was slippery and messy with the warm blood.

"And she told me to clean up the mess afterwards."

The man got up. He didn't want to get blood on his shoes. Put the knife next to Hillerström on the floor. It span around in the blood, like a lottery wheel in an amusement park. Then he emptied one of the cups of coffee into the sink, rinsed it, dried it with a hand towel and put it back in the cupboard.

He shut the door, took the stairs down and came out again into the lashing rain. The arm under his plaster cast was beginning to itch. The doctors at the Nobel Hospital had said two weeks. He'd just have to put up with it. In a week's time he would in any case be getting his reward: a break by the Black Sea, sun, peace and quiet.

YTTERHOGDAL
Wednesday, 13 November

For as long as she could remember, Tekla had been fascinated by the prospect of a catastrophe. Even as a child she used to imagine herself in extreme situations: how she would cope as the sole survivor on an island. It was no exaggeration to say that she adored *Robinson Crusoe*. Could she bring herself to eat her own friends if she were in an airplane crash in the Andes, like in the film 'Alive'? The answer was without hesitation yes, she would be the one who took the initiative. Because she had created make-believe worlds, she knew, at least in theory, what it would be like to survive a forest fire in a cave, cut open the belly of an elk and creep inside the warm innards when the winter storm hit – like Luke in 'The Empire Strikes Back' – or build a parachute out of old windcheaters, something she maybe didn't really think would work in practice. Maybe it was the fact that she had had to manage on her own early in life – Simon wasn't exactly much help, her mother was incapable, and her father was either at work or drunk. Maybe it was simply in her D.N.A., an impulse to see herself in extreme situations. Or maybe just a sense of existential dread that she tried to keep at bay by planning how to survive the Apocalypse. Later, as a medical student, she dreamed up disaster scenarios, each more implausible than the last, so that she would be well prepared when the trauma alarm sounded in A. & E.

But even *her* imagination couldn't have come up with this: a woman she had met only a few hours earlier, in convulsions on a rag rug in a cottage in a remote corner of Jämtland. And with no medical equipment to hand.

Tekla threw herself onto the linoleum floor and held Maria's head, which was twisting back and forth. Lundgren sat beside her.

"Tell me what I can do," he said.

Tekla pushed away the coffee table and grabbed a cushion from the sofa next to her, slipping it under Maria's head. The very worst of the fits was tapering off but there was no doubt that she was having a generalised seizure. Maria was unconscious and both her and the baby's lives were in danger.

"What can it be?" Lundgren asked.

"Wait." She tried to concentrate but her mind had been exploring so many aspects of the hunt for the Norrland family during the past day that she was unable to focus. The only thing she knew, intuitively, was that they needed help if they were going to save Maria's life.

"Can I have your phone?"

Lundgren gave it to her and Tekla called Emergency Services once more.

"Emergency Services, how . . ."

"We already called once before from Ytterhogdal about a woman in an advanced stage of pregnancy."

"O.K. That was probably my colleague, but—"

"Whatever," Tekla interrupted. "Check on the computer, we rang just now. The woman is heavily pregnant and cramping. She has to get to a hospital."

"It's difficult to dispatch any ambulances right now because the roads haven't been cleared yet."

"But get someone to plough them then, for . . ." Tekla took a deep breath. "Just hurry."

"Absolutely. We'll try to get a vehicle out as soon as possible. I've registered your location. Call back if her condition worsens."

"I don't know how much worse she could get," Tekla said and hung up.

Maria was shaking less now. The cramps stopped after another minute. She began to snore deeply. Postictal, unconscious after seizures.

Tekla rolled her onto her side so she'd have a free airway and not inhale any vomit if she should suddenly be sick. Maria was lying on the rag rug and although the floor was cool, but not ice cold, there was a risk that she would soon be losing body heat. A stove stood nearby, an iron one with a sizeable stack of firewood carelessly piled along one wall.

Tekla got to her feet and took down a knitted blanket from a cupboard. She covered Maria with it and brushed the hair from her face.

Tekla wanted to call Silva but couldn't because it was so difficult to get a signal.

She knocked back one of her energy drinks, hurried around the little house and raised the temperature on the electric radiators. Luckily the person who lived here had at least left the heating on low. But it was still draughty inside. She spent a few frantic moments getting the stove going in the living room. Every now and then she darted over to Maria to check that she was breathing and not cramping. There was every chance that the seizures would start up again. She had a hunch that she knew what Maria might be suffering from. It would be a nightmare, she hoped it wasn't true, but they had to be prepared for the worst.

Lundgren came in through the front door. He was completely covered in snow, stamping it off his shoes.

"I walked quite a distance, but it's stone dead."

"We'll have to try again," Tekla said. She rummaged around in some drawers, hoping against hope that she might find some medicines there – ideally some Stesolid, an antispasmodic. At the same time, she was calling up *Williams Obstetrics*, the 25th edition, in her head. She leafed through it, trying to recall the course in gynaecology and obstetrics, half of which she'd missed because she was working on the side and had slept during some of the lectures. That meant going through the entire mastodon of a book now in order to find the right page, the one on eclampsia. And as these were no ordinary cramps, Stesolid would no longer be an option. On page 998 she found what she was looking for: magnesium sulphate – treatment of eclampsia, cramps accompanying pre-eclampsia. How the hell was she going to get hold of magnesium sulphate?

There was a loud crack from the birch wood in the stove. A cosier, dry warmth spread quickly across the linoleum floor. Tekla dragged the entire rag rug, with Maria on it, closer to the fire. She breathed in the scent from the wonderful blaze, it conjured up images of security and childhood. Tekla pulled random twigs off a straggling birch log, let her finger tips glide over the spiky splinters, but did not allow them to penetrate her skin. The energy drink was beginning to have an effect. She had found four tubes of Solpadol in one bedroom. Somebody clearly suffered from chronic pain. Apart from that, there were few clues as to who lived in the house. The furniture presumably belonged to someone else, maybe the landlord, but she had seen the tenants' clothes in the bedrooms. There was no doubt that the boy who lived there was obsessed by superheroes of all sorts.

"Shall we try to get away from here?" Lundgren asked.

"It's too risky. What if she has a cerebral haemorrhage on the way. It's freezing outside. Here it's at least warm."

Lundgren did not object. The urgency of the situation had hit home.

"Besides, we probably can't get up that hill without studded tyres."

There was another explosion from the stove, and finally Tekla had an idea as to how she could set up a magnesium drip.

"Keep an eye on her airway," she shouted as she ran out to the hall. She opened the front door and almost had to retreat because of the storm. But she went out and pulled the door shut, holding her arm up to shield herself, stamping through the snow over to the barn where she had found the shovel. The big barn doors slammed shut behind her and she looked around, found a wicker basket and began to pick up the dry leaves on the ground, which had blown in during the autumn. She managed to half fill the basket, which she carried back to the house.

"She's moving," Lundgren said quietly, as if he were afraid of waking her.

Tekla switched on a kettle in the kitchen and found a large bowl and a colander into which she began to put the leaves. Once the water had boiled, she poured it on top. She left the kitchen and went back to the bathroom, where she found a lot of bottles, bandages, creams and shaving equipment, but no medicines and no syringes. She had to have a needle. Why couldn't someone in the family have had an allergy and needed to keep a syringe at home. Or diabetes.

"Tell me what you want me to do," Lundgren called out.

"Just keep an eye on her breathing. And check for a signal," she shouted back.

She searched through every cupboard and drawer but found nothing. Somebody in the household evidently liked to sew, however, because there were scraps of cloth, needles and thread on a table by a simple sewing machine. But no syringes or similar needles anywhere. In the kitchen, she found a number of tins and dry food items. A bottle of Vodka Explorer and an almost empty bottle of Baileys. In the refrigerator, some groceries like milk, cheese and vegetables, which suggested that somebody had intended to return to the house. Sweat trickled down her stomach and she pulled off her jacket. Her battery had charged a little but there was still no coverage. She needed confirmation that the ambulance was on its way, but sadly she had no magic wand. That meant making do with what she did have.

There was a sound from the living room and she ran there. Maria was moving. Tekla fell to her knees beside her.

"What . . .?"

"You were having seizures. But you don't seem to have hit your head."

"And . . .?"

From Maria's look, Tekla knew right away what she was thinking about: the child.

"Oh, I haven't examined you."

Maria tried to take hold of her trousers, but was too weak.

408

"I'll do it," Tekla said and helped to ease them down – they were stretchy jeans. Lundgren seemed uncomfortable with the situation and busied himself putting some more logs into the stove.

To her relief, Tekla saw no blood. No amniotic fluid either. She palpated the belly, which was large but soft.

"I've called for an ambulance, they're on their way," she said to Maria. In the same instant, the house creaked as a gust of wind slammed against the wooden façade. Tekla knew that no ambulance would make it there for quite a while. Not before the storm had died down. "And I'm sure there's no risk to the baby." Tekla knew she was bad at lying, and could tell that Maria had seen through her. Maria let her head fall to one side.

"How have you been feeling recently?" Tekla asked.

"A lot of headaches."

"Have you been checking your blood pressure?"

"They've told me that it's high, but that I should wait, it'll get better after the baby's born."

Why had Tekla not seen what was happening? High blood pressure towards the end of term, lower urine production, she did after all say that she hadn't "been able to pee so much", and then the oedema in the face and the whole body . . . all classic signs of pre-eclampsia. Were her misplaced priorities, her negligence, going to put this woman's life at risk? And the child's?

"You have eclampsia."

"What's that?"

"A condition during pregnancy where you risk having seizures. Like the ones you've just had—"

"Is it dangerous?"

Tekla felt the intense eyes staring at her from the side.

"Yes."

Maria looked at Lundgren, as if he might have a different answer. But he just stood quietly behind Tekla.

"Are there any medicines you can take?" Maria asked.

"Yes, something called magnesium sulphate."

"Sounds complicated." Maria looked about her. "There isn't any here, I guess?"

"Oh yes there is," Tekla said and jumped to her feet. She went to the kitchen and poured out some of the dark water from the leaves which had been soaking. She filled a plastic bottle with the help of a funnel and returned via the bathroom, where she pulled off the green water hose which had been used as an improvised pipe down to a floor drain.

Maria was lying on her side with the blanket drawn all the way up to her head.

"We just need to think outside the box a bit," Tekla continued once she was back, making sure to catch Maria's worried eyes. She held up the hose. "A little enema."

Maria wrinkled her brow and snorted. "Are you serious?"

Tekla produced the bottle of leaf water. "Leaves contain magnesium. And I can't find a needle to give this intravenously. I'm sure it'll work fine by absorption through the rectum."

Maria's eyes widened. She was almost expecting Tekla to start laughing.

"O.K.?"

Maria nodded slowly.

"And you'll need to get stuck in and help," Tekla said to Lundgren, who had barely moved a muscle.

Tekla squatted down and pulled off Maria's jeans. "This is the last thing I want to do, but you're going to start having seizures again otherwise. You absolutely need magnesium sulphate."

Maria did not protest when Tekla cautiously pushed the hard plastic tube into her back passage. Four, five centimetres, then she held the other end of the pipe to the bottle and began to pour. Maria squirmed at first, but realised she had to lie still.

"Warm leaf water up my bum, what could be better?" she gasped resignedly.

Tekla smiled and stroked Maria's forehead.

"You Norrland people," an impressed Lundgren said.

"Jämtland," Maria corrected him, closing her eyes.

"Sorry," Lundgren said.

Tekla stopped pouring for a while and put the bottle aside.

"Is this going to cure me?" Maria asked.

Tekla considered telling a white lie but knew she was dealing with a very alert and clear-eyed Jämtland woman. She went back to pouring the magnesium brew up into the gut.

"No. You have to give birth to the baby."

"What?" Maria widened her eyes and stared at Tekla.

"I know," Tekla said. "But we're buying time till the ambulance gets here."

If it gets here, she thought, but she did not want to contemplate that alternative. When she went to check that the hose was still in place, she saw blood in Maria's underwear.

Wednesday, 13 November

Silva aimed for the gravel patches and avoided the ice which had formed on the flagstones during the night. He showed his I.D. to the person in charge, who was holding up the police barrier.

"Are the criminal technicians here yet?" he asked.

"They've started with the kitchen." The police officer nodded towards the left-hand side of the brick house. Silva carefully climbed up the four steps and looked around. Villagatan in Stuvsta lay deserted, not even any dog-owners were out and about. Cold and dank, soon dark. Now he knew which of the five vehicles on the street belonged to the technicians – the grey minibus. He was pleased that the door-to-door enquiries had yielded such quick results. He loved nosy neighbours – the old lady opposite had told him how she had been intrigued by the elderly man and younger couple with a boy who had arrived at the rented house the previous Wednesday.

He stepped into the entrance hall, put on the blue shoe-protectors from the bin liner on the floor and unbuttoned his duffel coat, though he kept his gloves on. Immediately to the left there was a large kitchen with a black and white chequered floor. He nodded a greeting to one of the technicians, who was busy photographing something. Silva carried on straight ahead into an enormous living room. There was a faint smell of wood smoke mixed with something else, something chemical. The parquet flooring was real, these were no floor tiles. He stopped and drank in the volume of the house, appreciating the architectural style and wondered if he would be able to afford something similar in a remote, small Swedish town. But then he thought how depressing it would be to live all alone in such a large house. He heard more technicians chatting further away, at the other end of the house. His phone rang – unknown number. For a few seconds he considered declining the call, but in the end he answered.

"Alvaro Silva."

"Hi, it's Rebecka."

Silva's head fell forward. He immediately regretted having picked up. Who had he been expecting?

She went on: "Do you know how I can get hold of that doctor, Tekla Berg? She's not answering her mobile. And at the hospital they say she's taken overtime leave."

"No idea," Silva said, walking towards a long corridor to the right of the living room. Four doors in a row. Bedrooms, no doubt.

"If you're in touch with her, can you tell her I've been trying to reach her?"

"Absolutely," Silva lied. He wondered what would happen when they found out what he was up to. But then again, he knew he didn't have much to lose. What could they do? Chew him out? Sack him? No, that would never happen, they were short of experienced investigators. Crime clearance statistics came before office politics.

Silva looked into a bathroom, where a technician was just getting to his feet and came towards him. "Superintendent Silva!"

Silva held up his hand and continued along the corridor.

"Where are you, by the way?" Nilsén asked.

"Just a routine case."

The line fell silent. Could Nilsén be checking his location on G.P.S. or something similar, Silva wondered.

"O.K.," she said. "Let me know if anything crops up."

"Of course," Silva said, poised to end the call.

"You know that we've taken over the dioxin side of the investigation?"

"You don't have to keep repeating it," Silva said.

"And that the C.B.R. group is dealing with all the biochemical stuff?"

"Naturally," Silva said.

"And, Alvaro?"

"Yes?"

"I don't suppose you're keen on being castrated?"

"What—"

"Just so you know what'll happen if you're messing with me."

"I have work to do," Silva said, ending the call and turning off his phone. He wondered if he should take out the S.I.M. card but refrained. That was overkill, perhaps. Instead, he went on admiring the '60s architecture. An entire wall of cupboards in the corridor, dark, solid wood, none of that phoney IKEA stuff that breaks up with the damp. Fibreboard . . . Silva sniffed, his whole apartment on Brommaplan was one long IKEA catalogue, he had never been able to afford anything else. The beige wall-to-wall carpet looked tidy. Generally, the house was clean and empty. Very little furniture. Nothing in the cupboards. It must have been rented out for a long time. According to his colleagues in the Söderort district force, a neighbour had said that a somewhat older man was renting the house. A man who happened to fit the description issued by the police when they conducted a house-to-house enquiry while investigating the accident at the bus stop. An "older man with white hair and a long coat". Silva had checked with the staff at the Nobel Hospital's Orthopaedic Department. A tall man, muscular for his age, with white hair. He had given a name, Spiro Lazarov, from Serbia. It didn't sound Serbian, but he could be wrong.

Silva went to the kitchen, where the technicians appeared to be finishing their work.

"Anything interesting?" he asked.

A small, sullen man in his sixties by the name of "Lelle", whom Silva had seen at numerous crime scenes over the years, stared emptily at the kitchen table.

"No radioactivity anywhere in the house."

"Well that's nice," Silva said, looking around.

"Mushroom fricassee in the fridge. The remains of mushrooms in the rubbish. We're going to run some tests," Lelle said.

"The last supper, in other words?"

414

"Looks like it," Lelle said and nodded.

"Nothing else?"

Lelle suddenly smiled. "As always, I saved the best till last."

He turned and left the kitchen. Silva followed. They passed several storage rooms and entered a large double garage which was standing open. Two technicians were busy with something over by a long bench.

"What have you found?" Silva asked.

Lelle raised a hand. "Hang on. Isn't the N.O.D. in charge of this investigation?"

Silva's worst fears were justified. "Together with us. We're working together."

"Would be the first time in the history of the world, if so," Lelle said.

Silva took a step to the side, tried to see what was in the lockers behind Lelle.

"Do you know what's worse than a lie?" the technician asked.

"No?"

"A half-truth. Those sticky half measures people come out with when they want to keep a foothold in the truth. As if that made the sin only half as bad."

"Sounds like you're religious."

"My uncle was a priest." Lelle seemed to have all the time in the world. Silva was in a quandary.

"What do you want?"

"What's on offer?"

Silva pondered. "A case of good red wine."

"Not one bottle under a hundred kronor."

"Deal," Silva said.

"Do you know what hydrofluoric acid's used for?" Lelle asked, letting Silva see what was behind him.

Silva shook his head.

"Dissolving organic material." Lelle squatted down and pulled out one of the large drums.

Silva took in the information and ran the sequence of events in his mind. What was going to be dissolved? Or who? The man or the woman? Because it was becoming obvious that this old man was no ordinary pensioner. He had rented a house in Stuvsta and ended up in hospital after being run over by a car while in the company of a man who was then murdered by his girlfriend – or wife. Of course it was all connected. The only question was how. All he knew, and he knew it in his bones, was that this old man, or the murderer, or whatever, was now far away, at a safe distance from the Swedish police, probably in a large country to the east, a land where one could hide away for ever.

Silva had heard from the hospital that the man had discharged himself at lunchtime. He had ordered a nationwide search, but his guess was that this Spiro Lazarov moved quickly, he might even already have left the country. Maybe with the assistance of the woman in the white fur hat who appeared at the hospital the same day as the car accident, whom they had found on the hospital surveillance camera. He had clearly had help.

"Thanks," he said and backed away.

"One case. I'll send the address."

Silva nodded and took out his phone. He had to call Tekla and tell her she was on a wild goose chase. Then he needed to find out who had access to dioxin and who his colleagues thought might be behind the poisoning. Beata Ernryd had not given him any of the crucial details he needed in order to work out who the old man was. Although he knew where the information was to be found, he was equally certain that Nilsén was not going to be forthcoming. Not under normal circumstances. When all was said and done, it all turned on delicious meat and good red wine.

YTTERHOGDAL
Wednesday, 13 November

Tekla got to her feet without meeting Maria's eyes. She went to explore the house. There were only two bedrooms and a living room, the kitchen, a few small storerooms and an unexpectedly big bathroom, which was freezing cold since Tekla had smashed a hole in the window. Snow had piled up, half filling the opening, and a powerful draft drove the snowflakes all the way to the washbasin. She continued into the hall: a door that Tekla had missed at first. A cellar. She opened it, keen to delay the discussion with Maria for a little while. Tekla would never put off a difficult encounter. In A. & E., if a child died and all the staff were downcast and in tears, Tekla was always the first to go and speak to the relatives and look them straight in the eye. She knew that conflicts and trauma only escalate if you fail to get to grips with them right away. If you're quick off the mark, the person who puts their hand up to start reading in class, expectations are lowered, everybody knows how hard it is to go first.

Tekla pressed down the door handle and was immediately hit by the smell of a mouldy, freezing cellar. The door had proved surprisingly good at sealing it off from the narrow hall. She went down the cold stone steps and ended up on dank concrete in her Stan Smiths. To the right an oil-fired boiler and, behind it, large patches of damp in the mortar. The roof was just high enough to allow Tekla to walk upright. A cracked window at ground level was the only source of light and she saw a carpenter's bench cluttered with old tools: nails, hammers, some chisels, a packet of razor blades, a broken folding rule and two rusty saws. She rifled through some moist cardboard boxes on the floor, but it looked as if it was just old clothes and discarded kitchen equipment from the '70s.

She went back up to Maria and sat down on the rug.

"I'm bleeding," Maria said without attempting to raise herself. She was lying with her head on one hand, looking dangerously relaxed, as if she had already given up and was waiting to die. What a contrast to the young woman who had radiated so much spirit during the short time they had spent together in the car.

"I'll take care of you and the baby," Tekla said, but she heard that her voice did not sound totally convincing. She swallowed heavily, cleared her throat, looking for something to add, but Maria laid her cold hand on Tekla's. "Let's hope they come in time."

In time. Otherwise . . .

"Tekla . . .?" Lundgren began, but she just needed to think.

"Wait."

She had her eyes fixed on a piece of firewood, intending to throw more fuel onto the dying blaze. But her limbs wouldn't do as she wanted, she felt completely paralysed. Saw in front of her her father's cold hand after he had died in the hospital in Östersund. His liver failure had got the better of him. Although in reality he had assaulted his liver with alcohol for years. He was to blame. Maria had done nothing to deserve this fate. If, that is, a doctor was entitled to take such a simplistic view of cause and effect. But right now, Tekla was more than a doctor, she had a young woman before her. Dying. It could have been her.

"Never," Tekla said. She felt that her body was now obeying her once more. It was as if somebody had replaced a blown fuse. "This won't work. We have to get that sodding ambulance here."

"But you said they're on their way."

Tekla deliberated. Were they really? Could she rely on them? Yes, probably. But there was nothing she could do about the bloody storm, which just got worse and worse. Were there any other houses in the vicinity? Someone with a better car than theirs? Tekla already knew that Lundgren's old banger out there wouldn't even get them five

418

metres. And it was pointless to try to shovel snow, or find sand, or somehow get back up the hill they had driven down. It was she who had brought them into a death trap and she couldn't get them out of it. And she knew it. In her head she brought up the map she had briefly seen on the way here: there were no small black dots for several kilometres around. No neighbours they could get help from.

She had to fix this herself. Tekla carefully loosened the blanket and pulled Maria's knickers down a little further. There was no blood on the rug.

"Your waters have broken," she said. "Are you feeling any contractions?"

"I've had some but not that bad . . ."

Tekla weighed all the options. Her concentration was being disturbed by thoughts about the woman, the man and the boy. Silva had said that they'd also found dioxin in the man's body. So he too had been poisoned, but hadn't had time to develop any symptoms before the woman stuck the knife into him. It was not a crime of passion, then, at least not obviously so. They had been poisoned by somebody. But by whom? And the boy, had he too been poisoned? It didn't seem likely, he'd been perfectly well several days after the car accident. But why not? How did it all hang together? Her intuition told her that the boy could be in danger. She had to protect him. Could it be some sort of family feud? But in that case, would an innocent child be involved? Perhaps she was worrying unnecessarily.

"The baby has to come out," Maria wheezed.

"I know," Tekla said. "Is it O.K. if I feel around a little?"

"As if I have any choice," Maria said, smiling.

"You're dilated five centimetres. Shall we try to get the little fellow out?"

"Fellow? Sounds like a boy."

"My sense of touch isn't that good."

"And here's me thinking all along that it's a girl."

Tekla covered Maria with the blanket and laid her hand on her shoulder. "More than anything, we'd like the ambulance to get here.

I'm just going to check if I can get a signal." As she brought out her phone, the young woman caught her wrist.

"You know as well as I do that they're nowhere near."

"That remains to be seen. Do you have a phone?"

"I didn't bring it with me."

"O.K. But I'm just going to—"

"You . . . it's Tekla, isn't it?"

Tekla nodded.

"I can see you're frightened. That's fine. Just try to save the baby, please."

"You're forgetting yourself." Tekla remembered that she had to top up the magnesium. She took the bottle from the table and filled the hose. Every now and then a gurgling noise could be heard as Maria passed gas. Brown water ran onto the already brown rug. "I'm going to take care of you *both*!"

"The baby first."

Tekla gritted her teeth. She made a last attempt to get coverage, tempted to call Silva though it wasn't her first priority. The entire countryside was blanketed in snow and the mobile telephone masts might even have been knocked out. Tekla went back to Maria.

"Would you like something to drink?"

"Yes please."

Tekla fetched a glass of water from the kitchen and began to prepare herself. How would she cut the umbilical cord? She ran down and got the packet of razor blades from the cellar. She sterilised one of them by burning it with a lighter, just as her father used to do when he was going to remove a splinter for her or Simon. "So it doesn't get inflamed," she told Lundgren.

"What are you doing?" he asked in a hushed voice.

"You'll see."

She thought back to her father again. "Infected" was the right word. Tekla smiled at her silly, inner dialogue. She balanced the razor blade on the edge of the glass, so that it wouldn't touch anything, not even a sheet of toilet paper would be sterile enough. Sterile scalpel:

check. Then she went to fetch towels from a linen cupboard and several cushions with which to make Maria comfortable.

"Are you cold?"

"A bit," Maria said. Tekla collected several blankets from the bedrooms. A thought occurred to her: had the woman and the man had sex in this room? When she pulled the sheets off the beds, a notebook fell to the floor. It had been pushed in under the mattress. She picked it up: it was a diary, neatly written with dates, pleasing handwriting, easily legible. If only she knew some Russian. Damn, why hadn't Tekla taken some evening classes? She flicked through to the most recent jottings. Last Tuesday. Two days before the accident. So they'd been here as recently as that. Had they taken a car or the train to Stockholm? And why had they gone there? She tried to decipher the Cyrillic letters, but without success. Then she saw a short piece, about twenty lines, written in perfect Swedish. It was about an argument during a walk. The last sentence read: "Sasha is angry as usual."

Sasha, was that the boy's name? It was a good name, it suited him. So did he have a problem with his temper?

Maria cried out from the living room and Tekla closed the diary. She would go back to it later.

Maria was having more contractions, which was good. Now maybe they would be able to get the baby out. Tekla knelt down and put her hand on Maria's large stomach. The uterus was hard and contracted. Tekla explored with her fingers. "Good, six centimetres." Then she felt something she absolutely did not want to feel.

"Hell!"

"What?" Maria asked.

"A foot. A goddamn bloody breech presentation."

Maria's head fell back and Tekla wondered for a second if the cramps were setting in again. Then Maria's voice could be heard.

"You know best what needs to be done."

"We'll wait," Tekla croaked.

"For what?" Lundgren asked. She heard his heavy breathing

beside her. There was a smell of sweat, perhaps from him, perhaps from her. All their body fluids were melding into one common vapour in the midst of the living room.

"No, true, there's not much to wait for," Tekla finally said. "But how the hell am I supposed to do a caesarian on a bloody rag rug without any equipment?"

"A caesarian?!" Maria and Lundgren asked simultaneously.

STOCKHOLM
Wednesday, 13 November

The old man walked slowly down towards Norr Mälarstrand. It was raining, so he had to get out an umbrella. He drew up the handle of his suitcase and continued to pull it along. There weren't many people around. His earlier impression seemed correct, this part of Stockholm did not appear to be one of its restaurant districts. On previous trips to the city, he had always stayed near the Central Station. And once in Södermalm. But never in this neighbourhood. It was dreadfully cold, the wind blew straight through his coat and froze his thighs, which felt stiffer than ever. The cold in St Petersburg was never as penetrating as this. Was it the damp? Was it perhaps drier back home? He stopped by a red light and waited. Occasional cars drove by, but he had to wait ten minutes for a taxi, and by that stage he could barely move his legs for the cold.

"There aren't many cars around here, I see." He pushed the seat back and looked at the name plate on the dashboard. *Ali Hussein.*

"What did you say?" the driver replied in English.

He had to force himself to speak more slowly. "Banbyggarvägen in Stuvsta."

The driver keyed in the address on his display, put the indicator on and drove off.

The air in the car was musty, a mixture of unidentifiable herbs and other smells ingrained in the leather. Hussein presumably didn't know how to clean his car properly. They never did. Not back home, either.

He went through what had happened. The woman who had rammed them at the bus stop. Unfortunately she had not killed the man, though she did finish the job off later herself. So far, so good. But his own injuries had got in the way, they had held everything up. The woman was also dead. The Swedish healthcare system had seen to that. The only thing they had not been able to produce was the protected address where the boy was. But it was only a matter of time before he found it.

A boy. Was there anything that would stop him from killing a child? He tried, wanting to find even the slightest reason why that would be a problem. But there was none. A part of him was disappointed.

"Slow down," he said and held up his hand when he recognised where he was. Segerminnesvägen, he had walked down it a number of times. It was almost exactly one month since he had come to Stuvsta for the first time. They turned left into Banbyggarvägen. He leaned forward, said "Slowly, continue slowly along here", and saw from several hundred metres away what he had already feared: blue-and-white-striped police tape.

"Drive on, don't stop."

"But . . .?"

"Don't you get what I'm saying?" he hissed. "Drive on."

Hussein accelerated again, keeping both hands on the steering wheel. He looked curiously at the number of the house, then at the man's face.

"You shouldn't have done that," the man said. And then he added in Russian: "You just dug your own grave."

"What?"

"Drive to the city centre instead." He wrote a text message to his contact: Need a hotel quickly. Central location.

"Drive to the T-Centralen Tunnelbana station and drop me off."

Hussein keyed the data in on his display again, his hand shaking, seeking the comfort of the steering wheel.

The man went through the list of people he might need to get rid of. Who else could he have revealed his identity to? The nurses in the department? Despite the morphine and the sleeping tablets, he knew who he had spoken to. But Hillerström had coaxed something out of him, had got him to talk about the summer house by the Black Sea. He hadn't been so open with the staff, though. He was sure of that. But what about that doctor, how much had she really understood?

He was waiting to hear from his contact. He didn't know where she was, presumably in some rented apartment nearby, and in any case he couldn't just turn up there. That wasn't part of the plan. He needed only one more night to complete his assignment.

There was a tone from his phone: Stockholm City Hotel.

And in the next message: Call me.

He paid in cash and got out of the taxi, committing the driver's name and registration number to memory, and watched him drive off before he got out his mobile.

"What's happened?" Her tone was hard. That bothered him.

"The police have found the house."

"How do you know?"

"I was there."

"And the police too? Did you risk . . .?"

"They didn't see me. I drove past in a taxi."

"But how could they have found the house? Damn!"

"Tell me about it."

He was stamping his feet. Annoyed that he hadn't checked where the hotel was before calling. Which way was it?

She kept repeating "This is not at all good", as if she were about to lose her grip. He wanted to say something about bad leadership, but decided it wasn't worth it. He was getting help with the logistics, but that was just a bonus. The only reason for not breaking off contact with the woman was her role as guarantor, ensuring that he would be paid the rest of his fee. "We may have to pull the plug," she went on.

"No."

"What do you mean, 'no'?"

"We're not going to do that. I have absolutely no intention of giving up."

425

The woman gave a dismissive laugh. "It's not up to you."

"Yes it is. In the field, it is."

"Just a moment. I don't think your client would be happy to hear this conversation."

"Do you honestly imagine I'm worried what the client thinks?"

"But you do care about money."

"I'm pretty sure I'll get it in the end."

"Is that a threat?"

"It's a fact. I'm going to finish my assignment and so I'll get my money."

"You're not particularly worried about your reputation."

"Do you think I care about consequences?"

Silence on the line.

"Are we going to pull out or not?" she said, slightly more restrained.

He thought again about the Black Sea. Knew he needed the money.

"We're not going to stop now. I've got the situation under control."

"O.K. But it's not good that the police found the house. That makes you a suspect and they'll be guarding the foster family."

"Doesn't matter."

"What do you mean?"

"This is my last job. I'm retiring after this."

His feet were frozen stiff.

"I'm hanging up now."

He ended the call. Looked at his phone to see where the hotel was. Finally began to walk.

STOCKHOLM

Wednesday, 13 November

"Rebecka Nilsén."

"Can we take a walk?"

"Alvaro?" Nilsén said in surprise. "Where are you?"

"Outside."

"What do you mean, outside? Here, on Kungsholmen?"

"I'm waiting outside the main entrance, on the street. Don't feel like coming up and begging on my bare knees. And it would be good if you could join me. Alone."

There was silence for a few seconds. Silva could feel he was nervous, and not only because of the investigation. He wondered if Nilsén was just being bloody-minded, whether she was deliberately keeping him on tenterhooks.

"Of course," she said at last. "I'll be down in five minutes."

A quarter of an hour later he saw her come out through the swing doors wearing the coat with the cow-skin pattern. She glanced left and right as she crossed the road and walked calmly towards him. He began to fantasise: they had just seen each other at some work conference, they were madly in love and were going out to eat for the first time. Maybe they were in Paris, had booked a room together for a night . . .

"I thought you'd quit," Nilsén said, cocking her head to one side. She looked happy.

"I smoke when I get nervous."

Nilsén smiled. She looked a little tired, but attractive as ever. He remembered: she had always chosen warm, cheerful colours for her make-up. A very original hairstyle, with big barrettes. It seemed like a joke that she was as old as Silva. How could two people age so differently?

"It's actually great that you called. I needed an excuse to leave the office. And I was thinking about taking a long walk home." She began to stroll slowly away from the Police Authority headquarters. There was no wind, but it was still drizzling – ice-cold rain that could turn to snow at any moment. "Would you like to keep me company?"

They went along Kronobergsgatan and then right onto Hantverkargatan. Silva wanted to suggest a drink as they were passing a restaurant full of people but decided to steer clear of anything awkward. Assumed that their earlier flirtations no longer counted.

"Sorry to have been so prickly earlier today," he said grudgingly. He found it hard to apologise, the words somehow stuck in his craw.

"Oh that, not at all, it wasn't exactly the first time." Nilsén put her hand on his shoulder. "Or rather . . . I'm sorry, that sounded unsympathetic. Thanks for apologising, one should never underestimate how hard it is for a man to do that."

Silva felt shorter than he usually did as he walked along beside Nilsén, who was wearing high-heeled boots. It was as if her hand were pushing him down a whole ten centimetres. He let it lie there.

"It's just that I—"

"Get very wrapped up in your work," Nilsén filled in.

"*Sí. Mucho.*"

"And that's O.K. You wouldn't be Alvaro Silva if you weren't like that. But you're with the Söderort force now and it's not O.K. to freelance the way you do."

"I know."

"You know?"

"Yes."

"But you can't help it?"

He nodded.

"See how easy it is when you're not in attack dog mode," Nilsén said.

They passed Fridhelmsplan in silence. Silva felt even more like having a beer when they passed the old Löwenbräu pub, but he sensed that it wasn't the right moment. Instead, they continued across Rålambshovsparken, where the wind picked up. He was cold and wished he had an elegant hat like the one Nilsén pulled out. Perhaps not in the same bright yellow colour, but it looked warm and comfortable. His hair was starting to thin.

"Are you happy at the N.O.D.?" he asked.

"Apart from the fact that they skimp on our traditional Christmas lunches . . . Yes, it's good there. I like the cases. And I have a boss who lets me spend two weeks every winter in our apartment on Mallorca."

"That's right," Silva said. "I'd forgotten that." But he had noted that she said "our".

"So you're still married?" There was no point in beating about the bush. Just rip off the plaster.

"Carin and I separated two years ago, but we're good friends. She has somebody new who I know from before. We're going to Mallorca together this winter for the second year running."

Silva turned to Nilsén. "Are you serious? You go on holiday with your ex and her new partner?"

"Is that so odd? Life's too short for hatred and conflicts. We've kept what was best about our relationship, our common interests and friends, but ended the actual . . . more intimate side of things. I can now satisfy that with others."

Silva felt old-fashioned, ashamed of his spontaneous reaction. He wanted to say something more in keeping with the times, something he truly meant, but he couldn't bring himself to do it.

"Whatever makes us happy," was all he managed, and it sounded very clichéd.

They struggled on across Västerbron. The odd bicycle toiled

past. Apart from that there were few people out. Silva registered the beautiful view over the city but tried to focus his thinking on the real reason for his being there.

"What are your team's theories about the dioxin? Where's it from?"

"Why should I tell you?"

"Because . . ." He was searching for the right words, wanted to be as honest as possible. Nilsén had an uncanny ability to see through lies. "I really want to find whoever's behind it."

"Why has this become so personal for you?"

"Two reasons. In the first place, I genuinely believe the woman is innocent, caught up in some sort of domestic drama."

"That sounds like bias. Can't a woman be a criminal?"

"Statistically speaking, no. There's nothing to suggest she might be a criminal. No tattoos, no weapons, no money, no drugs in her blood. And with a small boy in tow. I think she's a normal mother who got dragged into something against her will.

"Fair enough. And number two?"

"Number two?"

"Secondly . . ." Nilsén elucidated as they reached the bridge support by Hornstull.

"Oh, O.K., I trust Tekla Berg's gut feeling."

"The doctor?"

"Yes. She has some kind of a sixth sense, and I've got pulled along by her obsession with finding out what happened."

Nilsén walked along in silence, apparently reflecting on something. Maybe it was to do with Tekla Berg. Silva knew that Nilsén too had been helped that summer by the doctor from the Nobel Hospital.

They crossed over Långholmsgatan and headed for Verkstadsgatan. Silva knew very well where Nilsén lived, but he didn't dare hope for an invitation to a late cup of tea.

Suddenly she stopped in front of an Indian restaurant.

"Hungry?"

"Always."

"They also have beer," Nilsén said with a smile.

"You're a mindreader."

She stopped with her hand on the door handle. "We think it's all to do with a power struggle between two Mafia bosses in St Petersburg."

Silva let the words sink in. What effect did they have on him?

Nilsén opened the door. "Smells good."

YTTERHOGDAL

Wednesday, 13 November

Extreme cold or extreme heat? Like one of those idiotic questions that people come up with when they're drunk: would you rather freeze to death or burn alive? Tekla wasn't quite sure how she'd answer, but she would probably be inclined towards cold. If only as a tribute to her heritage, her Jämtland origins. Winter, cold, snow, snow scooters and thinly sliced reindeer meat to top it off. But Tekla had never actually liked the climate when she was growing up. She blamed that on her bag of bones of a mother. Tekla had no subcutaneous fat and could never gain weight, however hard she tried. A trial for her, an insult to all her friends who struggled to keep the calories down.

Tekla drained her last energy drink and put on a dirty old quilted jacket she'd found in the hall. She wondered about the diary again, desperate to have it translated – maybe what had happened was written there in black and white. Was it prostitution or drugs? Human trafficking? The thought that the boy might have been exposed to something like that made her feel ill. Had he himself been prostituted? No, she simply could not bring herself to consider that possibility.

She went back to Maria, who was looking paler. "How's it going? More contractions?"

Maria nodded. "It's all going pear-shaped, isn't it?"

"Not at all. Come on, you're not the type to give up, are you?"

Maria beckoned Tekla to her and whispered: "You have to get the baby out."

Tekla felt a prickling in the palms of her hands. Then her whole body began to shiver. She was frozen right through to the core. It dawned on her that Maria too must be cold, even if she wasn't aware of it. "Can we get you up onto the sofa, do you think?"

"Maybe," Maria said. She tried with Lundgren's help to brace herself on one hand, but at that moment she had a contraction and fell back onto the rug. She screamed in pain, making no effort to restrain herself.

Tekla took Maria's hand and began to countenance the difficult decision which might put an end to all this. To Maria's life. To the child's life. To Tekla's medical career. She might even land herself in prison, but that was really the least of her problems. She let go of Maria's hand. "I'm just going to fetch something."

Tekla ran out into the hall to open the front door, but the snow was piled high on the porch and she had to push several times before it would give way. She waded through the snow, the car was barely visible. She had to grope to find the door handle and had great difficulty getting in.

She searched among maps and pill bottles in the glove compartment and, when she had found what she was looking for, she ran back to the house. Maria lay on the rug, recovering between contractions.

"Shall we give it another go?"

Maria crawled onto her knees, paused for a few seconds so as not to faint, and then managed to haul herself up onto the sofa with Lundgren's help. The hose in her rectum fell out and brown water spilled onto the linoleum floor. With no time to be put off by the sight, Tekla held up a glass of water. "Here. Take six."

"What is it?"

"Oxazepam. And I've dissolved four Solpadol in the water. They contain codeine, like morphine. You're going to need it."

"For what?"

Tekla knelt down and stared into Maria's eyes. "The caesarian. I have to do it. Otherwise, the baby will die."

Maria stared back. Terrified. "Surely you need to be put to sleep for that?"

"That's why you have to take these pills."

"But it's going to hurt."

"Yes. Like hell. You may even pass out from the pain."

Maria already looked as if she were about to faint.

"Shall we?" Tekla asked.

Maria nodded.

Tekla held out the glass and the tablets.

Maria did as she was told, swallowing large mouthfuls of the dissolved Solpadol, and leaned back in the sofa. It would be a while before they took effect, but Tekla couldn't wait. She dragged away the coffee table, pushed aside the armchair and fetched a floor lamp from a corner. She opened the curtains wide to let in as much light as possible. Then she hurried out into the kitchen and fetched the bottle of vodka.

"And now a few large gulps."

Maria took the bottle. "Feels like we're at sea and you're going to amputate my leg."

"Kind of," Tekla said. "Drink up."

"How's that for . . .?" Lundgren looked deathly pale.

"For the baby?" Tekla asked out loud. "It'll probably just get a bit drowsy. No worries."

Lundgren shook his head. "Are you sure about this?"

"I'm sure that both the baby and Maria could die if I don't do a caesarean."

Maria swilled half the bottle, suppressed a retch and kept on drinking large mouthfuls. She dried her lips. "Yuck," she said, shivering so hard her whole body shook.

Tekla had found chlorhexidine and cotton wool balls in the bathroom, which she used to make Maria's stomach as sterile and clean as possible. She had even found a whole roll of adhesive plaster.

Maria had another contraction. She did not hold back the scream.

"Go for it," Tekla said. "Enjoy the fact that Gunilla isn't here nagging you."

Maria laughed and cried between the screams.

434

"What's the dad's name?" Lundgren asked.

"There isn't one. Didn't think there was anybody suit—" She screwed up her face. "Suitable. I just went with artificial insemination."

"You don't need one. You'll manage just fine as a single parent," Tekla said. She had boiled the electric kettle and poured the hot water onto a clean towel which she now put on Maria's forehead.

Maria pulled it down over her face. "I'm feeling dizzy," she said, sounding slurred. "You'd better start now while I'm . . . as far gone . . . as this."

"Let it get a bit worse."

"Worse is the last thing I need . . . right now."

Tekla smiled. "You're as crazy as me."

"Let's do it," Maria said.

"Just one more second." Tekla fetched a needle from the sewing table and found a coarse thread. She tried to bend the needle slightly but couldn't. She then washed her hands thoroughly with soap in the bathroom and rubbed them with chlorhexidine as well as she could.

"How are you feeling?" Tekla asked.

Maria still had the wet towel over her face. "Everything's spinning . . ."

"O.K. Let's go, in that case."

Tekla closed her eyes and went through all the steps in her head. Looked up the right page in Williams' book on obstetrics. There were good pictures, instructive diagrams showing how to perform the procedure. Layer upon layer, all the way in to the uterus.

Then she asked herself one last time: was this defensible? What if the ambulance were just about to appear?

But it didn't.

She took a deep breath, opened her eyes and grasped the razor blade between thumb and index finger.

"Tell me if you want me to stop."

"Do it!"

She held out a handful of cotton wool balls for Lundgren. "You'll have to press where the bleeding is at its worst. And also keep an eye on her breathing. If she vomits, we'll have to turn her onto her side."

Lundgren nodded, staring down at the large belly.

Tekla's shoulders dropped, she held the razor blade in a steady grip and got to work. She placed the incision horizontally in the bikini line. There was surprisingly little bleeding. Perhaps Maria's blood pressure had plummeted, despite the eclampsia. Or else she had bled so much that there was nothing left.

The razor blade was good, brand new. Tekla had no difficulty getting down to the next layer: connective tissue and muscle. But there it became harder. She had to use her fingers to pull apart the muscle fibres, which first ran along the mid-line, and then like a fan down towards the pelvis.

Maria gave a loud shriek. A heart-rending yell which Tekla tried to shut out.

Now she had arrived at the point she feared most: the womb – it loomed large under the thin peritoneum. Tekla made a careful cut before tearing it open. There was now a different tone to Maria's screaming – it was a cry for help.

"I have to get the baby out, otherwise it could die," Tekla shouted. She saw Maria's twisted face. It was completely distorted by pain. Then she seemed to faint away. Maybe she had passed out, or the pills had begun to work.

"Make sure you keep the airway clear," Tekla said to Lundgren, who did as he was told. Now only the thick, glistening pink muscle mass of the womb lay between Tekla and a living child. Maria moved again, writhed on the sofa and bellowed out her agony through the Oxazepam and the alcohol.

Tekla knew that this was the critical moment, the point of no return. She took the razor blade and cut horizontally across the womb. The bleeding was profuse. She was forced to rock the blade and push down one corner so as to get through the muscle. Then she put the razor back on the edge of the glass, stuck her index finger down into the little hole and pulled. As she had read in *Williams*, one could tear the womb open completely, it had an amazing capacity to heal later, with just a few stitches. And, right now, the chances of Maria being able to have more children didn't seem the most important consideration. Or whether she would be able to keep her womb, since there was a risk that sooner or later she would need a hysterectomy. Only one thing counted: life, instead of death. Two lives.

Tekla had to stand in order to pull apart the thick muscle, but she managed it in the end. The blood was flowing and she pressed down a towel, right on top of the wound. Now she saw a leg. Somewhere underneath it was a head. A living foetus, she very much hoped.

She extended the opening in the uterus by a centimetre and took hold of both legs, had to manoeuvre slightly to pull one foot back out of the cervix. Then she rotated the entire baby, as she had read in *Williams*, and suddenly the body and head freed themselves from the sea of blood down there. No umbilical cord around the neck.

The child was alive.

STOCKHOLM

Wednesday, 13 November

He recognised the smell in the hotel lobby, the same as in all the others he'd been to. He wondered if there was some sort of international agreement on the kind of cleaning products one was supposed to use. When the glass doors slid shut again behind him, he understood: it was the rubber in the lobby carpet which gave off that distinct smell. Slightly mouldy notes, that no detergent in the world could get rid of.

"Can I help you?"

He answered in English. "A room. One night."

The woman had blond hair in an updo fastened by two gold-coloured clips. She peered down at her computer screen. He stood right in front of her. "What do those cost?" He pointed at a bowl with small bags of crisps, two kinds, yellow and reddish orange.

"If you're hungry then we have—"

"What do they cost?"

"I thought you might be hungry since you asked what the crisps cost."

"It isn't good to think."

The woman glanced at the telephone beside her computer.

"And now you're wondering if you should call your boss."

"No, I'm not," the woman said, fiddling with a ring on her finger.

"So what do they cost?"

The woman glanced down at the screen again. "Do you want a room?"

"Why would I have changed my mind?"

"No, I was thinking . . ." The padded shoulders on her jacket shot up a centimetre or so. "We do have a room available."

"Good."

"What?"

"That you didn't try to pretend and say you're fully booked."

"Why would I say that?"

"Because you find me obnoxious."

The woman's small, pointy larynx bobbed up and down several times. She didn't seem to know where to look. She turned and took out a plastic card which she put on the counter in front of him. "Room two hundred and seven."

"Do you have any other rooms?"

"Well . . . yes . . ."

The woman checked her screen again. Then she retrieved the plastic card, turned her back once more and got him a new one. "Three hundred and fourteen."

"Seven's my unlucky number," he said with a smile.

"Is it?" the woman said, trying to smile but managing only to look pained.

He picked up the plastic card. "So what do they cost?"

"Well . . ." she said and picked up two bags of crisps. "They're on the house."

"Absolutely not. How much?"

"Twenty kronor."

"A bag?"

"Yes."

"I guess that makes forty in total, since you've given me two." He took a one-hundred-kronor note out of his wallet.

The woman accepted the note without a word and quickly found some change.

"You can keep it."

She looked confused.

"This is where you say thank you." He bent down to pick up his suitcase.

"Th ... thank you," the woman stammered as the man walked away towards the lifts.

It was too cold in the room. He found the thermostat and turned the heating up to twenty-four degrees. Cheap bloody hotels trying to save money everywhere, he thought, sitting down in a comfortable armchair next to the window. He stretched out his stiff legs. The plaster cast on his left arm was itchy enough to drive him mad, it would have to come off as soon as possible. He opened the yellow bag of crisps and tried them. Normal, thin, ready salted. Nothing special, no real taste. Perhaps a bit too greasy. He opened the reddish orange bag. Ridged crisps – pickled onion flavour. In a different class altogether. He opened the minibar under the desk and took out a bottle of citrus-flavoured mineral water. It went well with the onion crisps.

When the bag was finished, he removed his coat and hat. Then he laid out his equipment on the bed: weapon, silencer, bugging device and sleeping tablets. He picked up the dossier he had been given. Took his time running through it, putting together a plan for the coming day. Tomorrow evening he would take the ferry back.

When he had finished reading, he put the papers in the bathtub and set fire to them. Once they had all burned, he washed away the ashes with the shower attachment.

He had the information he needed: the husband, Andrus Gudaitis, worked as a cook in a restaurant in the city centre. It was now nine. Might he still be at work? That was the key to finding out where the foster family lived. Then he thought about the doctor, Tekla Berg. Did she have any family? Children? Did she live alone? He did a quick search on the net. Gullmarsplan. Where should he begin?

He put on clean underwear and combed his hair. Then trousers, shirt, coat, gloves and scarf. After that, he put the equipment in a rucksack. He left his case, thinking that he would most likely get back in time for a shower before the ferry tomorrow. He left the room, took the lift down and found himself once more out in the chill Stockholm night. Next stop: the Gökuret restaurant, just a few hundred metres away. He looked up at the sky. The rain had turned into snow. All it had taken was a tiny shift in temperature. Maybe he did actually prefer snow to rain. It reminded him more of home.

YTTERHOGDAL

Wednesday evening, 13 November

The girl was breathing but had not yet cried. She was making lip-smacking noises now Tekla had wiped the meconium and amniotic fluid from her face.

Maria carefully turned her head towards Tekla. "Is it . . .?"

"Here," Tekla said, laying the girl against Maria's chest. She wiped sweat and blood from her face with sheets she had found in one of the bedrooms.

Maria took the baby with shaking hands. She was weak, completely drained of all strength, and didn't dare move because of the pain from the open wound in her abdomen.

Tekla cut the umbilical cord with a new razor blade and then tied the stump with sewing thread. She separated the placenta from the mucous membrane and placed it on the floor, like a large cuttlefish on a shiny boat deck. Then she turned her attention to the wound. It did not look pretty – the uterus was bleeding heavily and she had to hurry. All she had to work with was some very coarse sewing thread. It was a challenge, to say the least, since the needle was straight and the thread made for thick woollen jumpers. But, with an unorthodox technique, she finally managed to create a zigzag pattern in black thread running across the womb. Lundgren began to relax, it was obvious that he wanted to help but had no idea what he should be doing. "Difficult business, all this," he remarked drily.

Tekla carefully felt her way up to the cervix, to see if it was still bleeding. She wiped with the cleanest sheets she could find, washed with lukewarm water and tidied up as best she could. This would leave permanent marks on Maria, Tekla realised that. But right now the only thing that mattered was that she survive. That the bleeding stop.

Tekla was exhausted, as thirsty as if she had spent three hours in a Finnish sauna, but she gritted her teeth and kept going. She left the muscle tissue as it was – it would probably fall back into place and heal by itself – but she did close the thicker fascia above the muscle with the help of the coarse thread and did a reasonable job repairing the connective tissue. Finally, the skin, which was the hardest job of all, but she did not devote too much time to it, she just needed it to hold together until Maria got to the hospital. They would have to open up all the layers and redo the work in any case. Tekla wiped the stinging sweat from her eyes. She listened to the girl, who had found Maria's breast.

"Is something coming out?" Tekla helped the baby to find her way.

Maria did not seem to be present, but had clearly heard the question. "You'll . . . have to ask . . . Alva about that."

"Alva? What a lovely name. Had you already decided that before?"

Maria nodded with her eyes closed.

Tekla breathed in deeply through her nose. There were some smells in the house she hadn't noticed before. The most obvious was the metallic and slightly musty scent of blood and placenta. There was even a faint whiff of excrement and urine, but the most obvious was Maria's sweat. It was feral, pungent, oddly invigorating. She wished she could capture it on a towel and take it back to her library of olfactive memories in her flat on Gullmarsplan.

"There we are," she said, putting down the needle. "No master-piece, but it doesn't seem to be bleeding."

"Does she have any blood left?" Lundgren asked.

"A cupful or two, it appears to be enough." Tekla wasn't going to tell Maria how pallid she looked. The pale blue vessels in her forehead and temples shone through the paper-thin skin.

"She'll have to eat a lot of black pudding when she gets home," Lundgren said, drawing a hint of a smile from Maria.

"Black pudding, God how delicious," Tekla said. She was starving. She could eat half a kilo of black pudding with a packet of crisp fried bacon and a litre of milk. She got up but had to hold on to the sofa to support herself because of her stiff knees, which were crying out with pain. Lundgren remained sitting with the patient.

Tekla went into the kitchen and scrubbed the blood off her arms. She drank some apple juice straight out of a packet in the refrigerator and that gave her an energy boost. Then she boiled some water and made two large cups of instant coffee. She gave one to Lundgren and then walked around the house turning on all the lights she could find. It was pitch dark outside but the wind had slackened. The snow was falling vertically. Tekla could see through the kitchen window that the flakes were now bigger, perhaps because of a slight rise in temperature.

Tekla went into the second bedroom, a small, square space with a bed in one corner and a desk. There wasn't room for much more, apart from a crate full of plastic toys, mostly Avengers heroes in shrill colours. On the walls, there was an Avengers poster and one with Yoda sitting in the lotus position, hovering over a rock.

At last she could stop worrying about Maria, if only for a short while. The young mother had to get to a hospital, be given some antibiotics and probably undergo another operation. So long as she wasn't bleeding, however, she would survive. Now Tekla could go back to concentrating on her primary task, the reason they had found themselves in this remote Jämtland cottage: the mysterious family. The woman and the man had been poisoned with dioxin, and she understood from Silva that foreign involvement was suspected. Dioxin as a poison was not something that was readily available. She thought about the Ukrainian president Viktor Yushchenko and the murder of Alexander Litvinenko. Whether the perpetrators were the Russian security services or somebody else, however, the question still remained: who were these people? Were they even the boy's biological parents? Was he adopted? Why had they lived in different cottages in Norrland over the last few years? Were they hiding from something – or someone? Were they criminals? Spies? But in that case, what had they been spying on and who had killed them? Or attempted to, at least? And why then had the woman run over the man? And the old man, was he just collateral damage or part of the equation? What had happened in this cottage little more than a week ago?

She had to get hold of Silva.

She went back to Maria, who had fallen asleep. So had the baby; she lay swaddled in towels, snug between Maria and the back of the sofa. Both of them were breathing, which was enough for Tekla for the moment. Lundgren had gone to clean himself up. Tekla carefully felt Maria's wrist. The pulse was a little fast, around one hundred beats per minute, but it was strong. Maria could not have lost more than about twenty per cent of her blood volume, which was of course a lot, but not life-threatening for such a young and healthy woman.

Lundgren returned and sat down in the armchair, threw a few logs of wood into the stove.

Tekla put her hand on his shoulder. "Thank you."

"For what?"

"For coming with me on this little weekend trip."

"The best ever," he said and smiled.

"I could never have done this without you."

Lundgren laughed. "Yes you could, unfortunately. I was totally helpless. Never felt so lost. I just wish you could follow me on a raid once so I can show myself in my true element."

"I'd love to." Tekla went into the hall, put on another jacket and found a cap on the hat rack. She had to wrestle for a while to push the door open.

She emerged into a fantastically beautiful winter night. The snowflakes must have been at least half a centimetre in diameter and floated slowly down, like ash after a volcanic eruption. The storm had subsided. The car was just a blurry mound, and a big overhang of snow already clung to the gutters of the barn. The temperature had risen, but Tekla's breath cast plumes of steam in whichever direction she turned. She held up her phone but there was still no signal. Tekla began to suspect that the Emergency Services had not identified their location, that they simply did not know where the house was.

She set off up the road. It was hard to follow its path, but at least the tree line gave her a vague idea. Tekla remembered how far down the slope they had driven in order to get to the house, recalling the little hillock to the left of it, which no longer seemed to be visible. It was pitch dark, so she reluctantly sacrificed some of her phone's battery to light the torch. The snow had long since found its way into her trainers. Her feet were stiff and had passed the last stage of cold. Now there was only pain and numbness.

Every now and then she looked at her phone, waiting for a signal bar to appear and show the extent of her coverage. Nothing yet. Had the mobile masts blown over? Were they surrounded by a layer of snow which blocked transmission? She struggled on, turning off into the forest where she saw the ground beginning to rise. Now she was surrounded by fir trees and a vast ocean of new snow. Twenty-five years ago, her joy would have been absolute. She and Simon would have charged out into the forest, each with their own little sledge, a torch and their ski pants tucked deep into their tall boots. They would have found the highest point and from there started their races. Two hours later, drenched in sweat and exhausted, they would have collapsed in the hallway of their house, calling for hot chocolate, and their father would have met them with a smile.

Tekla was frozen. She stopped to catch her breath. She was hopelessly unfit, breathing in cold air mixed with snow and coughing while continuing to walk uphill. Finally she reached a plateau, free of trees. Maybe a rock ledge just before the top of the hill. She held up her phone and, at last: two bars.

She called Emergency Services and got through after three rings. They had registered her earlier calls but hadn't been able to send an ambulance because of the snowstorm. The roads along the lake were being ploughed at that very moment and an ambulance would be sent from Östersund in a few hours. Tekla hung up, realising that would take too long. She tried another way. After four ringtones, a familiar voice answered.

"Tekla? Where are you? You keep breaking up."

Tekla briefly explained to Carlsson about the cottage, the pregnant woman and the caesarian.

"But the ambulance won't get to us in time," she concluded.

"And the woman ... wait a second ..." Carlsson's voice was muted. Was she tired from the morphine? Tekla gathered that she was still in hospital, perhaps in Intensive Care. "Did you say you carried out a C-section? Are you in the hospital, then?"

"No, in a cottage in the woods. I don't have time to fill you in but ..."

"Is she alive?"

"Yes."

"And the baby?"

"Also. They're asleep now." Tekla was surprised that Carlsson had even asked about the baby. "But we have to get her away from here quickly. The ambulance won't arrive for another few hours, that's not going to work. And I also have to get to Stockholm as soon as possible."

"What's the hurry?"

"Please Monica. Just this once, I don't have time to explain. All I can say is that it *may* be a matter of life and death."

Carlsson was silent. Then she cleared her throat.

"I'll arrange for an ambulance helicopter to pick up the woman and the baby and take them to Östersund. Send me your location from your phone and leave the rest to me.

Tekla felt the tension in her shoulders relax. She had no idea how she'd be able to thank Carlsson, but she'd find a way.

She had one more call to make. She asked the switchboard at the Nobel Hospital to put her through to Orthopaedics. After a bit of back and forth, Tekla was given the name of the patient who had shared a room with the old man from Serbia. "He's called Enok Hillerström," the nurse said.

Tekla thanked her, looked up Hillerström's number and after two rings a young woman answered:

"Hello?"

"Yes, hi. Tekla Berg here from the Nobel Hospital. I'm looking for Enok Hillerström, have I got the wrong number?"

"It's Linda Svedén here, duty officer from the Södermalm police."

Then the phone died.

SÖDERMALM, STOCKHOLM
Wednesday evening, 13 November

Jennifer was freezing, even though she was wearing the woollen slippers Andrus had given her the Christmas before. She wondered whether to plug in their extra radiators, but she knew that Andrus would make a fuss over the electricity bill. Rightly so, they were trying to keep costs down. She stole into the bedroom to fetch another cardigan, wrapped herself in it and left Agnes in their bed. She didn't have the heart to carry her across to her room, was afraid she would wake up and cry when she realised what her mother was doing. Ever since they had taken in the boy, Agnes was more restless at night when Andrus went to work at the restaurant.

The boy. Why wouldn't he tell them his name? It was all a mystery. Jennifer closed the door as carefully as she could, but it creaked anyway. Everything did in this late-nineteenth-century apartment. The floors, the kitchen cupboards, even the damper in the tiled stove. But she liked it, a building that was alive, giving out small signs of life. Jennifer went into the drawing room and lowered the volume on the T.V. It was the late evening current affairs programme "Rapport". She had already seen the news, but there was something comforting about hearing the reporter's voice. At the same time, she kicked herself for not being able to get over her fear of being alone. It made her feel too dependent and old-fashioned. She wanted to be one of those people who were happy spending time alone in a cottage out in the woods. Who enjoyed their own company.

She went into the kitchen and put on the kettle. Her favourite mug was the one with the large leaf pattern. She loved it, not so much for its value as a collectible and the famous designer as for the thin,

449

rounded rim and the way it sat so perfectly in her hand, index finger nestling in the smooth porcelain handle. She brought out the rooibos tea, which was also her favourite. She could hear the boy rummaging about in his room, but she did not want to disturb him, she had quickly come to realise that he was something of a night owl, that he preferred late evenings when he could play on his own with the Star Wars Lego bought for him by Andrus or flick through the illustrated Harry Potter books which strictly speaking belonged to Agnes.

She poured water into Oliver's bowl, carried her mug of tea to the coffee table and looked out at the street lights in Swedenborgsgatan. The dog followed her and found a comfortable spot to lie on next to the sofa. It had begun to snow. With her hands on the window sill, she leaned against the window and gazed happily at the large snowflakes falling down onto the still-damp tarmac. Maybe they would wake up tomorrow to a winter wonderland Stockholm. She wondered how much snow the boy had experienced in his life. They still didn't know where he came from, where he had spent his winters, who his parents had been and whether they had played with him on the ice and slopes. It was a strange and slightly unsettling mystery. She and Andrus had taken care of three foster children before, for different lengths of time, and to be sure those children too had had their traumas. Drugs. Gang violence. Abuse at home. But they had always been given some information about their backgrounds. They knew what they were dealing with. But this boy . . . she turned and saw him walk from the desk to the bed . . . this boy was a riddle. He had no scars on his body, no signs of mistreatment, but he was clearly carrying some mental trauma, that much she could tell from his mournful eyes.

She picked up the mug and went into the small room. They had been using it as a study, but now it was temporarily given over to the boy. It was clear early on that for him and Agnes to share a room was not a good idea. Neither of them would fall asleep, so they separated them. The boy usually dropped off around midnight.

"Are you tired?" she asked, seating herself on the office chair by the desk. The Harry Potter book lay open at a dramatic picture of a wizard. She closed it.

The boy sat in his bed with the golden mask on his knees. He would hold on to it whenever he was nervous.

"Do you want something to eat?" she continued. "An evening sandwich?"

He shook his head.

"Maybe you should sleep. Have you seen that it's snowing outside?"

He turned, looked out of the window.

"Who knows, maybe we can get out the toboggans tomorrow. Agnes would love to show you where she usually goes. There's a slope in a park not so far from here. Would you like that?"

The boy nodded carefully. Then he laid the mask aside on the bedside table.

"Thirsty," he suddenly said.

Jennifer gave a start. "Of course. Would you like water or something else?"

"Water."

She felt happy as she walked away to the kitchen to get some. That was perhaps the tenth word in total that he had spoken. And now two at the same time. Maybe he was beginning to open up, to feel more secure in their home. If only Andrus could change his shifts and work nothing but lunches. She really disliked him being away so late in the evenings.

She returned to the boy's room with the glass of water in her hand but almost dropped it when she saw him.

"Careful!" she said, much too sternly, and put the water down on the table. Then she hurried over to his bed. The boy was standing on the window sill, pressing the whole of his body against the window. It was closed, but Jennifer could picture it giving way and the boy falling headlong down into the street and killing himself.

She grabbed his pyjamas and pulled him down onto the bed.

"You must never do that. Never stand in the window." She clasped him tightly to her. The boy was relaxed. Wasn't shaking. Didn't resist. He looked up at her face. "I'm sorry," he said.

Jennifer felt tears running down her cheeks. She shivered. Hugged the boy even harder and patted his mop of hair. Then she composed herself, aware that she'd overreacted.

"I just got such a fright."

The boy reached for the glass of water and drank calmly while Jennifer wiped the tears from her cheeks.

"Shall we go and brush our teeth?"

The boy got up and went to the bathroom.

Jennifer followed him but first went into the hall and double-checked that the door was locked. The chain secure. Couldn't he come home a little earlier just for once?

Wednesday evening, 13 November

Getting down from the top of the hill was easier. Tekla slid, rolled and ran by turns, high on her pumping adrenalin. Now the situation was under control: the woman and the child would be saved and she and Lundgren could set off for Stockholm, perhaps even that night if they could get the car started. She sent thoughts of gratitude off to Carlsson in her hospital bed.

After just a few hundred metres, she caught sight of the house. The outside lighting at the back was like a beacon in the darkness. She jogged down the slope and was feeling warmed through by the time she arrived. She brushed the snow off in the hall and saw that Maria was awake.

"How's it going?" Tekla asked.

"She's sleeping."

"And you?"

"I'd be lying if I pretended it's not hurting. But it feels fine. You saved both our lives. With a razor blade."

Tekla waved with her phone. "I'll try to recharge it in the car. A helicopter is on its way. It'll take you to Östersund."

Maria nodded carefully. "Thank you for everything. That sounds like a breeze compared to what we've been through today."

Lundgren nodded and smiled. "You're awesome, Tekla, do you know that?"

Tekla went up to him. She didn't hesitate this time but leaned down and kissed him on the lips. Then she went out to the car and managed to clear away enough snow from the driver's door to squeeze in. She crossed her fingers, hoping that the old Ford was not angry with her for having bad-mouthed it during the journey. First try, only the starter motor turned over. Second try, the engine gave a wheeze. Bloody ethanol cars, Tekla thought. Third try, she kept the key pressed in extra long and the motor started. She pressed the accelerator, made sure that the engine didn't die and put the heating on full blast. She found the charging cable and plugged in her phone. After a while, the screen lit up. Tekla fidgeted with the phone, waiting for a signal. After a minute or so, it appeared: one thin bar. She got the number of her Chilean police buddy.

"I've been trying to call you all evening," Silva answered testily.

"We haven't had any signal."

"How's it all going?"

"I'll tell you later. We're waiting for a helicopter, then we can get going. I'll be in Stockholm tomorrow morning."

"A helicopter, what—"

"You'll hear all about it," Tekla interrupted. "Tell me what you've found."

"A house in Stuvsta, where the family probably stayed together with that older man who was brought in injured to the Nobel Hospital after the hit-and-run."

Tekla felt a spasm across her shoulders and a crick in the neck. "They were staying with him? We thought it was a coincidence, that he just happened to be at the bus stop at the same time."

"It was no coincidence. There's more to come," Silva said.

He told her about the remains of the mushrooms in the kitchen and the drums of hydrofluoric acid in the garage. "You know what that means?"

"Hydrofluoric acid? What's that for?" Tekla asked.

"Someone was planning to kill someone and dissolve their body in the acid. Or bodies."

"Jesus," Tekla said.

"We've put out a search for him."

"Do you have any idea who he is?"

"No."

"And the motive?"

"I'm working on it," Silva said. "Think I can get an answer tomorrow."

"Good."

"Just one more thing," Silva said.

"Yes?"

"So, the boy isn't in fact the biological child of the man and the woman."

Tekla considered this. What difference did it make, actually? A big one, in terms of the police investigation and the background to it all. But when it came to her own feelings for the boy, they were unshakeable.

"O.K., I'll call when I arrive," Tekla finished.

Forty minutes later, a helicopter landed on the slope beneath the house, but the pilot was anything but happy as he helped to strap in the patients. He turned to Tekla. "You seem to have friends in high places," he said angrily, and pulled the side door shut. Tekla knocked on the windscreen and waved at Maria. Then she backed away from the helicopter and stood by the house, watching as the aircraft lifted into the Jämtland night.

"Shall we head off?" Tekla said to Lundgren.

"First we have to see if we can get up the hill."

Tekla had had other things to worry about. But the road was piled high with snow. They made a fruitless attempt to force their way through the heavy drifts but got stuck and the wheels just spun. Tekla swore and rang 112 again. She was put through to the rescue services in Sveg, who told her that they were hard at work clearing the roads. She told a white lie and said that Lundgren was having chest pains and needed to get to a hospital. They promised to give priority to the road down to the house, but said it wouldn't be for a few hours.

There was nothing they could do about that, so they went back into the house and refreshed the fire in the stove.

"Typical," Tekla said, accepting a cup of tea and two digestive biscuits which Lundgren had managed to find. He lay down on the rug in front of the fire and fell asleep after a few minutes. Tekla picked up the woman's diary and flicked through it. She had begun it four years earlier, writing exclusively in Russian, but after about two years she had switched to Swedish, though there were still occasional passages in Russian, the last entry, for example. Perhaps she was upset and therefore reverted to her mother tongue.

Tekla's thoughts were interrupted by her phone: Silva. She went into the kitchen and closed the door so as not to wake Lundgren.

"He's called Leonid Golitsyn and he's a former K.G.B. agent."

Tekla saw the sinewy old man before her in his hospital bed, with concussion and a broken forearm. Confused. Tired.

"But it's been a long time since he worked for the State. He's been freelancing, taking on assignments in return for money. He travelled into Sweden as Spiro Lazarov, a tourist from Serbia."

Tekla thought she knew where this was going, but she still wanted Silva to say it out loud.

"What do you mean, freelancing?"

"He's a hitman. He kills for money."

"And who's he meant to kill?" Tekla swallowed heavily.

"Looks like his main target is the boy from the hospital, Kolya Mischenko."

"Kolya . . . so not Sasha, then . . .?"

"What?" Silva asked.

"Nothing. But why is he supposed to kill the boy?"

"Kolya's the son of Anatoly Mischenko, who was killed in a shooting this summer. Anatoly controlled a Russian Mafia network and now his enemies want to make sure that even the heir to his empire is rubbed out."

"Kolya . . ." Tekla whispered.

"What's that?"

"So that's his name . . . Kolya . . . and is he really the heir to a Russian Mafia empire?"

"Like I said . . ."

Tekla could almost feel the boy's thick mop of hair as he sat on her knee in Swedenborgsgatan.

"And the man and the woman?" she managed to say.

"I don't have any names," Silva said. "But I assume they were bodyguards who were hired to protect him. Sweden's a large country where it's easy to go underground. It's not the first time this sort of thing has happened. But this Golitsyn guy finally found them."

"Obviously . . . the money . . ." Everything was starting to fall into place. As far as Tekla could see, the woman was not the boy's biological mother and she was living with the man, Sasha, in Sweden on some kind of assignment. But to think that she might have been a bodyguard or in some way connected to organised crime . . . that did seem bizarre, given how warm and loving her diary entries were.

"Maybe some kind of bribe," Silva suggested. "We can only speculate."

"Thanks. I'll be there as soon as I can."

Tekla ended the call. Just as she was about to put more wood in the fire, she heard a noise from outside the house and flew to her feet. Through the window she saw the yellow flashing lights of a snow plough.

"They're here!" she called to Lundgren.

DRIVING BACK TO STOCKHOLM
Wednesday night, 13 November

Tekla took a run at it, managing to keep the car on the road despite a lot of skidding, and after a short while reached the main road a few hundred metres higher up. She tried to stay calm, knew that she mustn't drive too fast, better that they should arrive in one piece. But she wanted to read a bit more.

"Can you do the driving?" she asked Lundgren, stopping the car in the middle of the road. It was still dark. She threw open the door. A cold, still night. Already five in the morning. She walked around the car and changed places with Lundgren.

"But drive fast," she said as she got out the diary.

"What's that?" Lundgren asked, accelerating away.

"Don't talk, just drive," she said without taking her eyes off the text.

"Your wish is my command," Lundgren said.

Tekla searched out the passages written in Swedish.

Sasha came home this evening. He had sweets from the airport with him but I felt like talking. He was tired and wanted to sleep, he said. He got angry when I asked if he had seen her. Said that all I did was nag. I cried half the night.

Tekla imagined the scene. They had been a couple, the man and the woman, but the man, Sasha, had had a family in Russia. The woman was jealous and tried to persuade him to leave his family. He was apparently away for long periods of time, so the woman must have lived alone in the different cottages with the boy, brought him up as her own son, educated him and been everything to him. Her love for Kolya shone brightly through the pages.

We were out walking today. Everything felt fantastically wonderful. I told Kolya about how I used to hike with my father in the forests back home. He's grown so much this last year. So curious about everything. It feels good that he doesn't ask about his background, but I wonder if he thinks about it. He obviously understands who the person is who sends him large parcels for Christmas. Surely? I've promised myself a thousand times that I'll tell him, but at the same time I'm so scared of what it will lead to. Maybe our relationship will change. At the same time, it feels so dishonest. I'm torn between the truth and my own hopes for the future.

Tekla stared out at the dark forest. A pale light was beginning to appear in the sky. A new day.

"Can you drive faster?"

Lundgren ignored her. He was doing the best he could with the scrapheap they were sitting in.

Tekla thought about the boy. The woman saw him as her own. In one passage she wondered – ashamed to be thinking that way – whether she could adopt him. There was no reference anywhere to the names of his biological parents. It was as if the woman had first seen the whole thing as a job – "our assignment", as she called it – but had then gradually come to realise that this was their life for the indefinite future, and started to make plans for the years ahead, for how Kolya would be able to study, maybe they could move to Stockholm "once everything has settled down". What might she have been referring to? Was it the prospect of a happy conclusion to the conflict between the Mafia families in Russia , or was the woman just trying to fool herself so she could endure the gloom and loneliness of the small Jämtland villages? There were long gaps in the diary, maybe this was not the only one she was keeping, but the last entries, from the autumn, were full of anxiety and apprehension. Something was going on between her and Sasha – there was more and more anger and frustration in her words.

Tekla closed the book and caught sight of a road sign. Soon they would be passing Gävle.

Suddenly she sat up. "We have to go straight there."

"Where?"

"To the foster family. We have to stop that hitman. That's where Kolya is."

"But the address is secret," Lundgren said.

"A person like that is capable of anything."

Tekla picked up her phone and called Silva. Despite the early hour, the Chilean superintendent answered.

"You have to fetch the boy."

"Tekla, now you really have to—"

"No!" she yelled. "Golitsyn's not going to give up."

"He's probably already back in Russia by this—"

"You don't know that! You have to go there."

"There's no need to worry."

"I am worried!" Tekla shouted out loud.

"But what do you expect me to do then?"

"Go there and fetch the boy. Take him to a safe place."

"*Loca.* It isn't necessary."

"Just do it!"

There was a few seconds' silence. "O.K. I'll go there myself if that makes you happier. *Puta madre . . .* do you have any idea what time it is, you lunatic?"

Tekla did not hear the last bit. She had already ended the call and turned instead to Lundgren:

"Drive. Faster. Thank you!"

SÖDERMALM, STOCKHOLM

Thursday morning, 14 November

If only his legs were not so stiff. He'd had problems with his knees for years, arthrosis the doctors said. They had offered him replacements but he was not interested. The mere fact that they would have to be explained at airport security checks every time the X-ray machine beeped put him off having the operation.

He did the circuit one more time. He had managed to find out the entrance code to the building and made sure that it worked to get into the back garden, if some sort of escape route might be needed. There was a gate out there leading to the next-door garden, which offered a way out into a side street with the strange name of Wollmar Yxkullsgatan. He longed for the Black Sea – just a few more hours now till he could take a shower and then the ferry back across the Baltic.

It was six in the morning. He stood on the corner, diagonally across from the entrance, and peered up at the second floor. At last, a light came on in one of the rooms. Just a minute later, another one, two windows away. He caught a glimpse of a venetian blind, perhaps it was a kitchen.

The woman, Jennifer Holmgren, worked as a social welfare secretary in Norrmalm. She started at eight and should be leaving the apartment in roughly an hour and a half.

He waited for a rubbish lorry to pass and crossed the street, keyed in the door code and walked into the stairwell, which lit up automatically. Irritating, he thought as he looked for a fuse box. Nothing. He followed the wires up to the ceiling. They were slightly awkwardly placed, in a corner, but he should be able to get at them. He brought

461

out a small pair of pliers and, with a certain amount of bother, managed to put the stairwell lights out.

After a little while, sounds could be heard from the top of the stairs. The old elevator shook for thirty seconds and stopped with a thud. Metal wrought-iron gates scraped open and a middle-aged man in a raincoat and brown boots stepped out.

The old man retreated into the corner by the exit to the back garden. He hoped that this individual was not going out to fetch his bicycle this November morning. The street door banged shut and silence fell again. Distant voices from one of the apartments on the next level up, but no children. Once the woman, Holmgren, had left to go to the office, only the husband, Gudaitis, would be in the apartment. He was probably asleep after his late night at work and wouldn't present a problem. The old man had followed him when he left the Gökuret restaurant at one o'clock that night.

The plan was simple: he would get into the apartment, surprise the boy and anaesthetise him. Then he would calmly and quietly take him away. His contact claimed that she had organised transport. A white Nissan van. He was close to completing his assignment. Was already sitting on the beach by the Black Sea with a good book resting on his knees.

Ten to seven. He considered his next move. Naturally, he would try to stick to the plan, but he knew from long experience that one always needed an alternative, reality rarely followed straight lines.

He took out his pistol and screwed on the silencer.

STOCKHOLM

Thursday morning, 14 November

"It's getting brighter," Lundgren said.

"Shit," Tekla snapped.

"Aren't you happy to see daybreak?"

"He's not answering. How hard can it be? Shall I call via 112?"

"I don't think they'll patch you through." Lundgren blew past Upplands Väsby at one hundred and fifty-five kilometres an hour. "You have to trust the police."

"But you are the police!" Tekla shouted.

"And what do you want me to do about it?"

She unbuttoned her down jacket. It felt as if the chill of the night had never existed, her body was boiling from the adrenalin pumping through every vessel. "Can't you drive a bit faster?"

"A hundred and fifty-five. Don't think this can do any more."

Tekla was too wound up to care how hard the Ford was being pushed.

"Besides, I already stretched my authority to the limit when I called and warned them that I was on the way in by private car."

"As if you'd never done that before," Tekla snorted and saw the sign for Norrviken flash by on the left. A faint, pale blue hue could be seen to the east. "I just need confirmation that Alvaro's there."

"You'll have to trust that he is."

"How hard is it to pick up?"

"When we're in the field we turn our phones off."

"But surely he must be in the apartment."

"I have no idea," Lundgren said, hitting the brakes for a Danish articulated lorry.

"Drive!" Tekla urged him on. She wanted to reach over and floor the accelerator herself.

"Seriously, Tekla. I'm going as fast as I can."

The traffic got heavier by Hagaparken.

"Fuck!" Tekla yelled. "Now what?"

Lundgren threw the car out into the bus lane.

"Finally a bit of moxie," Tekla said. She called Silva again, who this time rejected the call. "At least he has his phone switched on."

Lundgren wormed his way in past the N.S.K. to Dannemoragatan and Upplandsgatan and on towards Odenplan, Norra Bantorget and Vasagatan.

"Christ, what a lot of traffic," Tekla said, about to go to pieces. She had texted Silva but still not received any answer. Once they had crossed Centralbron and Lundgren had shot a red light at Slussen, she was ready to jump out and run the last bit. She undid her seatbelt to be able to get out quickly.

They turned left at Mariatorget, and when they reached Swedenborgsgatan, the street was bathed in the blue lights of at least five police cars. From a distance it looked as if a film were being shot in the early morning hours. The windows in the houses on Swedenborgsgatan were brightly lit and Tekla saw police officers stopping nosy Södermalm residents from coming closer. Lundgren drove up onto the pavement before Sankt Paulsgatan and turned the engine off. Tekla had already thrown the door open and nearly stumbled in the snow.

"Wait!" She heard Lundgren's voice behind her but she was already halfway to the police barriers.

"Nobody's allowed across this line," she heard the police officer before her say. He was stretching blue-and-white tape from a pole across to one of the police cars, which was blocking off the whole street.

"But I have to get in," Tekla said, doing her best not to yell. They were unlikely to let a hysterical person past the barrier.

"This area is off limits," the young police officer said.

Lundgren came up to Tekla. "Hang on a moment ..." He was panting, holding up his I.D.

"She's with me." Lundgren lifted the tape and got a nod back from the police officer.

"But you have to stay close." Lundgren took hold of Tekla's jacket. She was already poised to run away from him, like a disobedient dog.

"Get a move on then."

They half-jogged over to the next cluster of police cars. Tekla also saw two ambulances parked outside a restaurant a little way off.

"Alvaro," she managed to say. "Have you seen Alvaro?"

"I don't know what he looks like."

"But what's happened?" Tekla called out. Two police officers turned and looked at the woman in civilian clothes. One of them obviously recognised Lundgren and nodded.

Lundgren held Tekla tightly by the arm. He walked slowly towards his colleagues.

"How's it going?"

The police woman looked sceptically at Tekla.

"It's cool," Lundgren said.

"There were shots fired half an hour ago."

"What?" Tekla burst out. "Is anyone injured?"

"One dead," the policeman said.

Tekla tried to free herself from Lundgren, but he had a firm grip on her. "So tell us!"

Lundgren added: "Have you seen Alvaro Silva?"

"He's in there."

"Can we go in? Has it been secured?"

"Yes, it's O.K.," the policeman said. He either didn't know who was dead or didn't want to tell them. Tekla had only one thought in her mind and when she felt Lundgren relaxing his hold on her she ran for it. She heard him shout but already had a head start. She raced over to the door but was immediately stopped.

"Tekla?" Rebecka Nilsén said.

"Who's dead?" Tekla managed to utter, gasping for breath.

Rebecka pointed in towards the dark stairwell, but that didn't tell Tekla anything.

"Who?!" she screamed.

"Calm down, Tekla," Nilsén said, holding up both hands. "You have to take it easy. This is a crime scene."

Tekla tried to push past Nilsén, who grabbed her by the shoulders as Lundgren caught up with them. She saw the old man from the hospital lying on the stone floor at the foot of the stairs. He was motionless, face turned away, but Tekla could see the blood on his throat.

"Is it for sure?" Tekla asked, hearing her voice break.

"What?" Nilsén said with a smile. "That he's dead? Yes, it's for sure."

Just then, the ambulance staff came down the steps. They were carrying someone on a stretcher who was wrapped in a yellow blanket with something orange around their right leg. Tekla was aware that she was confused and anxious, but even her worried mind could not identify this as a child. She began to breathe again.

"Who . . .?"

"The husband in the family," Nilsén said. "He was shot in the leg."

A few seconds later, Tekla saw Andrus' face. He looked to be in pain, his eyes half closed. He had probably been given morphine at the scene, when they stabilised his leg. Perhaps his thigh bone had been shattered by the bullet.

"And Kolya?"

"Kolya?"

"The boy."

"His name's Kolya, is it? He's fine," Nilsén answered. "Or rather . . . as well as can be expected in the circumstances. At least physically unharmed."

"Can I go up?" Tekla asked.

"Yes that'll be fine. You've got your buddy up there."

At first Tekla didn't understand what Nilsén meant, but once she had fought her way up the two flights of stairs and walked into the yellow hallway she saw.

466

"I couldn't take your call," Silva said and held up two bloodied palms. "Kind of had my hands full."

"Are you hurt?"

"No. It got a bit mucky when I tried to put a compression bandage on Andrus." Silva gave a broad smile.

"What luck," Tekla said, looking around her.

"You can say that again. One doesn't get to pull out the old service weapon every day."

"But you drew the long straw," Tekla said.

"This time. Now's the moment to retire, I suspect."

Tekla scanned the room. Ambulance staff, white-clad criminal technicians and at least four people from the emergency response team were still in the apartment. Now she could also smell smoke, or gunpowder. The oiled parquet floor of the living room was sticky with blood. There were footprints in it and masses of soiled compresses, bandages and cannulae, as if an amputation had been performed right there.

Then she saw the boy on the sofa.

Tekla went and sat down beside Jennifer, who had bundled Kolya up in a blanket. Ignoring her own tears, she put her hand on Jennifer's, which was resting on top of the blanket.

"The old man is dead," the boy suddenly said.

Tekla stared into his brown eyes. For the first time she saw something approaching joy. At the very least, there wasn't as much fear there as before.

"The old man is dead," Tekla whispered back, nodding.

"Palpatine," Kolya said.

"Palpatine," Tekla answered.

EPILOGUE

The scent from the flowers wafted all the way to the pulpit. Tekla avoided looking at the coffin, first she wanted her eyes to get used to the inside of a church: the large altarpiece in some dark grey material, decorated with golden angels and an oil painting representing Jesus ascending to heaven. It looked as if He were launching Himself off the shoulders of the Roman soldiers below. Shafts of light fell through the large windows onto the aisle of Grangärde church. It was eleven o'clock, one hour to go. Tekla tried to concentrate. She sent a text message:

It starts in an hour. Where are you?

She stopped by the first bouquet, red roses surrounded by some white flowers which she could not name. She bent forward, read the card: *Rest in peace. Lars and Agneta.* Tekla had no idea who they were. The next one was a mixture of mauve, yellow and white flowers and a mass of green leaves. *Kajsa. Anna. Frida. In loving memory.* Maybe some of the staff from her care home? Tekla was conscious of how little she had seen her mother in recent years. Might that explain why she felt so lost? Why she had experienced more worry and stress than sorrow and regret since her mother died?

She continued until the last floral tribute, next to the coffin. *Monica Carlsson. Warm greetings.* Tekla was surprised. Very kind of Monica, but how could she have known . . .? Tekla tried to imagine her snapping at some poor physiotherapist at the rehabilitation centre in Saltsjöbaden as she tottered along with a walking frame whilst asking her secretary to order the largest bouquet with white and blue flowers for Tekla's mother's funeral in Dalarna.

"Well, here we are," she heard someone say behind her. The priest had appeared soundlessly and joined her by the coffin. "How are you feeling?"

Tekla briefly met his penetrating look. He seemed tired, but she

471

didn't feel like getting any more closely acquainted with him. Couldn't they just get it over and done with?

"Lots of flowers."

"Yes, one's often surprised to see how many people the deceased actually knew. I mean ... you're probably familiar with all these names?" He looked at one bouquet.

"No, not all of them."

The priest got out his phone. Tekla wondered what he was doing. Checking his calendar or perhaps his emails?

"Half past eleven."

"Gosh." Tekla looked at her phone. No reply from Simon. "I have to make a call."

"Go ahead."

Tekla left the priest as music from the organ filled the vault of the church. She went out into the anteroom, which was much cooler. A welcome relief, Tekla had begun to sweat up there by the coffin. Maybe it was the synthetic fabric of her jacket, which didn't let any air through. She could feel the hard object in the inside pocket chafe against her breast. She made sure that it could not be seen, buttoned up her jacket.

The church doors opened and two elderly people came in. They gave Tekla a neutral look and then concentrated on taking off hats and scarves.

"You can go in," Tekla said and got out her mobile. After two rings, Simon answered.

"Yes?"

"Where the fuck are you?" she hissed, and then checked herself. The old couple hadn't heard her swear.

"Calm down. I'm just parking the car."

"Lucky for you," Tekla snarled, cutting her brother off.

More people were coming into the church now, and Tekla took the opportunity to nip into the toilet next to the priest's office one last time. She drank some water and swallowed a bomb from her Lypsyl tube. Then took two Oxazepam and rinsed them down. What she really wanted was to drink half a bottle of wine but she didn't feel like putting up with Simon's jibes.

About fifteen people had gathered in the church, none of them under eighty. They hobbled forward to the pews at the front.

Finally, he appeared. Tekla didn't know whether to laugh or cry.

"Here," Simon said, holding out a Visa card.

"What did it cost?" she asked, staring at her brother, who was swamped by an oversized suit from the Dressman chain store in Ludvika.

"Two thousand."

"O.K.," Tekla said. "But didn't you ask them about sizes?"

"Oh come on, I like it when it's not too tight."

Tekla helped Simon straighten his tie. A simple knot. She did up the top button of his white shirt. Patted his smooth cheek.

"Thanks for shaving."

"You did threaten me otherwise," he said and smiled so that his large wolf's teeth were bared. He was as brown as a pepparkaka biscuit and his pale blue eyes sparkled like never before. At the same time, his face was swollen, she had heard him crying the night before.

"You look well," Tekla said.

"Sadly I can't say the same about you."

She punched him gently in the stomach and looped her arm through his.

"Let's go and sit down."

They went over to the front row and took their places in the uncomfortable pew. Every now and then Tekla turned and saw some older person slipping into a seat. Several of them nodded in her direction, but she didn't know how to return the greeting.

"Shit," Tekla said and took Simon's hand. It was ice cold, and nowhere near as sweaty as hers.

"It'll soon be over," he said, putting his phone on silent.

"Did you find an outdoor jacket?"

"Yes," Simon replied, and pointed past Tekla.

"What?"

"Look who's here," he said in English.

Tekla turned. Lundgren. She got up and gave him a hug.

"Thanks," she said, fighting back the tears.

Lundgren sat on her other side and reached his hand across to Simon. "Hey bro. Looks like you had a good time in Spain."

"Can't complain," Simon said.

When the ceremony was over, Tekla led Simon away to an empty space by a gravestone. A wooden peg had been pressed down in the snow.

"What?" he asked.

"This is where her grave is going to be."

"Nice." Simon looked up. "With a view onto the campsite."

"Dad would have approved." Tekla smiled, opening the jacket under her short coat. She brought out a little shovel and squatted down.

"What are you doing?"

Tekla began to dig. Fortunately, the cold weather had only hit during the last day or so, and the frost had not yet taken hold. But it was still hard to make any sort of dent in the ground.

"Can you please tell me what—"

"Just warn me if you see anybody coming."

Simon looked around and took out a cigarette.

Tekla had managed to scoop out a small hole and now produced a bottle from her jacket pocket.

Simon crouched down next to her. "What's that?"

Tekla held up the empty little vodka bottle. A rolled-up piece of paper had been stuffed into it. She had screwed the capsule back on. "Just a greeting from Pappa to Mamma."

"Christ that's great," Simon said, taking a deep drag on his cigarette. "Am I allowed to read it?"

"No," Tekla said, pushing the bottle down into the ground. Then she brought out a packet of More cigarillos and placed it alongside the bottle. "In case she feels the urge."

"Perfect," Simon said approvingly.

Together they filled the hole again with earth and snow.

CHRISTIAN UNGE works as a senior doctor at Danderyd Hospital in Stockholm. He spent the early part of his career working for Médecins Sans Frontières in Congo (DRC) and Burundi, later publishing a memoir about his experiences. *A Grain of Truth* is the second in a series of thrillers starring ER doctor Tekla Berg. Film/TV rights have been sold to FLX, producers of the Netflix series *Quicksand*.

GEORGE GOULDING's translations from the Swedish include *The Girl in the Spider's Web*, *The Girl Who Takes an Eye for an Eye*, *The Girl Who Lived Twice* and *Fall of Man in Wilmslow*, all by David Lagercrantz, *The Carrier* by Mattias Berg and *The Rock Blaster* by Henning Mankell.

SARAH DE SENARCLENS was born in Sweden and educated in Sweden, Austria, England and Switzerland. After a career as a simultaneous conference interpreter based in Geneva, she now works as a translator of fiction.